Divine Memories

James F. Bender

ISBN 979-8-89112-654-1 (Paperback)
ISBN 979-8-89112-655-8 (Digital)

Copyright © 2024 James F. Bender
All rights reserved
First Edition

This book is a work of fiction. Unless otherwise indicated or stated, all the names, characters, businesses, places, events, and incidents in this book are either the product of the author's imagination or used in a fictitious manner. Any resemblance to actual persons, living or dead, or actual events is purely coincidental.

All rights reserved. No part of this publication may be reproduced, distributed, or transmitted in any form or by any means, including photocopying, recording, or other electronic or mechanical methods without the prior written permission of the publisher. For permission requests, solicit the publisher via the address below.

Covenant Books
11661 Hwy 707
Murrells Inlet, SC 29576
www.covenantbooks.com

Thank You

If I learned anything at all, it's that there are about eighty thousand words between a good idea and a published book. Some days, the words come easy, and others, they don't. The journey through that is fraught with doubt and fatigue constantly nagging at you. If it weren't for the support of my wife, Kim, and a host of good friends, I'm not sure this endeavor would have been completed.

To my wife, thanks for constantly rereading the same chapters and acting like it's a pleasure. And all the people behind the scenes reading and supporting my efforts, a special thanks. The list, I hope, is complete, and if I missed anyone, I'll throw you in on the next book.

I would sincerely like to thank God first, for any talents he has loaned me. Second, comes the list of friends and family, Brittany Bender, Brenda Bender, Vicki Remlinger, Kelsey Bailey, Barbara O'Rourke, Michelle Kelly, Gail Lorton, Timothy Hurt, Tina Campbell Hefner, Jayne Rayhel, Debra Wineinger, and Angela Setzer. Thanks for all your efforts and encouragement; it means a lot to a simple struggler.

And last, I would like to thank Covenant Books for all their support and guidance in bringing this journey to completion.

1

Stepping down from her penthouse perched high above the rabble of the city, Nevada exited the lobby ready to kick the world a new one. The crisp early morning air burned as she drew a deep breath, releasing it back to the night sky. More of a "long white sandy beaches" type of girl, she wrestled with a strong desire to return to the sultry nights spent in the Caribbean. She frowned as the first flakes landed on her upper lip. With the first snow of the season tumbling from the sky, ready to complicate her day, she was right as far as she was concerned.

Crunching the white-littered ground with each step, she marched to the stretch limo parked idling at the curb. With the prospects of another chance to thumb her nose at the world, it should have brightened her mood. It was going to take much more than that today—much more after this hellish week was unpacked.

Glancing at her phone, she thought, *It's 2:58 a.m.! I really have lost it.* Hours before she would arrive at ground zero, she had definitely slipped a cog.

Stationed by the limo's open door, standing tall and rigid as any soldier on the parade field, he planted a huge smile in her direction, hoping for a peaceful trip.

She shivered as she brushed the flakes from her Canada Goose parka. The flash out of the corner of her eye was answer enough. *Good grief, Jerome. Give it up. It's three in the morning.*

"Good morning, Ms. Barrington," said Jerome, giving his cap a generous tug.

"Is it?" she asked, blanketing him with her usual early morning "gee, you're an idiot" pre-coffee-deprived glare. Lingering by the open door, she stomped the wet snow off her Jimmy Choos. She then fired off a withering scowl down upon her whipping boy that could easily blanch a scorpion. "Do I have everything I asked for? And I mean everything."

Great! The witch is in rare form this morning. Jerome dipped back behind the driver's door, ready to take cover. "Yes, ma'am. Everything as you ordered. Right-right there, next to your paper and beverage." He stammered as his backbone took a sudden vacation.

"Good. Let's get this fiasco started." She dropped down into the plush seat, settling in for the ride. "I wouldn't want to get fired for being late on my first day of this mind-blowing job." Then she muttered under her breath as she racked open the pages of her *Wall Street Journal,* "Good grief. I must be nuts."

As they rumbled over the George Washington Bridge, she looked up from the opinion section and gazed out of the rain-streaked bulletproof glass. Crossing into Jersey, she felt dirty already, grateful the sun hadn't risen to shine on the seedier side of life lurking just beyond the interstate.

Nothing but trash.

Taking a cautious sip of the ridiculously overpriced cappuccino, she settled back in the heated leather, already letting second thoughts invade. She fought the urge to cancel the mission and go back to her warm bed high in the sky. What did she actually have to prove anyway? How she had ever left a piece of her soul dangling out there unprotected was beyond her.

It was a hostile takeover. That's exactly what it was, and he was the king of it, she surmised.

Everything in her life was a hostile takeover. That conniving preacher had lassoed a tiny portion of her soul, his words blowing right through her normal defenses somehow.

Good luck, preacher boy, she thought with a twinge of guilt. Shame on the man for trying to squeeze the last drop of mercy or compassion out of her. He had somehow weaseled his way past fifteen years of calloused layers of pitiless living, but she would lay waste to his efforts. If she was honest, she would have to admit, she had no use for them anyway. Souls and a conscience were a liability in her line

DIVINE MEMORIES

of work. The circuit breaker for hers, deactivated years ago, allowed mercy and compassion to die on a brittle vine.

The sleek black limo, dominating the passing lane for the last three hundred miles, plowed through traffic, inching ever so closer to ground zero. She kept her head buried in the documents, profoundly uninterested in the patchwork of endless fields and dirty farms dotting the New York countryside. She put the finishing touches on her latest mission.

She came up for air, rubbing the sleep from her eyes. *What a pitiful, dreary existence these minions exist in*, she thought as the rural countryside sailed past her command vehicle. She had nothing but contempt for the rolling fields of farmland, and she already yearned to return to her concrete jungle. More accustomed to the thirty-thousand-foot view, she longed for one of the jets parked back in the hangar.

The sun, breaking over the horizon, made its presence known for the day as Jerome braked for the exit ramp into the rest area. Handling traffic with professional ease, he brought the stretch to a smooth stop. He lowered the partition, bringing their worlds to one. He silently took a three-second count first.

"Ms. Barrington, are you absolutely sure about this?" asked Jerome. "I just mean I don't want any…well, you know…problems." He braced for her ire, locking his eyes on the package with a surplus of worry and greed. He had no desire to see the wrong side of the bars. Had his meal ticket finally gotten in over her head?

Scooping up the stuffed manila envelope, she launched forward. "Jerome, don't get weak on me now. You promised!" she screeched. Letting the package of instant loyalty slip through her fingers, it tumbled down to the front seat. "Take that carrot and just keep that mouth of yours shut. Especially to my uncle," she snapped, adjusting the wig for the third time. She pulled up the fictitious driver's license and credit cards out of the bag, giving them a close once-over. "I hope everything is good to go with these."

Scrutinizing her new name and address, as usual, the reaction was swift. She scrunched up her face. *The new name sounds weak*, she thought, flinging the IDs back down.

3

She dropped them in the pitiful handbag she had ordered online last week from Target, and she grimaced at the new handbag. Ripping the tags off, she was astonished any self-respecting woman could carry such a monstrosity out in public. Dumping the rest of the contents out of her Gucci, snatching up the mere basics, she readied her attack. She closed her tired eyes from the boring drive and stole another deep breath. *The crosses I bear to prove a point,* she thought.

The thick packs of Benjamins felt righteous in Jerome's hand. More than enough for a man to disappear for a year. *Maybe two. If he drank cheap beer,* he figured. Being a witness to the mountains of pain she could dish out the door, he cringed at the thought of getting sideways with her. She would leave others to carry a banner of mercy or remorse as she paved the highway with her adversaries.

"Don't know what this is all about. Uh, well, please don't make me sorry for helping you create this Emily Parker identity." He stared at the transformed woman in his back seat. Heaven help anyone who gets in her crosshairs. Hiding lurking eyes behind his Oakleys, he admired his boss. *With that face and body, she looked good as a blonde or any color for that matter. If you take a leap and get past her moods,* he thought.

She adjusted her latest purchase in the mirror. Could people truly think these monstrosities looked good? *Sure, but they'd have to be suffering from a mental illness if they did,* she thought. Making sure the auburn locks would stay tucked under, she finally approved. "Jerome, you're rambling again. You make sure your butt makes it back here at the proper time on Friday."

Taking one last look in the mirror, she cringed at the reflection. Satisfied no further improvements were possible, she stepped out into the blustery cold and slammed the door on privileged living— the only life Nevada Rayne Barrington, one of the richest and most powerful women in the world, had ever existed in.

She sprinted across the parking lot as the taxi sat idling, waiting to launch the interloper among the masses. Dodging a truck camper, she officially abandoned her security and all the luxuries afforded a woman of her means. With each step, the carefully orchestrated layers of security were cast to the wayside, allowing the real world to seep in.

Unaccustomed to public transportation, she suffered for the cause, wiping the seat coated with foreign matter and managing the indignities somehow. Stepping gracefully out of the taxi, she felt no guilt at the deception about to unfold. In fact, each step closer to their corporate offices brought that old exhilarating desire to crush the world.

Man's world my ass.

Strolling through the front doors of the corporate offices of Atlas Omega, she tugged on the wig one last time. Smiling inside as she entered enemy territory, she sauntered up to the receptionist, ready to blend in to this filthy world she held in contempt. Adjusting the most hideous glasses she could muster the strength to parade around in, she patiently waited for the receptionist to finish up her call. *Yeah, first time for everything.*

"Oh yeah. Can I help you?" asked the receptionist, popping her gum while counting down the days to unemployment. Peering out over the top of her glasses, she reeked of cheap perfume and stale cigarette smoke. "Well, can I help you?"

And I thought I was rude, she mused to herself. Clearing her throat, Nevada held back the urge to come unglued, rip the wig off, and fire the gum popper on the spot. "Yes. I am uh, uh…Emily Parker. I was hired to support HR through the layoffs," she said stiffly, still morphing into her new identity.

"All you new temps meet in room 235. Down that hall and to your right." The receptionist pointed nonchalantly, mentally dismissing her fellow minion while already handling the next call.

Slow-walking it to room 235, she couldn't help but admire the decor. As if the broken tile floor, circa 1970s, wasn't enough, the peach-colored walls brought out the beauty of the warped drywall. She'd seen better decor in halfway houses.

Walking into her assigned room, she grabbed a seat near the back, avoiding eye contact with the other forty nameless rabble of temps. She eyed the twentysomething to her right. *Blue jeans. Really!* Swinging to the bleached blonde on her left while unwrapping her second piece of gum with unmanicured nails, she had surely peaked in life. Scraping her fingernail against her thumbnail, she waited for the show to get on the road.

With a room full of strangers, the room remained fairly quiet, each concerned with their own pitiful existence. The first possible hiccup of the mission came bustling through the door. Tucking her head behind the mindless drone in front of her, she blocked the speaker's direct line of sight.

Clearing a scratchy throat full of depression, the man said, "Good morning, everyone. I am David Brooks, CEO of Atlas Omega. I'd like to begin by thanking each of you for responding to the needs of our company." With a pasty face covered in a light sheen of sweat, he took a deep breath, fighting emotions that begged to come to the surface. "As you have been briefed, we are terminating over four thousand employees this month. I want this done with the utmost dignity as possible. I want you to put yourself in their place when you are letting them go." Feeling the cracks forming, he prayed the dam held a few minutes longer as he choked back a sea of anger. "These people are family to me, and some have been with us for decades. Please remember that," he said, walking off. He wished to say more but ignored a follow-up question.

He had been duly warned about her tactics and amazing abilities. Allowing a dazzling smile to camouflage her real agenda, he had let his guard down. Guilty in the first degree of bringing a knife to a gunfight, he had taken his eyes off the prize. The culmination of eighteen months of fierce negotiations would officially flow down the drain this week. At forty-five, being at the helm when the ship had run aground was going to be hard to swallow. Shouldering the responsibility for letting the dreams of his grandfather end on his watch was even harder. The one saving grace was his death so many years ago. It spared him the agony of seeing the business he had carved out over seventy years ago being fought over like hyenas on a zebra kill. The business was being dismantled and the pieces auctioned off to the highest bidders for pennies on the dollar. Outmaneuvered and outwrangled at each turn, she had beat him to the punch every time. The reputation of Nevada Barrington had been woefully underestimated. More aggressive than a time-share salesperson, she had cleaned his clock.

Assigned to cubicle J in room 250 with ten other HR temps, she sat at her assigned wooden desk with its fake oak finish. Cracking open a Diet Coke, she couldn't wait for Friday to roll around. The thought of forty hours of mind-numbing work just to prove she wasn't a monster made her stomach turn. Arranging the cheap pens by color, she heard the shuffling feet coming closer as they dragged across the broken tile floor.

Peering over the top of her cubicle wall was the peculiar smiling face of one Reggie Lions, her first official customer. "Is this J?" he asked with a goofy grin.

Rolling her eyes, she stabbed a finger toward the foot-tall *J* on the wall behind her. If this was the cream of the crop, it was going to be a long week. "Reggie? Can I call you Reggie?"

Wiping a sweaty palm on his torn jeans pants leg, he said, "Uh, yeah." He sat up a little straighter in his chair as she prepared to callously spoon-feed out the first wave of misery for the day.

"Looks...uh...you have been with the company for a little over three years. Your package will include a year of paid insurance and one thousand dollars per full year worked. Your last day will be December 30. Any questions?" *This isn't as hard as I thought it would be.*

Swallowing hard, his face fell. He knew it couldn't last. His luck never did. Tugging nervously on his scraggly chin hair, he slumped back down in the chair. "Uh. You mean I'm getting fired in less than two months?"

She turned from the monitor. "I'm sorry. What did you think was going on today?" she asked flatly, annoyed at his inept ability to grasp calamity in his life. *Where do they find these overachievers?* she wondered.

Rocking back and forth in his chair, he felt the air slipping from his chest. "We were told to report for severance discussions? I support my grandma. I'm all she's got. What am I going to do about her?" Catching his face in his hands, he allowed the gravity of her words to convict him.

7

Good grief! This was pathetic on so many levels, she thought. "Reggie, this job paid you what, eighteen dollars an hour? Surely you can replace it." *Maybe Grandma needs to get back in the workforce*, she reasoned. Looking at the line forming, she needed to wrap this up. "Here is the release for you to sign." She motioned for the next person to move forward.

Working throughout the day, word had circulated throughout the plant. She couldn't believe how much these people were living under a rock. Hearing a commotion at the door, she saw the problem steaming her direction. With her hair on fire, the redhead wasn't going to go down without a fight. Yanking the seat with little mercy, the attitude radiated from the woman.

"Let's get this over with," she barked, cracking her index knuckle.

"What's your name?" asked Nevada, matching the attitude.

"Matty Baker."

"Okay. Matty, I—"

"That's Mrs. Baker to you," demanded Matty, her icy stare begging for a challenger.

Caught in midsentence, Nevada stared back across the table. She was frosted by the audacity of this—for want of a better word—peasant. She forgot her vulnerability in this part of the new world. Raised in a world where her bark sent the underlings scurrying for cover, she hesitated. *Obviously, these people hadn't received the memo yet.*

Leaning over dangerously close, Matty said, "Listen, HR woman. Break that stare or I'll reach across this table and pull that blond hair out by its bloody roots. When I'm done with your hair, your pretty face is next."

Having never been in an actual fight in her thirty-five years, Nevada knew it wouldn't be wise to pick Matty Baker as her first bout. Seconds away from her first black eye, she scrambled for common ground to protect her scalp. "Mrs. Baker, it has been a long, tough day for everyone. I'm sorry."

"What's your first name?" asked Matty, reeling it back in a bit.

"It's Nev—" She faked a quick coughing fit. "I'm sorry. It's Emily."

Dropping her eyes to the floor, she could feel the heat from the other woman branding her as a failure. She was better than this. Replacing anger with a healthy dose of reality, she reflected over how fast their dreams had just been flushed down the toilet. Tired of fighting to make ends meet, they had been so close. She was dreading the conversation over the dinner table tonight; her Mike deserved something good in life. No shortage of bad news of late, she would have to tighten the belt up a bit.

"I made line supervisor last month," Matty said, smiling down at the floor. She shifted her gaze. "My husband and I scrimped and saved for eight years to scrape up a down payment on our house. We closed on it three months ago." Dropping her head down into her hands, she felt boxed in with no escape. "Ma'am, let's hear the offer, please."

The generous offer was a lifeline. Just that—a lifeline, not an answer.

Standing up, Matty flicked a stray tear away. "Mike and I will lose the house, but I'll not lose my decency. Emily, you didn't deserve my crap. I know it's not your fault." She extended her hand, dredging up a forced smile as she garnered the strength to leave. "It's not fair. We know how to do better. Management is inept."

Scribbling down Matty's personal information on the pad, she dropped it in her hideous purse. Releasing a heavy sigh, she launched her pen across the room, sticking it in the unfinished drywall at a strange angle. Emily Parker was in unchartered waters and sinking fast. The thought brought an uncomfortable wrinkle to her plan. Stowing her keyboard under the PC, she was already tired of how feeble and weak Emily Parker was morphing out to be. If she didn't find a way to clamp down on ole Emily, she'd be giving the store away by the time Friday rolled around.

"You can't fold up like a cheap tent at the first sign of a sad story," she murmured to the screen. Shutting down her computer, disgusted, she called for a ride to her hotel. Day one may have scuffed up her armor a bit, but a few stiff drinks should restore it by morning.

Back at the hotel, polishing off drink number four, she collapsed on the bed. She had nothing in common with these people, so why try forcing it? *If I say it enough...* Pulling the covers up to her chin, she closed her eyes.

One by one, his words returned, taunting her life. No, more of a deep burning haunt, much more than a simple taunt. Thrashing back and forth, she yanked the covers over her head as his words convicted her time and time again. She punched the pillow as his words strangled the strength from her. Business was business; it always had to stay impersonal. Reaching out, sloshing half of the last swallow down her negligee, she fell into a fitful asleep with one leg hanging off the bed.

As Friday morning rolled around, Emily Parker had an empty gas tank from witnessing a steady stream of lives caved in by greed. Putting faces to collateral damage was a dangerous endeavor. What could they expect to happen when you lived paycheck to paycheck? *For crying out loud, who does that?* she asked herself.

Emily Parker would need to be put out to pasture; she wasn't suited for this kind of work. She was soft, dangerous to a high financier. She had been forced to endure and be subjected to over a hundred heartbreaking stories, and these had smothered her. Ground zero had turned into a smoky crater of pity, and it was looking pretty ugly from her side of the desk. Glancing at the wall clock, she was banking on Jerome to rescue her from this train wreck. She had almost met her mandate.

A world away, seated at her Midtown Manhattan ivory tower, with a single stroke of her white crystal Caran d'Ache & Lalique fountain pen (a gift presented for torpedoing a behemoth last year), she had launched her initial strike package. A pen worth more than what a working-class man brings home in a month had tragically set these latest four thousand stiffs on a collision course with financial disaster. Forced to witness what a cruise missile armed with pink slips could do to the masses, she bit her lip, fighting to tremble. Would a wee bit of messy business, throwing the masses out in the cold, move the needle on an icy soul?

Coming back from lunch, with less than an hour left, she couldn't get out of this dreary experiment quick enough to suit her. She had fulfilled her mission. She had met her self-imposed obligation of facing the carnage she had generated. She created Emily Parker, and she planned to leave here without her. *She had no permanent place in her part of the universe.* Changing her spots once again, she would return as Nevada, the leader of one of the most powerful firms in the world. She couldn't let some sad stories interrupt her life. Running Barrington Enterprises, with assets approaching the one trillion mark, she had more than her share of the planet.

Glancing at the clock for the umpteenth time, noting the fifteen minutes left in this self-loathing saga, she could almost taste the sweet bite of the first of many martinis waiting for her in the limo. She was hoping her last customer had just taken the hot seat. The man appeared calm and collected. The tired expression accompanied with the blank stare, his avoiding eye contact, it all brought the hair up on the back of her neck.

Smiling at the thought of walking out of the nightmare shortly, she said, "Hi. Could I have your name to start?"

Tapping his fingers on her desk, the man refused to look her way. "My name?" he asked, eyes glued to the floor. "What's in a name?" He was gathering strength, allowing the wheels of retribution to lurch forward. "Joseph R. McGee. I guess you deserve to at least know who I am." He sighed. He was rubbing the salt-and-pepper stubble along his jaw, his closed eyes waiting to take orders from his lost soul.

"Okay. Thank you." Preparing to input the information, she saw the instant message pop up in bold letters: *McGee is a hothead. Be careful with him.* Looking back at the potential hothead, her heart sank. *Too late!* The butt of the pistol peeking out from his waistband ignited the first flames of fear, bringing her world to a grinding halt.

Mustering up a smile, masking the warning bells blaring in her brain, she continued. "Mr. McGee, what is your date of birth?"

Nothing! Unhitching his cart from the rest of the universe, he clasped his tired hands together, his hope in life bounced on empty.

Trying her best to remain calm, she typed the prearranged emergency message: *Code Omega! Room 250 cubicle J. Subject Joseph McGee, pistol in waistband.*

He broke the silence with a hoarse voice that would never again be heard by any other. "I'm fifty. I can't start over," he said as he prepared to close out their lives together. He was bobbing his head up and down to a rhythm he alone tuned in to. "I, uh, was hoping…you know…uh, you would be a little older."

Pulling his hand back off her desk, he took his first good look at the one person he chose to take with him to the other side. The poor thing was melting in front of him. He didn't want it to be this way. *Didn't she know it would be painless?*

"You saw it, didn't you?" He snatched the gun from his waistband, and the soft pop of the leather holster released its grip on death. "Do you have any family?" he asked, his voice an emotionless deadpan, void of compassion.

The ominous words of finality rocked her world, sending chills rippling through her body. With a weak nod of acknowledgment, she struggled to focus, losing peripheral. She was fighting to breathe as her chest tightened, squeezing the life out of her. Alone and unprotected for the first time in her life, her fear tumbled off the charts. With no hope of escape, she was at the mercy of the man with the thousand-yard stare. The ugly dark opening of the muzzle paralyzed her. Tracking her every move, it locked on, targeting center mass. The thought of the bullet ripping into her chest brought a sickening ache in the pit of her stomach. Time and reality clashed as her life slid onto the auction block of insanity. So many regrets, so many missed opportunities to make a difference. Her mind was issuing marching orders, but her body had closed up shop for the day.

"Mr. McGee, please…I have twin girls. They're barely four years old," she pleaded, lying in the name of survival, praying for compassion to ooze past his insanity.

Raising his hand to stifle her plea, he said, "Shh! The final bell for us has rung." He rested the pistol on top of her desk; the instrument of death loomed front and center. "Let's sit and talk for a bit. I promise it will be painless."

"Please, Mr. McGee. I don't want to die," begged Nevada. She was twisting in her chair, making her body as small of a target as possible. Her voice was reduced to a mere whisper.

DIVINE MEMORIES

Every fiber of her body cried out, pleading with her to flee. She was helplessly seeking pity from a man who just gave away his last ounce of compassion at the kitchen table that morning as he kissed his wife of twenty-eight years, Judy Lynn, goodbye for the last time. With her time ticking away, she grasped for a lifeline. She never took her eyes far from the pistol, which was now close enough that she could smell the pungent odor of fresh gun oil.

Keep it together, Nevada! The words roared through her brain. Trying to fight its fear, the trapped rat frantically searches for an escape clause. Something she was famous for in another time and place. Staring down the muzzle, she had four pounds of trigger pull separating her life and her death. She searched for the words to right his world again. She was stalling for time, probing for a fatal flaw in his plan. Doing her best to get to his level, she was grasping for a connection. Her world was a blur as the minutes ticked off while she searched the horizon for any sign of hope.

Out of the corner of her eye, she caught a movement. *Had that been there earlier?* She couldn't remember. The dark sleeve, exposed along the neighboring cubicle, disappeared back out of sight. Was that the cavalry coming or her imagination working overtime for a miracle? She voted for the cavalry. Desperate to stay aboveground another day, she, for the first time in her life, realized she couldn't buy her way out of trouble.

"Mr. McGee, I can get you a much better job if you just give me a chance," she pleaded.

He let out a mirthless chuckle. "I think we know how this is going to end. Close your eyes!" he commanded, stretching out his gun hand.

"Mr. McGee, my real name is Nevada. I can—"

The deafening back-to-back booms shook her to the core. Blown back by the horrific muzzle blast, she felt the first biting sting. Struggling to rise, she turned to confront the officer as McGee struggled to bring the Glock back up. The endless volley of incoming rounds struck down Joseph Robert McGee, forever ending a good man's life. A man who had been steamrolled by a world hell-bent on greed. He pitched over backward, breaking off the plastic chair leg as he got off one more round before collapsing through the cheap cubicle wall. Falling in the hallway, he was just another statistic, another evening news filler that lay sprawled on the floor dead.

"Ma'am, are you hit?" yelled the officer, fighting down his own panic.

Wiping spray off a face stricken with terror, she raked her hands over her torso, frantically searching for injuries through the acrid gun smoke. Unable to swallow, her mouth devoid of moisture, she pushed through the nightmare, fighting the onslaught of what-ifs barreling her way. "I...uh. Oh my god! I think I am good," she said, breathing a sigh of relief.

Pulling the wood slivers out of her blouse, she fought for air, amazed that she had escaped death. Her eyes locked on to the nasty jagged groove in her desk. McGee's final act, stubbornly refusing to be defeated, was plowing a six-inch gash in her desk. It halted mere inches from her stomach.

Snatching her by the arm, officers attempted to shield her past Mr. McGee. Facedown, a small trickle of blood rolled down the bridge of his nose, dripping thick drops on the bill of his worn Mets ball cap. Stealing a glance at the crumpled body, she might as well have pulled the trigger. No doubt, he had to have been someone's loved one. Now he was just a future memory to be forever misunderstood.

Stepping over the shell casings littering the floor, she knew her world had tilted. As she was being escorted down the hall, the adrenaline dump ran out of steam, and she was leaning all her weight on the officer. Close to collapsing, she fought the uncontrollable shakes as she fell into the seat.

The swarming police officers were armed to the teeth, with hardened faces refusing to acknowledge the danger they faced. Hiding their fear behind crude comments whispered to one another, they stripped off their raid jackets. All were thankful knowing they each had dodged a bullet. Once again, they would be returning home, delivered safe and sound back into the arms of loved ones.

Taking a few sips of water, Nevada came back to earth. Going through the debrief before filling out her statement, she couldn't help being distracted by the officers as they packed up their equipment. She was wondering what made a man or woman risk their life for a stranger. Lost in thought as she filled out her statement, she failed to see a problem headed her way.

"Ms. Parker, if you need anything from the company or me personally, don't hesitate to ask. Here is my personal contact information. We are a family here, and we will go down as one. It's been a tough day for everyone."

Surprised that her hand trembled, she pinched the business card and turned on the waterworks. "Thank you, Mr. Brooks. I will be fine," said Nevada, partially shielding her face with a tissue, hoping the bloodshot eyes and wig would do the trick. She winced at her adversary's kind words.

Shattered, beached on an island of broken lives, she sat surrounded by a sea of carnage brought about by her own devices. Forced to take ownership for the colossal mess, she wasn't proud of herself, which was a first for her. Finishing up her statement, she punched in the text. *Be there!* she pleaded to herself.

Hustling three blocks, sloshing through puddles of melted snow, she found Van Buren Street. The gentle flurries fought valiantly to paint a fresh coat of virgin white over the dirty piles of stacked snow. With a guilty conscience in overdrive, she wanted nothing better than to sneak back home, jump in bed, pull the covers over her head, and shut the world out.

Rounding the corner of Fourth and Meadow Avenue, the sight of her sanctuary idling on the side street brought a wave of unwanted emotions. *I hate Nevada Barrington and all she has become.* The thought came as she played the endless loop of the shootout over and over in her mind.

Jumping out to open her door, Jerome made his first mistake. "Hope you had a fine week, Ms. Barrington," he said with a warm smile, hoping the cougar would be peaceful on the ride back.

"Get me home!" she growled, dropping down in her seat. She slammed the button to raise the partition, cutting off any further conversation. Raking the useless glasses off her face, she showed no love for the wig, flinging both across the interior. The wig ricocheted off the side window, and she stomped it into the floorboard, assigning blame. She had created a raging storm for herself next month. Dark clouds were building, and she didn't see a path around it. The reckoning at the board meeting would be brutal. Running her fingers through her plastered hair, she realized she hated that preacher for the seed he had planted.

As she woke up the next morning, Nevada Rayne Barrington, accustomed to seeing defeat in the eyes of others, saw a mirror full of it. Staring back at her was a broken woman that grieved a distant memory. Heavy times, when life zigged instead of zagging, always brought their memories flooding back. Gone these many years, ripped from her life just when she needed them the most. Stolen from this good earth, leaving many more questions than answers—answers she would trade all her billions for.

With the walls closing in, she would seek refuge where she felt closest to them. Looking down, she could hear it beckoning her to come and rejuvenate. Even ninety-five stories below, it still brought back childhood memories during the good times. Reaching for her phone, she hoped Jamal was free.

He picked up on the first ring. "Hello?"

"Jamal, I know it's Saturday, but would you be free for a quick security detail?" she asked, crossing her fingers.

"You know it. When and where?"

"Come to my penthouse. I want to go to Central Park for a stroll," she said with an unexpected giggle. It had been a while since her last visit; maybe her world wasn't lost after all. She shook off the foreboding thoughts. Next week would take care of next week. It always had. "Jamal, dress warm!" she added.

Walking through Central Park, she never could understand the fickle math in life. She watched the children playing, accompanied by young parents as they frolicked in the foot of fresh powder. Red snotty faces plastered with big smiles—the cruel math wasn't fair. She was rich beyond most people's imagination, and they had nothing. Once, long ago, she was one of them. Trading life's simple pleasures for her billions now was tempting. They were happy, and she was a sad sack of gut-wrenching emotions that needed a bodyguard.

Watching the mothers with their babies, she knew her biological clock was ticking louder with each passing day. Would she ever truly be happy? Would there ever be a partner? Would she ever have children in her future? At thirty-five, working seventy-plus hours a week, there hadn't been time.

Watching a helicopter mom pick her son up from a tumble with tender care, she thought about it. What kind of mother would she be? *Will I ever hear the music of the pitter-patter of feet in the morning?* she wondered silently. Next year, she would be the same age as her mother when she disappeared off the radar. No amount of money had ever gotten the answers she longed for.

Surrounded by all that happiness, it dragged her to that all-too-familiar dark place. "Jamal, let's get out of here," she said, not waiting for an answer. She brooded over next month's troubles. She hated being living proof that money couldn't buy everything. Surrounded by the best money could buy, she'd trade it all to uncover one simple mystery. If no man and no amount of money could provide it, she knew she would finally be forced to seek answers elsewhere. Times when the world was packing it on always brought her to this fragile crossroads. Up against the ropes, she was one punch from going down, disgusted at how high the mountain of hypocrisy was going to be to climb up. She had stumbled to the foot of this mountain many times, but at the last minute, money had always found her a detour around it.

Taking refuge in the penthouse, she curled up in the fetal position on the daybed. She pressed up against the huge window, daring it to fail, allowing her to tumble over a thousand feet and splatter down onto Park Avenue. Exhausted from the turmoil and a healthy dose of depression, she came to an hour later. The power nap felt good. Waiting for Chinese to be delivered, she parked herself by the window, witnessing the lights of the city come alive. The cool touch of the glass felt comforting as she rested her forehead against the massive window. "This is all I know. This is where I thrive," she whispered.

Dining alone, she prepared for the most important negotiation of her life. She couldn't do it unassisted, keeping a tight hold of the wine bottle. She tried to recall her earlier teachings. The rules had always seemed ridiculously complicated and, in her opinion, unnecessary in many instances. Exhausted and suffering from the full effects of a bottle and a half of wine, she was ready. She knew the negotiator on the other side had never lost a decision, that he was tough but fair—if he bothered to show. His answers were known to be short and sweet, if he gave you one.

Dropping the wine bottle unceremoniously in the trash can, she swayed to the bed. Lying in the dark, she searched for any overlooked detour around the mountain. One that didn't involve groveling or begging. One that didn't have her upending her life needlessly. Trapped in a quagmire, his last brutal moments floated through her mind. Paralyzed by his senseless death, out came the white flag as she closed her eyes to the old world.

Fighting every instinct in her life, having exhausted all worldly options, she took her first step upon Mount Hypocrisy. Tormented by the never-ending visions of Joseph McGee, she closed her eyes tighter, shutting the world out. With the sharks circling closer each day, she crumbled, letting the world crush her down. Bowing down, she let the darkness consume her as she officially reached out to pull the card marked *religion* from the deck. Weighing her options to speak or suffer many more years in silence, her voice sounded foolish and small to her ears.

Some will one day tell you, he smiled when the knock on his door arrived. He had waited with a mountain of patience known but to him. Others will one day tell you he dropped everything to hear her tender voice searching for him in the dark. Placing the universe on hold, he strained to hear every word she spoke from her mansion to his.

They say he had to hush the heavens when her lips parted. Beckoning the angels, he dispatched them with haste to be by her side, giving her strength to ready her for the rocky path she would travel.

"God, it says you know my name and all I have done. So I guess I don't need to explain what brought me here. But I hope you have thick skin because I'm mad. You give with one hand and take with the other." Sucking in a deep breath, she let the pillow take care of the tears. "I don't know what the rules are, and I don't care. You started this war with me. You allowed them to be taken from me," she cried.

Thrashing back and forth, ashamed of the first sob, she opened the floodgates, holding nothing back. "I'll give up all my possessions in this world for it." Her soft voice was breaking, a mere murmur. "I'll use anything I have to point lost souls to you. Whatever you need," she bargained.

Wrapped in darkness, swiping a tear off the tip of her nose, she continued, "Lord, did you really form the mountains? Do the oceans really listen to your voice alone? Did you really hang the stars in the sky?" She faltered at the enormity of her next words. "Father, if you can really hear me, show me this awesome power, and I'll get out of your way."

Double-parking her soul at the intersection of Desperation Street and Hypocrisy Boulevard, Nevada Barrington had heard of humility. She would now take a bath in it. "Father, whisper in my ear. Where do their bones lie?"

Sliding the pillow over her head, Nevada allowed exhaustion to win the battle.

2

Joseph McGee's heirs would never forget the sleek black stretch limo rolling in at the last moment on that bitter cold December day.

Strolling out across the cemetery like royalty, with her small entourage at a respectable distance, Nevada was unknown to all. Standing silently near the rear, her face masked by the veil and dark sunglasses, she fought the desire to flee. She spoke to no one.

Had she been someone famous? they speculated. Maybe she was at the wrong funeral. They would always tease Joe's widow afterward about him having a secret rich love child—maybe. Whatever or whoever she was, they would always be grateful for the large anonymous endowment given in Joe's honor.

Holed up in her penthouse, shedding layers of smugness at an alarming rate, she orchestrated her escape, pondering the collateral damage. Perched high above the city of millions, looking down at the masses, she would miss it terribly. If she abandoned her concrete jungle filled with glitz and glamour, where would she land? She prepared for one last endeavor to tilt the scales of justice. She couldn't correct past transgressions, but she could halt the wholesale destruction being prepared to steamroll the common man.

Poring over the pile of spreadsheets, she would do what she did best. No general on the battlefield had anything on her. No detail was too small. Stripping mercy from the bones of her enemies, she would plan for any counterattack. Pulling the rug out from under the other guy would be the lunch special of the day. Surviving in a mecca that housed the most brilliant financial institutions in the world, she had slayed most of them. In a male-dominated world, she was fearless and feared in any boardroom she chose to grace, racking up countless notches on the ladder of success.

Annoyed at the intrusion, she glanced over at the monitor. She tipped her chair over as she bailed, scrambling to rake up the precious spreadsheets into a pile. He wasn't going to be put off again. She gave the room a quick once-over before opening the door.

"Well, hello, Uncle Charles."

"Hi yourself." He shifted his weight to his good leg, annoyed at her smirk. "Well, can I come in?" he snapped with a pinch of annoyance added in for good measure.

Stiff-necked from head to toe, she couldn't wait to see him lose his mind. She hated every drop of English blood in her body. Luckily, half of it was American. Bowing at the waist, sweeping her arms open wide, she braced herself for the snarky lecture.

Raking his eyes over the 4,300 square feet of prime New York real estate, he was dumbfounded. He zeroed in on the stack of spreadsheets encircled by a plethora of empty Chinese-food containers with a stray pizza box or two thrown in for good measure. He deployed his famous scowl, complete with that stupid teeth-sucking noise he was known for.

The neat freak in the poor man must be going bonkers, she thought.

He was careful not to commit the toe of his Kiton wingtip too far as he lifted the lid of the nearest pizza box. You'd have thought it was a land mine as he lowered the lid with caution. Proudly displaying the bones of a two-day-old half-eaten anchovy-and-sausage pizza, the smile was getting harder to conceal.

Plopping down on the barstool, she enjoyed pushing his pompousness over the cliff. He always resented her American half, and he delighted in reminding her of the proper way an English lady should perform, never failing to highlight the unfortunate fact that her pedigree was not pristine.

"I'm kinda busy. What can I do for you?" she asked stiffly, picking a spot of dried ketchup off her pajama top. She flicked it off her fingernail. It missed the trash can and sailed across the room.

Gazing down his long thin nose, he knew he could push her no further. Her mother, even though American, had been shrewd. "You look like a vagabond living in this pigsty," he bellowed, reaching for a spreadsheet that had strayed from the pile. Riding her coattails, while degrading for a gentleman, had garnered magnificent rewards.

"Huh-uh! Those are for my eyes, period," she shouted, snatching it out of his bony fingers.

On thin ice, he ventured with care, scratching the side of his goatee, "What are they? If I may be so bold."

Letting the smile take its time, she lifted her eyes from the floor with a healthy dose of mischievousness. "Pet project," she offered, opening the door.

Seething at her level of indignation, he grabbed the doorknob. How could this little ragamuffin dressed in bedclothes at midday be his superior? he thought. "Nevada, my dear, you have been absent. Refusing to communicate with anyone these last few weeks, among other notable discrepancies."

Popping the monogramed handkerchief out of his breast pocket, he prepared to clean that invisible speck from his glasses. This was number two on her list of Uncle Charles's most annoying habits, ranking just under teeth-sucking.

"Do you need to be reminded you are in charge of an eight-hundred-billion-dollar empire?" he asked.

Cocking her head to the side and squinting, she said, "I certainly don't. Do you?" She worked the door closed, bruising the sleeve of his Armani and letting the door say her goodbye.

The games would be fierce, stripping her enemies of their wealth and ill-gotten gains with a well-deserved stretch in an eight by ten courtesy of the Federal Bureau of Prisons. Violators knew the consequences for disobedience.

He is in deeper than his norm, she surmised. In her world, the eyes told it all. His spoke of a tale of woe. Like flipping a coin. Would it be a call to the Securities and Exchange Commission or a dish best served up cold?

Less than seventy-two hours till showtime. She needed to put the finishing touches on her surprise. An urgent call to housekeeping was in order first. Uncle Charles was right about one thing. It was a pigsty—a calculated pigsty.

Arriving fifteen minutes early, she strolled back to her usual table, signaling Jacob for the usual. Parking the martini by her glossy folder and his cranberry tonic next to hers, she waited. He was more of a father to her than just a board member. Her rock during rough times. Punctual as always, he came through the door on the hour.

"Hi, Lawrence." She leaned in for the mandatory peck on the cheek and gracious hug.

"Hello, sweetheart."

At seventy-one, he could pass for fifty. The daily workouts since the heart scare had certainly agreed with him. Eyeing her up close, she looked immaculate, maybe a little tired around the eyes. The complaints were overblown. The innocent-looking folder told him everything he needed to know. She was going to war.

"Thanks for coming on short notice. I need to share something with you." She caressed the folder containing her battle plan. Would the man of few words have her back? "You better have a sip or two first," she said with a wry smile.

She was her mother's daughter all right—straight and direct. He watched her torture the unlucky olive with her toothpick. Had she found a new level of vengeance? He was wishing this time, she wouldn't go for the throat. Draining the last of his cranberry tonic, he put in a rush order for another. It would be needed. He knew the glossy folders were reserved for her pet projects.

Unsealing the folder, he'd been here many times. The opening sentences sent his world spinning off its axis. She would leave no bridges unmarred. She would mete out punishment to those she felt worthy of it. Crushed, he ran his eyes over the last few sentences. Halting on the last page, he brought the folder closer, rereading the last paragraph a third time. He was hoping the words were wrong. Could his goddaughter leave this life!

Letting the folder slip through his hands, his long face matched his mood. "Honey, where would you go?" he asked, trying his best to conceal the heartache.

Clutching the hand of the one man she trusted in the world, she pressed it to her lips. He cared about her, no questions asked. Ignoring all the other noises in the world, he never faltered.

She replied, "To the first wide place in the road where someone is good to me and money doesn't rule their lives. I mean it. I really want to go where no one knows my name or worth." Cracking when the gentle hand caressed her back, she added, "I also…I hate everything I have become, Lawrence."

The gut punch left him empty. She kept him young. Didn't she know that? The closest thing to family, had his little fiery spark finally burnt out? Clearing his throat, he agonized about the allegations. Rubbing her shoulder, he couldn't help but notice the weight loss. He pulled back, giving her one last pat. "Your uncle Charles came to me with some disturbing tales. Are you okay?"

Refusing to take the bait, she continued working on the olive's demise, stabbing it with renewed vigor. "You know how much I hate him," she said, daring to be challenged.

"*Hate* is an awfully strong word," said Lawrence, flirting with disaster.

"Yeah, that's what the preacher said." Mortified at the slip, she hoped it slid under the radar.

Cocking one brow skyward, he mused, *Was it possible?* "Nevada, have you been going to church?" He'd be shocked at the possible depths of her problems if she had resorted to this. "You are really scaring me now."

Squirming under the interrogation, she sought sanctuary from the last sip of the martini. "What if I have?" she asked, slinging a bit of attitude across the table. She yanked her chin back in place when no return fire materialized.

"Nothing, sweetheart. But we both know how you felt about church. Why the sudden course change?"

Oh, Lawrence, you poor dear. You have no idea, she thought. Twirling the delicate stem of the cocktail glass between her fingers, she struggled to come up with a skillful dodge.

Reaching out for a hand, feeling the tremor, he said, "Nevada?"

Scanning the crowds coming in for lunch, she knew she deserved what was coming. Biting through the tortured olive and flipping the toothpick back down, she said, "Not here." She scooped up her bag. "You're not going to want to hear it."

"I'm sure it's not that bad, Nevada," he said with a nervous grin, pulling her chair back.

"That's sweet of you, Lawrence, to think that." Dropping a twenty down for Jacob, she said, "Let's go to the office."

Stepping out on Fifth Avenue, the sea of controlled chaos engulfed them. The lingering sweet smells of the shops pitted against the odor of horses and exhaust vied for their attention. Spreading his arms wide, Lawrence asked, "Can you give this all up, Nevada?" He was shouting above the screaming sirens in the background.

Looming above them, the monumental icon—a testimonial to man's ability to build skyward—stood silent, gazing down at the chaotic street scene. The cacophony of the never-ending traffic jam, the lifeblood of the city, would soon be a distant memory.

With a love-hate relationship with the inner city, she fought to maintain control as she took in the all-too-familiar scene. "Lawrence, I will miss the hustle and bustle of this great city, especially the Empire. But I have to move on." Stepping into the crowded reception area, she attempted to make a beeline for her office.

"Ms. Barrington?" said Marjorie.

"Yes, Marjorie. What earth-shattering problem exists now?" grumbled Nevada, biting her upper lip and holding her annoyance in check.

"These two gentlemen are from the Securities and Exchange Commission," she said, releasing a grimace behind their backs.

"Follow me. Five minutes and not a second longer," she offered, never breaking stride as she continued back to her office.

Closing the door and activating the smart glass, she said, "Have a seat, gentlemen." Tapping a perfect manicured nail against the mahogany desk, she asked, "What brings the United States government to my door today?" She fixed a bored stare on the closest agent.

"I'm Agent Wilson, and this is Agent Braxton. Before we get started, I believe this conversation should be for your ears only," said the agent, eyeing Lawrence.

"Lawrence stays. Continue."

"Okay then. Well, we are looking into trading irregularities in a company your company is possibly foreclosing on."

"Well, two things first, agent. One, you know I can't discuss anything in regards to unannounced decisions by this corporation. And second—and this is a big one—you know full well if I knew anything about irregularities, as you call them, I would have already dialed your number," barked Nevada, a veteran of unannounced government fishing expeditions. She rose to her feet. "I think we're done here."

Pitching a look over at his partner accompanied with a slow nod to the door, the agent replied, "Okay. Just trying to give you a heads-up. Good day."

"What was all that about?" asked Lawrence, breaking the silence.

"The glossy folder left out a lot of details on purpose." Cracking open a chilled bottle of Iceberg, she waited. "Well, that didn't take long."

Poking his head into the office, Charles asked with a puzzled look, "What did they want?"

Enjoying his fear, boiling just under the surface, she said, "Wanted to congratulate me on being nominated for the CEO of the Year award."

Flipping a major portion of his comb over back in place, Charles said, "I'm serious, Nevada."

"Oh, something about irregularities in trading." Leaning to the side, she asked, "Is that the Bankhill brothers in your office? Do you think that's smart business?" asked Nevada.

Sucking on his front teeth, the wall of nerves was headed his way faster than he could process. Turning without a word, numb to her question, he shuffled back to his office.

"Lawrence, let's go into the SCIF. I called Larry on our way over and had him sweep it for us." Slinging documents right and left at a furious pace, she came up with a foot-thick pile of papers. "I'm also going to need you to permanently take over operations in a few days."

Stung by the revelation, his eyebrows headed north and his chin flying south, the first salvos in her private war were coming much faster than he had counted on. "Nevada! Nevada dear, a board member is one thing, but to take over operations," mumbled Lawrence.

Walking into the SCIF, at a cost north of twenty million, the sensitive compartmented information facility allowed her to safely unload without fear of electronic intrusion.

"Did you see the looks we got from Uncle Charles and his two flunkeys?" Dropping the pet project folder on the conference table, she continued, "I am going to war, and it's not going to be pretty."

Crumbling inward, did he have the fight in him? Listening to the firebrand unfold part of the battle plan, could he handle the stress of running one of the world's biggest empires? She was built for war, but was he?

He asked, "Where will you be? I mean, after this blows up."

"Not sure." Snagging his hand, the gentle squeeze back would be missed. "But I promise to take care of the problem first before I hand it over to you."

Sinking back into the cushion, letting the air out of a sail or two, he hazarded a sliver of a smile. "Well, I thought you had something worse to talk over," said Lawrence. Her downturned smile revived his fears.

Clenching her teeth together failed to hinder the trembling lip as she lowered her eyes to the police report. "We aren't done yet."

"If it's about the church comment, I didn't mean to—"

Eking out a smile doomed to fade, she cut him off. "No. No, it's not that," she said hoarsely. "Not totally anyway." She braced herself for the oncoming flood of ugly memories starring one Joseph R. McGee. Haunted by the crumpled bullet-riddled body, she let it consume her. *Time to face the music*, she thought as she sank deeper in the cushion, devoting her attention to the chip in her nail. She let the steam build up as the images turned her stomach. Flinging her mop of auburn hair back violently, she blew. Raking the file off the table, she screamed, "I got a man killed!"

"What?"

Caught flatfooted, the next few minutes were earmarked for a new low in her life.

"Who?" asked Lawrence, summoning up the strength to face her next revelation.

Pitching forward, collapsing into her folded arms, she hated the sound of it. Recoiling from his touch, the hand withdrew. Shunning his love, she could only imagine the thoughts racing through his mind.

Letting the emotions drain, she leaned back to face her godfather. Ripping a tissue free, dabbing gently, she went to work on the damage. Gathering up a handful of hair, she managed to convince the stray tendrils to stay in place. She nibbled on her thumbnail, working up the nerve to meet his gaze. "I don't even know where to begin." She couldn't keep the once proud chin from nosediving. The sterile room with multiple layers of soundproofing magnified the painful rush of air slipping through her teeth.

Not since her parents went missing had he seen her so broken. "Start at the beginning, and we'll see where it takes us."

Surrendering, tired of the mental battle tormenting her 24-7, she tilted back in her chair, clamping her eyes shut. But still, the ugly images wrought havoc upon her soul. "Okay. But have an open mind."

Drawing back his hand, fighting the urge to reach out for her arm, he sat stoically. "I would hope you know me better than that, Vada."

She allowed a trace of a smile to bubble up from the dark depths she was enduring. The mention of her nickname let a slice of goodness invade her thoughts. She hadn't been called that since childhood. *He always knew what to say*, she thought. Sliding an arm over toward the sound of his voice, searching blindly, she felt the reassuring squeeze she had always leaned upon. How her life would be without him, she couldn't imagine. The best business decision Byron and Julia Barrington had ever made. They would never know what an amazing godfather he would become.

Taking a generous sip of water to clear the crying sludge from her throat, she said, "I guess it began a few months ago. I-I got these." She was struggling to climb back up that mountain of hypocrisy.

The gentle voice of reason always brought her to the top. "Whatever it is. Just say it, Nevada," he whispered.

DIVINE MEMORIES

"You were right. I did go to church a few times. A little country church a few miles out of the city. I can't explain why. I got these feelings I should go there." Dredging up the strength to reveal more, seeking the comfort of darkness, she covered her face. "Oh, Lawrence. I thought I was doing right, but it all fell apart," she mumbled through her hands. "I foolishly got in a disguise. I infiltrated Atlas Omega posing as an HR person. I just needed to see firsthand the results of our hostile takeover, and a man was shot and killed by the police as he tried to murder me."

Under the false impression the wind had already been knocked out of him with the first revelation, he couldn't prevent the last gasp from slipping out. "Nevada, why?" he asked, threading fingers through the salt-and-pepper hair earned from almost forty years of babysitting the Nevadas of the world. "Are you in any trouble?"

Cracking open one eye, she stole a peek at Lawrence. "No. I gave a statement and was released," she offered, waiting for the other shoe to drop.

Parking his hands on his head, he leaned back. "How did this fiasco not get its day in the news cycle?" he asked with a hint of suspicion.

Sneaking a hand down to slow the shaking of her leg, she replied, "Well, uh, before I tell you, I plan on straightening it out."

The whistle come out loud and clear in the SCIF room as he let the latest revelation rattle around in his brain. "I almost hate to ask. No, let me rephrase that. I do hate to ask, but let's hear about the man that was killed."

Conjuring up the images, her stomach rolled as she loaded up the nightmare. "He came to my cubicle and, from being so distraught at losing his job, pulled a gun on me. Lawrence, he tried to kill me. He shot at me just as the police shot and killed him." Wrapping up the well-rehearsed tale, she closed with a bang. "I gave a statement under a false name and came back home. End of story."

Wading out into a sea of troubles coming down the pike, he said, "Oh, Nevada honey. You know that's far from the end of the story. Let's get it all out there. What about Charles?"

29

The reprieve from her stupidity to zero in on Charles was a welcome distraction. "You remember Johnny Coopertown down at that sleazy operation Hicks and Larkins Securities? Well, he gave me a heads-up that Charles, the Bankhill brothers, and a few others have been illegally shorting Atlas Omega stock from 190 bucks down to under 2 dollars so far. That's what the two agents were fishing for."

Hurling the cheaters across the table, he did his best to rub the misery from his eyes. "Can this crap show get any worse?"

Regretting the excursion into Alpha Omega territory, she was desperate for a redo on the last two months. She hated the thought that she had dropped the ball. "Uh, possibly. Right now, from my research, if they covered all their shorted stock under ten dollars, the profits would be immense. In fact, the profits would be great enough to purchase enough Barrington stock to gain control of us."

Stretching out to retrieve his readers, he pored over the battle plan one more time. Taking a hard look at the youngest female commanding a Fortune 50 company, he said, "Are you sure this will work? Nevada, they won't take this lying down."

At 5'10", standing eye level to Lawrence, she replied, "By five o'clock Friday, they will be drowning their sorrows in some crappy bar."

"Okay. I'll meet with the other friendly board members and get back to you," said Lawrence, holding the door open.

"Good. Don't tell them the whole plan though."

"Nevada, I don't even know the whole plan. Do I?" he asked with his first real smile of the meeting.

"Sorry. No, you don't. It's for your own good," she said, planting a kiss on his cheek.

Making her way back to her office, seeing the cluster of scum in Charles's office was almost offensive. The brothers stared her down with a vengeance. *What pitiful minions*, she thought as she passed the doorway.

"Did you see her?" said Charles, almost gleeful. "She's ready to tumble and collapse."

"Yeah. Crying session for sure," said Amos Bankhill.

With a full chorus of the knuckle cracking of stubby fingers, Liddy Bankhill chimed in. "Yeah! She's crumbling for sure. You positive you heard her say she was handing over the reins to Lawrence?"

Snapping his head around, ready to pounce, Charles growled. "You want to hear the recording again, Liddy? You think I haven't wanted to hear those words for the last fifteen years? Her personal life is crumbling. We must strike immediately."

"Sorry, boss. Let the excitement overload me a bit," said Liddy, who was more muscle than a thinker. He bounced a look over at his big brother, Amos.

"We been this close before and got cocky," warned Amos.

The ominous warning shook the mood back to ground level.

Swiveling around, turning his back to the Bankhills, Charles peered out the window, daydreaming of her corner office. He had underestimated her once before. Spinning back, he muttered, "Don't bring that up again."

3

Agonizing over the next few minutes, his words would capture all the turmoil in her life. She had run it through her mind night after night, each time coming up the villain. The brutal sting of his words would be earned. All doubts must be bulldozed away, and there would be no crawling back. When she fired this bullet, there would be no future for her.

Drawing the business card between her fingers for the third time, she wondered. Was she ready to come off the throne? With two numbers punched in, the financial papers would have a field day next week.

Sucking in her bottom lip, she waited, almost glad if he wasn't available. She was half hoping to get his voicemail.

"Hello…this is David Brooks. Hello?"

Hearing his voice again regurgitated the painful bundle of emotions. "Mr. Brooks, uh, this is Nevada Barrington. How are you today?" She was cringing, waiting for the sting, knowing what she would be sending his way if the tables were turned.

Unconcerned about her wants or desires anymore, the sigh might have come out a little louder than intended. "Well gee, let me think about that for a minute. How would you feel if I was about to gut and destroy everything your family struggled to build over the last seven decades? You won. What do you want now?"

"I know that it must seem bitter on your end, but I would like to discuss some things with you. Are we on a secure line?"

"Bitter. Seriously? If you've called to gloat, I've got better—"

Drawing in her last breath as a firebrand, she cast away a life of power. "I need you to file an 8-K with the SEC today announcing an emergency board meeting at our headquarters here at the Empire for six a.m. tomorrow. I also need to have you assemble your full legal team two hours earlier."

The cold call threw his game off. "Humph. And why on earth, pray tell, would I do such a thing, Ms. Barrington?" asked Brooks. Enjoying the exchange, he was sniffing out the possibility she might have overshot somewhere, scouting out a sweet strategic moment to click Ms. High-and-Mighty out of his nightmare.

She rubbed her tired eyes, the result of too many sleepless nights. "Brooks, do you want your precious company back?" she asked, holding back a tongue more famous for its ferocity than its mercy.

Spilling his morning coffee, he snagged the receiver out of the cradle. "I'm listening."

"I can, uh, only imagine what you must be thinking, but I mean to surrender my hold over your company, Mr. Brooks," she said, leaving the door open for his wrath.

Shaking the coffee off the resignation draft, he said, "Ms. Barrington, I don't think your imagination is that vivid. But I'll listen for the sake of my employees. But hear this. I don't like you personally or anything you and your company stand for. If this is a game you're running, I'll go to jail if I have to just to get even with you."

"Fair enough. I'll see you and your team tomorrow morning. One more thing. Could you also bring Matilda Baker with you?"

"Who?"

Scanning the scribbled note again, she said, "I believe she goes by Matty Baker. She's a line supervisor on B shift."

"Why?" asked Brooks, trying to recall her face.

"Good day, Mr. Brooks."

With her bags already packed, she looked out over the sea of buildings. She would miss the city life, the excitement of the deals, the lure of the mighty dollar. Cleaning out her desk, the crumpled Polaroid fell to the floor. Crunched behind a sheaf of papers all these years, the sweet memory rocked her world. She was displaying her newly acquired driver's license. That was almost twenty years ago, and the happy trio was smiling proudly. One last group hug that would ultimately have to last her a lifetime. Who knew, one week later, they would be gone forever?

Camp Scum was a beehive of activity as she departed the office, receiving a smirk from the younger Bankhill brother as she passed. *Here's to your best efforts, minion*, she thought as she fired back a smirk, pondering just how much retaliation they would generate.

"Did you see that? Box in hand. She be done, brothers." Liddy beamed.

"She knows and she's gonna take a walk? Is your guy sure, Charles?" asked Amos.

"As much as you can be about that little viper. My guy assures me that her plans will fail to stop us."

Stepping into the limo, she threw the box down on the floorboard, allowing the plaques to tumble out. "Jerome, take me to the corporate attorney's office over on Sangamon Street." Bracing herself for a fight to the finish, she hoped her parents would approve.

As she walked into the plush offices of Hackett, Hackett, and Moore, she flagged down Andrew Moore, a senior partner. She closed the door immediately, taking her last official breath before the world got its first hint of her war.

"Nevada, we're amongst friends here," said Andrew, smiling as the young upstart took a seat.

The dark circles around her eyes told the story of a woman tormented by a world of constant distrust and a lack of love. "What's a friend?"

Reaching for the sky, Andrew said, "I surrender! Must be serious, huh?" He wiped the smile off his face.

Sliding the sheet of drafts across the massive oak desk, she said, "Make those official at precisely 8:01 a.m. tomorrow. Not a minute later."

Scanning the documents quickly, the magnitude of the news made the wily veteran sit up a little straighter. Dropping the drafts down on the desk, he leaned back, tilting his head forward, peeking over the new readers. "Nevada, are you absolutely—and I mean *absolutely*—sure you want to do this?" asked Andrew.

"Yes."

"Who knows?" he asked, firing off questions quicker than answers were going to be forthcoming.

"Two people on this planet know about it, and they're eyeing each other right now. Keep it that way till 8:01 a.m."

"Nevada, don't go off half-cocked."

"Sorry. That train has left the station already," she answered, pulling the door open. She left him with questions that would never get any answers.

Sliding back into the limo, she eyed the suitcase. "Jerome, did you have any trouble at the bank?"

"No, ma'am," he said, giving her a warm smile in the rearview.

"Good. Now take me to that little strip mall up on Route 1. You remember where?"

"Yes, ma'am. Pickup two hours later like before?"

"Right."

Browsing through the store, she kept a watchful eye on the limo as it disappeared out of sight. Leaving the store, she snuck down the usual path. The rusty hinge filed a loud complaint as she pulled the door open. The stale air rushed out to welcome her as before. Working overtime, the furnace was losing the war. Her stilettos, striking the ancient and worn varnished oak planks, echoed loudly in the sparsely furnished room. Brushing a layer of dust off, she chose a seat in front. She let her head fall back, and she shut the world out. The world felt right in this little house. One speck of quiet tranquility among the immense noise of the universe. Soaking up the serenity, she lowered the barriers, breathing in the peace only found here. Startled by a noise, she sat up quickly.

"Don't feel bad. You're not the first to fall asleep sitting there."

Taking a quick swipe across her face while mentally gathering up her string of grievances, she faced the man that started it all. In three simple sermons, he had done what the most conniving scum couldn't do. With all the emotions pulling her in a thousand different directions, she couldn't keep her anger toward him focused.

"Are those pieces of insulation stuck to your face?" she asked, replacing the frown with a smile.

"Yeah, I guess," said Pastor Rick, a bit red around the gills. "That's what I get for trying to save a dollar. We should get another year out of that decrepit furnace though." The shepherd—with a flock of twenty-five on a good Sunday, thirty on a major holiday—remembered the face. "The kids love the new playground equipment."

"You're welcome. Now buy a new furnace with the rest." Charmed by his pleasant charismatic way, she wrestled with her attack, its strength withering away by the minute. "I came here to pick a fight."

Cocking his head to the side, he squinted out of one eye. "You don't look much like a fighter."

"That's got many before you in trouble," she said with a smile that had foiled more than its share of plans in this ugly world.

"Humph. I'll just bet you're right." Trading in the grin for a wrinkled frown, he asked innocently, "But what do we have to fight about?"

Abandoning the smile, she said, "Ouch! Where do I begin?"

He dropped down in the next pew. "Try the beginning. It always works for me."

"That's the second time I've been told that." Listening to the comforting sound of the air whistling out of the floor duct as the furnace tried to prove its worth, she teetered. Could he be trusted? "Preacher, do you know who I am?"

"I guess I don't. But why you landed here is more important to me right now."

Leaning over, she tapped the tip of her JINsoon-coated nail across the back of his hand. "Has God ever mocked you, preacher? I mean, really shoved life down your throat. Casting you in the darkest pit he can find. Then stand by, cheering for the rest of the world to pile on?" Allowing her head to settle against the pew, she was staring at everything and nothing. "Has your life ever sank to depths so deep, light can't penetrate?" she said, trailing off. She waited on his words of salvation as she watched the ancient ceiling fan rattling overhead.

Staring into the red-rimmed pale blue pools of agony, a storm was clearly raging. He tiptoed through the minefield. "I doubt if God

DIVINE MEMORIES

knows how to mock. Jesus warned us. If you try to follow his teachings, it won't always be smooth sailing."

"Please tell me that's not all you have to offer," she replied, picking a piece of insulation off his collar.

"Sheesh. Cut me some slack. You heard, what, three sermons?" he fired back, saddled with a grin. "You know, I find when it looks darkest for us is the time when we seek the Lord out most earnestly."

"You got me in this quagmire, and I've been sinking ever since." Defeated, his words rang hollow. "You preached to search yourself with regards to greed and one on compassion. I did and boy did my world blow up. I prayed, and my world sinks to depths I can't fathom. Is that the message I am getting from your loving God? Do as I say and, oh yeah, hang on for dear life, huh?"

Taking a moment, he raked a tooth across his lip. "Do you believe there is a God and that he sent his son down to this earth?"

"On good days, I entertain the thought he might exist," she said with a stitch of guilt.

Wobbling on the tightrope, he ventured out farther. "Don't feel bad. That seems to be the human default for most people when it comes to faith, whether they admit it or not."

Slipping a glove over her fingers, she said, "You cry to have faith, but I am more of a 'touch it, smell it, see it' kind of girl. I was doing fine before I stepped into this house."

He tapped his nose with an index finger. "Oh, so you're one of those that gives the wind a free pass. Huh?"

Giving up on the glove, she asked, "What's that supposed to mean?"

"You've never touched, smelled, or seen the wind. But I guess you believe in it."

Rocked back on her heels, she hesitated. "But I-I uh…. Oh, I feel the wind, and I know it's real. I see it affecting things by its force," Nevada stammered, recovering.

Tapping the back of her hand, he smiled. "I see faith do the same thing," said Pastor Rick, coaxing the words out one at a time.

She stuffed her fingers in the glove. "Did I mention I hate know-it-all preachers?"

A quick study of the humankind, he witnessed a mountain of pain wrapped up in the bundle of mankind before him. She surely didn't want or need for material things by the look of her clothes and jewelry. What she desired, obviously, wasn't on sale. Whoever drew her number had better be a good partner with the Lord. *Peeling the many layers of disappointment from her will be tough*, thought Pastor Rick.

"Emily, do you lump God and the tooth fairy in the same category?" he asked.

With a crumpled-up smile, she replied, "When it comes to answering my prayers, I have to announce that the tooth fairy is tied with your God."

"Maybe God is preparing you for the answer to that prayer," he offered.

She was stunned at his suggestion. "I doubt it, but I'll keep it in mind." Taking one last look around the little church, she felt drawn to it. If nothing else, it was the best forty minutes of sleep she'd had in weeks. Hesitating at the door, she spoke without turning. "And if that's true, then what?"

"Depends on the prayer. It's the journey that follows that can be difficult to navigate sometimes. One never knows the path he will use to accomplish his goals. His way can sometimes be painful and costly but will always achieve his desires. That is, if he chooses to grant your prayer and your desires align with his," he said as the door clicked shut.

Sneaking back down the beaten path, late for her pickup, she dodged the muddy rut. Skirting behind the Marathon station, she tried to shake the ominous feeling. Had she opened a can of worms in her life? Lodging the tip of her high heel in the crack, she catapulted forward, landing on her knees. With the cold air sucking the life out of her, she made the last one hundred yards, limping on what was left of her Gianvito Rossi pumps. The ever efficient Jerome, parked front and center, spied her immediately and wheeled the limo across the parking lot.

Settled in on the heated seat, gasping for air, she stowed the broken evidence away. "Let's go home, Jerome."

"I thought you were over—"

Rubbing her big toe to work the feeling back in, she barked, "Home, Jerome."

Working through the evening, she went over the timeline incessantly. Timing would be crucial tomorrow. One glitch and the rest of her life would fold.

Less than four hours before the meeting, she sat alone in the dark, pondering her fate. Ready to implode her career for the sake of others, she felt a slice of peace for the first time in a long time as she fell back on the pillow. The shaky timbre of her voice betrayed the desperation. "Father, I am keeping my word. Don't abandon me."

Sailing out of bed, fighting the clock, it was the worst day to oversleep. The fatigue felt like a wet blanket, smothering her efforts, conspiring against her. At least, Jerome was on the ball as she sent the text, updating him. Not her best look, she thought, raking the brush against the sleep lines one more time. It would have to do.

Walking through the doors at 4:05, she could hear the contingent of lawyers and Atlas Omega board members grumbling at the delay. Wading through the crowd, she unlocked the SCIF, ushering the group inside.

"First, I want to thank each of you for making the time for this impromptu meeting," she announced. "I would—"

"Is this facade really necessary?" interjected a young lawyer just to the right of Brooks.

The anguish of weeks of planning, lack of sleep, and fear of failure—each begged to be the first to rocket to the surface as she let her eyes lock on the young hotshot lawyer. Rising, the alpha female sensing her next meal, she placed her hands flat on the table. The chit-chat around the massive conference table came to a screeching halt. Using the back of her legs, the innocent chair crashed over backward, taking out the coffee machine as she leaned forward. The small pop of her knuckle could be heard throughout the room as her hand flexed against her weight. "If you speak directly to me again, your ass is out of here! I don't care how important you think you are. I can turn the lights off, go back to bed, and take over your company later today for pennies on the dollar."

Clearing his throat, hoping Stewart's untimely remark hadn't dashed his hopes of saving the company, Brooks said, "Sorry, Ms. Barrington. Emotions are running high. Please continue."

"As I was saying, thank you for everyone's efforts." She gathered the paper sack and folders under her arm. "I need to have a private meeting with Mr. Brooks first, and then we can proceed with your board meeting. Refreshments should be in the next room."

Out of her element and thrown into the arena of the rich and powerful, Matty Baker was embarrassed at her outdated outfit, and the bright office lights highlighted the stain in her blouse. She took a seat at the head of the table in the small conference room. Alone some seventy or eighty stories up in the Empire State Building, she glanced at her reflection in the window. She didn't realize what a country bumpkin she was until today. The four-hour drive to the city allowed her imagination to run amok. Could the world screw her life over any further? What could summon her to this jungle?

With seating for twenty, she felt small and insignificant at the conference table. Her first trip to the Big Apple, she toyed with the tissue box as she heard voices headed her way. Her briefing for the meeting didn't allow for kindness.

"Mrs. Baker?" Extending her hand, Nevada said, "I am Nevada Barrington. Nice to meet you again."

She's like they said she would be—powerful, confident, and amazingly beautiful, thought Matty. "Call me Matty, ma'am." Cocking her head, perplexed, she noted that Nevada did look familiar. "Again?"

With a smile that could charm the spots off a leopard, Nevada said, "We will get to that in a bit. Call me Nevada." She gave Matty a nod. "Nice seat choice. Shows initiative."

"Oh my gosh. I-I'm sorry," stammered Matty, rising out of the chair. The hot blood racing to her face painted streaks of red up her neck. "I-I was nervous and wasn't thinking. I will—"

"Never mind. You're fine." Nevada dropped the paper sack on the finest exotic wood the world could exploit from the rainforest. "I hope to never sit at the head of one of these overpriced ridiculously long tables again. After today anyway."

"So. What's this all about?" asked Brooks, leaning back.

Her nostrils were flaring with shame as the air escaped back out. Dipping her eyes to the table, Nevada said, "It's about a lot of things."

With a weak promise to the wife to watch his mouth, he could feel that mountain of passion sprinkled with a heavy dose of guilt and anger clawing its way upward. "This isn't just about money. It's caused many people to suffer and some even more."

She was lining up to take it right between the eyes. "I know that."

Controlling his embedded anger with hope for the future, Brooks said, "I seriously doubt you have a clue." He let the clutch out easy on a truckload of hate headed her way.

Dipping a toe in enemy territory, looking across the table at one suspected of living a life of privilege, Matty said, "Nevada, you can't possibly have any idea what living on our side of the fence really feels like. We have had tragedies come out of this takeover."

With one last spin of her pen on the legal pad, she braced for the storm headed her way. With a dip of the proud shoulders, she replied, "I do. I was there that day. I have lived with the carnage."

"Huh! I'm calling BS on that," huffed Brooks.

Reaching into the paper sack, donning the wig and glasses, she turned to face them. "Brooks, that's twice you have misstepped with me. Don't try for a third."

Staggered by the reincarnation of Emily Parker, disbelief, anger, and confusion all raised their hands to go first. The silence was broken by the rattle of the paper sack as the props disappeared back out of sight. Stunned by the deception right under his nose, he sank. The pop of his wedding ring striking the table startled Matty.

"Ma'am, why?" cried out Matty, the lines of pain etched deep on her face. She believed humanity had already hit rock bottom in her life. "Was it a game for you?" Pitching forward, she stared down the one she held responsible for all her woes. "Maybe, uh, oh, I don't know, something rich people do for kicks. Watching us trailer trash suffer, fighting over crumbs you people dribble to the floor. Is that it?" Demanding answers, she fought the urge to reach over and extract justice for Joey McGee.

"I'm here to save a company," interrupted Brooks. "I don't' really care—"

"I am too, Brooks!" screamed Nevada. "But I owe Matty an answer. Whether she appreciates it or not is on her."

"I'm all ears, lady," said Matty, crossing her arms, daring the answers to be lame.

"Me too," chimed in Brooks.

Ready to launch into her well-oiled and rehearsed speech, Nevada hesitated, never considering plan B until now. How does one admit you are the monster in the room? How do you acknowledge you have made a wonderful and comfortable life stepping on the backs of the little people, destroying lives at a wholesale rate to fund your extravagant lifestyle?

The painful silence was pierced by the first honest words she had allowed to escape in a long time. Pressing her knuckles against her lip, she unloaded. "I went there to prove to myself I wasn't a bad person, only a good businesswoman. I wanted to see firsthand how my decisions affected people."

Fighting to push aside the memories of that day overwhelmed her. She failed, free-falling into the abyss. Ignoring her rule of no tears in a boardroom, Nevada fought on, swallowing all remaining pride. "I...I uh...saw the look of defeat in his eyes and knew it was my fault." Her voice trailing off, she tried to rip a tissue from the box, ignoring it as it tumbled to the floor. "I knew right then I was the monster and needed to make amends to the world. I'll be doing that at 8:01 today."

Hoping there was still some good under that hard exterior, Matty asked, "How?" Bringing the attack down a notch or two, she chipped some of the ice off her barbs.

Dabbing an eye, inspecting the tissue for mascara, Nevada said, "I'm resigning my position."

"Don't see how that makes my world any better," scoffed Brooks.

Shoving the folder across the table, she said, "That's how your world gets better, Brooks."

Opening the folder with a healthy suspicion, he spied the figures first, ignoring the verbiage. With "fool me once" rattling around in his brain, he tried to put the brakes on his hopes. Rereading the document slower, he couldn't see a downside, only the ability to fight another day. The revelation brought many questions. Had he missed the rabbit hole again? Out of bullets, her motives to make such a sacrifice were immaterial now.

"Are you dead serious about this?" he asked.

"I need two signatures and your bank routing number. The money is parked and ready to wire within the hour."

Struggling to keep it in check, he took a turn, swallowing his pride. "Thank you."

4

Walking into the Barrington boardroom, Nevada had never felt more alien. The Atlas Omega members sat quiet as church mice, darting hostile glances her way. They were waiting for the hatchet to drop, ending the seventy-year legacy of Atlas Omega and reducing a once proud dynasty to a mere blimp of information on Wikipedia. Declining economy and outdated equipment had led them to brutal distasteful lending terms.

"Ladies and gentlemen, we have one item on the agenda. This corporation has missed payment on a second forbearance agreement. Barrington Enterprises has started legal proceedings to recover the outstanding balance of 590 million dollars. Nevada Barrington has graciously gathered us here to propose a solution—one I believe we need to take seriously," warned Brooks, ignoring the hand shooting up.

"Wait! Let me get this straight. We sit in enemy territory and expect to be saved by the same jackal that has her jaws clamped around our throats already. This I gotta hear," said Mirah Johnston.

Nevada was stunned by the sheer ignorance. *No wonder they have failed*, she surmised. Rising from her seat, she said, "Thank you. I think of myself more as a lioness than jackal. And if you will be quiet and let Brooks finish, you'll get an answer, sweetie."

"It's 5:45 people. We have a little over two hours before Barrington board members will sit in these very seats and vote our final demise. I have viewed a copy of her offer, and I will be voting in favor of it. Nevada, the floor is yours," said Brooks, offering her his seat at the head of the table.

Stepping into an arena where she was the alpha female, she took over the controls. Savoring some of her final moments as an apex

DIVINE MEMORIES

predator, she cleared her throat. "This isn't a popularity contest. This is business. The last time I checked, your stock was under one dollar from a high of just north of two hundred less than six months ago. You owe my company almost six hundred million dollars, and you can't even make the interest payment."

Looks of disgust pasted across the faces around the table brought the wheels to a screeching halt.

"Brooks, I'm about to pull this offer," she warned.

"Can we have the room for a minute?" he asked, splotches of crimson forming in his cheeks.

Letting silence infest the room, he rocked in his chair, staring straight ahead. Choking back words better thought than said, he read the room. The mixture of nerds and hotheads, loyal to a fault, couldn't know how close they were to bringing rain to a warm sunny day.

"Hear me and hear me good. When that lady returns to this room, you will not show any emotions or make eye contact with her. Don't ask me why she would offer us this chance, but we must take it," pleaded Brooks.

Nevada entered the room again, and the muzzled members toed the line as she scanned the room, searching for violators. "We now have less than two hours before my board meets to officially discuss foreclosing on Atlas Omega. Your stock is now under fifty cents a share." With an avalanche of mixed feelings raining down upon her, she pulled the final thread holding her in command of Barrington Enterprises. "I am proposing to make you an offer to personally purchase fifty million shares for twenty dollars a share. Your proceeds would be one billion dollars. You will repay all loans to Barrington Enterprises and reinvest the rest to modernize Atlas Omega."

"Why on earth would you overpay for something you will get for pennies on the dollar in the future? What about your conflicts of interest? Your ouster will be swift, won't it?" asked Larry Fromworth, Atlas Omega general counsel.

"Those are my concerns." She darted a glance Brooks's way.

"Okay. Ms. Barrington, give us a few minutes to review the details," said Fromworth.

"I'll be back in the other conference room with Matty Baker," said Nevada.

She hesitated by the glass doors leading into the conference room. What could she possibly be thinking? Would she trade lives? Shoving the thick glass doors, she entered the room, bypassing the head chair now left vacant by Matty.

"We don't have much time. The lawyers are on the job now," said Nevada, reaching across the table and taking the calloused hand into hers. "Matty, regardless of what you think of me, I never meant you any harm. In fact, I never forgot you that day we met. I will soon wield considerable power within Atlas Omega, and I have insisted on you being promoted above your peers to a management position." Reaching into her file folder, she continued, "I also want to give you this incentive. Open it up."

Sliding the envelope through her fingers, the raised embossed letters reeked of money and power. Staring at the woman known to all as their nemesis threw her off her game. Is this how it is with her?

"Go ahead and open it. I need to explain."

"Okay."

The trembling fingers struggled with the seal, tilting the envelope. The letter slid onto the table, allowing the check to peek out. Fighting to focus on the two paragraphs, the check screamed to be noticed. Hardly a financial expert, the words were foreign to her. Dying to flip the check over, she seized it, raking it back two-fingered. Staggered by the number, she refused to be tricked, and she flipped the check away from her. "No!"

"Matty, let me explain. I need—"

"No! Why me? Tell me that."

"You may think it is a gift, but you will earn it. Believe me." Sliding a bottle of water over as a peace offering, she waited for the attitude to come down from DEFCON 1. "The agreement is simple. If you and management show one dollar or more of profit within the next four business quarters, the money is yours. My one stipulation is that the money must be used to pay off your mortgage. I never want your home threatened again."

Matty was fighting to keep greed's claws out of her back. "Nobody gives this much away without wanting something in return."

"You're right. You have been swept up in a much larger game being played out. I hate to admit it, but I am selfishly trying to change my life while also simultaneously punishing some people responsible for shorting your stock into the dirt."

Matty shook her head. The terms of the rich meant little. "Shorting?"

"It's a strategy of borrowing stock and selling it to drop the price of a stock and intending to buy it back cheaper, pocketing the difference. They search for companies in distress and hope the stock plummets or, better yet, goes bankrupt. For example, you sell company ABC stock for $200 a share and then hope the price drops to, say, $100. You tell your broker to buy the stock back. You pocket the difference between $200 and $100. You can only lose if the stock price rises higher than what you sold it for initially," explained Nevada.

Launched into the dark world of finance, the gaping mouth, partnered with her wrinkled nose, spoke a true understanding of how the rich got richer. "How can that crappy cheating game even be legal?"

"It is, unfortunately for Atlas Omega. But you can't use inside information to accomplish it."

The word *bankrupt* brought dread to Matty's ears. With a fresh memory of searching for their own lawyer to file, she had her back up against the wall. So far out of her element, she felt a trapdoor in every direction. Separated from the herd, she could see the predators singling her out. Which way to run for safety? "Nevada, I want to trust you, but all I've ever heard was bad about you."

The words penetrated through the thick skin, piercing one of New York City's coldest hearts.

"Up until the last few weeks, I would have had to agree with whoever told you that," said Nevada. The accusations haunted her. The stripes of shame were deserved. "Listen and listen good. I have vowed to reverse the misfortune of Atlas Omega before I am through."

Reaching up, pulling her sleeve. A sleeve designed for the rich. Closing the gap, forcing their bodies closer, the expensive perfume filled her senses. "But, Nevada dear, why I am really here?" demanded Matty.

"Frankly, I admire your moxie."

Teetering on what little pride she had left, she needed a win in her column. "Okay. Here's my deal. You will have my loyalty. But, Nevada, if you are tricking me, I'll hunt you down and make you pay for it. It won't have anything to do with money either, period."

"Fair enough. Let's go. Here comes Fromworth."

Taking her seat, Nevada took a quick read of the room. The dour faces revealed little.

"Okay. Everyone, let me summarize the offering, and then we can vote," said Brooks. Shuffling the papers, he looked for the term sheet. "Let's see. Ms. Barrington is offering to immediately purchase fifty million shares of Atlas Omega common stock for the purchase price of twenty dollars a share. Which represents a substantial premium over the current price. For that, she wants to replace four of the nine present board members and have no further expansion of the board. Is that about it, Ms. Barrington?"

"You forgot Matilda Baker's contract agreement," said Nevada.

"Oh. Yes. And a condition to promote Matilda Baker to a management position. Anything else?"

Unleashing a gracious smile, she spread her hands. "That's it."

"Well, let's take a vote. All those in favor say 'aye'. Those opposed, say 'nay'. Ayes have it," said Brooks.

With the hook set clear to the gills, she dropped the unpleasant news. "I will need all members to sequester in another conference room until the Barrington board meeting has concluded. And all outside communications will be blocked during the sequester." Ignoring the grumbles, she rose. "Mr. Brooks, I need you and Fromworth to remain."

With light at the end of the tunnel peeking out ahead, Brooks asked, throwing out a hand to his newest partner, "How do you want to proceed from here?"

"You two are about to witness just how much carnage I will dump upon people that get out of line." Sliding the drafts across the table, she said, "I need you to approve these press releases. They have already been loaded up for release at 8:02 this morning, pending your approval. Second, have your check made out to Barrington Enterprises for the exact amount of the loan repayment. And last on my list, what is the current outstanding share count on the corporation? I don't want to own more than 5 percent of the corporation."

"We have over 2.2 billion outstanding. Your 50 million is well under 5 percent," answered Fromworth.

"I don't plan on stopping at 50 million. I will be buying up to another 50 million out of the open market today, regardless of the price."

"You have no problem playing with fire, do you?" asked Brooks, basking in the first rays of hope. "You realize whatever clearing houses are loaning shares to the people shorting the stock could topple?"

"What a bonus, for me." Looking up from the battle plan, she shrugged. "Believe it or not, I don't bet against companies."

"Shall we both attend your board meeting?" asked Brooks.

With a curt nod, she pulled up from the battle plan. "With your check in hand."

"It won't be any good," replied Brooks.

"It will be at 8:03."

Waiting to close the door to the SCIF, she spied the trio emerging around the corner. Reeking of confidence as they passed by her, she just caught Liddy's trademark smirk.

Taking a step back, Charles asked, sucking on his upper teeth, "Nevada, word is Atlas Omega board members are here somewhere. What's that all about?"

"Oh, a bit of a last-minute begging session," she said, refusing to make eye contact as she ushered the last member in.

"What came of that?"

"They begged. I listened," she quipped. Spinning around, leaving him to ponder the possibilities, she announced, "It's 7:55. Let's get this show going."

Looking out at the sea of attorneys, accountants, and various corporate members, she threw out the first curveball. "Heads up. The reason we are having the meeting in the SCIF is because of known security breaches. If, for some reason, you can't remain for the entire meeting, then you're excused now. When the meeting starts, you will remain here, out of contact with the outside world," said Nevada. Inspecting the agenda while waiting for a response, she snuck a glance at her watch. It was 8:01 already. How she would love to see some faces about now.

Moving through Barrington business, leaving the Atlas Omega item for last, she stalled for time, allowing the short squeeze to unfold. She was hoping her buying pressure, along with speculators smelling blood in the streets, would start the ball rolling on the Atlas Omega stock price.

"Our last item on the agenda is discussion on granting Atlas Omega an additional forbearance or push them into bankruptcy," said Nevada.

The clashing voices, each fighting to be acknowledged, were eventually toppled by the deep baritone of Charles. "I believe we have been more than generous with this corporation. I believe bankruptcy is our best and only option," he said, giving a bored stare in Brooks's direction."

The tug-of-war raged on, with a final 5–4 vote to force the bankruptcy. The bittersweet loss was expected. Bracing for the deluge of reactions when the SCIF door cracked open, it would allow the tidal wave of blocked electronic communication to breach the boardroom walls. Rising to conclude the meeting, she shifted her glance Brooks's way. Right on cue as he pitched the check on the conference table.

"Ladies and gentlemen, I believe that will pay for our freedom!" said Brooks, beaming with delight.

"Whoa! What's that?" demanded Charles, hustling over to the group. With the blood draining at a fatal rate, he eyed each and every zero on the bank draft. Puffing up, he declared, "This smells more of a stalling tactic than a good faith payment."

"I assure you it's good. I have our bank president on speed dial if you want to confirm," offered Brooks.

"Let's go and confirm the check and see what else this ole world has in store for us," suggested Nevada, opening the secure door like it was Christmas morning.

Seconds passed before the steady stream of urgent electronic SOS messages sailed in to their intended recipients. The steady dump of nauseating news feeds and emails and mind-altering texts filled the room. For certain members, the news caused levels of panic not seen since the crash of 1929. The endless string of alerts threatened to test the limits of man.

Long gone were the smirks as they melted off their faces, each stumbling blindly, glued to their phones as they exited the SCIF. Most notable were the miserable-looking brothers tagging behind Charles.

If looks could kill, she thought. "Have a good day, boys!" she said, ushering them out into the world for slaughter.

Engrossed in the endless news stories and stock price alerts, Charles never heard her snickering. His world was wobbling off its axis. With a trading halt due to order imbalances forty minutes earlier at sixty-five dollars, Atlas Omega stock was on fire, skyrocketing on the news. Locked out with no way to buy back the shorted stock, billions in losses were headed their way.

Barricaded in his office, he stared at the monitor, waiting for the trading to resume. "Liddy, shut up and shut that door," said Charles, weak as a newborn kitten. Nearing collapse, he cradled his head in his palm.

Popping a mint, Amos asked, "How bad is it?"

"Total loss of almost five billion in profits already. And if we could miraculously cover right now, we'd be sitting on a loss north of three billion. Hang on. It's getting ready to start trading again. Oh Jesus! I can't even stand to look at it."

Peering over Charles's shoulder, the news issued him a brutal slap. "That's 125 bucks! Is that accurate?" asked Liddy, wide-eyed.

"It's blowing by 130 now. We're dead!" screamed Charles, kicking the monitor off the desk.

"Somehow, she knew all along. I didn't think I had the capacity to hate that girl more than I did already. My mistake," said Amos.

Cracking the door open, she finished off the wounded gazelles. "Check's good," said Nevada, with sugar on top. She slammed the door shut before the news reached brains on fire with hatred.

Snatching up a glass, the impact marred the veneer, sending shards ricocheting throughout the office. "Somehow, somewhere... she will pay for this," vowed Charles.

*****

Taking one last look at the city, she felt free as she put on her coat. She slipped a copy of the eight-by-ten taken of her, Matty, and Brooks into her briefcase. The big smiles were worth it; she had righted a wrong in this part of the universe. Closing her office door for the last time, bittersweet memories of victories surfaced. Rubbing the raised letters on her door, she shuddered at what she once took pride in. Peeling back the covers a bit, it brought a healthy dose of shame.

Leaning on his doorframe, Lawrence was waiting. He asked, "Nevada, can I have a word with you?"

"Sure."

"Shut the door." Letting the overstuffed couch break his fall, he knew time was catching up. She had kept her word. They had been knocked to their knees. But he knew they would get back up. "Nevada, I told you they wouldn't take this lying down. I overhead Charles talking to the Bankhills. They are desperate and capable of anything."

She was shocked at the change. He was looking every bit of his seventy-one years. The last few days had not been kind to him. "I will be out of the city before dark. Don't worry. I'll land on my feet somewhere. You won't hear from me for a while."

"Good. Come here and give me one last hug." Struggling to rise, he felt a loss that would never be replaced.

*****

The deed was done. Escaping the city of her sins, she relaxed in the spacious back seat as Jerome navigated through the city. She kept an eye out for it. Coming up on the right, she spied it finally. "Jerome, pull into that dealership coming up on the right."

"Yes, ma'am."

Exiting the limo, she made her way to the showroom. Scouting out the new models, she waited for a salesman. Excited at the prospect of actually driving a car, she couldn't recall the last time she had driven. Upon hearing the sound of heels approaching, she turned.

"Hello, I'm Barb. What can I show you today?" Consistently the top saleswoman, she knew a potential buyer when she saw one, especially one packing a Gucci.

"Well, I need to buy a car today."

Unleashing a pleasant smile, she said, "Good! That's what we like to hear. But we close in thirty minutes, so we might have to actually close on the deal after the holiday."

"No! I need it right now." Cold fear struck as she felt the walls closing in on her. She couldn't spend another night in the city. Looking out upon the lot, she asked, "How about that car right there?" She was pointing at an older Chevy Malibu.

"That car?" asked Barb. Running her eyes over the woman dressed in one of Dolce and Gabbana's finest suits, she shook off the plea. "Ma'am, my family is waiting on me for the holiday. I just couldn't handle the transaction today."

"Please! I will make it worth your trouble," begged Nevada.

Spinning her rings on her finger, she hesitated. Finally moving her purse to the side, she said, "Have a seat. I'll talk to our manager."

Fighting down the second panic attack of the day, she tried to imagine life without Barrington Enterprises in it. Refusing to be thwarted by a saleswoman wearing more jewelry than your average pirate, she searched for a plan B.

She was launching into the rejection halfway across the showroom. "Ma'am, he insists you come back after the holiday," said Barb, displaying her standard fake smile.

"Barb, is that a real Coach purse?"

She burned a new shade of red through the fake tan. "Well, I think so," said Barb with as much guilt as a car salesman could muster up.

Patting her own purse, Nevada said, "This is a Sylvie, medium hibiscus, red crocodile Gucci. And I will offer to trade you purses if you can find it in your heart to get this deal done in the next thirty minutes." She was holding the piece of purse candy out for her to see. "It's all yours if you pull it off. It will be a cash transaction, by the way," said Nevada.

"Can I look at it closer?" Stroking the crocodile leather with passion, Barb ran her fingers along the stitching. Finishing up with a close inspection of the serial numbers, she said, "You realize your purse is worth a great deal more than the car you're buying?" She was giddy inside, holding the holy grail of all purses.

"I'll be out in that limo when you need me to sign papers." Getting up to leave, she added, "Also, if that car doesn't have GPS, I'll need an atlas."

As Nevada came out of the restroom wearing blue jeans and a sweater, he almost didn't recognize her. Saying a hasty farewell to Jerome, she officially embarked on her new life. Shedding her old life, she was now a new 2.0 version labeled Emily Parker.

She bounced over the curb as she pulled out onto the street, causing oncoming traffic to brake and unleashing a torrent of honking and choice hand gestures. Oblivious to her actions, she maintained a firm grip on the Chevy's wheel, aiming it west. Racking up more traffic violations than your typical carjacker, she began to appreciate Jerome's driving skills more and more. Darting over to the far-right lane, cutting off a garbage truck and squeezing in, she was able to make the exit for the interstate at the last second.

With the city miles behind her, a sense of independence overwhelmed her. Turning the heater down, she felt the rumble of her stomach. Finally locating the gas gauge, she took the exit. Pulling into a Shell station, she battled to outsmart the gas pump. She slipped the card in, praying it would go through as she punched in her zip code. The number was rejected for the third time, and she kicked herself, needing to be more careful as she remembered her new driver's license. Punching in Emily's fictitious zip code brought pay dirt, and she sighed with its approval. As she searched for the gas tank, her MBA was letting her down. She was parading up and down the side of her vehicle.

"Lady, it's on the other side," yelled a kid, smiling, as he filled up a gorgeous black GT Mustang over on pump 5.

"Thanks! Just got the car," said Nevada, rolling with the punches in her new existence.

Cruising westbound on I-70 near Columbus, Ohio, with the gas light on for miles, she coasted into the Sunoco station on fumes. Now a veteran of refueling, she smashed her last pit-stop times. Grabbing a sub sandwich, she made her way back to the one asset Emily Parker owned. The sanctuary of the Malibu brought a comfortable feeling as she studied the atlas. The warmth of the heater fought gallantly to ward off the bone-chilling temperatures outside. With a single desire to escape, she would let fate plot her destiny, which was still pointed westward.

With the initial excitement wearing off, the journey was starting to take its toll. She was fighting to keep her eyes open as darkness fell, magnifying her fatigue. Making good time on the all but deserted highway, she crossed into the Land of Lincoln. With the gas gauge past empty, she limped off the interstate at the first town in sight. Unsure which way to turn, scanning left and right, she was looking for an open gas station. Glancing at the dash clock (1:30 a.m.), she knew there was not an open station in sight. Flipping a coin and heading south, she pulled up to the Pepsi machine outside the first station.

Slipping the bills in and failing to find an option for water, she settled for a Diet Pepsi. Working on her second swallow, math caught up with the Malibu. Taking its last sip, the cough and sputter of the engine brought a stab of fear. Running back to the vehicle, she slipped on the ice, splattering Pepsi against the driver's window as she made a desperate grab for the door handle.

Cranking the engine, the last gasp of the engine confirmed her fears, and she collapsed on the steering wheel. Her spirit broken, she was hugging the wheel. She knew she had been foolish not to fill up at the last big town. Grabbing her coat, she prepared for a long cold miserable night. Looking over at the streetlight, the silhouette of the first snow flurry sparkled. "Lord, why me?" she whispered.

The snow coated the windshield in minutes, and she felt the first needles of misery in her toes. Stomping her feet on the floorboard only delayed the inevitable. Daylight, a wishful thought, was more than an eternity away. She longed for her penthouse so far away as she shivered under the coat. The incoming snowstorm blew across the prairie with a mission to drive living creatures to their knees. It happily partnered with Ole Man Winter.

Gazing out into the wall of white fury, she looked for a savior among the glow of headlights creeping past her on the interstate. Marooned on a frozen land, she'd have better luck catching a ride on the moon. *So close but so far*, she thought as they each continued on down the interstate to destinations unknown. In the fetal position, keeping as much of her body heat under the protection of her down coat, she waited for a rescue. Closing in on 4:00 a.m., refusing to move any body part, she heard the loud rumbling getting closer. Sitting up, she saw the truck's lone working headlight headed her way, shining through the flurries. The ancient ride had seen better days. Burning more oil than gas, the chariot looked beautiful to her as the brakes squealed, bringing the rickety Jeep to rest against the curb next to her DOA Malibu.

The big man struggled in the cold to get the machine to swallow his dollar. The vicious kick boomed. Startled at the sudden outburst, she held her breath as the man continued sweet-talking the machine. Turning the ignition on to clear the windshield for a better view, the loud chatter of the wipers scraping across the glass, alerted the man to her presence.

Whirling around, he spied her presence with military precision, gauging the threat level with an intimidating glare. Holding the stare delivered an uncomfortable ripple down her backside. Evaluating the threat as minimal, he turned back to the machine, continuing his pursuit for a 7UP. Taking out a second and third bill, he knew he was losing the battle.

DIVINE MEMORIES

Shifting her weight, she pulled the Sig Sauer 9mm out of the glove compartment, praying she had remembered to chamber a round in first. Slipping it in her coat pocket, she was evening up the sides with the hulk of a man a bit.

Weighing her options, she kept a healthy grip on the Sig's cold steel frame as she stepped out into the storm. She was little more than eighteen hours from the city, and she was already prepared to beg for help. As she looked past the ratty old parka, the face, covered with stubble, smiled back. As he towered over her, she knew it would be a challenge even with the firepower from the P365.

"Excuse me. Would you happen to have a couple crisp dollar bills?" asked the man. "I can't convince this blasted machine to cough up a 7UP."

He did have a great smile, but so did Ted Bundy, she thought.

Stepping closer, seeking refuge from the wind under the awning, she tightened her hold on the Sig. Alone, vulnerable, her whereabouts unknown to all, the thought ripped through her soul. The thought of disappearing from the face of the earth, like her parents, raised flags faster than a soccer linesman official. The claxon blared a warning to return to the safety of the Chevy. She stepped back, never taking her eyes off the man.

"I'm sorry. Didn't mean to frighten you, ma'am," he said, raising his arms and displaying empty hands.

Retreating to the driver's door, she couldn't let her last option vanish into the wall of snow. Reaching into the car, she snapped a picture of the man and his license plate. Keeping the phone trained on the man, Nevada demanded, "What's your name?"

Chuckling at the tactic, he wondered if his harebrained sisters would be as savvy. "You've got to be from some big city." Shaking his head, he said, "My name's Jack Webster. I live right here in Noble County, not five miles from here." Dropping his hands, he waited on the verdict.

"Okay. I sent your picture and video to the cloud. I'm sorry to be so untrusting. I have my reasons," she said, reaching for the dollar bills. "I do hate to see man defeated by a machine though."

Retrieving the elusive 7UP, he cast his eyes on the snow-covered Chevy. "How is that working out for you?" asked Jack, jerking a thumb in the Chevy's direction.

"Peachy. The poor thing died of thirst."

Arching a bushy brow, he said, "You're not totally out, are ya?"

With a bitter taste of failure, she hoped the mansplaining lecture didn't go on all night. "I'm afraid so. Are there any hotels around here?"

"Yeah, couple on down the road." Dropping the can of 7UP in his parka, he said, "Get your things. I'll give you a ride."

With her right hand firmly around the pistol grip, she said, "Thank you." Nevada grabbed the suitcases from the trunk with her other hand.

"Here, let me get those for you," offered Jack, reaching out for the first case.

Freezing her position, she turned her back to block his efforts. "No. I've got them."

Opening the passenger door brought a dose of embarrassment as tools and papers tumbled out into the snow. Grabbing papers before they danced across the drive, she managed to make enough room to squat down on the tattered upholstery once called a seat. She propped her feet up on the toolbox in the floorboard. It might not be a limo, but the heater felt wonderful as she shivered, letting the warmth envelope her body.

"Sorry about the accommodations. This was my dad's work truck, or what's left of it anyway," offered Jack, grinding gears, trying to find reverse. Pulling out on the state route, he glanced over. "You know my name. What's yours?"

"Emily Parker."

5

With an uncharacteristic full parking lot, business was booming. With the leading edge of the raging blizzard stalling over the Midwest, conditions deteriorated rapidly, driving interstate traffic to abandon the highway. Rooms were at a premium as each wisely waited out Mother Nature's latest show.

"Well, so much for Motel 6 leaving the light on for me," complained Nevada. Rolling the suitcases out into the foyer, she dropped down on what she took for a sad excuse of a couch.

"Sorry. I called the other motel. Same answer," said Jack.

Springing up from the couch on the third try, she sighed. "Well, uh, could you give me a ride back to my car? I'll just wait till the station opens and then get some gas."

Bone-tired, grabbing the suitcase handles, his hesitation set the stage for the next batch of good news.

"What's with the sad face? Now what?" she asked, exhausted, dropping the handles.

"This is New Year's Day. They won't be open today."

Teetering on a full-blown fit, she exclaimed, "Great! At least my luck is running pretty consistent."

Always the consummate professional, making split decisions daily, judging people by their actions, he looked right through her. He was searching for the reasons to not abandon her. A sucker for a lost cause, he grabbed the nearest suitcase. "Let's go."

They piled back into the Jeep, and he ordered the old four-wheel drive to fight the six inches of new powder in its way.

As they were pulling back onto the highway, her hackles rose, unleashing a myriad of dark thoughts. Rapping on the side window, she asked, "Isn't my car in that direction?" Her hand went for her coat pocket.

Scratching an itch under his chin between gear shifts, he said, "Yeah. We're going to your last option: my parents' house a couple miles down the highway. You're in for a real treat."

Running out of options, she sighed. "Okay."

They fought to stay on the highway as the winter wonderland blotted out all signs of the two-lane blacktop. Feeling the strong winds buffet the truck, she rode in silence, never letting her hand stray far from the cold steel.

The Jeep laid a solitary set of tracks in the blowing snow. Fighting to stay on the road, he slid past the driveway. Backing up in the whiteout conditions, he coaxed the Jeep into the driveway.

Cutting the ignition, he draped his hands on the steering wheel. "It's Emily, right?"

She pushed a bang out of her eye. "Yes."

"Well, here's the deal. My mom's kinda gruff but harmless. She's got no filter in life and smokes worse than a chimney." Reaching for the nearest suitcase, he mumbled, "You've been warned."

"I'm sure it'll be fine," said Nevada with a jaw-popping yawn. "Here. I've got that one," she offered, taking the suitcase from his hand.

Hesitating as he dropped one foot to the ground, Jack said, "One last thing."

Spinning around, she hoped this wasn't where it went off the rails. "What's that?"

Rubbing a stray snowflake out of his eye, he said, "I don't blame a female traveling alone in this day and age, but I can't have you carrying a gun around my mom."

With rosy cheeks that couldn't get any redder, she asked, "What do you mean by that? I don't have a gun." She allowed a dose of that New Yorker attitude to spew out.

"You can keep it until you feel the situation inside is safe. But you'll need to keep it in your suitcase by suppertime."

Surrendering, she brushed a handful of hair out of her face. "How did you know?"

DIVINE MEMORIES

"It's a hobby of mine to notice such things."

"Touché," she said, eking out a smile, which was rare these days. She was seeing the man in a different light for the first time.

Navigating back to her lair, the sweltering heat hovered around the eighty-five-degree mark daily. The hawk eyes, barely visible, missed little. Covered from head to toe with her favorite afghan, Mama Webster tore her eyes from the old rerun. Perched at her feet, weighing in at four pounds soaking weight, was her faithful companion Pearl. Rising to her full height, Pearl prepared for battle. Chattering her customary early-warning growl, she gave the newcomers a fierce once-over. With the heart of a lion but the teeth of a Chihuahua, she was ready to terrorize the stranger's ankles with little provocation. Recognizing Jack, she called off the attack, slinking back under the comfort of the afghan.

Walking into the living room, fighting to find some usable oxygen in the virtual petri dish of carcinogenic. The wood smoke from the stove, backed up by the endless supply of secondhand smoke from the Marlboros, did little for longevity. Each competing to do the most damage, they were her world. Stationed at her post, the piercing eyes, bloodshot from lack of sleep, locked on to the latest stray cat Jack had brought home. Manning the couch 24-7, she was just finishing up the latest *Law and Order* rerun. She flung the blanket off.

"Mom, this is Emily. She ran out of gas," Jack yelled over the TV, silently crossing his fingers, hoping the intrusion didn't ruffle too many feathers.

Coughing up half a lung, she motioned the stranger to sit. She silenced the TV. "What did you say?"

"I said this is Emily. She ran out of gas."

The look of disgust confirmed the worst. "Can't she read a gauge? Probably poor as a church mouse," she said, grabbing the *TV Guide*. Lighting up for the day, she blew smoke across the room as she dropped her lighter back onto the coffee table.

"Emily, this is my saint of a mom, Maggie," Jack said, shaking his head while mouthing an apology.

"It's nice to meet you, ma'am," said Nevada, wishing she could trade the Sig Sauer in for a gas mask.

"Get that 7UP?" asked Maggie, shooing Pearl off the couch. Firing a stink eye in Nevada's direction, she asked, "Know how to play pinochle?"

Sensing a possible thawing of Ma Barker, she opted for a well-intended lie. "I think so. But if not, I'm a fast learner," said Nevada, hoping for a little leniency from the warden.

She gained little traction with the matriarch, who said, "We'll see about that."

Nevada waited out the next few days, helplessly witnessing the blizzard compete to be the worst in decades. Paralyzing the Midwest, with highways littered with hundreds of abandoned vehicles and countless people stranded, she knew what a blessing it was she had found in the Websters'. Taking two days to chip the rust off Maggie, she was still laughing at her "poor church mouse" remark. She found a soft heart under that thorny and crusty exterior. The old woman still reeled from the loss of her husband of the last forty years. Maggie welcomed the distraction in life.

Staring out the bay window as the snowplow rumbled by, she silently rooted for Mother Nature as man desperately tried to get the upper hand on her. Counting the days, she listened to the steady plop of the water melting the life out of the icicles hanging heavily off the gutters, each losing their battle against the incoming southern winds. Her time was closing in for a decision. She saw little of Jack these last twenty-four hours, and Maggie was tight-lipped about his absence.

"Maggie, will Jack be by today?" asked Nevada.

Kicking Pearl outside for a break, she grunted. "Said he'd be by around noon with a surprise for you," offered Maggie. Struggling to slam the sliding door, she yelled, "Pearl, get!" She ignored Pearl's buggy eyes, which were hoping a for last-minute pardon.

"I can't thank you enough for, uh, welcoming me into your home," said Nevada, fighting a battle within. Sponging up anything resembling kindness, she faced the uncomfortable thought of going back into the world. Drying the last of the plates, she placed it next to the good china with care. "Hmm. Wonder what it could be."

Known to keep secrets better than the Manhattan Project, the information highway was closed. Handing Nevada the final plate to dry, Maggie mumbled, "Hard to say."

Trying her best to keep the vacuum sweeper going straight, Nevada tried putting Jack out of her mind. Drifting in and out of wishful thoughts, the sound of the news alert on her phone shattered her dream. Allowing New York to ooze in, it was trashing the mood. She was hoping the news cycle would run its course by the end of the week. With the entire eastern seaboard ravaged by the blizzard, the bloodlust for news on the Barrington empire upheaval was finally losing traction. With her picture plastered on every financial channel, she was thankful the Websters were money-under-the-mattress kind of people.

With a full-blown alert from the Webster home security system barking furiously, she pulled the curtain back. She was smiling as she recognized Jack coaxing her Malibu through the icy slush. Her heart was unprotected as she sat in a strange land, searching for positives to cling to. Bringing a sour note to the fantasy, she watched the sheriff's squad car turn into the drive, slowly following the Malibu. Clamping her mind shut, she refused to acknowledge any problems headed her way.

As Jack walked back to the squad car, the interaction did seem friendly. The deputy slapped Jack on the back as they powwowed; this definitely wasn't NYPD in action. Jack was motioning toward the house, and she slid back behind the curtain.

She could hear him stomping his boots off at the back door as she sat waiting at the kitchen table.

"Hey, did you see what I brought home? With a full tank of gas, I might add," teased Jack, dropping his coat on the back of the kitchen chair.

"Yes, I did! Thank you very much," she said, brushing her hand across his. "What do I owe you?"

"Nothing. Courtesy of Shallimar, Illinois, population 4,800-ish." Tiptoeing around her situation, he wished to spare her. "The City has a fund to help indigent travelers. No big deal."

Slapped with a label unfathomable to her, the poor church mouse tried to keep it together. "Oh my! No...no, I have money. Really, I do."

"Don't worry about it. Let's get out of here. Lunch is on me," said Jack.

Years of living in beautiful palaces towering above the endless rabble, existing in the dog-eat-dog world of the city, she had been a shining example for few. Where generosity started strong, it often failed to come to fruition, fizzling out as the wine and champagne wore off the next morning.

Pulling her jacket on, she caught a glimpse of the girl in the living room mirror. Ashamed, she slashed the image from her mind, uncomfortable with her past. "Lunch is on me or I don't go."

"Fine! I'm getting a steak instead of the meatloaf special," he threatened. Reaching out to help straighten her collar, he brushed up against her cheek with his hand. She was beauty and mystery wrapped in one package, and he hated to release her back into the wild.

Taking a booth near the back, she had never rubbed shoulders with this part of the universe. With a wobbly table crying for attention, the wadded-up napkins under the leg were falling down on the job. Squinting to read the daily specials on the chalkboard, she tried to ignore the overwhelming odor of grease wafting out of the kitchen.

Inspecting the handwritten menu, she grabbed the nearest napkin and went to work on the dried crusty mustard. She pushed her chair back. The loud scrape caught the lunch crowd's attention, bringing unwanted scrutiny. Whizzing by, the vivacious blond waitress broke up the gawkers hawking annoying glances her way. Apologizing for slow service and giving Jack's shoulder a friendly squeeze, she vowed to return shortly. Too friendly for some.

"She could be your daughter," said Nevada, never taking her eyes off the menu.

Waving across the diner at a quartet of businessmen devouring their slices of mile-high pies, he ignored the accusation.

"Okay. What are we having today?" asked the waitress, sliding to a stop and giving Jack a syrupy smile.

DIVINE MEMORIES

"Janey, I think I'll have the special today," said Jack, tapping the waitress on her arm with the menu.

She flashed a smile, proof the braces had been worth their money. "Okay. And for you, ma'am?"

Snubbing the stunning little blonde's request, she asked Jack, "I thought you were having steak?"

Lowering her order pad, Janey smiled. "Yeah right! Uncle Jack never gets steak," she teased.

Slamming the brakes on her tongue, Nevada pulled up before she crashed and burned. "Well, I'm having the rib-eye special. Remember, I'm buying."

Taking the order, Janey slipped the pad back down in her apron and moved to the next table. Turning back over her shoulder, she said, "Uncle Jack, if she's buying you steak, she must be a keeper." Her raised eyebrows begged for details.

"Okay. Make it two rib eyes." Waiting for the lady's club to pass, he gave smiles to the key voters. Ripping the paper from the straw and giving the Coke a long pull, he said, "Yeah. That's right. She's my niece."

The embarrassing faux pas raised red flags. Measuring words intended to roll back her mistake, she rocked the table as she plopped down an elbow, twirling an unruly strand of hair. "I'm sorry for that remark. I stuck my nose in where it didn't belong."

"No harm. No foul," he shrugged, trying to resist the allure of her beauty. Gleaning little about her past over the last week and a half, he had failed at filling in many of the empty blanks. Tall and leggy as any runway model, with speech of a corporate elite, how could she not be attached to someone already?

"How would you feel about—"

"Here we go. Two rib-eye specials," interrupted Janey, dropping the platters down. "Need anything else?" She was eyeing Uncle Jack, looking for any evidence of a juicy story.

"Nope. Everything looks great. Thanks," said Jack.

"Uh, yes it does, Uncle Jack," said Janey, dipping her eyes to Nevada.

"Goodbye, Janey."

Working on her second fry, she looked up, kicking herself for a second misstep. Halting her hunt for a third fry, frozen by the man across the table. Forcing the last bite down and dropping the fork on the napkin, she waited. She knew so little about him, but what she saw so far was a refreshing change.

Opening his eyes, he knew he had failed to protect himself adequately. He promised himself he wouldn't get attached; she would be gone any day. A prayer couldn't hurt though. Everything about her defeated his best defenses. The fancy hairdo, the perfect manicured nails—he couldn't find a flaw. With bangs hanging over the bluest eyes, she looked so innocent as she reached out a hand. Hesitating, his hand engulfed hers. His magnet had found her steel, and he never wanted to let go.

Cringing at the blunder. "I'm sorry. I should have waited."

Her hand, soft and dainty, made the walls crumble. Giving the hand a gentle squeeze, he thought, how could he do this to himself? The mystery woman would be on his mind for months after she disappeared.

"No problem." Taking a healthy bite out of the rib-eye sandwich, he said, "You were gonna ask me something before Janey brought the food?"

Taking a sip of Coke, she tried to wash down the lump rising in her throat. Unaccustomed to such vulnerability, could she take a hit that deep? Drowning her fry in a pool of ketchup, she was about to crack open a door for true happiness or heartache. A door that had remained tightly closed for several years. Latching on to the first happiness in years, she placed her bet, laying her cards on the table.

"What would you think of me relocating here?" she asked.

Fighting to keep the Coke from spraying out of his nose, he blurted out, "Right here in little ole Shallimar?"

Feigning her best pout, she said, "Yeah. I could find a house to rent."

He slid his plate to the side. "What would you do? What kind of work would you do? You've got 'big city girl' written all over you."

She lay down the first tracks of a long row to hoe. "I raided my 401k. I'm good for a while. Me and the big city had a falling out."

Not since the time he took four days to get up the nerve to ask Megan Cook to the school dance had he been so nervous. Casting caution aside, ignoring all his instincts, he said, "Tell you what. How about, uh, I take you out on a real date tonight, and we can work out your plan?" he asked sheepishly.

"It's a deal!"

Peppering each other with questions, sparring to learn the most while revealing the least, they were lost to the world.

Closing down the diner, Janey headed their way. "I hate to break this party up, but we closed up twenty minutes ago."

Hijacking her earlier offer, Jack motioned Janey over, handing her two twenties.

"Hey, I said I'm buying," yelled Nevada, forcing the card into Janey's hand. "You keep his money for your tip."

"I'm good with that!" Janey said, snagging the twenties.

"Fine. I'll be out in the car, warming it up," said Jack, shaking his head.

Turning toward the restrooms, Nevada nodded. "Okay. I'll be right out," she said.

Lost in a dream of a simpler life, she tried to imagine herself trading in the penthouse for a house and a picket fence. Floating on a cloud of possibilities, she made it up to the counter.

"I don't think I've ever seen a cooler credit card. Is it metal?" asked Janey.

Mortified at the blunder, Nevada said, "Yes. Yes, it is." She was calculating the damage. "Has the charge already been applied to the card?" she asked, holding out for a small miracle.

"Yep. Went right through. Problem?" asked Janey.

Exhaling, Nevada blasted some rogue bangs skyward. "Ooh boy."

Admiring the black card, Janey said, "I'll bet you could buy a house with this baby."

Cracking a polite smile for an answer, silently beating herself up for the gaffe. Had the dream been extinguished before it could ever sprout wings? She felt the blood drain from her soul. The blow staggered her world, and she was hoping all was not lost as she went out to meet Jack.

"Somebody let the air out of you or what?" asked Jack.

Forcing a feeble smile, lying in the name of love, she replied, "I got a disturbing text. My old boss asking me to travel to Los Angeles to, uh, put the finishing touches on something I was working on."

With hope slipping through his fingers, he asked a question he wasn't ready to hear an answer to. "Will you return?"

Cracking open the window to her soul, she allowed him the chance to destroy her emotionally. Dropping all her defenses, so perfected these last years, turning, she locked on to the man she had chosen. She was afraid to launch the words—words that would give him the keys to her life. "Do you want me to?"

Tormented, dealing with the cruel anguish humans perpetrated upon each other on a daily basis, the words couldn't be any sweeter. Hesitating, allowing his heart to recover, Jack knew life would never be the same. A man of action, less on words, he saw how fragile life was and how fickle fate could be. Drawing her hand to his, he said, "More than I care to admit."

She said, "I'll be gone for a few days."

"Work fast."

6

Landing the next day at Dallas, she weaved through the crowded concourse and slipped into the first shop. Browsing through the endless trinkets and garbage waiting to be bought by the gullible, she spied her target. She pulled the fuzzy bear plastered with a large red heart off the shelf, boldly swearing to love Dallas. Slipping the Black Card back into her purse, she refused to live life looking over her shoulder.

Grabbing a slice of pizza, she scouted out her connecting flight. Scrambling to come up with a plan, she dreamed of a possible new freedom, one anchored by love and trust, scraping away the years of living with constant treachery lurking around every corner. Boarding the 737, she settled down in first class. As it rumbled down the runway, inbound for LA, she allowed, for the first time, a hope for love.

*****

Tied to his desk, buried in paperwork, he couldn't shake the ominous feeling. Not a word for three days. He hung on to the one card in his favor: her abandoned Malibu.

"Jack, did you see the report on the double murder near the state line…Sheriff?" asked Deputy Brady, peering around the open doorway.

"Uh, sorry, Randy. What'd you ask?" asked Jack, swiveling around.

Second in command, he gave his boss these last seven years a critical scowl. "You good?" asked Randy.

As Jack leaned back, the swivel chair protested with a loud pop. "Yeah, I'm fine. Why the concern, Mom?"

Pulling the door shut, he said, "Well, the guys say you've been biting their heads off on a regular basis. And you have been grouchy as an old bear around here too."

"Well, sheriffs aren't known to be nice," countered Jack.

Testing years of friendship, Randy tapped the woodwork. "You were, up to about four days ago."

With a slight narrowing of his eyes, it was clear he felt the sting. "Leave the door open when you're done."

Spinning on his bootheel, Randy grabbed the doorknob, hesitating. "She'll come back," he whispered. With twenty-plus years of sniffing out the truth, Chief Deputy Randy Brady missed little.

"Thanks, Randy!" he yelled, relenting, as he watched his old friend amble down the hallway.

With a raised hand acknowledging the clean slate between them, he disappeared around the corner.

Puttering around the office, Jack tried to keep her neatly in a box. Refusing to be cast aside so easily, she had jumped to the front of the line in his life, trumping his career and his family and smothering his waking thoughts 24-7. Lost in thought, refusing to acknowledge the chirp of the incoming text, Jack headed for the squad car.

Wading into the gruesome double murder crime scene, once again, he was witnessing another of the countless acts of street justice meted out to the troubled. The duo didn't stand a chance. Both were snuffed out execution style with bullets to the back of the head. The never-ending supply of violence and cruelty chipped away at his humanity. Pitting countless tax dollars and manpower against an evil empire failed to leave few untouched. Crossing countless lines drawn in the sand, it was here to stay.

Stripping the latex gloves off, Jack washed his hands with the disinfectant for a second time, cradling his phone awkwardly under his chin. "Hello?"

"Jack?"

"Yeah, Jack Webster. Can I help you?"

"It's Emily."

DIVINE MEMORIES

Launching a finger into his other ear to block out the screech of the tow-truck winch struggling to hoist the car up out of the wooded ravine, he said, "Who?"

"It's Emily. Emily Parker."

Hotfooting it down the gravel road, he clicked off his portable radio. "Hey, good to hear from you," he said, breathing hard from the sprint.

Testing their fragile bond, she asked, "Are you okay? Did you get my text earlier?"

Stepping around the jet-black body bags, he was grateful she was miles away. "Emily, work has been crazy, and I missed it until now. I will—"

Stuffing the present in the trash can, she worked her way to the boarding line. "Fine. No problem. I'll hire a cab and—"

"Absolutely not! When will you be landing?" Jack cut in.

Spoiled worse than six-month-old lunch meat, the claws were fully extended. "If it's a bother, really, I can—"

Furiously bailing water out of his sinking ship, he said, "I...uh...I Just need a flight number and time." He was trying to plug the hole in the ship.

Memories of her calming voice, so long ago, echoed in her mind, beckoning her to use her words carefully. Casting away the anger first, she broke the silence. "Southwest 1235. Should arrive about four thirty." Pivoting around a mom harnessed to two rowdy boys, she rescued the coffee-stained bear from the trash. "Thanks. Sorry, I am exhausted."

"I'll bet you are. Have a good flight home. I'll see you at four thirty," he said, righting the ship again.

Nevada blotted out the safety procedures as the stewardess droned on with the oxygen mask application. Had she found a new home? Was this the wide spot in the road she so desperately hungered for? Wheels up, heading back to Indianapolis, the nagging demons started creeping out of their box. Awakened from their slumber, they refused to be quieted. They were standing at the ready to sabotage her life again. Inbound to a world foreign to her, unarmed, she was missing the tools to live life without drama.

71

Popping the belt keepers off, he allowed the weight of the job to slip away, slinging the gun belt around the scuffed-up bedpost. Breaking apart the Velcro straps, he let the bulletproof vest fall to the bed. Grabbing ole blue, he traded the bulletproof vest in for his favorite faded flannel shirt. He felt human again. Dipping the comb in the stream of water, raking back the shocks of dirty blond hair, he fought to erase the hat hair. Looking at his reflection, giving a thumbs down to a quick shave, he thought she could do worse.

Months before his second term was finished, the last seven years had been an eye-opener. At thirty-seven, wildly popular for his tough stance against crime, Jack was a shoe-in for a third term, but herding mankind was getting more difficult every day. Strapping on his backup gun, he walked out into the world, intent on seeking out the woman of his dreams.

Pulling into the cell phone lot, arriving early, he used the time to sift through all his flaws. Stacking them up to the ceiling, he calculated why anyone in her league would be remotely interested in a hick sheriff for very long. With a boatload of self-doubt reeling through his mind, he flinched at the cell phone's ring.

"Hello?"

Retrieving her carry-on from the luggage bin, she asked, "I'm in Indy. Did you make it?"

Hearing her voice once again launched another sizzling dose of giddy excitement for a new chapter in his life. Inching farther out upon the limb, he dared to dream of happiness. With one foot straying dangerously close to the trap, could he take it if it all tumbled back to earth? It would suck the life out of him.

"Yeah, just let me know when you're headed out, and I'll pick ya up at the curb."

"Thanks, Jack. I'll be right out. Maybe we can grab a bite to eat."

"You read my mind."

Enjoying a quiet meal together, bobbing and weaving between the lines of truth, she broached the continual lie. She placed the glass of wine down. "Did I mention, I'll have to make a few more trips out to LA?" she asked, wrinkling up her pert little nose.

DIVINE MEMORIES

Halting the fork's progress, he left it hanging motionless. "No."

"Yeah. It's going to take a few more meetings. But I'll be back the next day each time, if I can get early flights out," she said, hating the deception.

Venturing off, straying into one of her grayer areas, Jack asked, "What exactly is it you did for a living again?"

"You know, I realized something. I don't know what you do either," she countered. Cutting the filet, she stalled as she aimed her fork in his direction. "You first."

Taking the last pull from his draft beer, he said, "I'm the sheriff of the county. I have two younger sisters, Bell and Candy, both mean as snakes, and one cranky mother."

Swallowing her piece of steak a tad bit early, she snatched up the goblet of water. "Well, that explains a lot." Tapping her fork on the plate, she said, "Well, what do ya know about that? Me, with the high sheriff." Pushing her plate away, his face revealed little. Cocking her head to the side with a mischievous grin, she asked, "You serious?"

"Is that a problem?"

"No! No, I feel safer already." She laughed.

"Your turn."

Spoiling the laughter, she took refuge, ducking behind her glass of wine, allowing the cool Chardonnay to take its time. He would not be denied as he sat patiently. "I was a freelance problem solver in the financial world," she offered.

"Pfft! What's that even mean?" he scoffed.

"You know. I would help close difficult financial transactions."

"Who did you work for? Where did you work? Details, girl, details," he said rapid fire, pushing her further out into the open.

Clasping her hands together, she asked, coolly topping off her drink, "Sheriff, isn't this where you usually read me my rights?"

Breaking off the interrogation, he was teetering at the cliff's edge. "Sorry. It comes with the job."

Dodging the dragnet, taking slivers of the truth, she drew a line in the sand. Let's grow on each other a little more before I start handing out my details. Okay?"

Stroking his mustache, he grunted. "Sounds mysterious."

She threaded the needle carefully. "We come from vastly different backgrounds, that's all." Reaching across the table, she added, "I just need you to really see me as a person first."

Staring across a table at more women than he deserved, he retreated. "Fair enough."

Placing the napkin across her plate, she toyed with the corner. "Would you, uh…. Well, would you have time tomorrow to go with me to look for a house?"

Jack was thankful for the subdued lighting, which masked his eagerness at the revelation. Every fiber desired her to be closer—a mere three feet away yet so far. "How about I pick you up around eight in the morning?"

"Great! Let the hunt begin at eight."

Escorting her across the motel parking lot, life felt right. With each step, he prepared for his moment. Rehearsing his words, he imagined what her responses would be, where he would place his hands, the sweet touch of her lips, where he would sit in her room, and how far it would go. A pro at handling rowdy bar fights and a decorated veteran, he was a survivor of too many bloody gun battles in Iraq to count. His nerves joined forces, conspiring to create havoc as Nevada turned.

"Home sweet home," she said, pulling the key card out.

Swiping his hand down the side of his jeans, he said, "Hopefully, we'll find something better tomorrow." He was thankful for the young kid in the jacked-up Camaro blacktopping the parking lot with the smoky burnout. It shattered the painful silence as the master plan turned to mush. His sweaty palms allowed the reins to slip through his fingers.

Inches away, she came to his rescue. Putting him out of his misery, she grabbed the broad shoulders. The quick peck was a mockery of the kiss his master plan had promised.

Leaving the motel door open a crack, unleashing a playful giggle, she was enjoying his misery. "Pretend I'm a fine wine. See you tomorrow." She closed the door with a smile—a smile that would keep him staring up at the ceiling long into the night.

*****

Working through the rental houses early the next morning, she knocked them out of the running one by one. Most never earned more than a courtesy drive-by. Chewing through the local inventory, they rounded the corner. Turning up the lane, she came alive, giving the pristine driveway constructed of red pavers her approval as it came into view. Peeking through the ancient oaks, the McGregor Plantation's mansion stood defiantly resisting the unforgiving element of time. Built in 1859, time had robbed her of the glory she once commanded. Nestled on over four thousand acres of prime estate, she had managed to evade the bulldozers of zealous developers time after time.

She snared his hand. "Oh my. Can we go inside?" she asked, almost pleading.

With little appetite to extinguish the fire in her eyes as she gazed up at the behemoth, he would make his case later. "Sure. But you know it's unfurnished, and it don't come cheap," he said, letting some air out on her dream.

Halfway to the front door, ignoring Debbie Downer, she would have what she wanted. Waiting for the realtor to arrive, she walked around back, taking a seat on the stone bench under the pergola. Patting the seat, he relented, preparing for the disappointment.

Raking her hands wide, looking out upon the tree-lined meadows, she said, "Tell me you don't think this is anything other than absolutely spectacular."

"Oh, I think it's beautiful. But…well…" He wanted to pump the brakes on the fantasy.

Sliding the Ray-Bans down a notch, she asked, "What?" Her icy stare a few degrees cooler than the gentle winter breeze playing havoc with her hair.

"That right there might be a problem," said Jack, stabbing a finger at the spec sheet.

I spend more than that a month on shoes. Shifting all her weight on one foot, Nevada said, "I can handle that." She was looking for a fight.

Chewing on the corner of his mustache, he failed to see the sign warning everyone to enter at their own risk. "Emily, don't take this wrong, but the rent is $8,500 a month, and the utilities average over $1,500 a month. Who could afford that?" Driving the final stake in her plan, he added, "Rumor has it that the owner of this estate has turned down offers of over 50 million for this house and all the land. They won't dicker on the price."

"I want to see the inside of this house. Don't concern yourself about my finances, Jack," said Nevada, proud of the growth she exhibited as she allowed him to keep his skin intact.

"Fine. Here comes Milly."

Catching Milly's eye, Jack's questionable look signaled another wasted morning on another dreamer for the property. Going through the motions out of courtesy for the sheriff, Milly enthusiastically boasted of all the potentials for a renter to enjoy. Standing in the converted office on the third floor, she looked out upon the massive sprawling meadows and mature woods. Trading in skyscrapers for the towering oaks and maples would be a welcome change.

*****

Arriving early the next morning at Mercury Real Estate, Nevada scouted out Milly, waiting for her exit from the break room.

Exhausted from a sleepless night with the baby, the business smile was difficult to muster up before 9:00 a.m. Fighting a tough economy with home sales in the gutter, she didn't have time to waste on dreamers. Deliberately facing away from the receptionist, taking a much needed sip of inspiration, she made a late grab for her coat.

"Ah. Ms. Parker, good morning."

"Do you have a minute?" asked Nevada, taking a seat.

Continuing to button her coat, she inched toward the exit. "Well, uh, I do have a couple of appointments."

"Could we discuss the McGregor property? If you've got time."

Pulling her hair out of the coat collar, Milly finished snagging the keys out of her purse. "I don't believe that property would be a good fit for you."

Trying not to explode out of her skin, Nevada hissed, "Oh! And why's that?" Each word was loaded with a lethal dose of venom.

DIVINE MEMORIES

Taking a step back, plopping down on the corner of the desk, Milly said, "Ms. Parker, I am the treasurer of the local Administerial Alliance. I believe I wrote a check paying for your gas just a few weeks ago. How could you expect to—"

Lunging out of the seat, cutting off the rival cougar, Nevada went straight for the jugular. "Let me stop you right there, lady. That was a mistake. Jack should have asked first!"

Milly sabotaged the single biggest deal of her life as she heard the receptionist's preplanned office rescue page. Flushing down all chances with the richest female in the country, she snatched up the phone. Answering the fake page from the receptionist summoning her to the front desk, she walked away.

"Can I get the owner's information?" asked Nevada, ready to pounce.

Screeching to a halt, pivoting to face Nevada with a murderous look, she said, "Absolutely not! You need to leave."

Left alone, she rifled through the stack of files, cracking open one labeled *McGregor*. With a quick peek, she knew she would welcome the trip down to Atlanta. She vowed to give that box a new owner in a few weeks or her real name wasn't Nevada Barrington. With a grunt of satisfaction, she slipped out the side door.

Buying the ticket to Atlanta under the name of Emily Parker, she would lead the dogs of war away from her lair at all costs once again. Taking the first flight to Atlanta, she pored over the plan. They couldn't refuse.

Dotting the Atlanta area with purchases from the Black Card, she could remain no longer than a day or two. She wouldn't get many more chances to leave a meandering trail, he was at the end of his patience for her escapades. Slowing for the turn, she noted that the neighborhood looked wrong. One row of broken-down shotgun houses after another, and she had turned down millions?

"Cabbie, are you sure this is the right house?" asked Nevada, rubbernecking up and down the street. With a higher ratio of abandoned cars in the yards versus those on the street, it was hard to believe the rightful owner lived anywhere near this part of the world.

"Yes, ma'am."

Uneasy at leaving her mode of escape, she ripped five hundred-dollar bills in half. "I want you to stick around until I'm ready to leave. If you are here in one hour, the other halves are yours plus another five hundred."

Eyeballing next year's Christmas fund, the cabbie said, "Yes, ma'am! One hour, right here."

Navigating through overgrown crabgrass, she found the broken remnants of what once served as a sidewalk leading to the small box of a house. Knocking on the heavy steel screen door, she waited, crossing her fingers. Knocking for the fourth time, her hopes of a quick deal sank, and she started to turn. The faint thud from inside renewed her hopes. Knocking a little harder, she said, "Ms. McGregor? Ms. Lillian McGregor? I have come a long way. I just want to talk...please."

"Who are you? What do you want?" asked Lillian, hiding behind the walls of her fortress.

Clinging to the sound of her voice, Nevada said, "Ma'am, I am Emily Parker from Shallimar, Illinois."

"Not for sale! Not for sale! Go away," yelled Lillian through the crack.

Leaning heavily against the screen door, she said, "Please, Lillian, just hear me out. I want to help you save the mansion."

"How? Why?" demanded Lillian.

"Open the door and we can talk it over. No commitments."

With seconds ticking by, the silence either signaled hope or the final dashing of her dream.

"Lillian, are you there?" asked Nevada, keeping the dream alive.

With a loud pop of the deadbolt being released, her dream was still alive. Swinging the heavy oak door open, Lillian peered around the edge. Studying the woman with caution, she looked left and right for accomplices. Stepping out, she faced the latest threat. A scant five feet tall, the little Southern belle would not be intimidated. Dressed for church, she had no time for strangers. She drew her shawl tighter, and she pulled the door shut.

"Nobody is tearing down my Yankee Mansion while I'm still alive," warned Lillian.

Releasing the binder on her set of documents, Nevada said, "Could we speak for a few moments, Lillian?"

"No!" scolded Lillian. "You're gonna make me late for church. You're welcome to walk with me, if you still want to talk," offered Lillian, allowing a tight smile to escape.

Entering the Southern Baptist Church of Atlanta South, Nevada steered the unlikely duo to a couple of open seats in the back row. Reaching out, Lillian grasped her sleeve and pulled her toward the front pews. "I always want to make sure God sees me in his house," said Lillian with a soft chuckle.

With a packed house, Nevada hoped to slide under the radar. Nervous, fidgeting, and clicking the snap holding the documents in and out, she drew quick scrutiny, offered free of charge. Reaching over, patting her hand, Grandmother had spoken. The rebuking brought a lost fragment of a memory from her past. A time when the world looked so much brighter. A time when she could still be a child. A time before her heart was ripped out, derailing a life now hell-bent on one answer.

Nevada was a master manipulator and the queen at outmaneuvering her opponents. *Lillian should be a piece of cake*, she thought. Strolling back, the conversation finally rolled around to the property. Bristling at the idea of selling, Lillian had another side to be dealt with. Holding all the cards, she would have been right at home, knee deep in New York's dirtiest negotiations. Pound for pound, the New York titan had her hands full with the tiny Southern belle.

"Lillian, I think the offer is fair," countered Nevada.

Taking a seat on the bench, she said, "Let me see that drawing again." Raising the architect's drawing inches from her eyes, she could have her dream yet. Ignoring her mother's ignorance, she clutched the drawing close to her chest. "Would you build a small wing on this side of the house and let me live out the last of my days there?" asked Lillian, her eyes misty.

Cocking her head to the side, Nevada studied her opponent. This sounded too simple, smelling of a possible renege. "Do I have your word you'll sign the deed over to me on the day you move in?" she asked.

"Emily, as God is my witness, you have my word. At ninety-one, you won't have to put up with me too long," said Lillian with a twinge of guilt. "My mother will be rolling over in her grave when I do though."

Giving out a rare hug, she came up from the embrace. "Why?"

"My mother never forgave my great-granddaddy for building that abomination, as she called it. He was a prominent businessman that had issues with Southern virtues. Before the war, he and all his workers moved north and raised corn and grains for Union armies at the Yankee plantation. She forbade us to ever spend a night there."

"Whew! That's a long time to keep anger fueled," said Nevada.

Rubbing her hand across the drawing, she traced the area where the addition would be. "You never crossed paths with my momma," said Lillian. The iron hand of the woman still brought a flash of fear.

Taking her hand, the broken nails matched the broken skin from years of neglect. As she turned the corner, the cabbie sat idling.

Landing back in Indy, she hated the never-ending pack of lies. She still held out hope as she gave a weak smile to the stewardess manning the exit. Regretting the mountains of deception racking up in the name of love, demanding honesty from the other side but gushing out a life manufactured from wave after wave of untruths. Pulling out her cell, she was ready to add to the list.

"Hey, Jack," said Nevada.

"Hey you. Headed back already?" asked Jack, crossing Main Street, failing to see the hellion on the electric bike breezing by. "What flight are you coming back on?"

"Uh, well, here's the thing. I forgot to call you. I am already in Indy."

"No problem. I am heading there now. How was LA?"

Cringing while adding another log to the fire, she muttered, "Fine. Smoggy as ever."

7

As he paced the office floor, Charles's world was closing in fast. The plan of a financial empire and her corner office had crumbled overnight. With a torrent of countless legal and civil suits bearing down on the trio, her hand had clamped around their throats. Cloaked behind multiple layers of wrangling, she had broadsided their ship, blasting it clean out of the water. Dodging creditors, living on a meager hoard of cash, all he wanted was one last shot at her.

"Liddy, is there no word on her whereabouts?" pleaded Charles, miserable as the weather outside.

Liddy dropped the ashtray. "Nope. Our teams can't find her, but luckily, neither can the feds."

"Well, gentlemen, we have two weeks before the grand jury decides our future. She must be dealt with before then. We-we can't have her chumming up to the feds," stammered Charles.

"We've been close a few times. Charges on her Black Cards pop up every so often," chimed in Amos.

"Yeah, she's got an apartment rented in LA. But our team black-bagged it, and she has set up a phony appearance of living there. She has recorded charges on her Black Card all across the country, but nothing shows up on any airline tickets. We can't locate where she is living. She's being smart," said Liddy.

"Surely, after almost five months, she has slipped up somewhere," said Charles.

"Charles, we are waiting on a team to check in on a large land purchase near a town she used the card months ago. It could be just a coincidence though," said Amos.

"I'm putting pressure on my source too, but keep on it. It's all we have to go on." Easing out of his chair, signaling an end to the strategy session. Aiming a bony finger at the brothers, Charles said, "Find Nevada Barrington, or I'm afraid we're going to be guests of the government's penal institution."

*****

Walking arm in arm through the diner door, the happy couple's planets were aligned. Sliding into their booth, she reached over for his hand. "Jack, I have never been happier," said Nevada.

Pulling her over tightly, throwing caution to the wind as the kiss landed, he said, "Me too, Emily."

"Hey you two!" bubbled Janey, pulling out her order pad.

Sliding back, plastering his nose in the menu, Jack said, "Janey, I'll have the special."

"And for you, Emily?" asked Janey, losing her smile. She dropped her eyes back down to the order pad.

"Same for me. Is everything okay, Janey?" asked Nevada.

Forcing a smile, feebly covering the worry, she replied, "Everything's fine." She turned to leave, dodging any further questions.

Shaking the ketchup bottle, Jack said, "That was weird."

"Yeah, I know."

Refusing to dish out any details when she brought the meal, Janey agonized over the dilemma. Jack deserved happiness.

Munching on his last fry, Jack said, "Hey, you remember that big mansion you wanted to rent when you first come to town?"

"Yeah. What about it?" asked Nevada, fumbling with her bracelet.

"Word is somebody has been pouring millions into the total restoration of the place."

Busy watching traffic on Main Street, she struggled to make sense of her life. Her house of cards had no foundation. Had she stayed at the roulette table too long?

"Did you hear me?"

Breaking the trance, Nevada replied, "Yeah. Yeah, it's good that somebody saved that beautiful house."

"What's wrong?" asked Jack.

Watching Janey heading their way with the bill, she said, "Nothing."

"Here you go, folks," said Janey, handing Jack the slip.

"Jack, you go pay. I'll leave the tip."

Lingering near their table, Janey closed in. "Emily, I need to tell you something," she whispered.

Here it comes! "Yeah, honey. What is it?"

"A couple days ago, two men come in the diner asking about you," said Janey.

Going pasty white, Nevada said, "It couldn't have been me, Janey." She swallowed hard, fighting to keep the demons under control.

Shaking her head, Janey countered, "No. It was you. They had your picture."

Panic bombarded her from every angle, and she could feel the heat rising. "What did they say? What did you tell them?" asked Nevada.

She looked younger than her eighteen years as she held the broken smile. "I'm sorry. I told them I had seen you before."

Handing over a ten for the tip, Nevada mumbled, "It's fine."

Stepping out into the bright sunny spring day, she cast her eyes up and down Main Street. Paranoia filling in the blanks, she gave a hard look at the SUV parked around the corner. Slipping in the car with Jack, she scrambled to gain control. Already seeing danger in every direction, she struggled to stay afloat.

"Let's go down to the state park and walk some trails," said Jack.

Lost in thought, she was busy concentrating on the next string of lies to hide behind. His words sailed past her, leaving her vulnerable.

"Okay. What's the problem? First Janey, now you. Let's hear it," demanded Jack, pulling up along the curb.

"No, drive." Looking out the window at everything and nothing, she couldn't face him.

Slamming the shifter in park, he said, "Not yet."

Giving the green light for the latest lie, she traded regret in the name of love. "I have to make one last overnight trip, and then I am finished. I promise," she said, refusing to meet his gaze.

Giving her a side-eye, he said, "You promise?"

"Absolutely! If I leave this afternoon, I can be back tomorrow afternoon."

*****

Picking a random city, Nevada made a hasty last-minute reservation for Miami. Packing the overnight bag, she dug down in the sugar bowl, retrieving the hidden anchor to her old life. Rushing to stuff her old work phone from Barrington Enterprises, minus the battery, in the bag, she heard the back door slam.

"Ready to go?" yelled Jack, rounding the corner of the kitchen wall.

She nodded, swiping the spilled sugar off the counter. "Yep."

Traveling the last forty miles in silence, Jack wondered. Was he losing her? Clutching her hand, she was his beautiful mystery. Five months and he knew so little of her past. He could coax little from her as she craftily evaded probing questions with professional ease.

"Well, here we are again," he said with little emotion.

Snuggling up against his shoulder, she cried out, "I know. I know. This is it. I promise."

Irritated at the unexpected trip, Jack pushed harder. An open book by nature, he pressed further to penetrate the murky wall around her. At the risk of losing her, he couldn't fight the doubts anymore.

"Emily?"

Lost in the lies, she had hit the limit on the balls she could keep in the air. "Yeah. What is it?"

"Nothing. Have a good trip," he said, backing off, leaving the fight for another day.

Oh, please give me a little more time, my love. "No, what is it?"

Hitting the release valve, the frustration dribbled out. Jack hoped their relationship could weather the waves coming. "Well, Emily. Uh, well, it's hard work to keep things on an even keel with so much mystery. I mean, really. If somebody asked me about you, what could I tell them?"

Recoiling from his shoulder, she saw the passage to happiness was getting bumpier by the second. Tightening the grip on her bag, she popped the door open. "You could tell them I am a hard worker trying to navigate through a complicated life. But be careful what you wish for," she warned, yanking her travel bag over the headrest and scraping the head liner. Slamming the door, she escaped further interrogation and went stomping off toward the terminal.

Busting a knuckle against the steering wheel, Jack sighed. "How much more frigging romantic can this relationship get?" he complained to the remaining passengers. Looking into the rearview at the empty back seat, he said, "Yeah. I'm talking to you." He raked his hair back. "God, I'm losing it."

The thought of a life minus her brought a wave of nausea. Life before her seemed so lifeless and empty now. Life without her would be unlivable.

The annoying honk of the pickup behind him unleashed the boiling point. Backhanding the innocent package of Oreo cookies off the dash, it exploded into a thousand pieces against the passenger window. It would be a long twenty-four hours till her return.

Easing the SUV forward, he caught a glimpse of her. Slamming on the brakes, he waited for the door to be officially closed on the relationship. Better now than a twenty-four-hour wait, looking for any positive to cling to.

Wiping her eyes, making a comment about allergies, she slid the key into the lock hiding all her secrets. Leaning into the window, she would not turn it just yet. Was this the man and the wide spot in the road she risked everything for? The last five months had been the happiest since her parents' disappearance. What more could she ask of him?

"Jack, I'm sorry." Falling into his arms, Nevada started sobbing. "I'm so sorry."

"Come around and get in." Leaning over the console, he went to town on the Oreo mess on the passenger seat, raking crumbs everywhere.

Flicking stubborn crumbs to the floor, she squirmed. Battling her fears, she pressed her head to the headrest. Tipping the scales for honesty, she sifted through the lies, cherry-picking a truth from the rubble of her life. Clouded by months of deception, she struggled to unwind the saga. Couched between troubles brewing in the Big Apple and a trail of lies stretching from LA to Miami, he would need the patience of Job to understand.

"Jack, I…I lied to you. I am going to Miami, not LA."

Releasing five months of anguish and suspicion in one breath, it competed to drown out the rumble of the Fed Ex jumbo taking off.

Bracing for the bridge between their worlds to burst into flames, he had to take his head out of the sand, no matter the outcome. Fighting to ignore the attraction of her beauty and charm, he attacked. "What else have you been lying about?"

Snaking a hand over, Nevada gripped his wrist before the final bell rang.

Closing her eyes, she prayed for a sudden dose of grace to materialize magically. "You asked what you could tell people about me. Well, there are two things you could tell them. One is that I have fallen in love with you. But, other than my love for you, almost everything else out of my mouth has been a sordid lie of one sort or another," she said, ripping the Band-Aid off.

Breaking free of her grasp, he forced her face to his, even as she flinched at his touch. Jack said, "Who are you really? No more lies."

"Who am I? That's a good question." Measuring her words, still twenty-four hours out before she could come totally clean. "I'm a woman you are going to love the rest of your life and marvel at the life I can give you. Or you are going to reject me and cast me out of your life like a disease."

The words brought excitement but were piggy-backed with a dire warning. He stared at her. How could he ever cast her out of his life? "You know I love you. How could—"

Pressing a finger to his lips, Nevada said, "Stop! You love my beauty, my smile, my laugh. Not who I truly am."

"Shut up." Reaching out, intertwining his fingers in her hair, he yanked her closer. Crushing his lips to hers, he didn't care what her story was.

"I gotta get going. Give me another twenty-four hours."

DIVINE MEMORIES

Pulling her back in for a second embrace, Jack refused to believe he would allow her to escape. "Yeah right. When do you get back in tomorrow?"

"About one fifteen. When I get back, let's go out to eat, and over supper, I'll tell you everything about me. The good obviously. And the bad and ugly."

"You know I'm not going to sleep tonight."

Cracking the door open to leave, Nevada hoped their relationship hadn't taken on too much water to stay afloat. She knew she wouldn't get much sleep either. "Remember, I've always told you I wanted you to really see me before you knew about me. Well, tomorrow, you will really know me. Remember, the lies were told because I truly do love you," she said, allowing the door to swing shut.

He lowered the window. "Girl, you're killing me here. Hey, you didn't mention the other thing I could tell people about you," yelled Jack.

Walking toward the terminal, spinning, Nevada allowed a smile to replace her frown. "Jack Webster owes me a pack of Oreo cookies." Waving back, she disappeared into the terminal.

8

Coming back from breakfast, Nevada stuffed away loose articles strewn about the hotel room. Plugging the charger in, she grabbed the phone, treating the treacherous instrument gingerly. Anguishing at the implications, she was fearful of the beacon it would soon emit. Somehow, somewhere, eyes were glued to a screen waiting for this day. Perched in dark corners were men eager to report her location to vile men willing to do the evil bidding of others.

With a beep signifying the charging, the fuse was lit. Screens in dark places where evil flourished finally had something to report.

Loitering in the front lobby, she placed the long-awaited call. On pins and needles, she waited to hear a voice from her past.

"Hello, Lawrence?"

Kicking his office door shut, Lawrence said, "Nevada, thank God you're alive! Don't say where you are, honey."

With a rush of emotions at the sound of his voice, she collapsed on the nearest sofa. "Give it to me straight. How bad is it?"

"Well. I guess."

She hailed the cabdriver as he entered the lobby. "Lawrence, don't sugarcoat it. I don't have much time."

"Nevada, it's bad. I've got a stack of federal subpoenas on my desk a foot thick. Then there are the three maniacs across the room that would love to cut your heart out, literally, and tap-dance on your corpse. Take your pick."

"You could've led with the three maniacs first."

"Honey, I'm not kidding. You are just a step or two ahead of them."

Halting the cabbie's advance with a raised finger, Nevada said, "Lawrence, I know. I know. I'm being careful." Turning her back to the cabbie, she lowered her voice. "Lawrence, I found my wide spot in the road and the man I'm going to marry one day," she said, wearing one of the rare smiles she would offer the world today.

Parting the curtain at the sound of cheers, Lawrence witnessed the beehive of activity inside Charles's office. It brought a stab of guilt coursing through his body, one he would have to live with. "Nevada, trust nobody. I mean no one. And watch your back. I think they know where you're hiding. Goodbye, Vada. Don't call again." He was chock-full of guilt for a misdeed decades ago—one he would never outrun. Letting the phone slip from his fingers, it clattered down on the desk. It seemed the years were tumbling down upon him. "Please be careful, little Vada," he whispered.

"Lawrence? Lawrence, are you there?"

Nevada ran for her life. The movies made it look easy as she made her escape in the grimy cab. Seated alone, one against many, she would not bow down. Defiant to a fault, she drew the nail file from her purse. Using her best penmanship, she took her time, making each letter legible. She scratched the taunting message on the iPhone screen. The mocking would fuel their hatred.

Closing her eyes, she allowed the sway of the cab to rock her tensions away. Exhaustion won the battle, and she drifted off.

Cutting ties with her earthly thoughts, she stumbled through the darkness. She sought a channel to be heard, one discovered by few. Falling to the ground, she shivered in the darkness. The bitter cold gnawed at her bones, competing for her attention. With despair and desolation for traveling companions, life had been strangled from her. Clinging to a hope she never fully believed in, she marched deeper into the wilderness. No longer possessing the strength to continue, she once again fell to the ground. Rolling up in the fetal position, she surrendered. "Lord, I am lost. Where are you?"

Subtle at first, the warm breeze enveloped her. The warmth, ushering in hope, was welcome as she clawed her way back up. In a world devoid of light, the faint glow commanded her attention. As it intensified, she shielded her eyes. It burst into a brilliant sliver of light, and she scrambled, taking refuge behind the nearest rock. It was rapidly expanding, and she cowered as the light continued to evolve. Peeking around the rock, peering through the cracks between her fingers, she could barely make out the silhouette. A sharp voice penetrated her senses.

"Your cries have not fallen on deaf ears. The journey you'll travel will be rocky. Stay on the path, stepping neither left nor right from it," *the voice warned.*

Screaming at the fading light did little good as it disappeared, leaving complete darkness. Thrashing about, she felt the impact crashing into the Plexiglas shield. She came to as the cabbie braked, narrowly missing the rear bumper of the Ford Taurus.

"Sorry 'bout that, ma'am. Heard you yelling back there and took my eyes off the road a second."

Rubbing a red spot on her cheek, she said, "It's okay."

Springing back away from the shield, she let the embarrassment evaporate. Horrified at the makeup smear on the glass partition, she retrieved her compact. One look brought a resounding gasp. Looking more like an assault victim, she applied a fresh coat of Serge Lutens Allumete N°3. Satisfied at the repair job, she swiped the lipstick smear from the shield. Settling back in the seat, she hoped the rest of the ride to the airport would be uneventful.

The letters screamed to be acknowledged. Filled with the smeared lipstick, the words were visibly highlighted. In small shaky letters, one had to look twice to see them prior. Leaning forward, inches from the shield, she struggled to make out the second number. Punching in the words on her phone, she let Google do her dirty work. Riveted to the phone, Nevada was oblivious to all else.

"Ma'am, we're here." Turning to see the problem, the cabbie said, "Ma'am?"

She refused to pry her eyes from the phone. "Keep the meter running. I'll make it worth your while."

The words, rocking her to the core, wouldn't release her. Running wild, they coursed through her brain as she read the passage again. Running her fingernail across the scrolled words, she let her nail catch in the groove.

"That's some of Father Michael's handiwork." The cabbie laughed. "Brought him home from the annual bingo one night with a snootful, and he left that little gift."

DIVINE MEMORIES

"When you see him again, thank him for me," said Nevada as she exited the cab.

*****

Soaring at thirty-five thousand feet, Nevada let the words run through her mind. Sitting on the fence, she tried to justify her day, indexing the unexplainable incidents into a box labeled *coincidence*. Looking down at the mountain range, she shook her head. How could anyone move them? But then, how could anyone build them? Sifting through the last twenty-four hours, she was left with more questions than answers. Descending back into Indy, she would need an abundance of answers for the man she loved.

Working her way through the terminal, she couldn't shake the dream. It seemed so vivid and real. Shedding her skin and facing the lies head-on ruined her mood as she saw Jack waiting by the curb. She would need to deliver the performance of her life.

"Hey there," said Jack, smiling from ear to ear.

Leaning in, she said, "Hey there yourself. Did you miss me?"

She looked stunning in her black jeans and Milano silk blouse. Breaking from the embrace, he saw the fear in her eyes clouding up.

"You bet. Where to first?

Buckling up, she said, "Let's head home and meet back up for supper at that steak place out on Meridian Parkway about five thirty."

"Sounds fine." As Jack pulled out of the parking lot, the silence, filled with unspoken words, held the balance of their future. Merging onto I-70, he set the cruise as her phone rang. Catching bits and pieces of the call, he fought the desire to pry.

"Lillian, I am happy it pleases you. Yes, yes, you are more than welcome. Goodbye," said Nevada, rushing the caller.

Jack slowed down for the trooper hiding in the shade of the overpass, who was running radar. He waited for his moment. Clearing the rust out of his throat, Jack said, "Who was that?"

"That was my great-aunt Lillian. I helped find her a new place to live. Maybe you'll meet her someday." Like greased lightning, the white lie flew out of her mouth.

Coming up from taking a gulp of Pepsi, he remarked, "How nice." He overtook a convoy of 18-wheelers. "Emily, remember your promise."

Soaking in the veiled admonishment, she couldn't wait to remove the cloak between them. She had lived a lie for almost six months, and the toll was getting too expensive. "I tell you what. The next time we meet, these lips will reveal all."

"Good."

As they crossed the Illinois state line, she lobbed the grenade. "Jack, in a little less than two hours, I am going to reveal who and what I am to you." Hesitating, dodging details better said across a table, she continued, "I am going to pack up everything in my car and drive separately to the restaurant. That way, I can just leave town if things between us go south." She stared out the window at the rolling hills.

Taking the next exit to Shallimar, Jack said, "That has a bad sound to it."

"Not every man can handle who and what I am."

"Sheesh, stop talking. You're scaring the natives."

*****

Sprawled out, taking up room for two on the sofa, Amos said, "Charles, she can't be in two places at the same time. Everything points to Miami, and we have active movement finally on her phone."

"Mm-hmm. And exactly how close is the team in Miami?" asked Charles.

"Hang on! That's them calling in now." The sag of the shoulders gave Charles his answer. "You're not gonna believe this crap. She slid the phone down in a cab's seat. But not before scratching a message on the screen for us first. Something to the effect of 'Three Stooges nice try.'"

Wheezing from forty years of a three-pack of Camels a day, Liddy slid into the office. "Illino-Illinois team has her...has her spotted!" said Liddy, sucking wind faster than a four-barrel carburetor.

With little to smile about over the last six months, Charles spent the capital to paint one on his face. Putting the brakes on the smile, he said, "Liddy, you better be right."

"Nope! We're golden. A team of shooters saw her waltz in, happy as can be, to her place in that hick town," said Liddy, proud as a peacock.

Plopping both feet up on the desk, Charles said, "Well, boys. We might have lost a battle here and there, but we are going to win this war. With her anyway."

*****

Walking into the Bernigan's Steak House, he was early. Taking a seat over by the windows, Jack watched the highway traffic cruise by. He tried to imagine what her true story would be. A beautiful woman made out of 10 percent facts and 90 percent mystery with a pinch of imagination in for good measure.

"Sheriff, how many tonight?" asked Margo, dropping menus and coasters down.

"It'll be just the two us tonight. How about a Bud Light while we're waiting?"

"Sure thing."

Pouring the beer in the frosted mug, he took a long draw. Hearing the distant wail get louder, he shielded the sun from his eyes, catching a fleeting glimpse of the state trooper barreling up the highway at Mach 1. Glancing at his watch, Jack ordered a second beer. She was fifteen minutes late. Had she decided to bail?

Attracting the patrons' attention as the string of sheriff cars flew by, the lights and wailing sirens were a warning to the innocent.

"Here you go, Sheriff. Must be something serious going on," said Margo, leaning down to get a better view up the highway.

"It's Saturday. Who knows?" said Jack, not liking the odds.

Feeling the vibration of the incoming call, he wondered what her excuse would be. Taking a second look, the incoming call brought a dread his soul was too weak to stomach. There wasn't a good scenario for him being called in on a Saturday night. Dread was seeping in as he summoned the strength to take a call that would potentially derail countless dreams, hopes, and a love. Wading through other peoples' tragedies daily gave his mind plenty of scenarios to conjure up the imagination.

"Randy, is she…is she alive?" he asked.

"Buddy, you need to get over to the scene at Meridian Parkway and Twelfth."

Grabbing his jacket, he sprinted to the door. "How bad is she? What happened? What did she hit?"

"Jack, she has been shot several times. We have a Lifeline chopper en route."

Slowing to make the vault across the guardrail, he asked, "What? Will she make it?"

Waving traffic around the crime scene, Randy dodged the question. "She had blood pouring from her head. Hard to tell how serious," he offered.

"But she was still alive?"

Grimacing at the desperation in his voice, Randy said, "Yes, but that was about all. EMS is on scene."

Threading his way through the squad cars littering the landscape, Jack came squalling to a stop. He sprinted to her vehicle, where the blood-soaked seat and steering wheel brought him to the brink of collapse. Crunching through the broken glass on the pavement, he pivoted to the ambulance. He yanked the back door open. Her limp body was unrecognizable. The long and luxurious auburn locks, plastered to the side of her face, partially hid the hideous damage of the assassin's bullets. Blue eyes that could trick a sailor into telling the truth were now drowned in a pool of blood. Pale as a ghost, Jack reached out and squeezed her shoe. Fighting for her life, she stiffened as the paramedics attempted to package her for the flight.

Coming into the LZ, the heavy wop announced the arrival of hope dropping out of the sky. Blasting the highway clean, the chopper touched down gingerly. There he stood amid the horror, depending on others to put his life back to normal. Jack would never handle a crisis the same from this day forward. Seeing a heartache and feeling one became the same thing today. With a cold wind blowing a hole through his soul, he felt the strength slipping out of his body.

He turned his back from the prop wash as the chopper went to full power. Lifting off with the woman of his dreams, a cold desire to kill this dirty world started an avalanche in his life. No one connected would be spared. Standing along the highway with traffic backed up as far as the eye could see, he watched his woman disappear skyward, fighting for her life. Falling to his knees, the prayer began with a tearful request but jumped to begging within seconds. Ending with a human touch, he placed the list of promises at the feet of God in exchange for a concession.

The soft pat on the back, loaded to the gills with love, ushered a thousand tears. Deputies and troopers alike hemmed in tight, shielding one of their own. Each was uncomfortable witnessing a man who usually led the charge now reduced to a shell. Weighing the gravity of the situation, they were ready to charge hell with a bucket of water for him.

Hugging more than a boss, Randy said, "Jack, come on. We've got work to do, buddy." It was the sole hope of getting Sheriff Jack Webster to his feet this day.

Wiping snot from his lip, pinching his eyes tight, he turned. Searching the faces of the twenty-plus officers, Jack asked, "Randy, what do we know?"

He pulled Jack to his feet. "Two guys in a copper-colored SUV pulled up alongside of her and opened fire. Sped off in the direction of the interstate."

"Randy, make me a promise."

"What?"

He would muster up no sympathy for them and was only looking forward to inflicting pain in their lives. "When we catch these guys, don't let me in the same room with them."

9

Numbed by the anger being fueled by a fiery hatred, Jack blew through the red light, squeezing past the gravel truck's front bumper by mere inches. Straightening it back out, he threw up an apologetic wave to the driver. Warren would understand on his next trip to the coffee shop tomorrow.

Entering the outskirts of Indy, looking for the exit, he got her call, which was later than usual. Her gossip hotline rivaled Amazon Prime for efficiency.

"Yeah, Mom?"

"What's going on down around Meridian Parkway? Blanche called and said there was a woman shot. Anybody we know?"

Tapping the brakes, Jack slowed to make the exit. He refused to acknowledge the tragedy. Reducing it to words brought it to another level of reality. He would let his world ignore the ugly facts headed his way as long as he could. "Yeah, we know her. I gotta go. Bye."

Grabbing an open parking space near the ER, he mustered up the courage to face the news. Leaning back, he sent up the first of many prayers. He sought out the strength to handle the stake about to be driven into his heart. Spiraling down, he prepared to have the devastation invade his life. Evil had permeated his world, savagely ripping apart the best thing in his life. Pulling the door handle, he put one foot in front of the other, praying for the best, guiltily expecting the worst.

Checking in with the surgical host, he settled in for a long night. Trading in the steak dinner at Bernigan's for a microwaved abomination out of the vending machine, he ate the soy burger in silence. Letting the hate course through his veins, he searched for a path to vengeance. Coming out of the fog, the nightmare returned

DIVINE MEMORIES

as he made out the waiting room. The gentle voice calling his name stood by, waiting for him to get his bearings.

"Mr. Webster, Emily just came out of surgery. I believe Dr. Bradley will speak with you in a few minutes. He'll be able to answer some of your questions," said the surgery host.

Rubbing the gunk out of his eye, Jack nodded. "Okay. Thank you."

Glancing at his phone, he saw it was 4:00 a.m. and there were three missed calls from Randy.

"Hey, Randy. What's up?"

"Wanted you to know. We got the guys," said Randy.

Shaking off the drowsiness, he snapped instantly alert. "Who?"

"Couple of guys out of New York. Indy Metro got into a gun battle with them on I-465. Driver's dead and the passenger is critical, not expected to survive."

"How did you get on to them?" asked Jack, allowing some vengeance to seep out.

"An eyewitness that accidentally rear-ended their car just as they opened fire on Emily got their license."

"Good job."

Venturing out on a tortured limb, Randy asked, "How is she doing?"

"She came out of surgery a few minutes ago. I'm waiting on an update from the surgeon. Hey, I think he's headed my way. Thanks for the update, and tell everyone good job."

"Jack, the whole town is praying for her."

"Tha-thanks, Randy. Tell everyone thanks," said Jack, choking back a painful dose of life's bile as he stood to face Dr. Bradley.

"I'm not a sugarcoater," announced Dr. Bradley, pulling his bouffant off.

Sucking in air, Jack dreaded the words he knew bracketed a future of pain and heartache. "Me neither."

"She's been shot twice in the head."

Opening the gates wide, Jack gave misery a chance to march in and take up residence in his life. "Will she survive?"

Dropping down on the arm of the sofa, remembering his cardinal rule, Dr. Bradley said, "She is strong, and we got lucky in removing some of the fragments safely. Emily came in with Glasgow score of 9, which signifies a moderate TBI. Her cranial pressures are elevated but manageable at this time, so we are going to monitor that closely. It's a little early to call her out of the woods yet though, but she is one lucky girl."

"What are her chances for a normal life if she does survive?" asked Jack, inwardly wishing he could pull the question back.

Dr. Bradley shook his head as he had a thousand times at the question. "I would be somewhere between guessing and lying if I gave you a number. I've seen much worse live completely normal lives, and unfortunately, I've seen the complete opposite too. Just pray for a complete recovery, but be prepared to say goodbye to the woman she was yesterday." Rising to leave, he placed the bouffant back in place. "Any questions? I have to get back in surgery. I have to put a twelve-year-old young man back together who will wish the rest of his life he had worn a helmet."

"Thanks, Doc."

"Oh, I almost forgot. My nurse gave me this note to pass on to any family."

Sliding his finger through the seal, Jack heard the commotion coming down the hall gaining strength. Void of an inside voice, she would never change.

"Candy? What are you doing here?" asked Jack, looking her over suspiciously.

Hugging her big brother like she loved him, Candy said, "Bell is parking the car. She has Mom."

Shaking his head, he said, "Oh crap! Tell me you're joking."

"Wish I could, but this was her idea. And you are gonna get your butt ripped by Mom for not telling her it was Emily."

Running his hands through his hair, searching her face, Jack was satisfied she was on the level. "Can't wait for her grand entrance. My only saving grace, she won't last long in a no-smoking environment."

"Don't bet on it. She really loved Emily."

"Loves! She's still living, Candy," snarled Jack.

Reaching out, pushing the rivalry to the side, Candy wrapped an arm around her big brother's neck and squeezed for all she was worth. The rare moment magnified the depth of how serious the situation was. "I'm sorry. You know what I meant." She dabbed a tear from his face as his world collapsed in front of her.

"That handkerchief better not have had snot on it," he said with a broken smile.

"How is she?" asked Candy.

"Just wait. I want to tell the story one time. I think I hear the dynamic duo coming down the hall now."

Scanning the waiting room, getting ready to storm the beaches of Normandy, Momma Webster found the future victim of her wrath. "Robert Jackson Webster, how dare you not tell me it was Emily," she yelled across the room, startling the other exhausted family members lounging in the worn-out furniture. "If you weren't so big, I'd blister your butt right now!"

Ignoring the room full of misery, each suffocating from one dire situation after another, she lashed out. The sight and sounds of the little gray-headed lady reducing the big man to a pile of mush brought therapeutic grins and snickers from every corner of the room.

"Way to go, Bobbie," teased Bell, invoking his hated nickname.

"Out in the hallway. Now!" ordered Jack, red-faced, renewing his dislike for his baby sister.

He waited for the door to close. He knew they meant well, but he had chosen to suffer in silence. He would stand alone, leaning on no one. It was his way. "Go back home. You can't do any good here. We won't learn anything new for a good while."

Jack knew the words were wasted as he saw their hackles rising.

"Well, for one thing, we don't know anything as of yet. Haven't you gotten an update?" asked Candy.

The words brought the tragedy crashing home. "She was shot twice. She is stable, but they are concerned about swelling over the next few days."

"Is she going to make it?" asked Bell.

The hopeless shrug of his shoulders brought their greatest fears one step closer. "Please go home. All of you. I promise to call if there is any change."

"What's that letter you have in your hand?" asked Mrs. Webster.

"The doctor said it was a note for Emily's family."

"Read it. We're her family today," said Mrs. Webster.

Leaning up against the wall, he read the note, looking for answers. The hope for some sort of revelation fizzled. The words meant little. "Read it for yourselves."

As they huddled around the sheet of paper, Mrs. Webster smiled. "Jack, do you know what Psalm 91 says?"

"No. Why would she write that on her wrist?"

"It is the psalm you go to when trouble or fear surrounds you. It says God may even send angels to protect you in troubled times."

"I can't see how it's helped her so far," he said.

"Jack, as long as she's breathing, there's hope," said Candy.

Saying farewell to them finally, he continued the vigil, living only for the next update.

*****

In a medically induced coma, Nevada lay helpless, tethered to the conglomeration of tubes and monitors. The auburn locks, long gone, were replaced by sterile bandages. Her face was mostly shrouded.

After ten days, the initial shock of the constant heroic actions of nurses scrambling up and down the halls were no longer noticed. She was fully weaned off the coma medication and ventilator early in the morning, and Jack waited to greet what was left of Emily Parker.

He was no longer aware of the date as the days merged together, never-ending. And he dreaded the nights, each lasting an eternity. Bending God's ear daily, he stood watch, never taking his eyes far from the woman as she remained motionless. He was dreaming of the time he would once again see her million-dollar smile. The steady vigil, wrapped in an endless supply of stress and doubt, frayed nerves down on a man built more for war. Drifting off, coming to, catching the late-night show host signing off, the world was at it was.

Illuminated by the lone nightlight, Nevada remained as she was days ago, still as the night and helpless. A cacophony of sounds surrounded her, each spouting off, telling the world they were doing their part.

Beat down, marooned on an island of sadness and fear of the unknown, Jack cast another prayer fervently skyward. The discovery of the suitcase had ripped the fabric, holding his love in check. Boxed in, running the scenarios through his mind, he couldn't fathom how she could be as she said.

Weary from the roller-coaster ride fate had thrust upon him, he was bankrupt without her. Abandoning all he thought he stood for, he mentally weighed the love of his badge on one side of the scales and his love for her on the other. Stroking her hand gently, he wondered what would be behind curtain number 3 when she woke up. Taking a hard right off the beaten path, agreeing to travel down the unknown, he cast a painful vote against the badge.

"Father, I know your love for me has been pretty much a one-way street. With you doing most of the heavy lifting. And I am truly sorry for that. I know I don't have the right to ask, but I am. Father, give her back to me. I promise to never leave her side. Father, I've never promised you a thing in my life, and you know it. Through Jesus's name. Amen."

Opening his eyes, the world remained unchanged. He went down the hall. Punching in the last number for the bag of chips, he pondered life as a private citizen. Hoping Randy would take the nomination, he made his way back to the loneliest place on the planet. The chips, standing in as a poor substitute for the missed supper, took the edge off his hunger. Drifting off to sleep to the antics of the Beverly Hillbillies, he came to as the sun was busy ushering in another day. Rubbing the crud out his eye, Jack saw the most beautiful set of bloodshot blue eyes staring skyward.

He softly called out her name, but she maintained the thousand-yard stare, oblivious to her new world. Fighting through the fog of the medication, she blinked once.

Bending down closer, Jack whispered her name. Hitting the call button, he dropped his head against her arm. "I promise, Lord."

Fighting to climb a rugged mountain, Nevada broke out of her dark world, tilting her head a few degrees after two days. Looking everywhere and nowhere, focusing on moving objects, she closed her eyes for the day.

*****

"Dr. Bradley, will she ever talk or respond to my presence?" asked Jack.

"Jack, I think you should focus more on the positives. It's only been a couple weeks. Emily is responding to pain and is moving more each day. I am happy with that, personally. You have to remember, she has been shot in her brain, and it's not the same as waking up from a long nap. This is going to be a long process," said Dr. Bradley.

"I know. I just want her back."

"Remember what I said when we first met. The old Emily may never return as you knew her. The damage to her left temporal lobe is serious, but it is surmountable over time. One small fragment is positioned near what is referred to as the hippocampus. That may cause her some issues—recalling memories and her ability to learn. She will have a lot of work ahead of her," explained Dr. Bradley.

"Okay. Thanks, Doc."

Rising to leave, Dr. Bradley said, "My advice, if it's worth anything to you. Go home and get cleaned up. Visit with family and return in a day or two. This is a marathon, not a sprint anymore. We're dealing with a part of the body that we haven't unlocked all the mysteries yet."

*****

Pulling out of the hospital parking lot two days later, Jack struggled with the thought of abandoning her. As he waited and prayed for her to return, the initial waves of disappointment crashed down upon him. Turning the radio off, he traveled miles in silence before pulling into the rest area. With a gust of wind catching his door, the paper on his dash sailed out, skittering across the parking lot.

Grabbing the paper and stuffing it in his shirt pocket, he continued on up to the vending machines.

Backing out of the space, he made the slow drive through the rest area, and he pulled out the crumpled note. Slamming on the brakes, he maneuvered back into the last parking space. He reread the note, searching for her inspiration for it.

Typing the psalm in Google, he studied the words. Could it be that simple? *Are your promises really meant for a couple of broken toys, Lord?* He let the words gnaw away at his doubts.

"Lord, if you do half of this, I'll be happy," he murmured, pulling back into traffic.

With a quick shower and shave, Jack walked into the Sheriff's Department. Tolerating the well-meaning back slaps of encouragement, he gave Randy a silent nod.

Randy closed the door behind him. "Well, how is she doing?"

The hurt look said plenty. "Not good. Barely half-conscious. Nothing verbal, and I don't think she even knew I was ever in the room with her. I'm beginning to think—"

Kicking the trash can with the toe of his boot, Randy cut in. "Jack, don't start down that road. It goes on forever once you start down it."

"Randy…you haven't seen her."

Opting for brutal instead of kid gloves, he said, "What I saw was her leaving in a helicopter instead of a body bag. And for that, we were all grateful."

Jack sighed. "I buried my head in the sand on this one, for sure."

"Jack, give her some time. It's been, what, less than two weeks?"

Jack swiveled in the chair, gazing out over the parking lot at the fleet of squeaky-clean squad cars lined up with precision. The draw had come early. Always wanting to be the cop, refusing to ever be the robber. Never having enough caps for his silver six-shooter, shooting a week's supply up by the next day. First to hotfoot it to the edge of the highway when the lone wail of the sirens could be heard approaching in the distance. Holding his breath, he'd hope they would scream past his house. He would stand in awe of the men and women as they roared by in their shiny squad cars. The allure of the heart-pounding sirens screaming, demanding the right-of-way, set a hook to a little boy's dream.

Coming home from the war with a chest full of medals and a few scars inside and out, he knew the dream had to be fulfilled. Becoming one of the youngest sheriffs in Illinois, Jack flattened the crime wave, never wavering until now. The crick of the chair echoed in the small office as he turned to level with his best—and maybe only—friend.

"Randy, I need you to do something for me and yourself."

"Shoot."

"I need you to quietly file as a write-in candidate for the sheriff's race."

Juggling the words, looking for the hook, Randy said, "And why would I need to do that? You're a shoe-in for another term."

The words hurt. The dream had cast a big net in his life. "'Cause I'm moving on and…well…well, I've made some promises that I need to keep."

Standing to leave, Randy said, "Oh, Jack. Give it a day or two and see if you still feel the same way."

"Randy, sit down. I'm days ahead of you on that. Here's your paperwork. You deserve the job."

"What will you do?"

"I'm never leaving her side, and that's going to be job enough for me."

He allowed the idea to blossom to life in his own dream. "I'll do it if you'll not announce it until the last minute," demanded Randy.

"Deal!"

Stalling at the door, weighing the chances of bruising their friendship, he had let it slide long enough. "Jack, one more thing."

Jack looked up from his phone. "Yeah, Randy."

"Well, I been meaning to tell you something. Your mom and sisters always save you a spot in the pew each Sunday. It used to be funny, but it's just getting sadder each week."

Catching the phone on the second bounce, Jack felt the shock and sting. The words sliced through his rough exterior. His armor

DIVINE MEMORIES

had weakened lately, allowing the words to penetrate deeper than normal. "No promises. But tell them to keep it dusted off."

*****

They say Jesus rose from the dead in three days. *Surely, a girl could say a few words in that time*, Jack thought. Double-checking the parking garage level, he made his way up to room 3027. He was littering the hospital with prayers cast to the heavens as he closed in on her room.

Placing the roses on the table, he felt three days of hope slip out the back door. Nevada was in virtually the same place and position she was three days ago. Her color seemed to have improved, at least— the little bit of her that wasn't trussed up by bandages. Spreading the cover over the chair, he bedded down for the night.

Startled by the alarm, he cracked open an eye, watching the nurse change out the IV.

"Ma'am, has there been any change in her the last couple days?"

"Oh yeah. She's a fighter," said Nurse Mayer, resetting the infusion pump. "Emily is much more aware of her surroundings. We're all impressed at her progress."

Caressing her limp hand, he noticed the broken nail stood out among the others, crusted with dried blood embedded in her cuticle. What he wouldn't do to turn the clock back. Her body jerked slightly as he placed her hand back down. He longed to hold her. Her face, much less swollen over these last three days, told the story of a troubled future.

Watching the pigeons three stories below fight for the scraps, Jack's mind flirted with a dark thought. Living in a black-and-white existence, nothing happened without a reason. He sought answers as to the why equation. The suitcase brought in a whole new set of possibilities. Had she done someone wrong? Was she a thief? The runaway train was in danger of leaving the tracks until she provided answers.

Nodding off and on, he slept fitfully. Turning down the lights, he listened to the purr and mechanical rhythm of the equipment.

Waking to the soft snoring sound, he rolled back over, fluffing the pillow. He heard the door crack open, and the night nurse entered. Feigning sleep, he remained motionless, too tired to interact with her. Flipping the light on, the nurse checked the IV and vitals.

"Jack, are you awake over there?"

"Depends," he said groggily.

"Well, if you're not too busy, come over here. Emily is finding her voice."

Bailing off the couch and flinging the covers to the floor, he limped over to her bed. Fighting a painful charley horse in his leg, he watched her struggle to form her first word. The continuous sounds, slurred and choppy, meant little.

Cracking open one eye, Nevada raised her hand, instantly responding to his touch. With all her vitals spiking, he begrudgingly released her hand.

Too amped up to sleep, he listened throughout the night. Wandering aimlessly through the foggy darkness, she searched for the pieces to the puzzle of speech. Traveling back and forth, looking for the right pathway, she brought tiny new pieces of the puzzle with her each time. By the time dayshift took over, she had triumphantly formed a single word.

Repeating it over and over, she swiveled to the side, noticing movement for the first time. Locking eyes with the nurse, Nevada stared, processing the event.

"She sure loves that word for some reason, doesn't she?" asked the nurse. "Did Emily live there?"

"She was from New York. But she may have lived there at one time," said Jack.

"Nevada. N-N-Nevada. Nu…Nu…Nevada," she stammered.

10

As the weeks folded away, slowly stringing the months together, Nevada marched forward, gaining strength. It was a daily challenge to return to the starting point before that ugly fateful day. No longer dependent on machines to live, she now tackled the simple things in life. With a mission to think smarter, not harder, she navigated life looking through a different lens. Looking back over the last couple months, she really liked the man known to her as Jack.

Running her fingers through her short hair, she looked forward to the day it would grow out. Lingering near the area where the bullet entered her brain, she cringed, thankful for the hair taking on the commitment to hide the ugly reminders. Dragging out the book of pictures again, she studied them, hoping to trigger a memory. *He said they were where we live, my house, my car—they mean nothing.* They were memories cruelly locked away. The path to them remained elusive and hidden from her.

"Nothing yet?"

"Jack, I'm really trying. I…p-p-promise."

Reaching out, searching for forgiveness, he stumbled through the wall of guilt. "I couldn't be prouder of you. You have made awesome progress." He caressed her back, still learning and living with her limitations.

Breaking free from his embrace, the sassy look brought her alive. A fragment of her old self was breaking through, bubbling up on the other side of her prison walls. "I want to leave here im-immediately," she said, putting extra horsepower on the *immediately.*

"Sheesh! Aren't you the bossy one? Well, just so happens you are checking out of this hotel tomorrow. Will that do for you, my queen?" teased Jack, cracking a grin at her serious pouty look.

"You p-p-promise?"

"First thing tomorrow morning, we're blowing this pop stand. By noon, you will be back home."

*****

Up at the crack of dawn, she readied for departure. The thoughts of the outside both excited her and brought doubts crashing down. Buckled in for the ride home after hugging the staff and engulfing all the well-wishers, Nevada left the one and only place she knew. The overwhelming exhilaration won out. As Jack pulled away from the curb, she gave the nurses one last wave.

Having the reboot button hit in her life, she saw nothing familiar. Her new world was foreign. Traveling down the highway, she felt her world compressing around her, squeezing tighter and tighter as her mind failed to pick out anything remotely familiar. Sailing out upon a vast ocean, lost, she racked up one failed moment after another. She longed to return to the safety of her sanctuary.

"Jack?"

"Yeah?"

"C-c-can you…take me back?"

Pulling over to the side of the road, clicking on the flashers, he dreaded the next few minutes. They said she would be a challenge daily. Sweeping up her hand, which was shaking with fear, he searched for the right words.

"Emily, they held the keys to your life. I hold the keys to your happiness. Give me two days. Let me show you your world and the surroundings."

"T-t-take me back. Please!"

"You have to move forward, not backwards."

"Take me back. Now!" she screamed, grabbing the door handle.

Feeling the object rub up against her finger, the attraction was overwhelming. Drawn to the object like a moth to the light, she pulled it out of the door panel. Analyzing it, turning it over and over, the wheels broke free in her mind, gaining traction. Sniffing the object, she let her head fall against the window. Letting the fragment

DIVINE MEMORIES

of memory marinate, she wanted more. Working the fifty-cent claw machine, she couldn't hang on. The brief window was closed, denying her access.

Turning the object over, she saw it was only a stale Oreo cookie. "Th-this was mine, wasn't it?" she asked.

"Oh my god! Thank you. Yes, yes."

Seeing only a foreigner's reflection in the window, she faced life head on. "Take me home."

"Okay." Running it through his mind, he had uttered the words a thousand times in life. A convenient collection of three words to utter. Never aimed in the right direction. Clinging to hope of faith, a new wrinkle in his life brought a startlingly clear new perspective. "Emily, you know, I think I truly just spoke to God for the first time in my life."

"Wha-what did he say back?" she asked, smiling.

"He said take you home."

As they pulled into the apartment complex, she fought the desire to run back to the safety of the known. Entering the apartment, it might as well have been the neighbor's. Surrounded by all the unknowns, discouraged at her failures, Nevada collapsed on the couch.

Jack dropped down beside her, wrapping her up in his arms. The silence was broken only by the muffled sobs of fear. Facing a life where she must stumble blindly through it daily brought her close to the brink.

Dragging her back to her feet, Jack said, "Let's get out of here."

"Where?"

"My place. Your new home. You had a suitcase already packed. I'll get it," he said stiffly. The thought of the other suitcase in the sheriff's department's evidence room brought a rush of doubt. The answers he sought to the mystery may never be known.

Drawing a puzzled look, she asked, "Wa-was I...moving?"

Blowing the question off, he headed to the back bedroom. Coming out with the suitcase, Jack kept his head down, aiming straight for the door.

"D-d-did you hear me?"

"Uh, yeah. Not sure what you were planning. Let's go."

*****

Nevada was greeted by the ambassador. Rocky circled, lunging in to lick her hand, welcoming her home.

Walking into the modest ranch house, she looked about for anything to trigger a memory. "H-h-have I been here before?"

"Many times."

Defeated, she dropped down on the kitchen chair. The slumped shoulders matched her mood. It was like working with a kinked garden hose; the memories refused to trickle through, no matter how hard she concentrated.

Scooting the chair up to hers, Jack said, "Em, this is your first day. Cut yourself a little slack."

"I know. I...I just thought I would do better."

He planted a kiss on the top of her head. "Why don't you go lay down and rest. It's been a big day for you already. And by the way, don't think I didn't notice that part in your hair."

Spoiling her bad mood, the smile fought its way to the surface. Other than a slight droop around her right eye, she looked the same as the million-dollar smile surfaced. Fluffing her hair, she said, "Do you really? Be...be honest."

"It's the icing on a beautiful cake."

Trailing her finger along his arm, fleshing out any possible conspiracies, she asked, "W-w-why are you being so nice to me?"

Scooping up her hand, he pressed it to his lips. "The answer to that question is better shown than told. Give us time."

Plopping down in his easy chair, Jack waited as she drifted off. She crashed as soon as her head touched the pillow. He tugged the patio door open, slipping outside undetected.

Calming Rocky down, he threw the big shepherd his favorite stick of the day. Covering it with a boatload of slobbers, he was in heaven as he lay down to reduce it to splinters.

Walking down to the pond's edge, Jack took a seat in the rickety porch swing. He hid from the world's problems. The intrusion to his one slice of tranquility was untimely.

Squinting through the sunlight at the caller's ID, he rubbed his temple. "Yeah, Randy. What is it now?"

"Hey, catch you at a bad time?"

He glanced up the dirt path toward the house. "Yes and no. What's up anyway?"

Randy cleared his throat, leery of which Jack would surface. "Well hey. I'll make it fast then. Just letting you know we heard back from the crime lab on those pictures."

Jack bolted out of the swing. "Yeah?"

"Boss, you were right."

Pacing along the pond's edge, he looked back over his shoulder. "New York City?"

"Yep. View is out of the north side of the Empire State Building. Report estimates it's coming from an office somewhere between the seventieth and eighty-sixth floor."

Taking it out on the innocent dandelion puffball, Jack launched it across the yard, "Pfft. What, two months later?" he muttered, shaking his head.

"I know. Some rush, huh. Well, you were right."

"What about the other picture? The one where she's with the two people, holding that piece of paper."

"Not good." Tiptoeing across the minefield, Randy said, "New York says it could take months to do a manual lookup on a plate twenty years old. And they didn't sound all that confident at that."

Eyeing another dandelion, Jack muttered, "That's just great!" Dropping back down in the swing, sucking up the warmth of the sun, he stretched out his legs. "Well, keep on it. Put the pictures back where we found them. Uh, Randy?"

"Yeah. Hey, how's it going there?"

Jack wiped a stray bead of sweat off his forehead. "About half as well as I hoped." Whirling around at the crack of the storm door slamming shut, he said, "Keep it between us for now. Gotta go."

Gazing out over the hillside, Nevada spied the violator. Marching down the path, throwing caution to the wind, she crossed her arms stiffly. "When I woke up, I thought you had left me." Dropping her head down, fighting to sort out her emotions, anger and fear collided. "I...I don't think you realize how lost I am!"

"I'm sorr—"

Stomping the ground furiously, she shook her head. "Let...let me talk!"

Patting the swing, Jack said, "Come sit down with me."

Collapsing down, she pitched the swing dangerously to the side. "Jack, I...I don't even know my n-name. I don't know who I am or where I-I come from." Slipping her arm around his neck, she began tightening the vise. "P-p-please don't give up on me. You're all I have."

"Emily, look at me." Gingerly turning her chin, he pulled her closer. "Look at me. I know what you're going through."

Nevada yanked her head back. "How...how could you?"

Pulling up his shirt, Jack revealed the red nine-inch scar across his chest. "I spent thirty-three days at the Landstuhl Regional Medical Center in Germany recovering from a sniper's bullet. My first four days were in an induced coma. I woke up lost too."

Melting back into his arms, siphoning strength from his love, she cloaked herself from the world. Walling off her worries, if only for the moment, she reached up and pulled his lips to hers. "I d-don't deserve you."

Reluctantly coming up for air, caressing her back, he never wanted the moment to pass. Letting silence rule, savoring the moment, he knew this was a mere dream a few months ago. Closing out her first day as the painted sky came alive with the sunset, he stroked her hair, careful to steer clear of her scars. He held an answered prayer tightly.

With moans of approval, the empty swing blew in the wind as she trailed by his side. Heading back up to the house, hand in hand, no words were needed.

*****

DIVINE MEMORIES

Surviving her first week of freedom, Nevada settled in, allowing his love to envelope her. Coming out of the shower, gingerly brushing her hair, she said, "I am starving. How's supper coming?"

"Tacos in five minutes."

Planting a wet one on his cheek as she strolled through the kitchen, she eyed his gourmet skills. "I realize I don't remember my prior life, but I imagine I was this happy."

Dropping the spatula in the taco meat, Jack swept her off her feet. "You're right."

Breaking free from the bear hug, she threw back her shoulders, crossing her arms defiantly. "Jack Webster, have you noticed anything about my speech?"

Squinting out of one eye, he said with a smile, "I was afraid to bring it up. Didn't want to jinx a good thing."

Raking her fingernails across his shoulders, Nevada buried her face in his chest. "Since I got here, I feel different somehow. More at ease."

"We're gonna make it through this. The doctor told you to quit overthinking it, and it would happen for you. Let's go eat. I hate cold tacos."

*****

Recouping at Jack's ranch, the tranquil days flew by as summer prepared to hand it off to autumn. Preferring the hermit's life, Nevada challenged any efforts to socialize, keeping Jack to herself. As she was putting the finishing touches on supper, she heard his squad car rattling up the gravel driveway. Hiding behind the doorway, she waited. Hearing the doorknob rattle, she crouched, ready to spring. She would launch as soon as he cleared the doorway.

Jumping squarely on his back as he passed by, she said, "Hands up, Sheriff!"

Reaching for the sky, Jack replied, "Lady, I give. But, ma'am, I think you need to get out more often." Jack flung her on the couch. Sitting on her chest, he said, "In fact, little lady, since you're in such a good mood, we're going on a road trip after supper."

She squirmed out from under his weight. "Where? Tell me."

"Nope. Just wait."

"Pleeaaze?"

"What's for supper?" asked Jack, ignoring the pathetic little beggar. Doing an about-face, he left her to beg to the empty room.

Cleaning the dirty dishes off the table after supper, she stalled, milking the job as long as possible. Hanging up the dish towel, she headed to the back door, but not before the long arm of the law seized her shoulder.

"Wrong way, babe. Truck's parked out front, remember?"

"Jack, I'm not really feeling very well. How about tomorrow?"

Shaking his head, he expected no less. "Pfft. Here's your shoes."

Prying her off the couch, ignoring the growing list of excuses, he herded her kicking and screaming to the truck. Approaching the side road, he negotiated the hard right leading up the lane. Pulling over, throwing it in park, they tried it a hundred times at a hundred places. Batting zero, he forged on.

Sitting tall in her seat, cheating for a glimpse of what was up around the hillside, she asked, "Where is this place?" She was hoping he would slip up.

"Quit asking. You know the doctor's rules."

Bouncing down hard in her seat, Nevada said, "Fine. Be that way. It always ends the same anyway."

As they crept up the lane, making it around the final bend, the top of the mansion's roofline emerged, partially obscured by the massive white oaks. Astonished at the difference since his last visit, with the addition of the new wing and landscaping, Jack barely recognized the place himself. Running out of ideas, he parked in the circle drive. The rest was up to her.

Going through the motions, she gave it a few minutes before busting his bubble.

"Nothing." Tucking her arms in her pits, falling back, she said, "Get this broken toy back home."

Massaging her shoulder, he said, "I thought for sure this might be the one that brought it all back for you. Are you sure that you don't remem—"

Letting the breath blast out, tired of the routines and failures, Nevada said, "Jack, nothing means nothing, in my world at least."

"You're right. Sorry." Pulling on through the circle drive, he caught a glimpse of a curtain being pulled back in the mansion. "Hey, Emily. Do you happen to know that old lady waving at us?" asked Jack, slamming on the brakes.

"Uh...no. I-I don't think so." She sat up straighter as the woman exited the mansion.

Her hesitation brought the hair up. Fighting through an evil fog, he could see the wheels spinning in her mind. She wasn't sure this time. A first! Gone was the smart mouth that almost gleefully cheered when his ideas flamed out each time.

Leaping out of the car, he spun back. "Stay in the car. Till I get back."

"Okay."

Making her way down the sidewalk, wielding her cane, Lillian studied the young man sprinting across the yard. His pleasant smile put her at ease. He was her first visitor in months, and she was starved for company.

"Hello, ma'am," Jack said. "Are you the owner?"

"Bless your heart, no. I am just allowed to live here."

Gazing up at the renovated mansion, he said, "It's even more beautiful than the last time we were here." He was eyeing the addition. "That looks new."

"Oh. Yes. That's my living quarters."

"Ma'am, I'm sorry to intrude on your privacy. We'll be getting on our way." Angling toward the car, he waved over his shoulder. He couldn't ever recall the lady. Looking over at the sound of the truck door popping open, he said, "Emily, we need to leave."

Leaning against the open door, cupping her hands to her mouth, Nevada yelled, "Ma'am, do you know me by chance?"

Shielding her eyes and taking a step closer, Lillian stared at the young woman. The hair was shorter. Suddenly, her tired eyes flew open as she slid a shaky hand over her gaping mouth. Her Emily had surfaced.

"Emily? Emily, where have you been, darling?"

Skidding to a stop, Jack asked, "You, uh, you know her?"

Bouncing on one foot, Nevada's heart raced at the sound of her name. "You know me? You really, really know me? Like who I am, I mean," asked Nevada, taking a hard look at the woman. Not waiting for an answer, she bolted across the yard, zeroing in on the missing piece of her puzzle. The source of memories flowed down a one-way street, remaining blocked on her end of the equation as she stood next to the stranger.

"Oh my lans. Yes, I know you, child." Letting the cane fall, Lillian reached out. "I hope you haven't changed your mind on me staying here?"

"Who am I?" pleaded Nevada.

"Who are you? Why, honey, what on earth?" asked Lillian with a broken frown, turning to look Jack's way.

"Ma'am, Emily was attacked by two men who shot her. She's temporarily lost a great deal of her memories. Could you tell us how you know her? By the way, my name is Jack Webster, sheriff of Noble County."

Lillian took a second look at the woman who had made an old woman happy in her twilight years. Gone were the eyes blazing with excitement when she had laid out the vision for her Yankee Mansion. Had they robbed her of her spirit?

Taking Nevada's arm, she said, "Dear, let's go up to the porch. The bugs are horrible this evening. I have a pitcher of fresh squeezed lemonade dying to be drank. I am Ms. Lillian McGregor, Sheriff."

Jack pulled out the patio chairs for the women. The cold sweet nectar quenched the late summer heat. Placing the glass on the coaster, he cleared his throat of the citrus. "Ms. McGregor, we only meant to drive by this evening. I knew Emily loved this house, and I thought the sight of it might, you know, jog her memories," he said.

"Could you hand me my cane, Sheriff? I'll be right back."

Struggling to get fully upright, Lillian hobbled through the door and disappeared into the mansion. Accompanied a few minutes later by a member of the house staff who was carrying a small stack of papers, she rested her cane on the tabletop.

"I know she loves the mansion," said Lillian, putting on her reading glasses as she tested the pen's ink on a sheet of paper. Fulfilling her promise, she slid the papers across the table.

"What's this?" asked Nevada. Scanning the documents, she struggled through the legalese. Giving up, she handed the duties over to Jack.

Pulling up the slack in his jaw, he pitched in for a closer look. There had to be a mistake. It said Emily was the sole owner of the McGregor Estate. Someone's head would roll when they figured out Lillian had escaped from the loony bin and given the farm away.

Jack said, "Ms. McGregor, there has been a terrible mistake somewhere. Emily couldn't possibly come up with the kind of money to—"

"She's already paid for it in full. Check right there on page nine," interrupted Lillian.

Racing to page nine, the already wide eyes threatened to pop. "Sixty million...dollars!" he gasped. Taking a look at the woman of his dreams, Jack couldn't help but wonder. Who could she be? Reliving the last few months, the suitcase, the lies, the mysterious trips—"what was she?" might be the better question. Had there been sixty million reasons she was gunned down? He was scared for the first time. Would she be too toxic when the truth came to light?

"Now what?" asked Nevada, unfazed by the revelation, still wearing the deer-in-the-headlights look.

"Your rooms are ready anytime."

Lost in the fog, she said, "For what?"

Spreading her arms wide, Lillian cast her eyes out to the open meadows. "Emily, this is all yours. As far as the eye can see."

11

Overloading what was left of a fragile psyche, bombarded daily with doubts, Nevada retreated. As she strolled through the perennial gardens, the stone bench tucked in among the bold Chrysler Imperial roses called her name. Taking a seat, running a hand along the smooth granite, she sifted through the murky darkness for the memory. She couldn't resist. Snapping off one of the crimson blooms, guilty of no crime, she drew in the strong fragrant scent. Running her fingers through the velvety petals, she mangled their beauty one pull at a time.

She twisted for a better look about the gardens, and the pergola, heavily laden with an ancient stand of honeysuckle, drew her attention. Crossing over on the dirt path, brushing off a season's worth of old blooms, she clearly had been here before. Plunging down into the darkness, she unleashed her unquenchable desire to steal back what had been stolen. Nevada strained with all the might she could muster, but the curtain was unyielding. Surrendering, collapsing down across the bench, she felt its warmth across her chest. Pounding the unforgiving granite, she assigned blame to the rose, showering the blooms across the walkway.

"Emily?"

Flicking away the dirt from her knees, she said, "Over here."

Ducking under the hanging baskets of petunias, Jack said, "Are you ready to go? Lillian is out front." Squatting down next to an impossible situation, he pulled her over against his chest. Her rigid body was unyielding. He cupped her trembling chin in his hands. "We're in this together."

Her nod masked a thousand lies.

"Hey, is your hand bleeding?"

DIVINE MEMORIES

Pulling the thorn free, she said, "Yeah. But I deserved it." Kicking a couple of rose petals from the walkway, she sighed. "Take me home."

Much too quiet on the way home, she lay crumpled up against the side window. The sheen off her cheek, highlighted by the passing streetlights, spelled defeat. Her bloodied soul, cruelly blindsided by the darkness, now lay coiled, ready to strike. Bristling, when he cleared his throat, ready for the interrogation.

"Uh, what do you think the story is about you and that mansion?"

"How would I know? Maybe I was a drug dealer." Unleashing a vicious kick, she left a dirty streak across the glove compartment. "Right, Sheriff?"

As they waited on the red light to turn, the click of the turn signal roared. The twister was headed his way. The direct hit had sunk his battleship. "Nobody thinks that."

Lingering at the green light, she smelled blood. "Jack, take me to my apartment." Nevada fought to fit words between the racking painful sobs. "You...you...deserve...bet-better."

Skidding the tires on his prized Chevy Silverado, it bounced over the curb and came to rest in the parking lot. Slamming the center console in the upright position, launching a day-old Mountain Dew skyward, the promise must be honored. Locking on to a handful of her blouse, he dragged the thrashing bundle of arms and legs closer. Worse than a fleeing felon, she exploded as she fought against the steel vise clamped around her shoulders. Flailing about, releasing months of fear and doubt, the rearview mirror became her first casualty, crashing to the floorboard. Wrenching a hand free, the claws ripped an ugly red gash down the side of his neck. Allowing the vise to tighten, he cut the struggle short.

Heaving from the battle, she surrendered, slumping down in his embrace. Letting the gut-wrenching ugly cry run its course, he waited as the twister's fury faded away.

Jack kept stroking the damp hair. "Emily, look up at me."

Burrowing deeper, refusing to surface, she offered only a pitiful shake for an answer.

119

"I can sit here all night, Emily."

Muffled by his tear-soaked sweatshirt, she said, "You need to forget me and move on."

Recognizing the parking lot for the first time, the chill permeated through his body. "Sorry. Can't do it. I made a promise to the guy that lives in that house to never leave you."

Waiting for the turtle to poke her head out, the pull intensified. High up for all to see, the symbol looked down upon the sheep, calling them to safety. It was unwavering in its promise, welcoming to all.

Piercing the silence, he said, "Let's go."

Brushing the hair from her eyes, Nevada asked, "Where?"

Preparing for round two, rocking his head, he said, "In there."

She peeked over the dash. "Take me home." She rose to protest.

Grabbing a tissue, Jack patted the trickle of blood from the side of his neck. "You can walk or be carried over my shoulder." Looking down at the bloodstained tissue, he said, "The choice is yours for the next few seconds."

Finding an open door, the new-carpet smell greeted the prodigal son. As Jack pulled the massive doors to the sanctuary open, the years of guilt flooded down. Guiding her to the back, he fell heavily, rocking the pew. Soaking in the silence, allowing the atmosphere to penetrate his soul, he pulled her closer. "I'm going up front. Wait for me here."

Running her finger near the gash, she said, "I'm so sorry."

Pursing his lips, he exhaled the anger. "Be here when I turn around."

She let her fingers trail down his sleeve. "Go."

Asking too much of the old football injury to his knees, the pop corrupted the quiet serenity. Kneeling down beneath the altar, beckoning the Holy Spirit's presence, forgiveness was asked and given. Feeling the burdens lift, allowing faith back in the driver's seat, he melted as confessions were doled out.

Twisting the bracelets around her wrists till the red marks spoke up in protest, Nevada shielded her eyes as Jack collapsed. Languishing in the pew, hidden in the shadows, she searched for the light. Snapping the chains binding her world, she disobeyed and headed up the church aisle to her man. The faint rustle of her blouse was his only warning as she tenderly stroked his hair. The heat of her body brushing up against him brought it full circle. As he tugged her in tightly, she surrendered once again, slumping into his arms.

"Emily?"

Limp, sliding through his arms, she struck the floor. "Jack. Jack, something's wrong. My head's on fire."

He placed a hand down across her forehead. "You don't feel hot. Can you make it to the truck? Emily, no, no! Stay with me, honey. Please stay with me." Jack threw a wicked glance over at the cross hanging next to the altar. *Lord, don't make me go through this again.*

Reaching for his phone, he felt abandoned as he struggled to stay on faith's side of the fence. He was looking down at all he loved on this earth, and she was too weak to move as the light slipped from her eyes, trading one darkness for another.

*****

Following the chopper's path till it disappeared over the tree line, he could see its flashing lights disappearing over the horizon. This launched another tug-of-war for his sanity, knowing that her prognosis seemed grim.

"Jack, I've got everything under control. Get out of here," said Randy, shifting his weight on the other foot.

"Here. Take this."

"What's this about?" asked Randy, turning the gold badge over in his hand.

Clenching his jaw till his temple pulsed, Jack said, "I've got sixty days left in my term." Pulling his lip tight against his teeth, halting the quiver, he mumbled, "The day she dies, you're the sheriff." Not waiting for a rebuttal, he slammed the emergency room door with a vengeance.

Scarcely doing the speed limit, he let the what-ifs do their damage. If she died, no sunset would be the same. Letting the song "Cover Me Up" finish up on the radio, he had nothing left, and he stuffed the tissue in the trash. Afraid of prayer, he decided to go it alone as he entered the waiting room. Fragile, with no reserves left, he lumbered up to the hostess. He took in one final breath before anyone could shatter his world. "Yes, ma'am. I'm here for Emily Parker. They brought her in a couple hours ago."

Hovering over the monitor, stroking the keys with ease, the nurse said, "Okay, just a minute. She ah...she is—"

"Not dead, is she?" demanded Jack. Mangled by her hesitation, he reached for the counter.

"Oh! No, no. She's back in radiology," assured the hostess.

Nevada had been wheeled into room 3230 minutes before 3:00 a.m.

Cracking a weak smile, Jack squeezed her hand. As he reached down for a hug, he flinched at the sting as his shirt collar broke free from the scab on his neck. "Don't scare me like that," he said.

"Sorry." She was mortified at the stained collar that screamed psycho girlfriend. "Jack. Jack, can...we start over?" She fought the medication as the heavy lids that begged to stay closed started glazing over.

Brushing the hair away from her face, he said, "Sure. As soon as you wake up."

Draping a blanket over the chiropractor special, the futile battle was soon lost to the hospital recliner. Finally calling it a draw, he drifted off. Sailing through the clouds, flailing downward, his screams reached no one. Bailing out of the recliner, he wiped the drool off the side of his face. The pain behind his eyes, a bonus from fitful sleep, cruelly confirmed the hospital room.

Spying the single eye peeking out from under the sheet, Jack asked, "Hey, what are you doing awake?"

"Just waiting for Dr. Bradley to look the scans over. Did you get any sleep in that back cracker?" she asked, smiling as she reached out her hand.

He planted a tender kiss to the back of her hand. "How do you feel?"

Rubbing the sleep from her eyes, Nevada stretched out an arm. "Good, I think. Still not sure what happened. I walked up front, touched the back of your head, and my world exploded."

DIVINE MEMORIES

"Well, you're back, and that's all I care about." Pouring a drink of tepid water from the pitcher, he said, "Did they give you an idea when Dr. Bradley would call in?"

With a knock on the door for an answer, a doctor stepped in. "Ah, you're both up. Good. I'm Dr. Jensen, the resident neurosurgeon handling Emily's care." Releasing Jack's hand, he turned to Nevada. "How do you feel this morning?"

Elevating the head of the bed, she replied, "I feel good. Maybe a little tired. But other than that, I'm fine."

"I've been in consultation with Dr. Bradley, and we both agree. Other than a minor irritation near your hippocampus, the scans are unremarkable," advised Dr. Jensen.

"Could that have caused the spell?" asked Jack.

"I see nothing in the CT that would have caused it. But the brain is good at keeping secrets from us sometimes. Emily, we're gonna keep you here for another twenty-four hours for observation and then do another series of scans."

"Good. Am I free after that?" asked Nevada, shooting a smile the handsome doctor's way.

Sliding off the corner of the bed, Dr. Jensen said, returning the smile, "If the scans look as good as this one, then yes, ma'am."

Leaving the comfort of the recliner, Jack parked his arms across his chest. Trying to keep his fear at bay, he asked, "And if not?"

"Then we keep searching. But let's take it one step at a time," cautioned Dr. Jensen, working his way to the door.

Refereeing the battle between her imagination and reality, Nevada stowed away the truth. Nervous for her results, she clashed with the dilemma. It started infiltrating its way into her consciousness. Frightened by the unknown danger, she fled, drifting off to sleep.

*****

Finishing up her third crossword puzzle for the day, Nevada kept a steady vigil on the door. Pacing about, looking for an escape, she hung all her trust on the new scans to unlock her cage. Starting

123

a fourth puzzle, the boredom, combined with the rainy afternoon, melted the last of her strength.

Stroking up and down on her arm, drawing her out of the dark abyss, Jack said, "Emily, the doctor is here." He began patting her hand as the lids fluttered open.

Working through the fog, she shook her head. "Hey, how's my favorite cowboy?" slurred Nevada.

Running a hand through his hair, Jack felt the heat rising up the back of his neck, "Uh, the doctor is here."

"How we feeling today?" asked Dr. Jensen.

Bringing her A game, not letting the facts get in her way, she glossed over reality. "Good enough to go home," said Nevada.

"Well, we are concerned that something is going on with your hippocampus. But for now, we'll monitor it closely." Spinning the medical chart, Dr. Jensen said, "Dr. Bradley wants to see you in two weeks."

Scrunching his eyebrows, Jack asked, "What do you mean something is going on?"

Exhaling, Dr. Jensen dropped a shoulder. "Sorry. I know that's not much of a medical term. But when you're working with an unknown phenomenon, there's not much to say in the beginning."

Going to town on a thumbnail, Nevada asked, "What's your best guess?"

"It'd be criminal to do that at this juncture. Sorry. I've already signed your discharge papers, so you're all ready to go," said Dr. Jensen, looking for the exit.

*****

Loading up in the car, Nevada welcomed the freedom and the fresh air. Pressed for answers, she'd have none to offer. Asked to explain it, she'd be at a loss.

"Do you want to stop for some real food?" asked Jack.

Watching the raindrops channel along the windshield, lost in thought, she allowed the feeling to rob her.

"Emily? Food?" asked Jack, taking his eyes off the road.

Tearing her eyes away, she said, "Sorry. Yeah, food would be great."

Patting her thigh, he breached her defenses. "Penny for your thoughts?"

She fell against the passenger door. "I'll let you know when they're for sale."

Tortured over the next few days, every waking moment was consumed by the dread of her next visit. Swimming in an ocean of conflict, she searched the horizon for land. Blowing in the wind, she flailed about like a kite without a tail. Always behind the eight ball, she never saw the next misery in time.

Taking her seat next to Jack, she popped the napkin open. "Jack, what time are we leaving tomorrow for Dr. Bradley's office?" asked Nevada, passing the potatoes over to Momma Webster. Spicing up the traditional Sunday brunch, Bell and Candy perked up, trading guarded exchanges.

Dropping the butter knife in his eggs, Jack said, "Ah, yeah. About that. I forgot about a meeting scheduled for tomorrow. Candy is going to give you a ride tomorrow."

Giving Candy a side-eye, Nevada said, "Must be an important meeting." She continued piercing the life out of the Smoky Link sausage.

"Yeah, it's a can't-miss meeting," offered Jack, glaring at Bell.

Throwing the covers back on another day in paradise, she fought to stuff her foot down the pants leg. Hopping across the room, slamming the curtain back, she caught a glimpse of the squad car disappearing into the light fog. She pressed up against the window, witnessing fall show its presence as the leaves fluttered to the ground. Her life of late mirrored the maple leaf dancing in the wind across the yard, moving against its will.

Taking up her customary seat in the kitchen, Nevada doctored up her coffee with the last of the milk while staring at the empty chair. Glancing over at the clock on the wall, with the hum of the refrigerator her only company, the morning elixir was bland. Tracing the rim of the cup, the small chip ruining its perfection was comforting. As she halted the cup's advance, allowing the steam to rise, her world had tilted. She sprang up to the sound of crunching gravel, and the coffee cup took one for the team, bouncing off the sink and losing its handle down the garbage deposal.

Throwing a dish towel over his favorite cup, minus one handle, she sprinted out the door. Sticking her head through the open driver's window, she planted a wet one.

"Gosh, I was coming back in to say good luck."

"I know. I couldn't take the loneliness another second."

Yanking back a sleeve, he said, "I was gone, what, less than thirty minutes."

Rocking back and forth on the balls of her feet, she fidgeted with the door lock. "I know. I'm too needy."

"Hey, everything is gonna turn out fine at the doctor's office. You'll see." Sliding his raincoat across the passenger seat, Jack said, "I can't believe she is here on time." He could see Candy's Nissan pulling up the drive.

She started pulling his arm through the window. "What's so, so, so important, you can't be with me today of all days?" asked Nevada, remaining laser-focused on the raincoat.

"Emily, it's a commitment I am bound to."

With more focus than the Hubble Telescope, she searched his face for any deception. Analyzing every wrinkle, each individual pore, she compared it to all past history. The data was telling. Leaning in for a kiss, she said, "Okay. Wish me luck then." Stumbling as her knee buckled into the car door, the visions flashed vividly in her mind. Unsteady, she regained her composure.

"Emily, what's wrong!"

She was holding her forehead in the palm of her hand. "Little weak, I guess. Should have ate some breakfast, probably."

"Candy, watch her closely," ordered Jack.

Cradling an arm around Nevada, Candy said, "We'll be fine."

*****

Pulling out of the McDonald's drive-up, Nevada let her enjoy the first bite of her Egg McMuffin. Jamming the straw through the lid, she asked, "So, Candy. Where's Jack really going today?"

DIVINE MEMORIES

Choking down the last swallow, she was dreading the ninety miles of interrogation. "Oh heavens. Who knows?" murmured Candy, reaching for her Oakleys.

Nibbling the corner off the hash brown, shifting over, she started invading the suspect's space. "I saw the roses Jack tried to hide. Give it up, Candy."

Fooling with the earpiece on her sunglasses with one hand while adjusting the seat belt for a third time, Candy said, "I swear, Emily." Slamming on the brakes, she narrowly missed the bicyclist.

"For crying out loud, Candy. Take those stupid sunglasses off before you get us killed. You look like a rookie in a Texas Hold'em poker tournament," barked Nevada.

Unleashing a painful silence, Candy stared straight ahead, placing her loyalty to a brother on the chopping block. His words of desperation echoed in her ear. "I can't tell you anything, Emily. He'll kill me."

Smoldering under the surface was a fire ready to scorch the earth. "Tell me who the woman is. And what makes you think I wouldn't kill you?"

Kicking the cruise off, swerving to make the exit, Candy aimed the car up the ramp. Barreling into the gas station, she slammed the rolling car into park, skidding up against the curb. The Nissan came to a cringeworthy gear-grinding halt, causing the picnickers to abandon their blankets and seek shelter up on the picnic tables. Leaving kindness and compassion in the rearview mirror, she took the gloves off.

Candy pivoted around to face the trouble. "You really think it's another woman, don't you?"

The words sounded dirty to Nevada's ears. The three roses had been real, but the jury was still out on the visions. "I don't know what to think. I know what I saw."

Candy drew her lip back. "You saw nothing! My brother loves you more than life itself."

Betrayed by a weak quiver, blinded by doubt, Nevada asked, "The roses?"

Thrusting out a hand on a mission of peace, Candy said, "Oh, Emily. They are a symbol begging for forgiveness, not love."

Marrying their hands together, Nevada said, "Take me to him."

Pitching forward, turning the steering wheel into a makeshift altar, Candy prayed for guidance. "Uh, Emily, I don't think Jack is ready to reveal this burden."

Untethering her inner feelings, she placed them down at Candy's feet. "Jack still makes fun of me when he tells how we first met. How scared I was of him and how smart I thought I was. Ten months later, I once again am scared of him. This time though, it's because I'm afraid he will vanish from my life." Grabbing a second tissue, Nevada said, "Candy, don't make me beg."

Shoving off the steering wheel, Candy studied the headliner before clamping her eyes shut.

"Please, Candy!"

Oxygen-deprived, exhaling loudly, Candy said, "What about your doctor's appointment?"

Watching a kid launch off the picnic table and land squarely on the bag of chips, she hoped her next words tipped the scales. "If I lose Jack, I don't care what the doctors have to say."

Backing out of the parking lot, Candy said, "You got about as much chance of losing Jack as I have of winning the lottery."

"Where is he?"

She shook her head. "Here are the rules. I take you to him, and I reveal nothing further. Got it?" Candy said, her eyes leaving no room for further questions.

They turned onto the single lane where the ancient blacktop, broken from years of neglect, was now more grass than pavement. It was guarded by a black wrought-iron fence—fighting the rust, held up in places by the weed patches—that had been forgotten long ago. As they passed under the sagging metal arch, the letters, in need of a fresh coat of paint, solemnly announced the name of their final resting place. A mismatch of stones, leaning awkwardly, had the lonely task of being the lasting reminder for loved ones. Oddly out of time and place, the squad car was parked in the rear next to the three modern stones.

Blasting rainwater out of the potholes as they traveled down the lane, they shattered the quiet peacefulness. Popping up from behind the squad car, recognition was instant, collapsing down into his arms on the hood. Recovering, his spine forced his body to stand erect, ready to defend his covey of victims.

"He is furious. Let me talk to him first," said Candy, opening her door and wading into his fury.

With his eyes blazing a fierce contempt for a sister's betrayal, Jack said, "You had one job, Candy!"

Batting her hand away, Candy said, "I know. I know. But she saw the roses. Jack, she got the wrong idea, and you know how she can get."

"What does she know?"

Reaching out, wide-eyed, Candy was grasping for some middle ground. "She-she knows absolutely nothing. I-I promise," stammered Candy. She turned at the first crunch. "Here she comes."

Putting one boot in front of the other, Nevada ignored her fears. Trekking across the pea-gravel path, she stood before all she desired. Standing tall against the gently blowing breeze, she would not be forced to live without the truth. Competing with the incessant chatter of the red-winged blackbird perched on the fencepost, she pleaded her case.

"Candy, you can leave us," said Nevada, extending her hand over his. Overpowering his resistance, she wrapped his arm around her waist.

"Emily, I think it's best if—"

Halting the protest, Nevada pinned the silence with an index finger across his lips. Shifting her gaze over, she said, "Go!"

Making the final turn out of the cemetery, Candy disappeared out of sight.

"Don't be mad at her, Jack. I forced her to bring me here."

Pulling her in tight against his chest, surrendering to his will deflated all his anger. "Now what?"

Breaking out of his embrace, Nevada said, "You have always said we are in this together. So we're gonna go to whatever is on the other side of your squad car and trade secrets."

"Secrets, as in plural?" asked Jack, pushing away from the squad car.

Tugging his hand, she ignored the question. Rounding the front bumper, holding his hand, she spied the misery.

Dropping down on the poncho spread out on the ground, inches from the trio of stones, the stage was now set for act 1 scene 1 of her life.

Running a finger across the date on the first stone, four years ago today, Jack asked, "Do you want to go first or me?"

Gritting her teeth, she lay back flat against the poncho. "You already are. Just do what you would do if I wasn't here," she said with her hands over her eyes, blanketing out the world.

Venturing into the ring, hands pinned to his side, Jack gave permission for his memories of that fateful day to pummel and ravage his soul. Tracing the granite, first Isabel's then Jacob's—he saved hers for last, as always. Tucked in behind her mother, she would never experience a first love. Forever denied a child of her own to hold and cherish. Yesterday being her sixteenth birthday brought the next waves of sorrow piling on.

Jack asked, "Emily, are you okay over there?"

Recovering from the initial drain, she sat up next to him. "Yes. I'm here for you." He was a broken shell of the warrior she had fallen in love with. Was he too fragile to hear the revelation?

Wiping his sweaty palm off on his pant leg, Jack pulled out a handkerchief. "I do this every October the eighteenth. No matter how many times I'm told to get over it, I return on this date." Filling his handkerchief with four years of sorrows, he said, "I'm done here. What's your secret?"

Patting the poncho, she said, "Come lie down beside me."

Dropping his head in the crook of her arm, both stared skyward as the clouds broke up, allowing patches of blue to surface. He braced for impact.

"You remember when I had that spell, as you called it? The one at the church?" asked Nevada.

"Yeah."

"It started right then."

Rolling up on one elbow, he asked, "What started, Em?"

DIVINE MEMORIES

Making a meal out of her upper lip, she brushed an unruly bang from her eye. "I, uh.... Well, I don't really know how to describe them, but I see people's memories in my mind. Not all the time, just part of the time. Like here today, for example. I believe it is a gift and not a curse."

Chewing the corner of his mustache, Jack said, "Let me get this straight. You're saying you can read my thoughts?" Rolling back over, stroking his mustache, he stretched out with a huge grin. "Let's see a demonstration. If you're up to it."

Running her fingers through his hair, she drew her nails across the back of his neck. "I'm gonna scare you."

"Quit stalling."

"Okay. You asked for it." She closed her eyes to catalog the memories back in real time. Clearing her throat, she launched the salvo. "It was a Sunday evening, about five thirty in the evening. You were waiting for Momma Webster to cut her famous blueberry pie when the call of a domestic disturbance with a weapon rang out over the radio. The deputies were tied up on other calls, and you answered up for the call." Pulling up for air, she asked, "Enough or should I continue?"

"So far, Mom and a copy of the police report could have told you all that," said Jack, still wearing a smile.

"Okay. So let's see. You were eastbound on Route 17, going approximately eighty miles an hour, when you crossed over Mercer Avenue on a green light. The green Kia Sorento ran the red light, and your car struck the Kia square in the passenger door. You never got your foot on the brake."

The fading smile left room for doubt. "Again, a police report could give you all that." Rolling up into a sitting position, he pulled her up, surprised at the wetness of her hand. "Tell me something not documented in a police report."

Holding both of his hands as she sat cross-legged, she continued, "Here comes the scary part. Please don't look at me differently."

"I promise."

Wiping the streak of a tear off his face, Nevada said, "I know you're a good man because of this next memory. You secretly investigated Jacob and Isabel's background and discovered they were both orphans from Salina, Kansas. You took two weeks of vacation, traveled to Salina, searched for any lost relatives. Finding no relative, you returned and purchased these plots and tombstones for their graves. I also saw a fleeting memory of the receipts for the plots." Never seeing fear in his eyes before, she hesitated. "I have one more layer of proof, if you want to hear it," she asked.

"Yes...yes."

"Close your eyes and recall where the receipts are hidden."

Falling back on the poncho, Jack said, "If you tell me that, I'll believe."

Handling the drain much better now, she let the memory flow inward. Opening her eyes, meeting his flippant gaze, she held the key to her own sanity on the tip of her tongue. "They are in a little cedar chest locked up in the second drawer of your desk at work."

Releasing her grip, his smile fell off the cliff.

Cupping her hands over his eyes, she said, "Say something. And don't look at me like that."

Unmasking his eyes, he was stunned by her gift. "How on earth!"

12

Waiting in the elevator, she needed to control the narrative. Stepping through the open doors, Jack punched in for the fourth floor. She knew he meant well. Halting on the second floor, after releasing an exhausted mom and two rowdy boys, the elevator was theirs.

"Jack, I don't want Dr. Bradley to know about what I can do, you know."

The metal walls reverberated with his sigh. "Why?" Surrendering to her scowl, he said, "Fine. Why would we want to give the person solely responsible for helping you all the pertinent information available anyway?" said Jack, letting the sarcasm drip off.

Squeezing his massive hand with all her strength, she said, "I mean it."

Rolling his eyes, he said, "That's all you got?" He stepped through the parting doors.

Grabbing last month's issue of *Cosmo*, she brushed up on the hottest tips to getting the man of your dreams. Working her way through the three hottest ideas on how to lure and capture the man of your life, she felt the pinch. Trying to keep up with his size 14s, she shook Dr. Bradley's hand first. Keeping a short leash on Jack at all costs, she shouldered past him. *Such a child.*

"Emily, how are you feeling today?" asked Dr. Bradley.

"Fine. Never better," she answered, firing a stink eye Jack's way.

"I should have your final scans in a few minutes. Let's talk about mood changes or any unusual episodes. Have you experienced any feelings of lightheadedness or confusion since your last hospital visit?" asked Dr. Bradley.

She ignored Jack, who was standing behind Dr. Bradley, his hand inching upward while mouthing "pick me, pick me."

"No, I can't really think of anything," said Nevada, suppressing a grin, refusing to acknowledge Jack's exaggerated jaw-dropping performance. *And I love this idiot?*

"Good. Good. Hang out here, and I'll be back in a few minutes."

"We got scum locked up at the jail that can't tickle the truth that good. Sheesh," said Jack, taking a seat next to the examination table.

Flipping a cotton ball in his direction, Nevada hissed, "Remember what I said. Not a word."

Tinkering with anything not nailed down in the room, he began to plot a full-scale betrayal. Conjuring up a basket full of justifications to push his guilt to the side, he made his decision. With a knock on the door, he'd rather be back in Iraq.

"Sorry, that took a little longer than expected," said Dr. Bradley, shutting the door behind him. "Okay. Young lady, you are the special of the day. Probably more accurate to say special of a lifetime for an old neurosurgeon such as myself."

Hovering somewhere between absolute fear and complete devastation, Nevada asked, clamping a hand against her chest, "Is that a good thing or bad?"

"Right now, I can't say it's either. What I can say is your condition has never been witnessed in my twenty-seven years as a board-certified neurosurgeon. Your scans have revealed that you have a third hippocampus forming. It appears as a juvenile nestled up against your hippocampus on the left hemisphere of your brain. At first, we thought the bullet fragment was the culprit for your recent episode. But we are now hypothesizing that the sudden growth may have caused an increase in cranial pressure, causing temporary disruptions."

"Dr. Bradley, what's a hippocampus?" asked Jack.

"Without boggling your mind too much, the brain has one located in each hemisphere. It is responsible for storing recent memories, spatial memory, and learning. It does a host of jobs for the mind. But we only have one on each side of the brain, normally. Emily's brain has developed an additional independent hippocampus."

DIVINE MEMORIES

Suddenly wearing the label of freak, she couldn't stop her hand from touching the indention to her skull, inches above her left ear. "Is it a danger to me?" asked Nevada.

At fifty-nine, Dr. Bradley thought he'd seen it all. "Emily, right now, you're somewhere between mystery and miracle. Be honest with me. Have you had any unusual incidents?" he asked.

Sagging under the weight of the lie, white-knuckling the tissue, she felt the walls close in with haste. Her shake of denial opened the floodgate as she heard that all too familiar throat being cleared. *Great! Here comes the big mouth.*

"Emily, tell him." Ignoring the hot glare threatening to blister the paint off the walls of the examination room, Jack said, falling on his own sword, "Or I will."

Caving inward, she fell back on the examination table with a sigh from hell. Backhanding the pillow to the floor, she said, "No!"

"Dr. Bradley, she can—"

"Wait," Dr. Bradley interrupted, lowering his hand. "I'm going to hand off my next patient to Dr. James, and I'll be right back." Hesitating by the door, he added, "I want to hear it from Emily."

Rattling the paper on the examination table as she sat up, she gave the rat ample time to turn and face her. Pitching the box of tissues off the back of his head, she said, "What part of 'I don't want to tell him' didn't you understand? Huh?"

"I-I guess it would be the part." Spinning on his bootheels, unfazed by her unbridled fury, he continued, "The part where you let fear and common sense clobber you over the head."

Snagging the pillow off the floor, she took up her perch. "If I tell him, I have to own him first." Adjusting her head on the pillow, she knew there would be many prisoners in her war. Preparing for act 1 scene 2, she really did like Dr. Bradley.

Not bothering with a knock this time, Dr. Bradley entered cautiously. "Well, I don't see any blood on the floor."

"We haven't left yet, Doc," said Jack dryly.

Dr. Bradley rolled the stool closer to his star patient. "Well, Emily, what's going on with you today, darling?"

Backed into a corner, she would have no qualms in ruthlessly protecting her gift. Hardly a master of it, she still fought to gain control of the awesome capabilities it possessed. As she began to grasp the infinite intricacies more each time it unfolded, every fiber in her body told her to deny its existence.

"I've really nothing to report, Dr. Bradley," said Nevada, shifting her gaze to the rat in the room, who was priming his gums. "Remember what I said. I will make it painful for him."

Hitting the launch button, he jumped in. "Dr. Bradley, she can see other people's memories," blurted out Jack, looking into the most vicious set of blue eyes he'd ever encountered.

With visions dancing in his mind of the countless write-ups in the *New England Journal of Medicine*, he could feel his heart racing. "Will you show me?" asked Dr. Bradley, chomping at the bit to unwrap the mystery present.

Letting the uncomfortable silence become unbearable, her shoes hit the floor. "How bad do you want to see it? Before you answer, just know this. You will have skin in this game, Doctor."

Accustomed to being the captain of any ship sailed in his examination room, her words spoke of mutiny. On an ocean never sailed before, he failed to see the rocky shoals looming dead ahead. As he handed over the helm to her, he sealed his fate. "What did you have in mind?" asked Dr. Bradley.

Nevada towered over the doctor, erasing the anger from her face. "First, give me your word you won't reveal what you see or hear to any other person."

Surrendering a right hand high in the air, Dr. Bradley lied. "Done."

"Second, do you feel guilty when you tell a lie?" asked Nevada.

Scrunching his bushy eyebrows together, Dr. Bradley said, "Well, I try to avoid telling any. But if I did, I certainly would have a measurable amount of guilt associated with it."

"Good. That's good. Now I need you to have a seat and concentrate on two of the darkest secrets in your life. Ones that you have the most remorse for. Ones that you feel are completely hidden from the world. Ones that, when I repeat them back to you, we'll all be on the same page," said Nevada with an innocent smile.

"Right now? Just think about them and you can simply tell me what I was thinking?" asked Dr. Bradley.

Dropping back down on the exam bed, she had no time for doubters. "Yep. I want you to recall things in newspaper clippings, locations, faces, and specific actions, etcetera. Let me know when you're ready."

"Emily, I think I'll step out," said Jack.

Nodding as she stared at the doctor with his face buried in his hands, she said, "Good idea. I'm afraid this is gonna be messy. Grab me a Diet Coke, will you?"

Straightening back up, Dr. Bradley said, "I think I'm ready for this little experiment." He nodded, wiping the glossy sheen from his forehead.

Parting the gateways, she allowed the torrent of dark memories to rush in. Her brain was on fire as she ordered them each systematically cataloged. She massaged them in her mind till the chronological order dropped each peg in place. His deeds, the darkest she had encountered yet, fought to contaminate her soul. Using the last of her strength, she put up a mental shield between the memories.

"Well?" asked Dr. Bradley.

Wagging her finger, she said, "Whew! Doc, give me a second." Looking worse than a two-day drunk, she fell back on the bed. Letting her batteries recharge, she let the wave of exhaustion subside. The gift laid bare a tragic unintended consequence to the owner. Sifting through the memories, she got more than she bargained for.

"You 'bout done in here?" asked Jack, peeking through the crack in the doorway.

Rising up off the bed, she ordered her eyelids to obey. "Jack, step outside with me," said Nevada, drained from the exercise.

"Emily, I have other patients to attend to. Why don't we schedule you for another visit in two weeks?" asked Dr. Bradley.

"No, I'll just be a minute. We're not quite done here."

"Okay."

Returning shortly, pulling in Jack's hand for support, the iron grip lent her strength to continue the crusade. The crisp pop of the Diet Coke releasing her elixir of choice breathed new life back to the shell.

"Emily, sometimes with a brain injury as serious as yours, patients sometimes manifest—"

"Dr. Bradley, take a seat," interrupted Nevada.

Scratching the back of his head, still getting used to the new hair transplants, he said, "Emily, let me try to explain. When a patient—"

Kicking the pedestal out from under the monster, she said, "Ricky Moline, age eight, struck by a hit-and-run driver on that dreary, rainy Fourth of July. A driver long sought but never identified. Until now."

Picking the scab on a wound he had carried through life these last forty-two years, her soft voice moaned out the details. She never intended to destroy, only defend and ensure the secrecy of her gift.

She continued, "The next day, you drove back by the scene of the accident. The sheared-off bike pedal lying next to the white line screamed out your name. That's why you've kept it all these years, constantly punishing a seventeen-year-old kid for that one reckless moment in your life."

Dr. Bradley took the punches better than a heavyweight boxer. The blows met years of perfected denials. "As I was saying about patient manifestations, we can get therapy started to help with that."

Unfazed, she pried the covers off the second memory, allowing light to shine down upon the betrayal. "We'll come back to that memory in a few minutes. But for right now, let's discuss all those out-of-town symposiums you have been attending. Do you think your wife would appreciate the receptionist out front?"

Slipping a wicked left hook around his lies, she popped a chin that should never have stepped in the ring with her. Swaying in the wind, he saw a beautiful and comfortable life unraveling. Coming in second in a two-man race, he crumbled under the weight of her accusations. Juggling fears, the haunting truth, a constant seeker of the light of day bared its ivory fangs.

He stared at his double-tied Oxford, which was doing its best to hide the nervous shake of the foot inside. A head suddenly too heavy for his neck drooped with defeat. "Let's go into my office." Heading to the door, he barked an order to the receptionist to hold all calls.

With walls adorning a lifetime of accomplishments and hobbies successfully chased, it was home court advantage for him. The mounted twelve-point buck head on the wall stared back at her with anger. One entire corner of the massive desk was a dedicated shrine of beautiful grandkids armed with huge smiles, each frolicking in life.

"I'm not here to ruin your life."

Moving his wife's portrait to the side, he supported a trembling chin melting down on his closed fist. "Could have fooled me," muttered Dr. Bradley.

Unprepared for the head-on collision of darkness, she said, "I only meant to protect my secret."

"Where do…. Uh, I don't even know where to begin. Tell me what you're thinking!" demanded Dr. Bradley.

Scooting to the edge of her seat, she said, "I warned you that you would be putting skin in this game if you wanted to see my abilities. I…I know this will scare you, but it's not negotiable."

Tugging the life out of his earlobe, his blood became scarce as it thickened with the terror of her words. Lightheaded as he watched her lips move, he waited for the nightmare seated across the desk to offer her terms of surrender. "What do you want?" he asked. He tapped his pocket, confirming the nitroglycerin tabs, as the pounding in his ears intensified.

Reaching out over the oak desk, the small palm plopped down next to the portrait of the oldest daughter's graduation from high school. "Reach in your desk and hand me the pedal. I'm not here to judge, only protect my secret."

Rocking back in the captain's chair, Dr. Bradley asked, "What good will that do you?"

"Hand me the pedal, Doctor!" The sharp crack from her finger snap compelled compliance, ending the standoff. It paved the way for the small twisted pedal to come out in the full light of day. "Jack, video this exchange," said Nevada.

With the walls crumbling down all around him, Dr. Bradley made one last pitch for his salvation. Recalling that first night, crying out for forgiveness into a pillow already stuffed full of lies. Wandering the earth, looking over his shoulder as the story of the hit-and-run blanketed his life. The steady stream of denials that had dogged him these last four decades would end today.

Dropping the pedal down into her hand, he said, "Ricky Moline is the reason I am a neurosurgeon today. He, unfortunately, died in a car wreck a few years ago. I can never make this right now." Leaning back, interlocking his fingers across his chest, he waited helplessly for the other shoe to drop. "What are you going to do with...with it?" murmured Dr. Bradley, pointing a crooked finger at the elephant in the room.

No longer the flawless consummate professional in her eyes, she reined in a strong desire to viciously judge him. Refusing to speak until his eyes pulled down from the ceiling, she dialed back thoughts of justice for a little eight-year-old boy. Spinning the broken pedal, she held his silence between her fingers. Flipping the pedal over to Jack, she said, "Doctor, you will never utter a word about this afternoon to another human being as long as you live."

*****

Forty miles of silence from the city, he had run the apology around the flagpole a hundred times in his mind. Clearing a throat full of sorrow, Jack said, "Em, I just didn't realize the power and implications of your gift, as you call it. I'm truly so sorry. I wish I had listened to you."

Giving no indication of life let alone acknowledging the olive branch, she continued staring straight ahead at the eighteen-wheeler. The tough girl from New York City sat in a catatonic state, inhaling the darkness, torturing her mind with endless reruns of his memories.

Reaching over, clicking off Chris Stapleton as he was finishing up "Tennessee Whiskey," he asked, "Emily, are you all right?"

Untethered, navigating a life checkered with empty blanks stubbornly refusing to be filled, she cried out, weary of the search for the exit to the maze imprisoning her. "We both learned something today." Unbuckling her seat belt, drawing her long legs up into a fetal position, the first tear riding the rails, ricocheting off the console, cried out for her rescue. "Jack, I am in trouble. I've let a genie out of the bottle, and I can't control him."

"Hang on. Let me get you home."

*****

She was thankful for the days of tranquility around the ranch as she recharged from the train wreck with Dr. Bradley. On day two for the jeans and black hoodie, the gift had been silent. Grabbing the phone on the third ring, she thought of milking the headache. "Hey, Jack."

"Checking to see how you're doing. How's the headache?" he asked, holding his fingers crossed.

Refusing to take the bait, she dodged the cheese. "As long as we stay home, I think it will be totally gone by bedtime. If you catch my drift, bucko," she said with a throaty laugh.

The queen of chiselers and beggars, she was his force to reckon with. "Fine by me. But shed that black hoodie. I think it's day three for it."

"Day two and fine."

"And before I tell you this, don't…ask…me…a hundred questions. Okay?"

Perking up, she leapfrogged out of her funk at the first note of a mystery. "Uh, no promises. What is it? Tell me right now." Bouncing on the couch cushion, she said, "Tell me, please."

He shook his head at the oncoming interrogation. "You're so predictable. Uh, well, I'm bringing something home that is gonna take a bunch of explaining."

"Oooh! Jack Webster, you better tell me what it is. If you know what's good for you!"

"See you at five." He silenced the interrogation with a mile-wide smile visible from space.

*****

Nevada had been standing at the back door since 4:45, busting at the seams. Her imagination ran ragged. She stiffened up at the first crunch of the gravel as the Ford Interceptor halted, stopping at the mailbox. Further punishing her with the unnecessary delay, he would pay. Crawling up the drive painfully slow, activating his emergency lights, it seemed like he was mocking her misery.

She fumed at the delay as she hiked one leg up, leaning against the doorframe. *How could I love such an idiot?* she mused.

Fighting a smile as he tried to pucker up for a kiss that would never be delivered, Jack asked, "Miss me, darling?"

Searching him better than most police cadets in the academy, she asked, "Where is it?"

"Oh that. Let's do that tomorrow night." Clamping down on his lip, he tasted a hint of blood. Walking through the castle door, Jack yelled back out the doorway, "Get away from the truck. I was kidding. Let's eat first."

Going full animal on her cheeseburger and fries, Nevada peppered questions out at a rate of fire somewhere between that of an AK-47 and an M-16.

Jack said, "Don't choke to death before I go out to get it. Sheesh."

Finishing up the last fry and tossing her hair to the side, she said, "Quit jacking around and go get it."

Sucking his tooth with a loud slurp and failing with the toothpick, the Emily train tumbled over the cliff.

"Jaaack!"

Shoving back from the table with a tired grunt, he said, "Here's the deal. Go into the living room and wait for me. When I come into the room with it, let's take our time on the outside of it first." Holding up his hand, he halted the avalanche of questions. "Now go."

As he wheeled the mystery item into the center of the room, her eyes revealed little.

"That's it? A suitcase?" asked Nevada, the crestfallen look filtering up through the bangs. She dragged the case closer, running her finger across the red seal. "What's with the police evidence seal?"

"Keep looking it over, but don't try opening it yet."

Poring over the titanium exterior, she got bored with the exercise, and she drew a fingernail firmly across the seal. Failing to breach

DIVINE MEMORIES

the integrity of the seal, she allowed a thumb to stray into enemy territory, teasing the push-button release.

Rolling his eyes with the lame attempt, Jack said, "Didn't really think I'd give it to you unlocked, did you?"

"Worst Christmas present ever!" she moaned.

Pulling the key ring out of his jeans, he said, "Hand it over here." Slipping the key in the locks, he greenlighted the Pandora's box to reveal its story. Sliding the case over, he held it down firmly on her lap, smudging the light coating of dust. "Lay your hands on it, but don't you dare open it until I explain some things to you. You understand?" asked Jack, his green eyes flashing a warning.

Knowing when his line was really a line not to be crossed, the weak nod was all he needed. Releasing the case in her custody, he dropped down on the recliner.

Spinning one of the case's rubber wheels, she inspected the exterior for any of its secrets. "Whose is it?"

Dragging her hand away from the case, he engulfed it completely within his, blotting out the worries. "It's yours. You have always had it with you from the first day I met you."

He watched the confusion dance across her face.

"Why are you just now letting me see it?" Nevada asked.

Hooking a canine on the corner of his mustache, Jack explained, "I didn't want to know the answers to the questions we're about to have." Popping the top on a cold one, he said, "Let's get this over with. Go ahead and open it."

Back-to-back snaps echoed as the locks lost their final bid to hide the mystery. Inching the lid open, she peeked under. She slammed the lid back, rocking the bundles of Ben Franklins. Fanning a $10,000 bundle of hundred-dollar bills before burrowing down deeper into the cache of bundles. Coming down out of the clouds for a landing, Nevada asked, "How...how much?" She kept a watchful eye on the fortune.

"That's $948,000, give or take," said Jack, slow to respond as he saw her clueless look.

Running her hands through the mountain of bundles, she asked, "It's mine? Are you sure?"

"I can only assume you do."

Hammering the case shut with a vengeance, she disturbed Sheba, who hightailed it off the back of the couch to hunt for peace and quiet elsewhere. "Is this where we pick up the conversation of me being a drug dealer, Sheriff?"

Shaking his head, he said, "Aw, come on. You know I have never uttered those words. But I do have to wonder how a woman blows in town driving an older Chevy Malibu can shell out over sixty million dollars for an estate and have almost a million in cash lying around." He yanked the case off her lap. "We aren't done here yet."

Dumping the bundles of cash on the coffee table, he reached in, slipping the photos out from the hidden pocket. Anxious to know her identity, overriding the ample fear of it, he handed her the puzzle pieces face down.

Rocked by his words, she had no counter or defense. "What are these?

"Turn them over when you're ready."

Running her fingers across the back of the photographs, she hesitated, sensing a moment of finality. Turning the first photo over, the trio were a mystery. Bringing the picture closer, the teenager spoke to her through the wall of fog. "Is this me? Are these my parents?" Nevada asked rapid fire.

With a steadily rising pulse, Jack muttered, "We think so."

As she flipped the second 8×10 over, time dragged its heels as her world, wobbling these last few months, was brought back with clarity in an instant. As she dissected the second photo, the redhead standing in the picture jarred the rusty bolts open to the prison doors, allowing the memories freedom at last. Channeling them as they came barreling back into focus overwhelmed the once formidable titan. "Matty Baker!"

"Emily, you okay?"

Stretching out on the couch, kicking the throw pillows to the floor, she struggled to juggle fact from fiction. The trails of faint memories crisscrossed her brain, intermingling. Which to believe and which to doubt? Unleashing all her senses to parse out the truth, she sat up. "I'm not sure it's Emily anymore."

DIVINE MEMORIES

Rocketing out of the La-Z-Boy, Jack asked, "You remember who you are?"

"Well, I...I have it narrowed down to just two people and can't say they're my first pick of choice. Let's go to bed."

13

Nevada snapped her eyes shut as the morning sun assaulted her through the blinds. She smelled the trap; he knew bacon was her kryptonite. Counting the revolutions of the wobbly ceiling fan, she knew him too well. Yanking the covers over her head, this was her one last chance to stay as Emily Parker. She was unable to resist the trap as the aroma of the freshly brewed coffee chimed in. The covers got out of the way of a new day as they slid down to the floor.

Setting the last of the tableware, Jack called out, "Hey, sleepyhead."

Stretching arms to the sky, twisting as she groaned, she said, "What's sleep? I researched half the night."

He slid the peace offerings on her plate, accompanied by a steaming cup of coffee. Passing the butter over, he asked, "Are we ready to talk?"

With a look that'd scare your average hardworking junkyard dog, she replied, "Huh-uh. Not before coffee." She made a grab for the mug. Blowing on the brown liquid, she reached over, dropping a pile of papers on the table. "Don't touch till I say so." Sipping the coffee, she left it to rest on her chin as she churned the damning words through her mind. She only wished she was a drug dealer.

Pushing his plate to the side, Jack slid the pile closer. "Okay."

She pushed the plate back. "No. Eat while I talk." She took another sip of courage. After nearly eleven months, he deserved the truth. Clearing a throat that didn't need to be cleared, Nevada said, "I don't have all my memories back, but what I do have will give you a clear idea of who and what I am."

"Good."

With a failed smile, she said, "Careful what you wish for."

Snapping the strip of bacon in half, Jack pointed it at the sad sack at the other end of the table. "You always told me that you wanted me to see the real you before I knew who you were. You also told me I may love you for the rest of my life and marvel at the life you could give me."

"But if memory serves me right, I also said you may leave me too," Nevada said softly.

Washing down the bacon with a generous slug of orange juice, he asked, "Who are you, girl?"

She kept stirring the egg yolk with her fork. "Before I tell you that. I...I want you to know, I've never been happier in my life. I can take you leaving me for what I am but not who I am." Swallowing down the fear, she continued, "My real name is Nevada Barrington from New York City. Emily Parker was a false name I had invented."

"Why?"

The screech of the fork on the plate brought a painful reminder of what she faced. "I am an heiress to Barrington Enterprises. My net worth is north of numbers most people can't even correctly write down on a piece of paper. I left everything, searching for somebody to love and want me for who I am, not for my bank account. Promise me you won't let the money change your feelings for me."

"Oh, Em." Chuckling as he realized the mistake, Jack said, "I mean Nevada. That's gonna take some getting used to. So you're a filthy rich girl. What else?"

"Well, it appears, from some of the news articles, that the government might be looking to have a chat with me regarding insider trading. I launched a war against a group, which included my uncle. They were all indicted for illegally destroying a company by using insider information. I may have inadvertently done the same thing but not for personal gain."

Wincing at the news, he asked, "Have you been indicted?"

"No. I think it worries them I donated all the profits to charities the same day. They're probably scared of the Robin Hood effect."

Bobbing his head, looking for the next question, he said, "How bad did you hurt them financially?"

Pleased that he was still a part of her life for now, she replied, "Last count, the three brokerage houses and individual defendants were on the hook for close to eight billion in losses. I gifted the three and a half billion I made to about forty charities." She sighed. "Your eyes are scaring me when we talk money and numbers," said Nevada.

"No. I mean, well, the numbers are huge in my world. You know what I make a year as sheriff."

Sifting through the pile, Nevada took out the photos. "These were my parents, Byron and Julia Barrington. That's me proudly displaying my new driver's license," she said, reliving one of her last moments with them. She was unable to maintain the sad smile. "They're gone now. Kidnapped and never heard of since that day. This other photo was taken the day I executed my coup on the scum, destroying these two people's company." Flipping the photo, she nodded. "That redhead right there, Matty Baker, brought my memories back to me." She smiled at the memory of the rough, no-nonsense woman.

"I'd say it's not much of a leap to figure out who tried to kill you, is it?"

She slid the pictures back in the pile. "I know. Their day is coming, if I have my way."

Reading through the story of her life, one could only feel pity and a healthy dose of fear for those that had crossed her path. An orphan at sixteen, her path would be led only by her instincts and a strong desire to succeed. Educated at the best schools, she remained out of the public eye until her placement as CEO at the age of twenty-five. Kicking ethics and morals to the curb, she marched over those in her way daily. Until the "Day of Reckoning," as it was coined in the *Wall Street Journal*. The total meltdown in her part of the universe would leave only her standing when the smoke cleared.

Shoving the pile to the middle of the table, Jack went all in. "Phew!"

Wrinkling her nose up, she just missed his hand as he drew it back. "I know it's bad, isn't' it?" The face revealed nothing to her as he avoided her gaze. The stifling anxiety began to cripple her. Sucking in a ragged breath, she asked, "Jack...have I lost you?"

Shaking the kitchen table as his foot twitched, nervously bouncing off the floor, he blotted out all else except that fateful day. A man constructed out of honor, duty, ethics, and a generous dose of morals would keep a promise when others would have cast her away.

Clearing his throat, signaling his answer was headed her way, he rubbed the pain near the base of his neck. It was a chronic pain that he would, hopefully, live with for the next few decades, if he was a betting man. A pain that he hoped to marry one day. "The night you were shot, I searched for anything I could trade to get you back. I sat in that hospital parking lot for a long time, not wanting to come in to hear what awaited me. As the days went by and it really didn't look that good for you, I made a promise to God to never leave you if he gave you back to me. I also—"

"Jack, don't," interrupted Nevada.

Placing his hand firmly over hers, he said, "No, wait. I haven't told you this till now, but I am not running for reelection. Randy is taking over the first of December."

"Noooo." Nevada sighed.

He rubbed eleven months of worry from his tired eyes. "It's been a long time coming. I can always get a job somewhere else to support us."

With a loving smirk, she countered, "Oh, Jack. That's sweet, but it's my turn to take over in that department. Let's go to the living room, and I'll tell you what you're signing up for."

Dictating seating arrangements, she ran her fingers through his hair as they nestled on the couch.

He turned his face from hers, and she said, "Close your eyes as I tell my story."

Committing a cardinal sin as he held the power button on his phone, he barred the world from theirs. "Let's hear it all."

She released the sigh she had held ever since that first encounter at the Coke machine on that cold and snowy lonely night. "Okay. Well, remember this first. When you're as rich as me, you don't have to brag. Your mansions, luxury cars, and servants do that for you. I was born in New York City, as you know. When I was a little over sixteen, my parents and Uncle Charles were attacked in their limousine.

The limo driver was shot to death, and my uncle Charles was shot in the leg. My parents were never seen again."

Reaching back for her trembling hand, Jack said, "I'm sorry, Nevada."

Using a knuckle to clear a misty eye, she replied, "Yeah. Well, it's been so long, I have trouble remembering their faces anymore. Anyway, I went on to college and finally wrested the company back from my uncle Charles with the help of my godfather Lawrence. I rose in power quickly using legal methods never deployed before. I have houses in every corner of the earth. I have three corporate jets, cars of every design and speed. To explain the size of my wealth to you, I could spend five million dollars a day, seven days a week, for the next forty years and still have money left. But then one day, I heard a voice speak to me. It told me to go to this small church a few miles out of the city."

"Now we're getting to the good part," said Jack, turning to face her. He pulled her head down on his chest.

"I remember the first time I went there. I thought it was a condemned building at first. So I waited to see if anyone entered it on that Sunday morning. Well, I went in. My heels drew stares, as did my dress. The preacher was nice, and of course, the sermons were always on greed and loving your neighbor—things I wasn't excelling at then. From that day on, my life derailed with a vengeance."

"How?"

"I started questioning my life and the chaos I brought to others. I secretly went undercover to a company we were thinking about foreclosing on, and it unleashed a side of me I didn't know existed. I discovered an illegal plot by my uncle Charles and others to destroy the company. Through biblical-sized maneuvers, I foiled the plot, destroying the scums' financial positions in life."

"Did you and your uncle get along?"

With a look sour enough to curdle milk, she shrugged. "I can't stand that man."

"What brought you to my neck of the woods?" asked Jack.

"After I saw what a monster I had become, I made the plans to leave it all. I told myself I would seek a place where nobody knew me

DIVINE MEMORIES

or about my wealth. If I found someone to love me for who I am, not what I own, I would stay forever. Have I?" She looked deep into the eyes she longed to see each morning for the rest of her life.

Tugging her earlobe just under the cheap earring, he chuckled. "You have to ask?"

She rubbed her chin against the two-day-old stubble; the hoarse whisper was for his ears only. "Let's summarize this conversation. I am filthy rich—your words, not mine. I possibly might be a wanted fugitive in the near future. I might or might not have people looking to finish what the last two hit men screwed up. And the best for last. I have a weird uncanny mental ability to see other people's memories. You still willing to sign up for that ride?" asked Nevada, nibbling on the side of his neck.

The sparkles of golden flakes in her eyes flashed back at him. Could he be a kept man? "Here are my sticking points. One, I don't want to ever meet the Nevada that lived in New York. Second, I never want the one I met first to ever change."

Rolling over on top of him, pinning his arms down, Nevada chuckled evilly. "One last warning. I come with a no-return policy. Buyer beware!"

"Where do I sign? Or have I already?"

Singlehandedly yanking his 230 pounds off the couch, Nevada barked, "You're already bought and paid for mister. Let's go. I'm hungry."

*****

Looking at the black screen, Jack waited for the phone to come back to life. "I can't believe it's noon already. Hey wait. Oh crap." Reading the text messages, the frown washed away the happiness. "We've got to stop by the office first. Another little girl was snatched late last night, just across the state line."

Grabbing her purse off the chair, she made a last-minute stab at her hair. "I'm ready. I'll wait for you in the truck when we get there."

"Okay. It won't take but a few. Be right back," said Jack, looking down at his phone as the next blast of text chimed in, confirming more grim details.

Rolling down the window, allowing the cool breeze in, she couldn't say she missed the city. *A little fine dining wouldn't hurt*, she thought as she heard her stomach complaining with a loud rumble. Checking for imperfections in the visor mirror, she decided no improvement was needed.

Smacking the side window with a thud before he got back in achieved the desired effect. Startled, she spun, wearing a look that would make a serial killer move on. The grin, more of a confession in her eyes, deserved punishment as he reached over, flipping her visor up. "You look fine. A little scared but fine."

"Jackass."

"Hee-haw," said Jack, smiling into the face of death before spying the small mountain of wrappers.

Refusing to be a victim, Nevada said, "That's right. I ate every last one of your precious Life Savers. And the cherry ones were especially uncommonly delicious," She smacked her lips with pride.

"Glad I could contribute to saving your life. Guess we better forage for nutrients before you gnaw my arm off."

Doing as much damage as she could to the Beef Manhattan, she caught the heat of the man's stare out of the corner of her eye. Shifting in her chair, she blocked the unwanted invasion. "Jack, who is that man over my left shoulder wearing the wifebeater?" asked Nevada, hunkered down.

Looking over the top of his sunglasses, "Really? Wifebeater? Where would you have ever heard...never mind. Which one?" Scanning the tables, he said, "Oh, that's Percy Spivey. Our local Peeping Tom."

"He's creepy." Nevada shivered.

Taking a healthy sip of sweet tea, he clarified, "Dear, I'm afraid Mr. Percy Spivey left creepy in the rearview mirror years ago." Pushing the sunglasses lower as he swung to get a clear view in Percy's direction. He held the stare, ensuring the message was crystal clear to the opposing team.

Throwing in the towel on the Manhattan, she said, "I've lost my appetite."

Digging out the debit card as he stood, Jack said, "I've gotta talk to that group of fellas up by the counter for a minute. I'll be right back."

Taking a long taste test on Jack's abandoned sweet tea, she entertained thoughts on his last fry. The brief lull allowed her to catch bits and pieces of the child abduction as it blared out of the ancient TV hanging over the counter. Competing to be heard over the lunch crowd, the live shot outside the victim's grandmother's house gave out few clues.

Washing down Jack's last fry, she plotted her course to the counter, staying as far from Spivey's table as possible. Tilting a chair to squeeze by, she refused to give him the privilege of seeing her baby blues as she parked herself close to Jack's side. Hating herself for taking the bait, she swiveled to confront his stare. The empty chair registered as the aroma of gas and old oil hit her nose. Craning her neck, she felt filthy as he stood behind her, holding his check. The smile, a dentist's nightmare, dripped with vulgarity. He was undressing her with his eyes, and the scraggy whiskers around a mouth caked with gravy turned her stomach.

"Sheriff, do they have any clues on these girls?" asked Jess Watkins as he passed by.

"Yeah, but they're keeping them close to their vest for now."

Trying not to get high off the fumes, she spun, holding her breath as best she could. "You can go around. We could be here for a while," said Nevada, hoping the Manhattan stayed down.

"No hurry, ma'am," said Spivey, holding up a hand with enough grease under the nails to lubricate your average carnival ride.

Doomed, she turned back around, catching up with the conversation.

"Hey, boys. I just heard on the scanner a few minutes ago that they were narrowing the search down to an older model blue Ford F-150," piped in Gordy Neilson, who dropped his check and a twenty down on the counter.

"What happened?" asked Nevada, looking up at the crowd of gawkers.

"Here, take a sip of water."

"How did I get over here?" Taking a swallow, she said, "I'm fine. I'm fine."

"I don't know. One minute, I'm listening to Gordy. And I look around, and you had fallen into the arms of Percy Spivey," said Jack.

"Jack, we need to leave right now," said Nevada, shoving up out of the chair.

Snaking an arm around her waist, he asked, "Are you okay?"

Shaking her head to clear out the cobwebs, she said, "I'm more than okay." Shooing his arm away, she leaned in close. "I gotta warn you though. You're going to need to throw common sense out the window."

Jack stepped back, frozen by the whispered promise of foreboding troubles on the horizon. Giving Mrs. Peabody a reassuring smile, he helped Nevada stay upright. "Why?"

Tossing her head, she searched the crowd. "Where's that Percy guy?"

"After he got his grimy claws off you, he bugged out," said Jack with a disgusted grimace, pointing out the greasy smudges under her breasts.

She was seething at the greasy streaks, so painfully obvious upon her white blouse. It was a transgression against her that would be paid back in spades. A groping that would touch off the first shot in a campaign tailor-made for the destruction on one corner of man's evil. "That's one violation upon a woman he's just going to hate himself for," said Nevada through clenched teeth.

Braking for Widow Perkins, the town's most notorious jaywalker, to kick her walker in high gear, Jack asked, "What happened in there?"

"Percy Spivey has upped his game."

Returning Widow Perkins's guilty smile, he asked, "What's that?"

Officially raising the curtain on act 1 scene 3, Nevada said, "He's got that little girl hidden in his house."

*****

Startling the flag crew at the VFW as the Interceptor squalled, Jack made a last-minute request for the turn lane. Barreling to the sheriff's department, he knew better. But if it was his little girl, he'd flatten the earth to find her. "Are you absolutely positive, Nevada? I mean, this will immediately draw huge amounts of skepticism in your face."

Grabbing the armrest as he rounded the corner sharply, she said, "I know what I saw."

Jack pulled into his reserved spot. "Okay. Let's get it all down on paper. We'll need to get our ducks in a row before we let this cat out of the bag."

"Can't you just go out and arrest him?"

Shaking a head that knew only too well the tumultuous weather they were headed into, Jack explained, "It's not what you know. It's what you can prove. And people on my side of the equation are going to be our first hurdle. The Mercer County Indiana Sheriff's Department being first up."

Tapping a finger to her lips, she said, "Well, I guess I'll have to make believers out of them. But remember, I will always protect my gift."

"That's the part that worries me the most," said Jack, wishing poor Sergeant Janicky over at Mercer County the best of luck.

Spending the next hour detailing her visions, she waited for his return. Going over the plan, she would control the narrative as before, ignoring his pleas for leniency. No matter which flag they flew, she would not jeopardize the gift.

"You ready? I've set up a one-on-one meeting with Janicky. He's the detective spearheading the investigation. Remember the ground rules, okay?" asked Jack, dreading the wall of scrutiny they were about to walk into.

At forty-seven, Janicky had seen the worst of the worst, dressed down in his flannel and jeans. Finishing up his twenty-fifth year, he dreamed of retirement more and more with each atrocity he waded through. Seated toward the rear with his back against the wall, the friendly wave disarmed nobody. He was there to unravel a mystery.

Standing with respect, Roy Janicky offered his hand. "Sheriff."

"How's it going this morning, Roy? How's the twins and wife doing?"

Trained to miss little, he shifted his gaze to the woman obviously wearing a wig next to the sheriff. Foiling her identity with the mask and dark glasses, he would wait for the explanation. Going right for the jugular, he said, "They are fine…uh, just fine. Who do we have here, Sheriff?"

Grabbing the handle to his auburn-haired Pandora's box, he would set her world down on the table for all to see carefully. Taking a deep breath, letting it out with a little remorse, he allowed the words to leave his possession. "Roy, before we get to the who part, let's talk about the what part first."

"Sheriff, this is your show. Run it how you want," came Janicky's slow drawl. He hailed the waitress over.

"We've both been in this business a while, so I wouldn't waste your time. That being said, this woman has the ability to see or interpret things in ways others can't," said Jack, holding up his hand. "I know. I know. We've all had to listen to more than our share of the little old gray-headed ladies with no teeth proudly claim they communicate with—well, you fill in the blank, etcetera. At least, hear this woman out till your coffee cup is empty."

Up to his neck in the case, desperation and a healthy respect for the sheriff were Janicky's only motivation to stay seated. Not his run-of-the-mill nutjob, she didn't fit the profile. "Ma'am, I'm gonna be honest with you up front. I have less than zero faith in what I have heard so far. I've worked more murders and major cases than I care to acknowledge, and none of them were solved by noisy, pesky soothsayers, mind readers, or whatever you call yourself. We waste resources investigating vague information from people such as yourself. Information just believable enough to waste said resources on." Taking a sip of coffee, Sergeant Janicky warned, "Clock's ticking."

Narrowing her eyes at the dose of love being shoveled her way, Nevada quipped, "Well, quite the speech, Sergeant." She adjusted her N95 mask, for once, glad for the COVID-19 pandemic. "I guess we shouldn't waste any more of your precious time then."

Downing the cup and ignoring the searing pain, Sergeant Janicky said, "Time's up."

"Sorry, Roy. I'll buy the coffee for your trouble," said Jack.

He spread his arms wide with a whimsical smile. "Never know where that big break's coming from. Gotta check 'em all out, right?" asked Sergeant Janicky, grabbing his hat off the table.

Waiting to see the whites of his eyes as he slid his chair in, Nevada asked nonchalantly, "Sergeant Janicky, how are the twins this morning?"

Snapping his head over crisper than a Granny Smith apple, he said, "Excuse me."

"How's that little scamp Marjorie? Still butt-hurt at being falsely accused and spanked for her sister's lie this morning?" said Nevada, letting it soak in. "That's right. You better get another cup of coffee."

Jack wished for his own mask to slink behind as he witnessed Sergeant Janicky dissolve into a pile of goo. Unable to hold his own under the withering gaze, he tried holding the tiger at bay. "Let's all start fresh again," suggested Jack.

Sergeant Janicky plopped his hat back down. "Ma'am, I ran the information by the little girl's mother that you supposedly saw. I'm being told it's all wrong. The description of her panties and the Band-Aids are all wrong. I want nothing better than for you to know what you're talking about," he said.

Tipping up the bottom of her mask, Nevada took a long draw on the straw. "I hope she has your cell number." Tired of the stiff neck in the room, she asked, "Sheriff, may I proceed?"

"Hang on a minute. Roy, do you want to see a demonstration of her abilities? Think twice before answering," warned Jack.

"How does it work?"

"Roy, once again, think twice," said Jack.

Prancing at the starter's gate, she leaned forward, closing the distance. "I will need you to recall a memory of something that you feel guilty about. Simple as that. But I want you to visualize the place, the objects, the people, and such," Nevada said smoothly.

"Sure."

"Make sure it's nothing your family or anyone else would know."

"Sure."

One more "sure" from the stiff neck and I'm gonna scream. Nevada said, "One last thing. Lay your hand flat on the table and close your eyes.

"Got it."

Shielded behind the dark plastic, her eyes devoured him, ready to unleash her gift. "Begin whenever you're ready. You may feel the tip of my finger touch yours. Don't open your eyes."

Submerged in his memory, she strained to unravel the tentacles clinging to another memory. Slipping her glove off, she gently tapped her nail upon his wedding band. Clearing the logjam, she began ushering the memories to come crashing through. Feeling uncomfortable invading the man's intimate thoughts, she plodded on. Securing the picture of a simple theft and a long-running emotional battle, she opened her eyes. She was wincing as the gift drained her energy.

Letting his stare, famous for busting countless felons, land squarely upon her, Sergeant Janicky said, "What'd ya come up with?" He started digging his keys out of his pocket.

Frowning at the insignificant memories, she replied, "Well, I'm not sure your memories are dark enough to control you. I'll just wait till the mother calls back. Maybe that's her now, Sergeant."

She eavesdropped on the animated conversation, which was loaded with plenty of nodding and an abundant number of uh-huhs. Dropping the phone in his pocket, he ran a finger along the rim of the coffee cup. "Who are you, lady?" asked Sergeant Janicky, lowering the barriers between them.

Adjusting the mask, she said, "I'm someone unlike anyone you've ever known. You will never, ever know who I am."

With his tail in the crack, he shifted over to friendlier territory. "Jack, where do we go from here?" asked Sergeant Janicky, his words dripping with desperation.

"Does the mother know why you asked about the panties and Band-Aids?" asked Jack.

"No."

"Janicky, I make the rules on this side of the border." Gathering in the ramifications of widening the circle, Jack said, "I will hand you the guy that did this, but you will never reveal the conversation with this lady to anyone." And he gave Janicky his own version of a felon-busting gaze.

Bristling up a might, running fingers through his high and tight, he was beginning to dislike the tag team unfolding across the table. In enemy territory, far from his own playground, he couldn't go home empty-handed. Her eyes revealed little beyond the dark shades. They were living in a world where if it quacks like a duck, it's probably a duck.

"You know what worries me, Sheriff? This woman knows details only the kidnapper would know. I'm not leaving till I know her identity," snarled Sergeant Janicky.

Lunging up, she snagged her man's sleeve as he launched. "I got this." Slurping down the rest of her Coke, she let the straw hit rock bottom with a loud gurgle. "You want to unveil my identity, do you?" asked Nevada.

"Not just want. I will, lady," threatened Janicky. Those chilling words had brought down their fair share of the locals far and wide.

The mask failed to hide the smile slipping out through her eyes. "Okay. Let's play the game again, and I'll give you the option to ask me my identity afterwards. If you should choose that option, that is," said Nevada, removing her glove.

Spinning his wedding band, Janicky was trying to fit the pieces together. "Why?"

Reaching for her purse, she angled toward the exit, "You playing or not? If not, I'm gone."

Bellying up to the bar for one last round, he said, "Let's do it." He slid his hand out across the table. "I'm gonna be the tornado to your trailer park, missy," sneered Sergeant Janicky.

"Oh, you better check the weather forecast, Sergeant," said Nevada, pressing her acrylics in the back of his hand. "I take no pleasure in this, but you need to stay focused on the bad people."

"Sure."

Cracking open one eye at his "sure," Nevada pressed down harder. "Shut your eyes, Sergeant. This time, I want you to remember a time when you felt your actions endangered your pension and job. Put name tags on the people involved. I want you to imagine writing the details on a piece of paper, such as lies told, laws broken. Write down the people wronged. That's it, keep writing. Yes, yes. Keep writing. No, keep your eyes shut."

Pulling out from under her claws, the game was summarily terminated. It was too late to keep the deed hidden behind the layers of carefully constructed misdirection. No longer the biggest bully in the sandbox, he waited for her voice behind the mask. Rubbing the red dents from the back of his hand, he knew they were a lasting reminder of the yoke about to be placed around his neck.

Rattling the ice, she was looking for one last swallow. "Here's your deal. I have your complete silence. And for that, I won't publicly speak of your…let's call them indiscretions in your life," offered Nevada.

Stepping down into the depths of hell, he said, "If I don't want to sign up for your craziness, then what?" Sergeant Janicky drained the last of his coffee.

She licked her lip before leaning over to spin the coffee cup. She dropped the cup down, chipping the truck stop's fine china. "Times up! Do we start with the BB gun you stole as a kid? Maybe how you cruelly treat little ten-year-old Marjorie because she constantly reminds you of that sister-in-law that scorned you years ago? Or do you want to hear about Officer Jacoby and the missing cash?"

Wilting as the air was stomped out of his lungs, Janicky let the back of the booth stop the back of his head's freefall. "Stop."

Wading into the bloodshed, Jack said, "We only came here to verify the details, Roy."

Mired in guilt for a lapse of judgment over ten years ago, he sat there dazed. With Jacoby's death last year, he alone was still prone to suffer for his stupidity. Looking for his water glass, he couldn't rip his eyes from the black orbs obscuring hers. His fate saddled to her whim, he scrambled for options. "How do…you know…do it?" asked Janicky.

Releasing the withering storm from her eyes, she softened. "I have a divine gift. One I will guide and protect carefully," said Nevada.

14

With a few weeks left in his term, he had to leave with dignity. Plotting Nevada's safety, he worked the rescue mission for a terrified little six-year-old girl. One who was safely locked away down in the pits of hell, away from prying eyes. Listening to the lazy clomp of the bootheels headed down the hallway, he hoped his old friend would take it well.

"Randy, come on in and have a seat."

He dropped down on the worn-out sofa next to the wall. "What's up, Jack?" Randy asked with a five-gallon bucket full of suspicion.

Leaning on his palm, hoping Randy's pained look wouldn't reach out for anger, Jack said, "Shut the door. We need to talk."

Squinting, Randy leaned over, catching the doorknob. "Must be important."

Letting his hand freefall down to hit the tabletop, Jack said, "It is. Listen carefully. I'm only saying this once, and I'm not answering any questions. If things go as planned, I'm gonna hand you a search warrant to make an arrest on those missing girls. You will never know how it was solved."

Yanking a boot over his knee, Randy asked, "What? You don't trust me now?"

"That's not it. It's not my trust to give on this one. I don't have the authority to violate their demands, period."

"Whatever." Turning to leave, Randy growled as he jerked the door open. "Nice knowing I have your complete trust." The sound of the boots retreated with haste as the words fueled each clomp.

"Randy, wait!" Falling back against the rickety chair, Jack knew it would be a long day. Looking out the window, he saw the fall winds had managed to strip off the last of the beautiful maple's leaves. Gathering up his notes, he headed to the meeting.

Locking the door to the conference room, he turned to face the duo. Janicky, wearing a pinch of gloom on his face, sat next to the woman of his dreams. "Well, here's the first hurdle. The luck of the draw sucks when it comes to available judges today. We will have to apply for the warrant in front of Judge John R. Bowers."

"Tough, is he?" asked Janicky.

Shaking a head filled with the memories of countless rejections by the sadistic jurist, Jack complained, "*Tough* ain't the word. He protects the Fourth Amendment like it was his firstborn."

Giving the masked stranger a side-eye, Janicky said through pursed lips, "This will be brutal."

"If we don't get the warrant, we'll still go to the house and work as much magic as possible," said Jack, looking over at his beautiful mystery about to be unveiled.

*****

Pulling down the drive lined with the flowering pear trees, each naked, having surrendered their foliage to the coming winter, they stopped in the circle drive. The sentry on duty met them with an untrusting demeanor. Circling the vehicle, anxious to greet the strangers, the woman of the house ran interference.

"Macey, leave them alone. Come here, girl." Blocking the sun from her eyes, she said, "Good afternoon, Sheriff."

"How you doing today, Mrs. Bowers?" asked Jack with a gracious smile.

"Fine. Just fine. Need the judge?" asked Libby Bowers, holding Macey back by her collar.

"Yes, please."

She chirped a warning. "Good luck. He's grouchy. The Cubs are losing in the fifth."

Gritting his teeth, Jack yanked his head to the side. "Thanks for the warning," he said. "Janicky, give us a second." Huddling close, he muttered, "Nevada, you don't have to do this. Lillian calls me every

Monday morning wondering when you will return to her 'Yankee Mansion,' as she calls it. Nobody knows about any of this yet. You could live happily there without the biblical scrutiny headed our way."

"I couldn't live with myself if I caved in now. Go pave the way," said Nevada.

Only too familiar with the man cave, Jack knocked on the wall, pulling the judge's attention from the wide screen. Judge Bowers whipped his head over as he slashed an arm through the air. Court was closed. Sliding a coaster closer for his gin and tonic, he yelled, "Not today!" With forty-five years on the bench, the closest thing to God, he tamped down his fellow man daily.

With the roar of the Cardinal fans celebrating the final flame-out of the Cubs' cleanup batter, his blood boiled. The commercial brought a cooling-off period, allowing the blood pressure to simmer down a bit.

Turning down the volume, he would deal with the pesky intrusion. "What?" howled Judge Bowers, throwing the remote across the room.

With a dismal batting average against the judge, Jack's hopes for a home run were pretty bleak. "Judge I need a search warrant for a house we believe one of the missing girls from over in Indiana is being held."

"Who's this?" Judge Bowers growled, pointing a stiff finger in Janicky's direction.

"This is Sgt. Roy Janicky from Mercer County Sheriff's Department. He's the lead detective on the case."

Frowning as he retrieved the remote and hit RECORD, the judge was less than confident technology would allow him the right to the witness the Cubs rally back against the Cardinals at a later date. "What do you have?"

On a tightrope with no safety net, Jack ventured out slowly. The scowl forming on the only man legally capable of saving a lost little girl didn't stoke his confidence. "Your Honor, we have a confidential source who claims to have seen the little girl in the house we are looking at. She has provided details available to no one else.

Sergeant Janicky has confirmed the details with the family members of the little girl."

"What kind of details, and when was the last time the informant saw the little girl?" queried Judge Bowers.

"She identified what kind of panties she was wearing and specific Band-Aids on the victim's legs. Also, a very vivid description of the victim herself and the house has also been described to a tee," said Sergeant Janicky.

"I'm sorry. Did I miss the last time victim was observed?" asked Judge Bowers, looking up from scribbling on the legal pad.

Mentally installing earplugs, Jack could just hear the thunderous howl about to erupt from the grizzly seventy-eight-year-old. He gave Janicky one last look before plunging headfirst into the fight—one that would speak for an innocent six-year-old captured by a monster. He flipped to the first page of the file like he didn't already know the answer. "Judge, the confidential source saw a memory of the details involving the suspect this morning," said Jack, dropping the pen. He was waiting for the fuse to set off the fireworks.

Judge Bowers slammed the pad shut with a vengeance. Red being the new color for the day, it accented the bulging vein in his forehead. "Aww, what in blazes are you trying to jury-rig here! You expect me to trample all over the Fourth Amendment using the psychobabble of a psychic!" he screamed.

Swallowing his anger, Jack pleaded, "I realize it isn't standard evidence. I am only asking you to hear all the forms of evidence."

Looking for the PLAY button on the remote, Judge Bowers said, grimacing at the score, "I think we're done here, Sheriff."

The exchange had carried throughout the house. Strolling through the living room, the lady of the house apologized silently with a sympathetic frown as Jack passed.

As he was backing out of the drive, the chilling local radio broadcast renewed his fight. Turning, he said, "Are you absolutely sure, ma'am?"

"You know I am," said Nevada.

Pulling forward, he said, "Roy, stay in the car. It's gonna get ugly this time."

DIVINE MEMORIES

Silently counting to three before he kicked the rattler glued to the wide-screen TV, Jack knocked, bringing the love. "Judge, we're not done."

"If I have to turn this off, you may get a contempt charge on you," said Judge Bowers, refusing to turn.

Hoping his house would sell fast, visions of leaving town disgraced flowed like a river through his brain. "Judge, if you don't turn it off, I may put a bullet through it."

Recoiling, the gin-soaked eyes brightened at the prospect. "Did you just threaten me?"

"Pretty sure I threatened the TV's life." Taking a seat on the edge of the couch, Jack continued, "You know, Judge, you don't like me, and I have little use for you personally. But I'm not going to let your stubborn ass get another girl tortured to death. I have a proposition for you. A bet, you might say."

Missing the Friday-night poker game last night, he needed some action in his week. "Probably won't go for it, but as long as you are traipsing through my house, let's hear it."

Pitching the gold badge in the nut bowl, showering pistachio hulls across the table, Jack said, "Hear the lady out and then make your decision about the warrant. If you can honestly deny the warrant after hearing her testimony, well, the badge is yours, and I resign Monday morning. But if you grant the warrant, the badge is mine and you don't run for the bench again."

Working a piece of pistachio out of his molar, the judge asked with a smile creeping out from the corners of his mouth. "Let's summarize. I hear the lady out and make my decision to deny the warrant, and you resign Monday. Correct?"

"Yep."

"Get her in here. It's the seventh-inning stretch anyway," ordered Judge Bowers.

Motioning for her to lower the window, leaning in close, "Okay. He has agreed to hear your testimony. Before you get out, know this. He gives asses a bad name. He can't wait to make a fool out of you. And one last thing. No pressure, but I sort of promised to resign if he didn't issue the warrant in good faith."

165

Adjusting her mask, Nevada said, "Lead me to the pompous tyrant."

Taking a seat front and center, the duo took their places.

"I'm unaware of the rules of conduct for this kind of matter," said Nevada.

"I make the rules, you follow them," said Judge Bowers with an air of superiority.

"That's fine as long as we all remember our places in life," said Nevada.

Dropping the legal pad, the judge asked, "What's that mean?"

"You know. I'm an honest citizen trying to save a girl's life, and you are a local judge in a hick county in the middle of a state I would routinely only fly over."

Sneaking a hand up, Jack covered a grin that would have earned the average man a contempt charge. He could only admire the woman he would marry one day, even if she got jail time in the next five minutes. She was saying words to a face countless individuals would love to witness.

Taking the slap with little in the way of defense, Judge Bowers said, "My dear, you've got five minutes."

Eyeing her adversary, Nevada asked, "Do you want to hear what I saw or prove I saw it first?"

"Let's go with prove it first. Also, what is your name?" asked Judge Bowers, smiling at the prospect of the golden souvenir.

Powering through his glare, she replied, "I'll give you my name after you sign the warrant. If not, you don't need my identity."

He was coiling up, ready to strike. "Fine. The floor is yours. Dazzle me."

"I find proving it to you could only be accomplished by personally reading your own memories. Am I right, Your…Honor?" asked Nevada, choking out the respectful title.

Holding his cards close to his vest, pushing all his chips in, Judge Bowers taunted, "You do that, lady, and you got yourself a warrant."

"Great. Let's get started. I need you to lean back and shut your eyes. Now I want you to think of two of the most regrettable things you are guilty of."

DIVINE MEMORIES

"Oh, we're really going to go through with this dog and pony show?" asked Judge Bowers, straightening up his horn-rimmed glasses.

"Close your eyes please. Now reach back in time. Let the memories flow. Concentrate on your actions, people harmed, dates and places. Pretend you are standing in front of a chalkboard. Now write down the details for me to see. Quit trying to hide them. Let them come forward. That's it. One after another, let them flow out," coaxed Nevada. Dragging a set of nails lightly across the back of his hand, she summoned the final guilt-racked memories to escape his possession.

Doctoring up a sudden set of dry lips with a liberal coating of ChapStick, he fought to hide the tremors as he downed the last of his gin. "That it?" asked Judge Bowers, gloating at the potential win.

"Got what I needed," said Nevada.

Ready to rake in his winnings, Judge Bowers said, digging out the badge, "Let's hear what you got."

Looking down at her man's gold star, his reason for living, being coldly snaked back across the table, it turned her stomach. She was counting each vein as the bony hand clutched the symbol of law and order.

As he proudly held the trophy, the speech of his life driveled out. "Sheriff, will eight a.m. be too early for your resignation ceremony Monday?" asked Judge bowers, twirling the badge between his fingers. "I also think we—"

"Don't get too attached to that, Judge. We've got a lot to talk about," said Nevada, shutting down the victory speech.

"Such as?"

"One Rancy Meagerson, locked up in Menosha Correctional Center for a life sentence that's what," said Nevada, dropping the nuke on the pompous dictator known locally as Judge John Robert Bowers.

Crashing back to earth, it landed next to its rightful owner. Reclaiming his property, Sheriff Robert Jackson Webster said, "Go ahead, ma'am." He winked at the woman behind the mask.

"Judge, you purposely let your biased feelings against Rancy lead him down the road of devastation. You knowingly allowed tainted evidence against him, essentially framing him for the murders of his wife and son. You knew some of the witness testimony was suspect at best. And for your other memory—"

Pitching over against the table, closing the distance between adversaries, Judge Bowers hollered, shaking with rage, "You can't prove a thing."

Brushing off his unbridled anger, Nevada continued, "And for your second memory. One I believe we can prove quite easily, in fact. I'm referring to the cozy arrangement you have with another elected official. You know, the one where you two skim money from certain court funds. You ready to talk about that warrant now?"

With his world going pitch dark, the master of dictating rules to underlings now found that the tables had turned. His heart was racing to pump blood to a brain that was out to lunch with fear. Attacking from all sides, she had been underestimated, and he scrambled for survival.

"How about I cut you two in on the deal?" asked Judge Bowers, holding out a peace offering. Watching his chips being stacked up on the other side of the table, he waited for the jury's decision.

Sweeping her eyes past the sorry excuse for a human, Nevada said, "Sheriff Webster, he has a diary in his office detailing all his personal dealings."

Dusting the pistachio crumbs from his badge, Jack secured it back in its rightful place. Strangely enough, recalling all the verbal assaults he had endured, all the demeaning decisions thrown in his face, the words weren't as rewarding as he envisioned.

"Judge, we're heading to your office, where you will issue my search warrant and hand over the diary. You will also announce your retirement Monday. And lastly, you will assign the amount of your thefts to be paid back upon your death. Oh, one other thing. You will immediately seek to assist in getting Rancy Meagerson a new trial."

Busted out of the game, with no more capital, Judge Bowers could only nod. "Let me get my jacket."

*****

DIVINE MEMORIES

Armed with a warrant, the posse closed in on the ramshackle shotgun house surrounded by decades of junk. Receiving the signal that all four corners were covered, the ominous battle cry followed: "Search warrant. Sheriff's department!"

As the front door shattered off its hinges, the splinters rained down in the living room. They fanned out to secure the house, and one scared occupant in the shower was detained. The stringy hair, dripping water, hung down plastered to his back. Allowed to change out of the dingy towel for blue jeans, the contest between right and wrong unfolded.

"Uh, uh...Sheriff, what's this all about? Who's gonna pay for that damaged door? Is this because I manhandled your woman?" asked Percy Spivey, the crooked smile allowing his two remaining front teeth to shine.

"My, my, Percy. The only thing keeping me from knocking those last two yellow fuzzy teeth out of your thick head is a love of my freedom. No, Percy. We're here for another little piece of business. I think the warrant speaks for itself," said Sheriff Jack Webster, scratching the side of his eye socket while scanning the room for signs.

Struggling through the warrant's lingo, Percy asked, "Little girl! Is this a joke?" Wadding up the warrant, he threw it at the nearest deputy.

"Randy, I'll be out in the squad. Tear it up, boys!" yelled Jack.

The strained look worried her. Had her gift led her astray? The sudden squawk on the radio startled her. "How's it going in there?" asked Nevada, sneaking a hand across the console.

Longing for more than her index finger as he grabbed it, Jack was careful to maintain a professional front. "Oh, 'bout usual in these kinds of situations. Homeowner screams they're innocent until we drag them to jail. It'll take Randy and his team a little while to find her."

"And if they don't?"

Tugging on his mustache, he said, "I'll send in Wonder Woman."

She ran her eyes over the heaps of junk scattered throughout the empire of the crazed lunatic, complete with a slightly used Chevy

Nova up on blocks. "Great," she muttered. Shackled to a cause that would soon be unleashed upon the world, she would need to recharge. "When this is over, I need to go back to New York sometime and see a preacher friend," said Nevada, repulsed by the mound of trash bags strewn out across the yard.

"Do you want company?" asked Jack, turning at the sound of the screen door slamming behind Randy.

Pulling back her hand, she said, "Not necessary. I will have a lot of cleanup to perform when I get there. Maybe next trip back."

He gave the finger one last squeeze. "Okay. Here comes Randy. Don't look good."

Sauntering across the yard, he eyeballed the masked stranger as he gave the window time to open. Pushing his hat back, Randy said, "Well, we've come up snake eyes so far. Spivey's crying lawsuit and demanding we get off his property."

Facing a notion of failure, the thoughts of facing the smug judge crept in. Gnawing on a lip that had been gnawed on too much lately, Jack ordered, "Randy, go back in and gather up the deputies with Spivey. Everybody hole up in the back bedroom. I'm gonna bring her in to see what she can do. Don't let Spivey get an eyeball on her."

Tapping a knuckle on the side mirror, Randy sighed. "Jack, I thought this was my show."

"It is the second we find a little girl in that cesspool. Until then, it's on me."

Dipping lower, he gave the passenger a cool reception. "Give me five and then come on in. Good luck," said Randy.

Scouring the broken-down couch for a clean place, Nevada opted for the end rigged up with a brick for support. Listening to the mouth in the backroom complain about his rights being trampled on, she closed her eyes. Blocking out the tirade, she massaged the memories, molding them for her benefit. Round and round they go. Each time, shadows peek through, revealing more.

"Oh! Take me to the pantry," said Nevada.

Hitched to her train for survival, Jack asked, "Got something?"

"Yeah, we need to find a can of Van Camp's pork and beans in there."

Losing a head of steam in the survival department, Jack asked, "Huh?" He was drooping a set of weary shoulders.

"Just go…go," ordered Wonder Woman, shooing him back.

Slipping on the loose dog food, he finally found the string leading to a bare lightbulb coated with cockroach feces. Yanking the string brought everything the sixty-watt bulb had to offer. The pantry, littered with broken quart jars, would never pass the local health board. Kicking debris to the side, they finally made it to shelves lined with canned goods. Snapping on his flashlight brought another bonus as the cockroaches scurried off the shelves. Raking cans off the shelves, back against the wall, they noticed a lonely can of beans dying to tell a story.

Latching on to the can, he knew instantly. *Much too heavy.* The key to her rescue was one step closer. Lifting straight up on the can brought a metallic click as the cable tied to the can tightened, releasing a latch to the hidden door. "Randy, get in here!" yelled Jack.

The clatter of boots in overdrive skidded to a halt at the pantry entrance. "Yeah, got something?" Watching the half wall swing inward, Randy took a hard gander at the woman. "How did she?"

"Don't worry about that now. Watch my back," said Jack, drawing his weapon.

Raking the room with his tactical light, he spied the metal handle of the trapdoor back by the far wall. He nodded to Randy as he wiped a bead of sweat from the tip of his nose. The scrape of the trapdoor, muffled by the rotten wooden case, released its hellish nightmare for all to see. The pungent odor of urine assaulted his nose as it wafted upward. Leaning down into the darkness, he frantically bathed the dungeon with light. His heart faltered, sinking at the sight of the small lump on the filthy bed.

Vaulting down into a slice of human tragedy, he crab-walked over to her. She recoiled at his touch with a whimper through her gag.

Jack said, "Marci, sweetheart, it's over. You're safe now. It's over. I promise."

Cutting the clothesline from her wrists and ankles, he scooped up the last victim of Percy Spivey. He held her tightly as she remained motionless, unsure of her rescuers. Naked, bruised, and more dead than alive, she held her eyes tightly shut. The once bright eyes would take time to trust a world where monsters would always lurk in the shadows for years to come. Jack caressed the stringy blond locks as he untangled them from the matted food.

"Oh my god. I'll…I'll go get her a blanket," said Randy, smearing a glove across his wet cheek.

Rocking her slowly on his knee, Jack said, "Call for EMS and bring her a bottle of water too." He let her head fall against his shoulder.

"Got it."

"Randy, clear the house before I bring her out. I don't want to see that piece of filth anywhere."

Shielding her eyes, allowing the light of the day to witness the atrocities, Marci released her first cry.

Jack handed her up through the trapdoor. Seventeen years of witnessing the worst man could dole out couldn't prepare Deputy Angie Legion as she took the child. Clamping her arms around Marci, she was no less loving than she was for her three girls. Bundling the child tightly in the blanket, she couldn't whisk her out of the house of horrors fast enough.

"Jack…is she going to make it?" asked Nevada, choking back a sob. She was concealed back in the shadows of the pantry.

Falling hard against the wall, knocking a bowl of dog food clattering to the wooden floor, Jack felt the rage billowing up to the surface. Dropping down onto a pile of ancient newspapers, he allowed the back of his head to strike the wall in defeat. "I'm so sick of this world's ugliness. That girl is gonna have a long road to recovery. Her body will heal, but her world will never be the same," he said, unashamed, putting the handkerchief back in his pocket.

"She will never want for anything as long as I'm alive." Grabbing the sleeve of a sheriff on life support, Nevada said, "Get me out of this godforsaken hole, Jack."

15

The chimes boldly sang out her presence. Given new life, the Yankee Mansion could withstand another 150 years if she was lucky. The click of the heels echoed sharply off the marble as she ambled her way across the foyer. Peeking out the window, Lillian's eyes flew open with joy as she recognized the woman who was fidgeting with the door handle, struggling to outsmart the smart locks installed last year. Sweeping the door back, Nevada's hearty embrace seemed to straighten up her osteoporosis.

Looking older but spry for almost ninety-two, Lillian broke from the embrace. Taking a critical look, she asked, "Oh, darling. Where have you been?"

Holding a calloused hand that had served the poor, created more than it destroyed, and longed for rest, Nevada said, "I'm sorry I haven't made it over sooner, Lillian. Life has been crazy, but I am much better now."

"Well, Emily, you're here now, and that's all that matters." Lillian cackled. Not giving out options, she pulled Nevada inside. "Did that sheriff tell you I have been checking on you?"

Choosing to postpone the name correction, she forged on. "Yes. Yes, he did. I just got free from the world's claws last week and decided to come on over," said Nevada, allowing Lillian to lead her deeper into the mansion's interior. The millions had done the mansion justice.

Over sweet tea and hummingbird cake, she let her down easy as the futile request was repeated. Reaching out across the table, Nevada said, "Lillian, I'm not saying no. I'm saying not yet."

With defeat seeping in, Lillian sighed. "I thought we would enjoy the mansion together," she pleaded, feeling the fortress walls closing in. Escaping her grasp with a bitter smile, the hands clenched her cup of inspiration. "I don't understand why. We have plenty of room, like we planned."

Pushing back her sweet tea, Nevada rose. "It's for everyone's protection, Lillian. I promise to return soon," she said, hugging a dear soul that deserved much more from life. Pulling the massive oak door shut, she lingered on the covered porch. She pushed the sounds of the curtains rattling against the window behind her from her mind as she turned. Taking the steps two at a time, she headed into the storm.

*****

"Are you sure you'll be okay? I mean, this is the first time leaving town on your own since, you know…when?" asked Jack, loading the last suitcase in.

"Aww, isn't that sweet. You do love me," purred Nevada. "No, I'm good. I will be back as soon as possible. Believe me. Hey, while I'm gone, can you visit Lillian? She didn't take the news very well."

Wearing a "just whacked my thumb with a two-pound sledge-hammer" expression, he said, "Thanks a lot! You know how hard it is for me to escape her clutches."

"Pleeease!" She moved to seal the deal. "There may be something special in it for you when I return," she whispered with a teasing brow calling his name.

Hearing his name called for the gallows, he melted into her arms and placed his head in the noose. "Fine."

Gazing down upon Mother Earth, she sped to a destiny unknown. At peace as the clouds slipped by, she parted the cover. Gently separating the crisp new pages, she searched the tabs. Running a trembling finger down the page, seeking his words written so long ago. Grabbing the new Hi-Liter, she brought the words to life. Trailing a finger along, she guided her eyes across the psalm as the comforting winds blew her way. Ready to step into the lion's cage, she ushered the words to permeate her soul.

"It's one of my favorites too. Sorry. Didn't mean to intrude," said the man seated in 2B.

DIVINE MEMORIES

Jolted back to earth, she hadn't noticed him before. Snapping the Hi-Liter's cap back on, she pulled the earbud free. "Pardon me?"

"I'm sorry. I just said Psalm 91 was a favorite of mine." The infectious smile disarmed her.

"I find myself returning to it more and more these days. It does bring me comfort, especially verses 10 and 11. The thought that angels might truly be guarding me from harm helps me get through rough days," said Nevada.

"Had a few of those lately, have you?" asked the man.

"You wouldn't believe me if I told you. But strangely enough, a lot of good has come from those rough days."

"Even the finest swords have to be hammered first to bring out their best," he said, gathering up his papers.

"Well, if that's true, I should make a fine sword by now," said Nevada with a warm smile.

Slipping out of the row to head on up the aisle, he turned. "We think you will."

Watching his shoulders disappear through the curtain into coach, she tried to gather the strength to pursue. Starting behind her eyes, the sudden wave of fatigue played havoc with her senses. The jelly legs refused to cooperate, uninterested in pursuing him. As she was falling back, the words rattled around in her brain, rudely interrupted by the stewardess announcing the connecting flight information.

*****

Walking into her home away from home, the Sherry-Netherland was the one place she allowed for guilty pleasures. Tumbling down upon the bed, she knew she had better places to spend her money. But the allure of hiding in plain sight had its appeal. Clamping her eyes shut, releasing her feet from the bondage of the pumps, she stretched out on the California King. Once again surrounded by the hustle and bustle, a twinge of guilt filtered in as she took in all the city had to offer.

Tunneling under the throw pillow, she came to as the sun was calling it a day. She punched in the numbers, cancelling them as she let the phone slip through her fingers, bouncing off the throw pillow. He wasn't going anywhere, she thought. He'd still be there tomorrow.

Drawing a bath, escaping, she challenged the lavender to soak away the tension as she relaxed in the warm water. Using a big toe, she cracked open the hot water, allowing a loud trickle of water to drip down. Sliding down in the warm bath alone, one against many, she laid out the plans in her mind. Dropping the hot washcloth against her face, blanketing out the world, she mentally rehearsed the words.

With perfect timing, she snapped the blouse's last button just as room service arrived with her supper. The wine, being the first course up, went down easy. Finishing the sea bass, the evening invited the long shadows to blanket the city. Ushering the walls to close in, darkness dropped its veil over the city. Punching the pillows, with a power nap under her belt, sleep was elusive. She kept staring up at a ceiling that had been stared at for nearly a hundred years by weary travelers, and he came back to her.

With her nose buried in the Bible, she could have missed him taking a seat by her. It would be his words that finally made her abandon the bed. Pulling the lamp's chain, showering the lounge chair in light, she drew her feet up for a seat. Never venturing far from the psalm, the rest would remain foreign to her. The names and places carried little meaning to her. Only the author's words brought comfort.

Her soft words carried a message charged with fear as she held the book tight against her chest. Rivaling *Let's Make a Deal*, she cast off her burdens at his feet.

*****

With sunlight dancing in her eyes, she woke to another day. Stretching out a stubborn kink in her neck, she reached for the burner phone. Faced with crawling out from under the rock she had been hiding under, she punched in the last number.

"Lawrence?"

The gasp drew their attention. "Oh my god! You're alive! Where have you been? No, don't answer that," said Lawrence rapid-fire, drawing in air.

"Whoa, whoa, whoa. Slow down. I'm fine but I want to meet."

The silence telegraphed his fears. "You must be close?"

"Very," she said, clipping the emotions off.

Rubbing a silver temple fraught with worry, he asked, "Okay. Where?"

"Room 2103, 2:00 p.m. My favorite hotel. Come alone."

*****

The crisp knock, brought a twinge of fear. He had aged. Couldn't even call it salt-and-pepper anymore.

With the mandatory peck out of the way, he stepped back. "You look good, all things considered."

Letting his fingers slip through her hand, she wished she could say the same. "How have you been?" she asked, noticing the tremor.

The words no longer flowed easily between them. "Oh, you know how it is. The government has been hounding me for you, and the shareholders are on a constant rampage. It wears you down," said Lawrence, dropping down on the lounge chair.

Twisting the cap free from the bottle, she said, "No picnic on my end either." She was cycling through feelings she needed to set free.

Scratching a wrist that didn't itch, he stared at the floor. "They made me believe you were dead."

"Sorry to disappoint the scum. But I'm back."

Tortured by his weakness, he prepared the tale for release. "I think I led them to you." His tired draw offered up no further clues as he waited for her response.

With a lifelong friendship under attack, she felt the air slip out, crushing her spirit as only he could. Stacking all his good up against his next few words, she held back the legion of pain that waited in the wings to shine. Fading inward as her daggers spawned little love his way, he reached for a hand that would never trust him blindly again. He felt the sting of that ill-fated decision long ago as her hand wavered.

"You think or you know?" she asked, eyes reduced to mere slits. Brushing the hand away, she was waiting for his confession with one hand on the spigot, ready to unleash her anger.

Drying a clammy hand across his suit trousers, the betrayal snagged his heart on the way out. Facing a regret from two decades of silence, he would be making a down payment for it today. Fumbling with the gold tie tack, he sawed off the gangplank, tumbling from her life.

"I knew," he said, tasting the bitter words as the confession tumbled out for all to hear.

Chucking the water bottle into the air, it splattered against the vanity mirror. "I mean that little to you! Lawrence, they hunted me down like a filthy animal, shooting me in the head twice. I didn't know who I was for months. Thanks, Lawrence." Collapsing under the betrayal, she shuddered at the thought of falling into arms she had once trusted so completely.

Drawing back his arms, pinching a quivering lip, he said, "Vada, they were going to kill me if I turned the phone off. I tried to warn you when you called." Gathering up his jacket, he knew the damage had been done. "I'm truly sorry. I'll turn my resignation in Monday."

"No."

Hoping for a crack to open up, he asked, risking a glance her way, "If you say so. But why?"

"I have my reasons."

Looping the jacket over his arm, he delivered the bombshell. "Okay. One last thing. I am hearing through the grapevine that Charles and the Bankhill brothers are trying to get a deal to turn state's evidence against you."

Hiding fears behind the vicious smirk, she said, "Lawrence, you are friends with Director Kliner, aren't you?"

Witnessing her transformation, the question paved the road for his return in her life. "You talking FBI director Kliner? Why, Nevada?" asked Lawrence, returning to the sofa.

"Can you set up a discreet meeting with him and not reveal my identity?" asked Nevada, wringing the last bit of good out of Lawrence.

"When and where?"

Sweeping up the smashed water bottle, she shrugged. "His choosing."

"Okay. He happens to be in the city this week."

Ushering him to the door, she said, "Make it happen. I'll be around."

*****

She was impressed with the new look. He had used the money wisely. The new glass doors welcomed the visitors as they entered the building. The Sunday morning crowd had grown since her last visit. By the time he unleashed his sermon, the pews were full. Still sporting a mop of unruly hair no comb could tame, he flashed the boyish grin upon the flock. With unbridled enthusiasm, he garnered their attention flawlessly.

Wrapping the sermon up in a tidy bow, he issued his standard invitation to accept the Lord as he spied her near the back. Had she been there all along? The toothy smile reappeared as he tried to focus on his closing prayer. Brushing off the flock afterward, he waded through the crowd, blocking her escape.

"Good morning," he offered, waiting for her to slow the retreat and turn.

Stepping out of the exit line, she faced her toughest adversary and allowed a smile to blossom. "Oh, good morning," she said.

"What? You weren't gonna even say hi or bye?"

Overdressed for the local clientele, she attracted more attention than a four-car pileup on the interstate. Letting the choir ladies pass, she endured the gawkers, each turning the spit on the barbecue of gossip as they filled in the facts about the newcomer. It would be a bonanza for the lunch crowd later on at the cafe.

She raked her head back and forth, hoping the words were gonna have a truer sound. "Oh no, no. I was going to come back and see if you were free for lunch."

"It's noon," said Pastor Rick, letting his shirt sleeve slide back in place.

She was trying to find something for her hands to do other than get in her way. She hated the way he outmaneuvered her. "Well, so it is. I am hungry."

Drizzling ranch dressing on his salad, he fired off the opening shot. "What's it been…almost a year now?"

Taking a healthy bite off the breadstick, she asked, feigning innocence, "Since?"

"You know. Since your shadow last graced our presence."

She took her time on the breadstick as he wasted his time trying to throw a loop around her soul. "Oh, that. Yeah, once again your fault," she said, double-dipping the stick in cheese sauce.

"Hmph. How on earth is that remotely my fault," he scoffed.

"You remember our last meeting?"

Hoping his collar could take the heat, he said, "You're hard to forget."

Releasing her grip on her fork, she allowed it to pole-vault lettuce over the side of the bowl. "Remember that prayer? Well, uh… uh, I don't even know where to start."

"Why don't—"

Launching a hand, she said, "I know. I know. From the beginning."

Heading for seconds on the salad bar, he said, "Have it for me when I get back."

Why would you pair me with him? He's so pushy, she asked herself. Watching his ease with the locals, each so accepting of him regardless of their faith. Or lack of faith. Lending a hand to the little girls fighting to do the least amount of damage to the salad bar decor brought smiles from both. Had her money opened doors and hearts for him? The thought warmed her.

Returning with a naked salad soon to be drowned in ranch, the pastor waited, finally pointing the pitchfork her way. "I'm not eating another bite till you open up," he demanded, dropping the fork with a clink.

"Fine. I'm going to describe your way of life first. Then mine."

Answering around piece of pepperoni pizza, he mumbled, "Whatever trips your trigger."

"Okay. If I get off the mark, just let me know," she added, smirking slightly.

Shooing her into action, he said, "Fire away. Tell me what you think." He was amused at the little challenger.

DIVINE MEMORIES

"I think you see people all day long, hear their problems, say a thousand prayers a month. Can't recall what the last three prayers were that you feverishly sent skyward. Defend God to the nth degree. Believe you have witnessed miracles, but deep—and I mean deep down—they could have possibly been extreme coincidences." Putting it in park, she awaited his fiery speech.

It took thirty seconds to eat ten seconds' worth of pizza. The words burned. He let the smug drip off for a while. *God, why would you send her to me?* he wondered. Forcing the bile down with a sip of Mountain Dew, forcing his eyes to see past her beauty, he noticed a difference for the first time. "I hate that you might be right."

"*Hate* is a strong word. I'm sorry if—"

Shoving back from his plate piled high with pizza, he said, "I couldn't think of any better word for it. *Hate* seemed too weak."

"Don't beat yourself up too much. Wait till you hear my story." Munching on a pepperoni ripped off an abandoned pizza bone, she continued, "I've cussed God out so much over the last twenty years, he probably seeks out therapy afterwards. I ask for the same thing each time and never change the prayer. It's so monotonous, he probably sits up there mumbling the words along with me. It's no wonder he's never answered the phone when I call up there. Until lately."

He unrolled the napkin from the silverware and retrieved a new fork. The lights were getting ready to come on as the curtain started to rise. Attacking his salad, he was glad she had moved on with her imperfections. "Tell me about it."

Caressing the wound on the side of her head, she fell back to the difficult months. "I learned a valuable lesson."

"How so?"

"Well, for starters, don't ask a guy for a gentle nudge in life when he has the ability to move a mountain or hang a star. Unless you're ready. I don't think he knows his own strength sometimes."

"How did he answer you finally?" asked Pastor Rick, halting the advance of his slice of pizza.

Searching out a cherry tomato, she stabbed it finally. Stalling near her lips, she said, "The difference between you and me. You ask for miracles. I am one."

"Come on, girl! Don't be bashful!" he demanded, excited at her revelation.

"Let me see how my week goes. I don't want to place you in danger."

Cracking a smile intended to dislodge details, he muttered, "Come on. You opened this show."

With a growing list of broken lives mounting, she wouldn't be cajoled. "It hasn't ended well for those that know my gift so far. Don't push it."

Pulling the check closer, he nodded. "You probably know best. Maybe next time."

She held a hand out. "Give me that. I make more in a day than…well, give it to me."

"When will I see you again?"

"Depends on how my next meeting goes."

*****

Arriving two hours early, she scoured the crowd for his ring of security. Taking a table near the exit, she shifted in her seat as the waiter came for her order again.

"Can I get you another drink while you wait for your other party?" asked the waiter, reaching for her glass.

Beating his hand to the glass, she said, "No, I'm good." Mindful of her DNA, she tugged the glove on tighter. Adjusting the wig, she was rocking the sunglasses like nobody's business.

An hour later, they fanned out into the crowd. They melted into the scene, ready to spring at the first hint of trouble. Making a low-key entrance, he took a table in the middle, far from any exits.

Lawrence had come through. Now, to seal the deal, she would need to walk a careful line, placing her freedom at risk. Taking up her water glass, she slipped through the tables of the open cafe.

Swinging around at the last second, she said, "Director Kliner?"

Standing up slowly to alert the team, he nodded. "Yes? Do we have an appointment?"

DIVINE MEMORIES

She scanned the crowd; there was no movement from the agents yet. She would need to move quickly. Dropping down across from Kliner, she could feel their eyes boring holes in her back. They were lurking in the shadows, itching to pounce.

"Yes, we do," said Nevada, placing the water glass down in front of her.

Admiring the glass, Director Kliner asked with half a grin, "DNA?"

"Exactly. Wondered why I had the privilege of being the only patron to be served in a glass, not plastic," she said, scanning him with eyes filled with a mixture of confidence mingled with fear.

He finished the last of his coffee. "What can I do for you, ma'am?"

Building up to this moment, she hoped her knife was sharp enough to cut through the mountain of red tape most would be dragged through. "Director Kliner, is there any crime the FBI knows who did it and can't prove it? Or an incident that holds a special meaning to you? I mean, one that you would give anything to solve. One that keeps you up at night, a festering cancer that you beg to have stamped out of your life."

Looking past her shoulder, he was suddenly more interested in the men in the shadows.

"Why?" asked Kliner.

She was dying to turn and survey the crowd. "Director Kliner, if you make any attempt to identify me, you will never hear my offer, and it will be at a great loss to you," warned Nevada, throwing a shoulder back in defiance. "Do you have a case in mind?"

Somewhere between curious and annoyed, he eyed his table companion. He was trying to fit her into a category he could understand. She violated his norms. "Why should I waste my time on you?" asked Kliner, removing the lemon peel from his ice water.

"Funny. I was just thinking the same about you," she sniped back, refusing to give ground.

"I have a cold case in mind. But after forty-eight years, what could you do that the FBI hasn't?"

183

Starting at the pit of her stomach, hope rose at his words. Tamping down the emotions of breaching his trust, she needed more. "Give me the details of the case, and I'll tell you exactly what I need and what I'll accomplish with it."

Ordering another drink, he shook his head. "This is crazy. If it wasn't for Lawrence vouching for you." Drawing down on thirty-five years of crime fighting, he seared her with eyes that missed few deceptions. "I don't know you, and you're asking for what?"

"Reveal the case details. I solve the crime and then we speak about future cooperation."

Catching the eye of a waiter lurking nearby, Director Kliner said, "Baker, release the squad. I'm good to go here now."

Stunned as the three waiters revealed their positions, Nevada was caught off guard at the depths the FBI had prepared for her arrival. It rocked her back on her heels. Holding on tight to the glass, she met his gaze, giving a casual glance at agents handing aprons back in to management. "All for me? You needn't have bothered," she scoffed.

"Lawrence was mysterious on the phone. I don't live with mystery."

"Before you think of the details, make sure it involves something no one is familiar with. I want no confusion when I blow your mind."

Kliner did his best to clear a throat of forty-eight years of shame and anguish. The heat of the dance floor and the sounds of those voices having the time of their lives so long ago drifted back. Dressed in their best suits, paired up with girls twirling around the small gym floor in overpriced dresses, the world was right.

"Before I go any further, could you explain what makes you think you have more capability than the FBI?"

Raising an eyebrow at the door being opened, Nevada said, "It would be more of a demonstration." She scooted closer. "I can do that."

Leaning back, squeezing the life out of the lemon peel, he said, "You can do that right here?"

Channeling all her energy, she refused to blink first. "Yes. My gift is extraordinary."

Spreading his arms out, he knocked the napkin off the table. "Give it your best shot 'cause it's the only one you are going to get."

She slid closer, now an arm's length away. He seemed younger than his sixty-two years.

Comfortable in a position of power, he kept a close eye on her hands as she came closer.

She said, "I want you to think of a time when you have experienced that incident or major regret in your life. One that you are sure would not be known to me. Preferably one unknown by the FBI or anyone connected to your public life. Make it an incident so secret and personal that you will have no doubt of my abilities. Let me know when you have it in your mind."

Shifting in his seat, he tugged on his tie. "I have one."

"Okay. I want you to think back to the incident and recall the details. That's it, go back to the moment. Immerse yourself in it. Reach way back and recall the sights and sounds. Take your time. Recall their names and faces. Spell out the most important name in your mind. Pull back and scan the room. Now pull back again and look at the location from afar. Go ahead and bring in the problem causing the anguish. Include anyone responsible in your mind for the incident. Hold it right there," instructed Nevada as she lightly touched a nail to Kliner's hand. "Go back to the person responsible. How is the party responsible and why?" Her silence signaled the end of the torture.

With eyes pinched tightly, he left the small sidewalk cafe and immersed himself down into the quagmire of hell. A hell that had tormented one of the most powerful men in America for the past four decades. Rubbing his eyes, he said, "Well, great. Let me guess. You're what, a clairvoyant? Fortune teller?" asked Kliner, unimpressed by the performance so far.

"No, sir. Mine is a gift from God. One that I unknowing prayed for," offered Nevada.

Giving his security detail marching orders, he muttered, "Head out."

Rising to repair the bridge, she said, "Director, I can—"

185

"Stop!" Ripping the check from the table, Kliner said, "Thanks for making me late for my daughter's graduation." Sandwiched between his security detail, Nevada was already a distant memory.

"I-I can find Jaylene!" stammered Nevada.

Looking more like Keystone cops instead of elite FBI agents, they bumped into each other as the boss slammed on the brakes. Kliner screeched to a halt at the mention of her name, his back ramrod stiff as he pivoted toward her voice. "I'm not done here yet. You guys fan back out."

"I need but one agent to find her body. You've had forty-eight years to find her. Give me forty-eight minutes alone with Gant, and I'll promise you with all my heart, I'll bring her home after all these years," she pleaded.

"You know her name…his name too?" asked the king of the pessimists and the embodiment of the untrusting. He dragged the chair back out, caught somewhere south of sorrow filled. "Just know from this moment on, young lady. If you are a fraud, you may disappear from society," said Kliner, smooth as silk, under his breath.

Unfazed, she held out a gloved hand in friendship. "Where do we start? I can see memories."

Rubbing a chin that had missed a shave for this meeting, he said, "Tell me mine and we are partners."

Running her finger along the edge of the water glass, eyes cast downward, she said, "You promise?"

"I don't make promises."

Climbing back in the driver's seat, she asked, "Does anybody know how you feel about these memories? A wife or any confidant?"

Scooching in closer, now inches from the only hope he has had in years, he replied, "Not a soul."

The flecks of gold in her eyes sparkled as the words paralyzed his mind. "Jaylene Montgomery was your first love. You agonized for days, searching for the courage to ask her. It was your first school dance, and you were so proud to be seen with her. She was wearing a mint-green dress with flowers bordering the hem. You got jealous at her for dancing with other boys. You made a decision to not escort her back home after the dance. She was abducted and was never seen again. The one and only suspect was a mail carrier named Gant. To this day, you have never forgiven yourself for abandoning her."

"Son of a," exclaimed Kliner, staring back at 127 pounds of spookiness. "Can you really find her? Please…please don't jerk my chain," he begged, his face etched in agony.

"If he did it and knows where she is buried, I'll solve the crime in less the forty-eight minutes, not forty-eight years."

The driving force behind his career and climb to the top was her haunting memory. "What does the FBI have that you need?"

"Assign one agent to accompany me to go interview Gant. And one other thing."

"Yes?" he asked, his voice reduced to a raspy whisper, one coated with desperation.

"Give me your word to make no attempt to uncover my true identity until I am ready to reveal it."

Making it his business to never be outmaneuvered or out-thought, the challenge came with a sacred bond. One covered in dust from lack of use. One he used so sparingly, he had no memory of its last use. Thinking back to an innocent fourteen-year-old scrawny girl with big brown eyes, struck down cruelly before she had a chance to fulfill her dreams of being a veterinarian when she grew up, he said, "You have my word. If you bring her home, I want to use you to scorch the earth."

She dropped the water glass in her purse. "Can you put that on your tab?" Brushing past the last agent, she stepped back. "Get ready for a phone call for you to come running."

16

Breaking the last ties with the city had been a hard pill to swallow. Lying next to all she loved, the gentle hand caressed her arm. Did she really have the right to ask? Committing to travel down an unknown path, had she bitten off more than she could chew? The burdens of the future inched closer, weighing heavily upon her. The gift gave her unquestionable abilities, but it was still missing.

Has God forgotten me? she wondered. Slipping out from under his arm to snag her phone, she headed to a safe place.

Confirming the final details, she heard his toe crack as he tried to sneak up behind her.

"Who was that? Your boyfriend?" Jack asked, snapping up out of a crouch that would embarrass your average tiger.

Dropping the phone down on the table, she replied, "Would you really care? Get dressed. You'll scare the neighbor's dog."

He was trying to tame his hair with his fingers. "We don't have neighbors."

She popped some bread down in the toaster. "For your information, that was the moving company."

"Huh?"

Taking the corner off a grape pop-tart, she sighed. "That's right, a moving company. I closed out my penthouse in New York, and I'm having everything delivered to the mansion."

Releasing the refrigerator door as if it were on fire, he failed with the balancing act as the stick of butter went splat on the floor. "Are you serious?"

Executing a flawless pirouette, she said, "Meet the newest Shallimar resident."

Stepping around the mound of butter, Jack pulled everything he loved into his arms. "Girl, you're weird but lovely. I knew you were hooked on my home cooking but didn't know you were ready for that."

Pulling the hammer back, she armed her defenses, shoving him away. She let her eyebrows scream her thoughts. "Problem?"

He put the pin back in her grenade. "Absolutely not!"

"Good answer, buster." Scrunching up a lip, she pulled him back in. Her words were soaked in hope with a dash of love. "I'm going to make this my home forever. I need you to stay by my side through everything."

"You know I'm unemployed now. Right?"

"Yeaaah…we need to talk about that."

Licking a dry lip as he cradled her chin, he asked, "Problem?"

Pulling free, dodging the question better than a good politician, she said, "The eggs are going to burn. Let's eat and talk it over."

Somewhere between the weather and the latest talk of a new restaurant moving in downtown, he got the train back on the tracks. "Let's hear it."

With bets already placed, she worried her hole cards were weak. She looked out the window as a pair of cardinals fought for the rights to the bird feeder. Two against the world, secretly championing for a victory over the blue jay as the cardinals teamed up against him. Jealous of their love, each standing shoulder to shoulder, fighting to survive. Would he stay by her side? Could he stand up against whatever came their way?

She flinched at his touch as he tugged her hand closer. Dropping her shields, lowering the walls around a heart that had experienced little love, she asked as the blue jay flew away in defeat, "Are you going to marry me someday?"

"Look at me."

Shielding her eyes from the sunlight as the clouds parted, she looked younger than her years. "I'm sorry. I just—"

"Sit back down." The screech of the chair being dragged across the floor drove the cat southbound into the pantry. *Yesterday's perfume is still there*, he noted as their cheeks pressed tightly. "Nevada

Barrington, I've wanted to marry you since I first laid eyes on you. Remember my fight with the Coke machine?" He chuckled, feeling her smile form against his cheek. "Best night of my life. When I thought you were leaving, I...I was lost."

Clamping an arm around her anchor to planet Earth, she whispered, "Hold me." Trading a little trust in the name of love, she held on for dear life.

Being in love with a master manipulator was work as he realized she had conveniently danced around her latest mystery. Pushing back, Jack said, "Okay, dork. Let's really hear what's the problem. Answer your phone first."

With the final buzzer going off, she had run too much time off the clock. A glance at the ID launched her out of the chair. Pacing the floor, she smiled at the love of her life across the kitchen table. Using words sparingly as she agreed on the final plans, he was ready to pounce with the questions as she clicked off the call.

"Let me guess. That was the movers again."

"No. It was the director of the FBI."

Giving her points for originality, he snorted. "Pfft. You're such a liar." Rubbing his extensive interviewing skills in her face, he asked, "What's his name then?"

"Ronald Kliner."

Too fast. With his smile losing some steam, he analyzed her deadpan expression. She was not above jerking his chain, and he might be losing his touch. It was a toss-up as he held her stare; she was sneaky. "Okay. What did he need from little ole you?"

"Well, that's what I was just getting ready to talk to you about."

Plopping the gallon of milk on the table, not even wasting time to imagine the potential bombshell, Jack managed a shrug. "I'm all ears."

"Well, have a seat first."

"Oh geez. What's this gonna be?"

She tethered her life to his as she interlocked their fingers together. *Already skittish, better to know now*, she thought. Stripping her speech of the sugar, she voted for black and white. "I think I am going to be indicted on federal charges soon. I had a meeting set up with Director Kliner and proposed an offer for cooperation at a later date."

Fear tingled through her fingers as he watched her implode. "Is that what the trip back east was about?" he asked.

"Mostly."

Letting the answer slide, he pushed. "What do you have to do?"

Licking a tear from her lip, she said, "My-my plan is to solve a cold case he is desperate to solve and then offer to help further for complete immunity on any crimes I might have committed."

He was used to working with her puzzles handicapped, never failing to be shy a few pieces. "Where do I fit in?"

"If I accomplish this first mission, I want you by my side for the others. But I have one condition."

Jack rolled his eyes for the umpteenth time in the last hour. "Conditions? From you, that's hard to believe."

Going to town with a tissue, she replaced the tears with a fragile smile. "I want you to have that suitcase of money for helping me."

"No!"

Yanking back, she said, "Don't piss me off. You're taking it."

She reminded him of a timber rattler he had accidentally stepped on once, already coiled and ready to strike. Why couldn't he learn? "Why?"

"Haven't I derailed plans you had before meeting me? Please take the money. I'll feel better knowing, if something happens to me, you will be okay."

Trying for a dodge, he said, "I'll think about it."

"Good! You have about forty-five minutes before my jet lands at the local airport. We're going to handle it."

"Nevada!"

"La la la!" Plugging fingers in her ears, she marched down the hall. "You need to get out more. Pack some nice clothes. Scratch that. You don't own any. We'll get you new clothes in New York," she yelled back to the shell-shocked warrior who was nursing a serious injury back at the kitchen table.

"Nevada, get back here!" he yelled with wasted breath.

"You've got forty-four—no, forty-three minutes. Chop-chop!" she taunted, rounding the corner and lugging the suitcase.

*****

Strolling arm in arm down the busy Park Avenue sidewalk, her backyard stretched far from his. Meandering from one shop to another, she guided him through her city life. Setting up the account with Mellon's Wealth Management, he saw for the first time the awesome power she wielded. Mingled somewhere between exhilarating and exhausting, he survived day two—a day full of shopping and frolicking in the city.

He snagged the door of the nearest bar. "I'm ready to drop. Let's go in for a drink," he whined.

With a pitiful shake of her head, she sighed. "Lightweight. This has only been a mild excursion."

He dropped the coldest beer of the day on the coaster. "It's all lovely, but I am ready to sleep in my own bed again. Don't get me wrong. This weekend has been great, but when does our flight leave?" asked Jack.

"Thanks, Jack. You've been a good sport." Removing the swizzle stick, she sampled the martini. "Our flight leaves when I tell it to."

Tilting back the best hops he had drank in a long time, he grunted. "I'll drink to that."

The whirlwind affair had his head spinning as they headed back to Shallimar. Riding in luxury, he squeezed the leather as he gazed down on what he believed should be Ohio or maybe Indiana by now. Watching her work the phone, he couldn't even fathom such a possibility a few months ago. Jet setting from one world to another—he wondered if such a foreigner would always fit in her life.

Shattering the pity party, the pilot made an announcement over the intercom. "Ms. Barrington, we're fifteen minutes out from Noble County Regional Airport," advised Captain Calloway.

"Thank you."

"Ma'am, you and your guest need to buckle up for landing. This is more plane than their set up to normally land here. We'll be braking pretty hard," warned Calloway.

DIVINE MEMORIES

Nevada patted her seat. "Hey, come over here."

Snapping his seat belt, he asked, "Get everything wrapped up?"

Adjusting her seat belt tighter, she replied, "Just about. I'll be dropping you off and immediately flying out to Iowa to meet with an FBI agent, Calvin Jenkins. I have a meeting set up for one o'clock."

"Then what?"

"Playing it by ear after that."

Stepping off the jet at Shallimar, he could already feel the loss. With a last-minute wave, she braced for the takeoff. Leaning against the bumper of his Silverado, the Gulfstream's engines roared as the pilot released the brake. Sixteen seconds later, she was airborne, wheels up, streaking westward. Dipping into the clouds, she disappeared from him once more. He had all his eggs in one expensive basket.

*****

Dropping out of the sky ninety minutes later, taxiing into Sioux Gateway Airport, Nevada saw the note tucked under the briefcase. He was so predictably unpredictable. Seated in the cabin of a jet with a price tag north of eighty million, she had offered him a glimpse of her former life. Overwhelmed by his fear of abandonment, her eyes consumed the words, his fears were unwarranted. She stowed the note away for a conversation later at the kitchen table. They had lived in doubt long enough.

Twenty miles out of Jaime, Iowa, she reached for the phone. On the third ring, the voice of Agent Jenkins came on. The pleasantry was deceiving. It was a must for all of them, she thought as she recalled all the government-sponsored fishing expeditions in her office over the years.

Exiting the cab at the Monrovia Club, she grabbed a table near the back. He'd never do for any undercover work, she thought as he entered the establishment. He reeked of FBI in the suit and short-cropped hair. Nevada let him scan the room awkwardly before letting him off the hook.

Barely thirty, I bet, she surmised as he waded through the noon crowd. Cuter up close but still FBI to the bone.

193

"Ms. Parker?"

"Just Parker," she corrected.

Looking up from the notepad, he said, "Is that your first or—"

"Both. For now, that is."

Already in the hole, he ordered a drink. Tasting the sweet tea, Jenkins took a hard look at the informant. "Okay. Parker, how do we want to proceed?"

"I want to know about you personally first."

Only the outer surface betrayed his youth. With nine years on the job, he had dealt with his share of ugliness on this spinning rock we call home. Her file was scant for details of her first encounter with Director Kliner except for notations of rather unusual abilities.

"We don't work that way," he said, refusing to blink first.

Ordering a second martini, she smiled. "I have to know you can keep up with me. When I open up this ball game, I will demand to only work with one agent. Will it be you? That's what I need to know."

"Not sure that's a good idea."

"Where you from? Got a family? Kids? Wife? Your career in FBI…those sorts of things. And then I will open up too."

Already ditching the standard policy of dictating the interview, he opted for concessions. "If I do, will that include a discussion of all your abilities I see mentioned in your file?"

Rocking her head to the side, she allowed a piercing glare to accompany her words. "If you wish."

Bouncing both index fingers off his upper lip, he dove, leaping off the cliff. "Married, one little girl age five. Work out of the Sioux City office. Been with the bureau nine years and plan on making it my career. I believe in God first, family next, and FBI a close third," said Agent Jenkins, now unknowingly owned by the lioness.

"That's' going to come in handy for you later. My turn, I suppose? Lay your hand flat on the table, palm down."

"I want details of—"

"Shh. They're coming. I want you to close your eyes and recall any memory of anything that would affect your career. Perhaps a case you may perceive as damaging or an action that you hope never sees the light. That's it. Concentrate on that day," she murmured softly,

DIVINE MEMORIES

allowing her words to invoke his worst fear. Releasing the pressure, she raised her nail from his hand.

"Well?"

"In my world, you would be considered squeaky clean. But you aren't in my world, are you, Agent Jenkins? You lied during your polygraph. You failed to mention the fact you stole money from your neighbor's lockbox in your youth," she said to the saddest brown eyes staring back.

"I'm a good and honest agent," he offered, seeing the lioness emerge before him.

"For my silence, you will never reveal my gift to anyone other than Director Kliner."

Untrusting to a voice rampant with fear, he silently slid the dingy dog-eared file boldly labeled Jaylene Merci Montgomery Abduction across the table. Crumbling dreams of a long and storied career danced through his brain as she calmly pored through the forty-plus-year investigation.

"Here is what I worked up for a cover story when we meet Gant," said Nevada, sliding the scenario back across the table.

Scooping up the paper, he said, "Let's meet here tomorrow about eleven. Gant's place is up the road a few miles," said Agent Jenkins.

*****

Camping out across the highway at the Iowa Motor Inn for the night, Nevada longed for Jack's touch. Marooned on a deserted wide spot in the road, the demons began their assault. Restless, she kept the moon company, watching the sunrise finally take the handoff, ushering another day down upon the people. Grabbing a coffee and stale Danish from the highly touted complimentary breakfast, she trudged across the highway, more zombie than human.

Agent Jenkins was prompt if nothing else, arriving on the dot. Same suit, different man. He was not quite sure which path should be followed with the woman known to him simply as Parker. Would she be a direct line back to the director? How long would she honor her words?

195

"Good morning. You look tired," he said.

Breaking the morning sleep crust, she fired back, "Me? You must not have any mirrors at your place."

Letting the file thud to the table, he grunted. "Got a lot riding on this one," said Agent Jenkins, hoping the Tums kicked in soon.

She let the sugar dissolve as she stirred. "I know I rattled you yesterday. I'm sorry for that. When you see God channel his will through me, you'll understand why I demand your secrecy. I'm not here to derail your life or career."

Grateful for the pass in life, he nodded. "What do you think we can accomplish this first day?"

"I've got forty-eight minutes to find her," said Nevada, taking a cautious sip.

"Who?" asked Jenkins.

"Jaylene Montgomery. Who else? Hey, you're spilling your coffee," she said, wanting to reach out and slam his jaw back in place.

"You're joking, right? I mean, she's been missing almost fifty years."

Swinging her head to the side, offering little in clarity, she cradled her coffee cup. "Nope. Forty-eight minutes from the time we introduce ourselves to Gant."

Taking a dim view on stupidity, he hung a label out to dry for later. "I'm ready whenever you are."

*****

Jaime, Iowa, boasting 240 souls, had grown little over the last fifty years. With the shoe factory going bust back in the eighties, opportunity shifted elsewhere, leaving only the diehards to scrape out a living in the sleepy village.

Located on the edge of town, the Gant place was unremarkable. The single-story brown house revealed little, its immaculate lawn spoiled only by the crumbling sidewalk. Hunched over a riding mower near the unattached garage was the target of interest. Straightening up at the sound of company, he shielded his eyes.

DIVINE MEMORIES

"Cleaning her up for the winter?" Agent Jenkins asked with a disarming smile.

Fighting to straighten back up, Gant said, eyeing the agents, "Hope so. Can I help ya?"

Even after nine years, the jitters still surfaced on first contact. Agent Jenkins asked, "Are you Ray Gant? Mason Ray Gant?"

Dropping the oily rag down in the bin, he nodded. "Yeah. Who's asking?"

"I'm Agent Jenkins with the FBI. And this is, uh, Agent Parker."

Scrunching up a face full of wrinkles that took seventy-five years to accumulate, Gant said, "Awwww! You boys been here three, maybe four, times, hassling me over this case."

Surrendering, his hands raised high, Jenkins chuckled. "I know. I know. I'm just here to push paper and, hopefully, find a way to permanently close your file. Hear us out, and we'll get out of your hair," he said.

"At least, the agents are getting better looking," said Gant, running his eyes over Agent Parker. "Let's go in the kitchen. My neighbors are nosy enough already." Then he started hobbling away.

"Fine, lead the way. Anybody else home?"

"Just me."

Hoping her senses weren't affected too much by the cat urine, Nevada shooed the cat off the chair. Unshaven and smelling of gasoline, the thought of his ending the life of Jaylene with those dirty hands turned her stomach.

His eyes raked her up and down.

The animal should be in a cage, she thought.

Agent Jenkins said, "Okay. Mr. Gant, let me explain. Since the new administration took over, we have had a new directive to close out as many cold cases as possible. To do so, we have to make a final act of investigation. By that, I mean something not done up to this date. As I look at the file, I see only verbal interviews have been done. So, in theory, we have to do something besides that. Possibly a search or something similar."

Fidgeting with the salt shaker, Gant said, "So you want to toss my house?"

197

Sinking closer to his good ole boy mode, Jenkins said, cutting loose with a sloppy grin, "Oh! Oh no, Ray. Just enough of a search so I'm not lying to my superiors. You know how it is working for Uncle Sam."

Weary of government promises and intrusions, the sooner he got rid of the agents, the better. "And I won't get any more visits from the FBI?" Gant inquired.

Yanking hard to set the hook, Jenkins said, "Exactly!"

"Well then. Get it over with."

"Mr. Gant, we need to review the file first," said Nevada.

"She does speak," teased Gant.

Ignoring the barb, she went right for the throat. "I see on the night of Jaylene's disappearance, you were seen walking in the area that night."

"No crime against that," hissed Gant.

"Since then, you have been interviewed three times, and your version of the facts that night remain the same, correct?"

"Bet your ass you're correct."

Summoning all her might, she needed to knock it out of the park. Twenty-two minutes already on scene, and with time slipping, she had nothing. "Mr. Gant, during the search, we will be looking for articles of any kind we deem as potential evidence. To include Jaylene Montgomery. Do you understand?"

"Yep."

"Mr. Gant, imagine yourself as the person most responsible for Jaylene's disappearance. Where would you hide her body? Yeah, run that through your head a minute. What about taking a souvenir from her body, maybe an article of clothing or something else. How would you kill her?" asked Nevada, reaching over and brushing her nail against the edge of his hand.

"Lady, I got nothing to say. Just search my house and get out." Gant snarled, rubbing the edge of his hand.

"Sorry. I know this dredges up old memories. Let us go out to the car and get the form for you to sign, and we can do a quick search and leave you in peace," offered Agent Jenkins.

As they were huddling by the car, Nevada whispered, "Listen carefully, Jenkins. You will be looking for a rolled-up old tube sock

DIVINE MEMORIES

with two red stripes in his bedroom dresser. Hidden inside should be what I think they used to call an ID bracelet. It will have Jaylene's name inscribed on it. Grab it and let me have it."

Stunned, operating on a quart low of belief, he said, "Are you sure? I mean, you only—"

"Hurry. I only have fifteen minutes left."

"Have a good pow-wow out there?" Gant snickered, staring a hole through Nevada.

"Yeah. I got the job of babysitting you while my partner wastes his time searching your, uh, castle. I don't mind though," said Nevada, itching to make that call for the cavalry.

With eight minutes to spare, Jenkins called out, "Parker, can I see you in here? I need a signature for the paperwork."

She palmed the bracelet as she witnessed the form. Hidden from all who loved her these last forty-eight years, it would soon get its chance to speak for Jaylene.

Stepping outside, pressing the SEND button, she launched the first picture in her campaign. It was no less powerful than the launching of an ICBM as the target would soon be totally obliterated. The response was immediate as her phone chimed.

"Come running." The words rushed out filled with a bittersweet memory as she saw Jaylene's final resting place in her mind.

"I gave her that bracelet before the dance that evening. Do you know where she lies?" asked the hushed voice, haunted by years of pain.

"Director, I know exactly where she is resting."

"I am airborne already and just diverted our flight. I'll be there in less than two hours."

"Bring a team to exhume her body."

"Oh, don't worry. That sleepy part of the world will have something to talk about for a long time. Parker, I...uh...I want to thank you for everything. Her parents would thank you too. They died never knowing where.... I'm sorry. I never thought I would see this day," said Director Kliner, choking back emotions bottled up for decades.

"Hurry. She's waited long enough."

17

Calling in for additional support, the trio of responding Iowa troopers welcomed the assignment. The burly trooper, two weeks out from putting his papers in, had little love for Gant. He thought back to all the years his oldest sister suffered a broken heart at her best friend in the world being lost forever. He smiled as he showed little mercy, ignoring Gant's protest as he complained of bum knees from packing mail for thirty-five years.

"You guys got nothing on me," complained Gant.

Opening his palm, allowing the bracelet to see the light of the day, Jenkins said, "Beg to differ, Gant."

"I found that one day, packing the mail down Mulberry Street," huffed Gant, twisting his bent leg out straight.

Rubbing the tarnish from the inscriptions, Jenkins said, "Let's just see what this says, Gant. Well, look at that."

The cheap engraved inscription shone brightly now, screaming out the single word plain as day: *Jaylene*.

"Oh, let's see what it says on the back," Jenkins continued. "Well, lookee there. '*Love Ronnie*,' again plain as day. Gant, got any idea who Ronnie might be?"

His eyes pinned to the floor, Gant kept toeing the table leg. "Nope. Don't care."

"Ronnie's my boss, Gant. That's right. Director Ronald Kliner of the Federal Bureau of Investigations. You killed his first love, idiot."

Yanking a leg over his knee on the second try, Gant said, "He can be president for all I care. No warrant means you all need to leave, pronto."

Twirling the bracelet around his index finger, Jenkins chuckled. "Gant, got some terrible news for you. The warrant and Ronnie

DIVINE MEMORIES

are both on the way, along with about two-thirds of the FBI agents assigned to the area. And a convoy of mobile crime labs thrown in just for kicks."

"Some kid's jewelry I found don't mean jack!" screamed Gant, spraying a stream out across the table.

Walking into the kitchen for the kill, she couldn't take the lies and deception any longer. Older now but no less lethal when cornered, Nevada failed to find any pity for this repulsive example of humanity. Dropping down next to all she found evil, she would knock the wind out of lies that had survived for far too long. "Gant, it's not all bad. Just think. The place is finally going to get that new sidewalk you've always wanted," said Nevada, taunting the parasite.

"I want a lawyer. Right now."

"I bet you do," she said over her shoulder as she headed toward the sound of the incoming choppers.

Ballooning the population over three hundred in Jaime, Iowa, for the first time in a long while, the assault on the sleepy village staggered its frightened citizens. The side streets quickly filled up with black SUVs, and sprinkled in were a few massive mobile labs with a battalion of technicians deploying throughout the property. With a ratio of one agent for every five citizens, Jaime, Iowa, was one of the safest cities in the nation that day.

Standing out in the open field, the lone woman's hair blew freely in the wind as she waited for Kliner to notice her among the army of agents. Returning her wave, he broke from his entourage.

"My god. You did it," yelled Kliner over the whine of the chopper.

"Not really me. I'm just along for the ride. Now we need to talk."

"What will it cost me?" asked Kliner, holding jacks to her queens.

Turning her back to the wind and Kliner, with arms spread wide, Nevada surveyed the approaching waves of men and women descending on Gant's world. "This is all because of my gift. In forty minutes, it accomplished more than your entire machine could in forty-eight years. I can replicate this over and over."

201

"For?" asked Kliner, stepping nearer.

"Not much really." Spinning back, she said, "Complete immunity for any crimes I may have committed up till now and the termination of all investigations of any company that I have an interest in."

"Who are you?"

"Deal first. I'll also want everything protected under the State Secrets Protection Act," said Nevada.

"Is she near?"

Dropping the winning hand down, she said, "As soon as I have your word, I'll lead you right to her."

"You have my word. May I now have the pleasure of knowing who I'm doing business with?"

Almost feeling sorry for him, she pulled the mask down. "You want my name, Director Kliner? It's Nevada Barrington."

Suddenly realizing he was the guppy and not the piranha in the tank, he exclaimed, "Oh boy! My life just got complicated. You know the SEC is gunning for you with everything they have, right?"

"She's waiting."

Holding his cap down as the helicopter's prop wash rained debris outward, he yelled over the turbine's whine, "You don't realize how much effort is being expended to take you down. I'll try to get it wrapped up tomorrow."

Whipping the hair out of her mouth, she pointed. "See that cab over there? I have paid for him to stay there one hour. That's where I'll be when you get your answer. Jaylene can wait one more hour," said Nevada, leaving Kliner as he reached for his phone.

Forty-five minutes later and several lies told in the name of justice, he rapped on the cab's dust-streaked window. Allowing the window to lower, the lioness raised her eyes from her phone.

"It's done," Kliner said, regretting the bridges that were casualties in the pursuit of purer justice.

"Let's go get Jaylene."

"Before we do that, they have recovered some additional articles. We believe they could be from some other missing girls back in that time period. Can you talk to Gant one more time before he knows his goose is really cooked?" asked Kliner.

DIVINE MEMORIES

Slamming the cab door, she held out her hand. "Give me the articles."

Clearing the kitchen inside, Nevada took a seat closest to Gant as Kliner and Jenkins stood back. "Well, Gant, I'm back." Her sneer was FBI-approved. Taking out the ziplock baggie, she shook them like dice, casting the jewelry out on the table. "Oh look, Gant. I got a Yahtzee. I win!"

Shaking his head, fighting the noose, he muttered, "I found those over the years."

She fondled two of the rings as she allowed the fear to climb another notch in his brain. "Must have been a good year for mood rings. Now, Gant, where do you suppose the last owner of these little girl's trinkets might be? That's it. Let it flow right out through that demented, twisted mind of yours. Recall the last time you saw their broken little bodies. Remember that place where you shoveled dirt over their beautiful bodies. Remember this time as clear as this bright sunny day. A day that you stole all these girls from their families. One where our God will soon be having a conversation with you about it."

Reaching across the table, casting her nail out, she stabbed it into the top of Gant's hand. "That's it right there! Hold that thought," said Nevada, sliding back down in her chair.

"My chest hurts," complained Gant, sweating profusely while slumping forward.

Nine years in the FBI woefully prepared him for his new partner's gift. She was surgically slicing the truth from the suspect with her calm and soothing command. Respecting little in life anymore, he would never forget this day as he followed her outside.

Washing her hands of the man, Nevada spun out of the kitchen. She whispered words to Kliner that would finally bring five girls home. Jaylene was first.

Walking out into the blazing sunlight, burning off the stench of a pedophile, she halted a few feet from the front door. Looking down at the suspicious depression in the sidewalk, she noticed it was crumbling after decades of neglect, doing its best over the years to reveal the atrocity hidden under it.

203

"Jaylene is buried under here," said Nevada. The ugly memories of her final moments seized her completely. It was an unfortunate by-product of the gift, one that she would need to handle or be lost to their horrors.

With the grating bite of the backhoe's teeth against the concrete, the final resting place of Jaylene Merci Montgomery would be exposed for all to see. Gone for decades but never forgotten by the man standing at her side. Removing his hat, Kliner bit back the emotions. Holding up for documentation, the corner of a leather pouch surfaced on the tooth of the backhoe's bucket. They halted the dig, and the painstaking forensic exhumation of one Jaylene Merci Montgomery, forever age fourteen, began.

Photographed and videoed from every conceivable angle, the leather pouch was removed. The US Mail stencil was still legible as time failed to defeat the road sign pointing back to Gant. Riddled with holes on one end, the edge of a once beautiful gown poked out. No longer the vivacious teenager with dreams of being more than the sum of her parts, the bones would be reconstructed and cataloged for the prosecution.

Kliner took a knee by all that was left of his worst nightmare. Forty-eight years and one gut-wrenching regrettable selfish decision later, he grasped the edge of the gown. He pulled it gently, and the tattered material slid out of the gaping hole.

He hated this day. He hated the man who was leaving in the ambulance. He hated the job. He hated himself. "Jaylene honey, I'm so...so sorry."

18

Standing in front of the mirror, the auburn locks stretched below her shoulders finally. Touching up some pesky crow's feet, she smiled as she caught a glimpse of him in the mirror. The telltale crack of his big toe gave up his position once again. "I heard that, goofball," she said, dodging the dirty sock as he rushed her position.

Brushing away hair, he planted a scratchy kiss on her bare neck. "Marry me."

Grabbing the curling iron, she said, "Did you take the trash out?"

He disarmed her as he ran his nails up and down her back. The moan let him off the hook. "It's working its way up the list."

"Humph, so is marrying you. Mwa ha ha!" Laughing at her witty retort, she pulled him in hard. "You ready to go?"

"Just about. You scared?"

Letting the brush clatter in the sink, she melted against his body. "Not as long as you're by my side."

Stroking her hair, he knew she was a woman that wouldn't drop on any battlefield. "I wouldn't blame you if you were. I never got used to entering them myself, and I've never been to a max fed prison either," said Jack, cringing inwardly at the thought of the vicious animals they were going to share a cage with later.

Grabbing two masks off the shelf, she said, "Well, I've got to honor the deal. I trust Kliner and Jenkins. Let's go."

Cruising into the rest area, their target of interest lurked, seemingly harmless, in the truck parking. Beefier than your average motor home, only the government license plates gave one a clue. Packed with the best toys tax dollars could acquire, the best in class was escorted in. Typical manmade with plenty of stainless steel and security features (some obvious, some not so), it was more medieval than modern inside. There was a single steel table bolted to the floor with ample seats to go around and eyebolts to serve up to two guests at a time.

She let the first shiver escape. "Can the driver see me back here?"

"No," said Director Kliner. Shifting his gaze, he asked, "Who do we have here, Nevada?"

"Sorry. This is Jack Webster. He goes where I go," said Nevada, her eyes screaming *don't try me*.

"Fine. And you remember Agent Calvin Jenkins, of course. So let me brief you on what we are going to do today. The inmate will enter through that door and will be shackled down through the eyebolt on the table. He will be hooded and unable to see who is in the room. I'm sure you have reviewed his file, so I don't need to tell you how dangerous he is. He is a big, mean-looking guy that has absolutely no capacity to feel pity or remorse for his crimes. Be prepared for any combination of degradation he will sling your way. If, for any reason, you need to say anything out of his earshot, we can go in the next room, which is soundproof. Any questions?"

"Whew! I'll do my best," said Nevada.

She buckled up for the short ride to the infamous death house located at the federal maximum-security prison located near Terre Haute, Indiana. Annoyed by her heel clicking on the steel-plated floor, she planted more of her weight down, conjuring up worries and giving the demons a foothold. She closed her eyes, tugging skyward for more strength. She was chanting the words silently as she felt the vehicle chugging toward her destiny. Embarking on a crusade to lay waste to evil, she felt the warmth return once again.

Entering through the massive gates, they were escorted by a small contingent of security as the command vehicle rolled into the designated secure area. Looking for a game face, she fought the steady supply of doubt. Throwing her hand out, she felt the power in his grip.

Pulling her nearer, Jack whispered, "You've got this." He was supporting a shaky foundation, and he wouldn't let it crumble.

Trusting with only a shake of the head, she gave him the smile reserved for him alone.

DIVINE MEMORIES

"Nevada, we've got a few minutes before he is brought out. Do you want to review his file?" asked Agent Jenkins.

Releasing her lifeline back to all that was normal, she pulled her hand free from Jack's. "Yeah. Let's go over it once more."

"Okay. Ranky Lee Boushard is fifty-three years old, six foot four, and tips the scale at 325 pounds. Red and gray hair, normally in a ponytail. He was born and raised in the state of Louisiana. He has been incarcerated for 178 months and is due to be discharged soon. You can see in his file that he was arrested for kidnapping a woman from a gas station. A trooper stopped him for speeding and heard cries coming from the trunk. We believe that he is responsible for approximately seventeen other unsolved murders in a hundred-mile radius of the kidnapping," said Jenkins.

"Did the killings stop with his arrest?" asked Nevada.

"Fortunately, yes. The killer was dubbed by the locals as the One-Shoe Killer. Each victim was found manually strangled and propped up against a tree in a conspicuous place with her right shoe missing. Your job here today is to find those shoes. Nevada, you're our last hope. We will be freeing this animal in less than two months," said Jenkins, reaching for the intercom. Hanging up the receiver, he said, "Showtime in two minutes. He's on his way out." He too was scouting around for his own game face.

Looking for strength from a long pull of water, Nevada set the bottle aside, hoping the biscuits and gravy stayed down. "I'll do my best," she said. Looking over at the only friendly in the room, his smile calmed her. His slow nod gave her the fight to throw caution to the wind as she jumped at the loud bang on the door.

"Boushard, you've got two steps to climb, and then you're in," yelled the prison guard.

"In what?" asked Boushard. His gravelly voice, still hoarse from throat surgery last month, was muffled by the hood.

With a rock of the boat, Boushard was aboard. Guided to the seat of honor, the massive wrists were shackled to the table. Trying to chin off the hood, he racked the chains through the eyebolt, testing the tensile strength of the steel. Satisfied he was still a captive, he sat, waiting patiently for the exercise to begin. Soaked in the downpour, the rain magnified his body odor, turning the stomach of the weak.

"Boushard, I am Agent Calvin Jenkins with the FBI. We want—"

"I want my lawyer. Now!" howled Boushard, ripping the chains back and forth through the eyebolt.

"We're not going to ask you any questions."

"Hmm. I believe I do smell a woman amongst us. I'll stay for the show." Boushard chuckled.

Letting her eyes trail down the thick arms, she had doubts about the chains' capability to bind the bulging arms littered with tattoos. Studying the huge hams suspected of clamping the life out of his victims gave her a sense of renewed purpose. His ugly and vile voice, the last they would have ever heard, needed to be silenced. The weak would rise today. Snuffing the life from them with such joy, she found her mission and a voice for all his victims.

Clearing a throat dry as the Sahara, she inched closer, calculating his reach. "Mr. Bou—"

"You're scared!" taunted Boushard with a booming rasp.

She took refuge again from the bottle of water.

"The lady must really be thirsty today," Boushard sounded off, mocking his opponent. Leaning hard against the chains, turning in her direction, he said, "You're just another female begging to be put in someone's trunk. The world doesn't need another female wanting to wear pants in a man's world." Boushard had drawn first blood.

With the home team crumbling, Kliner shot a withering look Jenkins's way. With the star pitcher flaming out on the mound, they allowed doubts about her ability to seep in.

Clearing the sludge of fear, or maybe just disgust, she polished off the last drops the bottle had to offer. With Boushard about to tee off on her again, her smooth voice cut in. Flinging the bottle across the room and missing the trash can, she ignored the clattering sounds as it rolled across the steel-plated floor. "Mr. Boushard, I'll do the talking. You'll be better served to keep that ugly mouth shut tightly."

"Ahh. Honey, I could listen to you sweet-talk me all day," said Boushard, seething at the audacity simmering out of the female.

DIVINE MEMORIES

"Okay, let's take a look at this file. I see you had a good run for what, maybe five years? Looks to me like you were a mediocre garden-variety killer, in my mind, at best. You know, big dumb animal versus the weak. Probably trying to compensate for other, shall we say, deficiencies in other departments. Killing what you knew couldn't fight back. No comment?"

Shifting in the steel chair, Boushard said under a mask of fury, "Lady, I got nothing for you. Answers, that is. Now maybe when I get free, we can hook up and have a talk about any deficiencies."

Sliding her chair closer, the screech echoed off the steel walls. "Let's go back to all those poor victims that made the mistake of crossing your filthy path. We need to talk about all those shoes. You know the shoes I'm talking about? The shoes that will soon be scuttling your ship to the bottom of the ocean. Let's go to where they have been hidden from prying eyes. I mean, they are your trophies, right?" asked Nevada, pouring out her gift.

"Shut up. I could use a water?" asked Boushard.

Ignoring the request, she marched on down the road. "I need you to look back upon the collection. A hoarded collection for your eyes only. Like fine art, only you knowing their true value. Denied your presence all these years, waiting on your glorious homecoming. That's it. Let your eyes worship the memories. Let them come alive. Now focus upon their hiding place. Lift the lid of darkness hiding them. Let the light shine down upon them.

"Yes. Ahh…yes. Right there they are. Imagine the glory of running your hands down through them again. Remember the original owners as you slipped the shoes from their feet. The feeling of power that flowed through your body as you championed over them. Let's now imagine traveling to retrieve them. That's it. Watch for street signs. Look up and down the street out front. Back your view away from the house. Is that a mailbox? Look closer. Step inside and get them. Make it quick. This is your journey. Enjoy it. Unearth them. Bring them to the light," whispered Nevada.

"Lady, get your finger off me," threatened Boushard, the thunder and cockiness long gone from the rasp.

209

Pulling away from his hand, Nevada said wearily, "Get him out of here." She felt sapped from the drain.

Stumbling down the first step, Boushard broke free from the guard's grasp. "Lady, I really hope we meet for that drink. I'll make sure the trunk's cleaned out," he said, busting out with a laugh only a monster could own. Against doctor's orders, he convulsed into coughing fit as he lumbered back to his cage.

"That's it?" asked Director Kliner.

Running interference, Jenkins said, "Director Kliner, this is her first time in a hostile environ—"

"Whoa! You guys told me to find the shoes. What's the problem now?" asked Nevada.

Staring into each other's eyes, turning, their voices came out as one. "You...know where the shoes are?" asked Kliner.

"Think I would have kicked that piece of trash back to his cage if I didn't?" asked Nevada, sliding in next to Jack. "Grab your legal pad, Jenkins."

Flailing a hand back toward the exit, Kliner asked, "You-you got what we need from that?"

"Well, that abomination of evil that just graced our presence believes the shoes are there."

"Where are they?" asked Kliner.

"In a little town called Jesse in Louisiana."

"His hometown," said Jenkins, throwing the file across the room.

"It is a run-down shack on Bangler Avenue. I couldn't read all the numbers on the mailbox. Something with the numbers 540 should help though."

"It's 17540 Bangler Avenue. That house has already been searched years ago. I was there!" erupted Kliner, his enthusiasm nosediving.

Rubbing a forming migraine, she thought that maybe she wasn't cut out for government work. "Think what you will, but I saw a black tote buried under the crawlspace. There's also some kind of notebook with the shoes," said Nevada, standing and pulling Jack to his feet.

Divine Memories

Shoving the file across the table, Kliner said, "I'm heading back to Washington. Jenkins, follow up if you get any credible leads."

"Yes, sir."

"Kliner, I can have you both and a team of about a dozen agents in Jesse, Louisiana, by early afternoon. If you don't have those shoes in your possession by six p.m., we can part ways."

Exposing true bureaucratic leadership, he muttered, "I...I don't know."

Littering the table, the black-and-white crime scene photos cascaded down. One at a time, pictures capturing each victim's last moments of their nightmare pile up.

"Kliner, how much more egg do you want on your face? I'll get them by myself if I have to," threatened Nevada, looking Jack's way.

Jack broke his silence. He had been rubbed the wrong way by the feds more times than he cared to remember. "Seriously. You still doubt her gift. She has knocked down walls you and all your cronies couldn't climb over in forty-eight years, if I remember correctly, that is. Director, don't make me hold her hand while she shows you her true capabilities," he warned.

Her gentle squeeze of his hand green-lighted their future headaches. "I have one of my jets parked in Indy right now, Director."

One could almost feel pity for a leader putting his career on the scales. Kliner was weighing the witness of the unexplained up against the real world. Had she some hidden gimmick that would be the anchor around his neck, one that some hard-charging investigative reporter would uncover and gladly sell to the highest bidder? He could almost feel the hot lights as he imagined being interviewed by the *60 Minutes* reporter. The words "did you really fall for her scam" echo loudly in his ears.

"Jenkins, I think we—"

"Director Kliner, I don't need to read your mind to see you have doubts. I ask you to remember, I have done exactly what I said I would do. Quit thinking of yourself and think about the people you are paid to protect," said Nevada.

"Young lady, have a seat at the table," ordered Kliner.

211

He invaded her personal space as he inched close enough to see the gold flecks. The light fragrance of her gum, coupled with the sweet scent of her perfume, invaded his senses. Young enough to be his daughter, she held the stare. Molded by who knew what, she held ground he couldn't take.

Staring into a mystery he couldn't fathom, Kliner gave a command he hoped he wouldn't have to answer for in front of Congress one day. "Jenkins, get a team together out of Indianapolis. We're hitching a ride to Jesse, Louisiana."

She slid the pictures back in the envelope. "Wear nothing that identifies anyone as FBI when we get on the plane. My crew knows nothing of my involvement," said Nevada.

"Fine. Can we depart Indy by eleven a.m.?" asked Kliner.

Texting with as much precision and speed as any fifteen-year-old, she said, "I'm notifying the crew to ready for departure at eleven right now."

*****

Getting the agents settled in for the flight, she slipped off to her private room. She pulled him in close. "Jack, we have a planeload of FBI agents headed to, hopefully, not a blunder of biblical proportions, all on account of me. Am I doing the right thing?" asked Nevada, falling upon a shoulder that has heard a thousand sad stories.

Stroking her hair, he was careful to avoid her scar. "Does it feel right to you?"

Breaking from his shoulder, she replied, "I know what I saw."

Laying her head back down, he said, "Then march straight ahead. Don't listen to the noise on the right or left of you. Stay on the path you feel led to follow."

Interrupted by the knock on the door, she stiffened at the intrusion.

"May I come in for a moment?" asked Director Kliner.

"Yeah, were just talking," said Nevada in a tone that was reserved only for him.

Twisting his wedding band, Kliner was looking for an easy out that didn't exist. "Nevada, I owe you an apology. I want you to know

I want nothing more than for you to be real. I deal in what I can see, touch, and feel. You go against all that I know. But let me tell you this. If those shoes are found in that house, I will never again doubt your abilities—or gift, as you call it."

"You said we were partners before. I can't keep trying to earn your approval each time you have me use my gift," said Nevada.

"You should already be to that point, Director Kliner," Jack chimed in, standing by her side.

Grabbing for the doorknob, he nodded. "Humor me a little longer."

*****

Fanning out into teams of four, the caravan turned south of the airport and on to Highway 686, a never-ending ribbon of sticky blacktop running between ditches full of murky black water chock-full of cattails.

With a forty-mile jaunt ahead of them to the thriving metropolis of Jesse, Nevada felt the first demons coursing throughout her body. The weight on her shoulders became oppressive as she let the demons linger too long. Closing her eyes, she summoned the only antidote for them. Channeling all her fears and worries, she set fire to them as the warmth enveloped her soul. Recalling the dreams, she would stay on the path regardless of the pain or doubters.

Turning down the broken lane, she saw the cock-eyed street sign hanging on the broken post. As they dodged the potholes, she thought Bangler Avenue had seen better days. Front and center, the boarded-up shack sat defying the hot Louisiana humidity. Living on borrowed time, the shack had seen its fair share of big blows from the hurricanes that had ravaged the town time after time.

The faded graffiti was still partially visible, announcing the home of the One-Shoe Killer to the world. It had new meaning. Clashing with time, it lost some status as new crops of more vicious killers had been given their fifteen minutes of fame on the evening news.

Deploying around the one-time fortress of one Ranky Lee Boushard, the agents waited for marching orders.

Kicking the front door in brought a testament of the capabilities of the Louisiana termite. Shattering inward, it disappeared from sight as the subfloor gave way. Stepping gingerly on the floor, the agents navigated on choice floor joists missed by the termites. Drawing straws, the excavation of the crawlspace began. Within minutes, agents vaulted out of the crawlspace. Word of snakes traveled with warp speed throughout the group of city boys. As they called for local animal control, the search ground to a halt.

Armed with a dogcatcher's pole, local animal control officer Ramius Sneeder saved the lives of a mama diamondback and her den of babies, as well as the pride of a dozen FBI agents who were ready to retire early before being ordered to go back down in. Moving slower than a sloth, each agent prayed their light wouldn't puke out on them as they searched the crawlspace.

Working two hours with trench shovels in the tight quarters, the howl of an agent signaled either pay dirt or snake. The agents were freezing in position, pulling their shovels closer, each hoping the nightmare was over.

"Got something over here!" hollered Agent Mack Kelly, muddy sweat rolling off the side of his face.

Pulling back, allowing the evidence team to take over, Nevada waited. Pacing up and down Bangler Avenue, the place held a certain peace. The nearest neighbor was blocks away, and there was only wildlife for company as she heard the distant sounds of the water fowl arguing for their little slice of life.

Almost suppertime, she thought as her stomach rumbled. Walking back, she could hear the celebration half a block away.

Stretching out, just clearing the mud puddle, Nevada asked, "Think they found them?"

"You know they did," said Jack, yanking her closer.

19

She was lounging in the gardens of her Yankee Mansion. The last of the rare warm February day lingered, losing its grip to the setting sun. Sipping the tea, she couldn't get the call out of her head. Dragging the shawl tighter, the thought of meeting him face-to-face turned her stomach. Lawrence gave few clues. Not on her A-list anymore, could he be trusted?

"Sitting out here with all your friends?" asked Jack, laughing at his dad's old joke as he navigated the path.

Lobbing a menacing glare over the top of her cup, she replied, "Friends are overrated. So are wannabe husbands."

"Rrrr! Ratchet those claws back in."

Watering the ground with her cold tea, she folded up shop, bumping her head on an abandoned hanging basket as she rose up. She whipped a glance his way, ready to pounce if a smile materialized. "Sorry, got a lot on my mind. Shouldn't be more than a day or two. Will you miss me?"

He was mentally smiling from ear to ear. "Yep."

"Good. Kliner called earlier with an update," said Nevada, snaking an arm around his waist.

He cocked a nervous look her way. "And?"

With less emotion than your average attender at a goldfish funeral, she said, "Gant died before he got to the hospital. They found the other girls buried under his shed. Boushard's goose is cooked. The FBI has matched up over eight of the shoes with murder victims. And get this. The idiot took selfies of each victim and kept them in a scrapbook."

"Guess he won't be making it to have that get-to-know-you-better drink then," said Jack, ducking under a hanging basket. "See, that's the way it's—"

"Shut up," she said, rubbing the top of her head, letting the grin see daylight. "His patience is at a breaking point with me. He has scheduled an interview with that other inmate for the day after I get back from New York. If I don't make it happen, I'm fodder for his cannon."

"I'll be ready when you get back. But we need to work on your exit plan too."

"Way ahead of you."

*****

Walking into her Sherry-Netherland apartment early the next morning, Nevada cringed at the sight of the water spots still visible on the vanity mirror. The thought of his disloyalty to her left a crater in her life. Living a black-and-white existence, gray areas would never be tolerated in her world. Not when loyalty was the subject. Bouncing the phone off her knee, the urge to flee back to Shallimar rang louder and louder. In limbo with her deal for immunity, she flirted with her freedom.

He was prompt as usual; the knock allowed her hackles to flourish. Giving them permission to unfurl, enjoying their new freedom, she dredged up his banner of disloyalty. Pulling the door back minus a greeting, he stepped in. With hat in hand, he would try to settle accounts today. Primed for a fight, she wasn't a sixteen-year-old kid enamored with him anymore. Ready to receive his fate, he knew the routine. He'd heard of her abilities many times.

The silence rolled his world as she stared at her worse loss in life.

"Thank you for seeing me," said Lawrence, breaking the silence.

She was fighting the feelings from the years of love for him. *Could he know how deep the wound hurt?* Pitting them up against his transgression, love would take second place. "Anything comes out of your mouth that's untruthful and you're going to suffer for it." The wicked look withered the poor servant.

He was relieved to hear her voice pardoning him from the silence. Bobbing a head ready for the chopping block, he nodded. "Understood."

Leaving no room for lingering love, she rushed to the front, ignoring the years of loyalty. "What's this all about?"

With the air getting thinner, he fought to manage his words that would soon close the final doors between them. "No matter how mad you get, let me finish my story."

Pinching the bridge of her nose, she rose. She'd heard enough sad stories for a lifetime. Letting the silence guide her as she paced around the room, her mother's words rose to be heard. Clamping back the daggers, refusing to face him, she glanced back over a rigid shoulder. "As long as I hear what I think is the truth coming out."

Pulling in a ragged breath, he knew the deed had been hidden for too long. "Two days before your parents disappeared, Charles called me in his office and accused me of embezzling funds from the company. I had intended—"

Threatening to chip a tooth as she let anger boil over, she said, "You stole from my parents!" Clenching a fist as the words flooded her soul, she added, "You're lucky I've kind of found religion." With shame piling on, the weight of her anger drove his head down. "Ohhh no! Get that head up and face me!"

"He made a clear warning I should stay out of his way."

The revelation clouded her world.

Unblinking, she let the steam release. "Is there anything else?"

Coming up from the nosedive, Lawrence was hoping the information would get him some decent mileage. "Liddy Bankhill is in federal lockup, as you know. He contacted me and asked me to relay a message. He's says he needs to speak with you."

Sucking the life out of her bottom lip, she felt her skin crawl at the thought of Liddy's smirking face. Pulling back the window curtain, she noted that looking down at the life of the common man scurrying twenty stories down below brought more appeal daily. Could they have the capacity to understand a billionaire's problems? Would they jump for joy to trade her places, blindly running through the streets and shouting how luck had finally swung their way?

Letting the curtain go back to work hiding the world's lower class, she faced a man she loathed. "Make it happen and fast."

*****

Entering the Guantanamo of New York early before regular visiting hours, she shivered as she made her way through the levels of security at the Metropolitan Detention Center. Nevada regretted leaving Jack at home as she was led down the hallway that went deeper into the belly of the facility. Would she need a get-out-of-jail card herself before this was all over? Taking a seat on the cold stainless steel chair, she waited, shoulder to shoulder with a world she never dreamed of entering.

Liddy was no longer wearing a smirk but more of a little-boy-lost look as the guard brought him in. The tough guy no longer existed as he struggled to make eye contact. With his master plan unfolding, he felt the fresh air already.

"Hey there, uh, Ms. Barrington. Thanks uh…for taking the time to see me," said Liddy, fawning for mercy.

Colder than the steel chair, she could smell his fear. "Save your thanks. Bankhill, I don't really care for you, to say the least. To be completely honest, I'd just as soon pay your bond and hire two guys to put a bullet in your head. You know, like you did for me," said Nevada, having no eye contact issues.

With a master plan on fire, he said, "Ma'am…ma'am, that wasn't me."

She stabbed a finger up against the glass. "Shut your mouth!"

Slinking back, he let his body fall heavily against the chair. "Okay. Sure, sure, Ms. Barrington."

She swallowed down the bile of her hatred, inches from all she found offensive and vile. "Say what you have to say. But if I detect a lie, you're done. And if I detect a lie, I wouldn't leave this facility if I was you. Ever!"

Shaking the bushy locks of greasy hair, Liddy let a smile creep out past nicotine-stained teeth. "No, ma'am. No lies."

Stepping across a line beaten into his soul his entire life, the terms of future living arrangements blotted out the fears. Facing the rest of his life behind bars, he saw the hatred and contempt in her eyes. Her ears perked, just waiting to hear the truth get mangled. This being his only lifeline still in existence, he made the leap across that great divide between good and bad.

"Would you be interested in proving who paid to have you hunted down?" asked Liddy.

With her heart pounding under the cashmere sweater, she said yes, allowing the word to trickle through her lips.

Looking about the room, he lowered his voice. "Amos and Charles. Mostly Charles. You probably knew that."

Keeping her heel on his throat, Nevada said, "Put your hand flat against the glass."

She slammed her hand on the partition, marrying their hands. She pressed hard against the glass. "Close your eyes. Think about those months that they were plotting against me. How were they paid?"

Letting his hand squeak down the glass as he pitched forward, Liddy muttered, "Get me immunity for that proof, and I'll tell the world what I know."

"I'll be back. Don't go anywhere."

*****

Late for a shower to cleanse the jailhouse stink off, she hustled back to her apartment. Tidying up around, she polished the mirror, eradicating the stains of his betrayal. Calling the air crew for the flight back home, she would turn her back on a city filled with misery. As she stepped back into the Midwest, she drew in the fresh air as her man reached for her arm.

"Missed you!" Jack said.

Breaking from his embrace, she countered, "Missed you more."

He pulled her in close, hanging a thumb off her belt loop. "How'd it go?"

"I need a drink first."

"Okay. Let's go to Bernigan's for a steak. I'll drive. I want to make sure nothing happens to you this time," said Jack, tussling her hair.

219

Had it only been thirteen months since that snowy night? It had been littered with love and misery along the way with a miracle or two sprinkled in for good measure. Taking a seat, her million-dollar smile flashed a warning that she would be hard to get rid of.

"We haven't seen you in a while," said Margo as she opened her pad.

"Nope. Not since the night of the shooting. This is who I was waiting for that night," said Jack, reaching for Nevada's hand.

"Oh my, honey! You are truly an answered prayer. Look at you, beautiful as ever," gushed Margo.

"Thank you."

Looking for motives on her words, she listened to Margo assign credit for her healing to her Sunday school group's prayers. Still trying to field the honesty of the Midwesterners, the droning had to have its limits.

"I could go on and—"

"I'll take a water with lemon," said Nevada, shutting down the diatribe.

"Oh, I'm sorry," said Margo, parking her tongue. Spinning on her heel, she headed to the next table as she looked back over her shoulder, mouthing *sorry* to Jack.

Flipping a sugar pack across the table, she said, "Man, she can talk."

"She means well." Unable to walk back a rare case of impatience, he cleared his throat. "That Sunday school class you would bring judgment down on fed my family for days. In fact, if you look over there, those ladies right there ran errands for my mom while I stayed 24-7 with you at the hospital for weeks. The whole town was pulling for a stranger. Unlike the eight million gallant citizens of New York City," said Jack, leaving her to scrape some New York egg off that pretty face.

With nowhere to duck, she toiled with the wrapping on the silverware. His rebuke blasted through her armor, stinging her to the core. Always defaulting back to her old life, she longed for his goodness. "You're right. I'm an idiot. I don't—"

"Here's your waters. Ready to order?" asked Margo.

Sliding the menu back in the holder, Jack said, "Margo, give us two steak dinners, both medium rare."

Squirting out a smile like she loved her job and her feet didn't hurt from the new shoes, Margo said, "Got it." Swinging to take on the next order, an act that would have been unimaginable months ago, would be slow to unfold as Nevada's hand reached hers.

Shifting in her hot seat, choking down a bitter piece of humble pie, humility found its way to her tongue. "Ma'am, I need to apologize. I thank you and your group for all your prayers. I'm not used to people caring and loving without motives. It's a curse I am working on," said Nevada, gripping a hand knotted up with arthritis.

"Oh, honey. Don't think a thing about it," said Margo, patting her hand and marching off. With those words, maybe her feet didn't hurt so bad after all.

Two tables down, Margo glanced his way, recovering with a broken smile as she greeted her next guests. Turning to his own pet project, Jack said, "Wow! You can play nice."

She smeared a smile his way with an abundance of wrinkled nose. "Oh whatever. You knew I was a broken toy when you rescued me," said Nevada as the wadded-up napkin whizzed past his collar.

"Enough games. What'd you get out of your visit?"

"Plenty. If I get Liddy a deal, he'll reveal details about the scum who had me hunted down."

Chewing on the new wrinkle, Jack asked, "Do you think he is legit?"

She fished out an ice cube. "Before I start the session tomorrow, I am going to get Kliner researching it out first."

"Let's keep our heads down and march forward on your goals tomorrow. Did I ever tell you that you are my favorite broken toy?"

"Pot calling the kettle black, ain't it. Like you ain't broken," said Nevada, drawing out the word *ain't* with her best hick accent while lowering her standards.

He was smirking at the work in progress as she tried to Midwest up her talk a bit. "There's hope for you yet," said Jack, pinching the lemon peel her way.

The rest area was hopping with early morning travelers angling toward the bathroom, each oblivious to their proximity to a modern-day version of the Manhattan Project. Boxing out images of her next evil stepping stone to freedom, she sucked in the fresh morning air. It was the last she would get for the next few hours. Parked in the same place as last time, her escape plan housed inside brought an early morning ripple down her spine.

"Good morning, Nevada," said Kliner, unlatching the locking mechanism.

Somewhere between a smile and a moan, she took the steps up. "Good morning, everybody."

"Hey, Jack. How you doing this morning?" asked Agent Jenkins, offering a hand.

"Good, but it's still early," said Jack, playing the game.

"Let's hash over our target today before we head to the prison," said Kliner, cracking open the file. "The man of the hour today is one worthless human specimen. His mama gave the name Coy Will Haskins. Age 58, white male, about 6'9", weighing 170 soaking wet. He's been a guest of the system for the last sixteen years, for crimes too numerous to list. He's spent several bouts in the SEG unit for disciplinary issues regarding personal disagreements with his fellow roommates. He has been diagnosed with mental issues, as you can imagine, and sports an IQ near the 100 mark. He hates women, loves little girls, and could care less if the rest of us ever saw another sunrise."

"Nice guy. What am I looking for today?" asked Nevada.

Closing the file folder and tapping a middle finger down on it, Jenkins said, "His graveyard and, hopefully, twenty or so missing kids from that corridor of the United States during his reign of terror. When they searched his RV on the day he was captured, they found gas receipts close to several of the areas where kids had come up missing."

Sliding a glance Jack's way, Nevada said, "I'll do my best. Can we discuss something else first, Director Kliner?"

He dropped the pen as he lifted his eyes her way. "Yeah."

Not liking the resistance in his eyes, she said, "I need a favor."

Jutting out a perfectly shaved chin, he asked, "Haven't we done each other favors already, Nevada?"

"Yes. But what's one more?" she asked, hoping the chuckle would pave the way as she darted Jack a crushed look.

DIVINE MEMORIES

"Can't do it. I'm still stinging at the cost of your first one."

Coming to life at the sight of the hyenas circling his lioness, Jack charged the pack, letting his love guide the attack. Clouded by years of frustration with politics and backroom deals, he cleared his throat. A quick calculation and he launched. Scooping up her hand, he said, "Call us when you're ready to discuss her favor. If you feel you need to revive the prosecution efforts against her, go for it. We're done here."

Hiking a brow, Kliner warned, "You're going to be sorry."

With one hand on the door, Jack let Nevada through. "You already are," he answered. "Good luck with your next conversation with the attorney general." Letting the door slam, he caught up with Nevada.

Whipping around, she said, "Jack, are you sure that was a—"

Leaning out, Jenkins pleaded halfway across the parking lot, "Nevada...Jack, come on back."

Skipping a beat as the cloud lifted, she squeezed the hand representing 95 percent of the good in her life.

Retaking their seats, the searing glare from Kliner brought an end to the friendly partnership. "What do you want?" he asked.

Giving up on the dream of taking home Miss Congeniality, she wouldn't be stopped this close to the answers. "First, I think you need a math lesson. There are thousands of Jenkinses and thousands of Kliners in the world. There is only one like me in this world. Forget that again and you are going to have vacancies in your department. And second—and this is a big one. You ever do anything again to get in my way of discovering who did me or my family injustices and this friendly merger will evaporate. Also, I could care less about your prosecution efforts against me. I'll hire a battalion of lawyers and buy media coverage and destroy the government's best efforts before I ever see the inside of a courtroom."

Scared of little in life, he knew her threats had real teeth. "Nevada, what do you want?" asked Jenkins, recalling his first encounter with her. He wished Kliner would move on the demand.

"I need immunity for any charges against Liddy Bankhill for his possible involvement in the attempt on my life. I may also need a sweet deal for his involvement on the insider trading charges he is being held on currently."

"What happens if you find out that he was actually the one that tried to have you killed? He will walk scot-free," said Kliner.

"I'll take my chances. Go make your calls. Jack and I'll take a walk."

Choking down his second cup of rest-stop coffee, he dreaded the winter. With a twinkle in his eye, the TV weatherman enthusiastically announced the next storm of the season headed their way next week. Dumping the coffee, giving his stomach a reprieve, Jack asked, "Do you think he will come through for you?"

"If not, I'll buy us an island, and we can rule it together."

He was hoping there were no bugs on the couch as he let his head crash back. "I'm being serious."

Twisting sideways, giving him a side eye filled with attitude, she said, "I am too." She pulled her phone up. "Let's go. He's ready to talk."

His poker face revealed little as they settled in. Pushing the stack of files across the table, he allowed the pile to topple over. "Help me with those and we have a deal," said Kliner.

Reaching out for the stack of misfits, she put the pile in order before hurling them back to the owner. "What's his deal?' asked Nevada.

"He gets his immunity."

"Get it papered up with his attorney before the end of the day. If I need something else in the way of a favor later… Don't make me ask twice. Well, let's get going. We're late for our chat with the next psycho."

Pulling into the prison, her thoughts strayed from her. *When would he make her whole? Had he changed his mind or, better yet, never heard her prayer in the first place? Could he not see she was holding up her end of the bargain?* Rocked back in place as the doorway darkened, she silently watched as the guard helped the shackled human beanpole enter the chambers of his horrors. The games began.

Dropping into the hot seat, the standard defense jumped out. "Is my lawyer in here?" demanded Raskins from under his hood.

DIVINE MEMORIES

"No. But we won't be asking you any questions," said Jenkins, avoiding the Miranda warning.

"I still want him here. I can't breathe under this hood."

"Boo-hoo! Probably nothing compared to little Jessica trying to pull air through a crushed windpipe with your filthy hands clamped around her precious neck," said Nevada, driving a stake through the giant's scales.

He racked the chains back and forth through the eyebolt, flaking metal shavings off the eyebolt as the chain bit deep. "Lady, come closer," threatened Raskins, turning toward her voice.

"Don't worry, Coy boy. We're going to get closer. But first, let's talk about little Jessica Stout. You remember her, I'm sure. The coroner's report says—"

Kicking the panel with a deafening bang, he screamed, "Tell her to shut up!"

"Looking at this report, you really are a hands-on man. Especially when it comes to frail little girls' throats. Must be especially rewarding to stand by and witness the life drain from their tiny bodies. From the psych report, it appears you might have a problem with big girls. Looking at you, I can—"

Ripping at the cuffs, his skin was the first to give. Shaking with rage, he allowed a slobber to roll down his neck past the hood. "Lady, if I ever find you, I'll enjoy—"

"Oh, Coy. I'm much too old for your liking. I'm a big girl. As I was saying, I'm sure Jessica was your last, not your first."

Allowing the gift to draw the misery in, she hesitated as he allowed his hate to marinate in their horrific demise. Jumping from one act of barbarism to the next, he was silent.

"That's nice, isn't it? The begging and whimpering only sweetened the deal back then. You were the end of their world, grossly putting your desires above their pain and fear. The power to invoke your will over their cowering bodies. Performing your evil deeds and then discarding them like trash. Do you alone know where they are hidden? Now look down upon their final resting place. Imagine trying to find them again. It must be a struggle to remember after all these years. Could you even do it?" asked Nevada, baiting her hook.

225

The numbers scribbled on the scrap of paper faded as he fought against the gift, slipping from her sight. Pushing the gift harder to give her more, she reached a hand near the killer. Tapping her finger on the back of his hand, the reaction was instant as the killing machine roared to life, wrenching fingers back, hoping to come up with her flesh.

"Please try it again!" bellowed Raskins, rearing up out of his chair.

This brought Jenkins to his feet. He hoped the cuffs were as strong as advertised.

Wiping a strand of hair back, drawing in the scent of cheap prison soap, she leaned forward with a sneer. "Coy, Coy, Coy. Guess we'll be making a jaunt out to Oregon. Or it could be Idaho maybe? Geography was never one of my favorite subjects."

"Take me back to my cell. Now!" screamed Raskins, swinging his head at the sound of her mocking voice.

Allowing the predator to exit, she scribbled the numbers down. Releasing a shiver as the immense display of human wickedness screamed bloody murder outside, she tried to place a value on what the families would do with the knowledge about to be handed to them. Would the peace of mind be more than the pain of the old wounds being ripped open again? Handing the paper to Kliner, she awaited their skepticism.

"What's this?"

"I think those are GPS coordinates to their gravesites. That's how he found it each time," said Nevada. Standing with wobbly legs, she added, "I'm done for the day. I could just puke."

"Could it really be that easy?" asked Jenkins, floored again by her gift.

She slid her jacket on. "I hope it brings some peace to the families," said Nevada, her voice trailing off with exhaustion.

Losing the fear of her prosecution, he teetered on a rocky cliff as he tried to stay on her good side. One that would be difficult at best. "Nevada, about that. I think you should know how that will unfold," said Kliner.

Halting with an arm halfway up the sleeve, she asked, "Now what?"

"I want you to understand. We don't want your abilities known until we have accomplished as much as we can. We will immediately try to locate these girls and anyone else we discover. But we will do it clandestinely. We will gather all the victims' families later to announce the finding of their loved ones all at once," said Kliner, bracing for the blowback.

Slipping the arm on through, she said, "Fine."

Pulling into the Shallimar city limits, looking out the window, she was lost in thought. How many encounters with evil memories could she absorb before she faltered?

Turning up on Maple Street, waiting for the green light, Jack asked, sliding an arm over, "What kind of island would you buy? Nevada?"

Tearing her eyes from the little girl pedaling the tricycle for all its worth up the sidewalk, she asked, "What? Sorry?"

"What kind of island?"

Ignoring his words, she turned back. "It's hard to believe there are monsters out among us that would destroy a precious little girl like that one. How could you crush the life out of her? Look at that cute smile. How could you?" asked Nevada, lifting her hand to wave back, smiling at the infectious mischievous grin.

Little one, watch out for monsters, she silently warned. Biting down on a nail, she choked back a barrel of tears, each ready to spill again for a little girl recently wrestled from evil.

"Don't' let this destroy you, Nevada," said Jack, pulling through the intersection and patting her hand.

"Secluded from the human race, my house would be one that would shame the Swiss Family Robinsons—but equipped with modern conveniences, for sure," said Nevada, scrambling away from his warning.

Crossing Jackson Avenue, he said, "Huh?"

"My island of choice," said Nevada, letting the words come to life.

20

Marching into the Metropolitan Detention Center for a second time, popping a second aspirin, Nevada caught sight of Agent Jenkins loitering in the foyer with a cluster of suits. No doubt, Liddy's legal wranglers were waiting to hear the juicy details, each trying to justify their worth, ready to pounce on the government if any attempt to color outside the lines occurred. Ignoring the defenders of the scum in this broken world, she gave it even odds the interview would go off without a hitch as she parked a weary soul by Jenkins.

Proudly displaying a man bun and sporting a ten-thousand-dollar suit, Micky Smitley, New York's go-to choice of the wrongly accused, opened the show. "My client is ready to reveal details that I presume you are looking for. As of this time, I am completely in the dark as to the nature of those details though," said Smitley, swimming in unchartered waters.

Jenkins said, "Your client chose to not reveal the nature of this discussion to anyone."

"As long as immunity covers anything out of his mouth today, I couldn't care less," said Smitley, dropping the file down on the table with his standard bored expression.

Shuffling into the room, outfitted in the prison garb, Liddy made little fanfare as he took a seat next to Smitley. Introductions were made around the table, and the two sides prepared for battle.

"Okay, gentlemen," said Smitley, "I believe we—"

"Smitley, do I have my immunity?" interrupted Liddy.

"Liddy, as far as I can tell, you do for anything you were involved with regards to Nevada Barrington. But as far as—"

"All my team can leave the room. I'll call if I need you," ordered Liddy, cutting off the thousand-an-hour mouthpiece.

Shaking his head at his latest client to earn the title of moron, Smitley began to protest. "Liddy, I don't think—"

"Goodbye!"

Sweeping the door open wide, shooing his cocounsel out, Smitley hesitated. Turning back, he said, "Liddy, not sure if it would be of any interest, but a certain client of mine bonded out late last night."

Inflating an upper lip, he let the air escape with a squishy gush. The gut shot hurt. With a little less color, as the blood struggled to stay above the shoulders, he said, "Keep me on the clock. I'll see you after this."

A veteran of being third flunky to Charles's criminal enterprise for years, the shift in the tectonic plates of his world brought a hot fear. Charles's long reach, when motivated to strike those that wronged him, had military precision. Trapped behind bars, he would soon feel the tentacles reaching out to earn their fee. Seated across the table was his ticket to freedom—if she had the right motivation.

Rubbing the red marks left by handcuffs on his wrist, "We're gonna have to reshuffle the cards and come up with another deal. I can't stay behind bars while Charles is out of jail. Ms. Barrington, you can understand that, can't you?" asked Liddy.

Flinging the legal pad across the table at the chiseler, "Liddy, you got your deal."

With a well-timed smirk, he said, "Well, I'm pulling it back."

With the one iota of goodness going up in smoke, she let the dogs of war attack. "Agent Jenkins, have the guards take this piece of trash out of here. I'm going back home. Liddy, have a good life while it lasts."

Rousted out of his chair, the slow march to the door with the leg shackles dragging on the floor allowed the last fragment of mystery to blossom. He halted at the door. "Ms. Barrington, would you care to really know what happened to your parents?" asked Liddy, holding his smirk with pride.

Nevada froze. These were the words she had longed to hear for the last twenty years. Had her answers been this close all along? With her world suddenly entering the eye of the storm, the calm invaded her world. She resisted the urge to strike out, pointing a finger capable of anything the mighty dollar could buy in his direction. "I feel I should warn you. If you mislead me. I...I will have you released from here," said Nevada, shaking as she grappled with an avalanche of emotions, each competing to speak for her. Anger was in first place with revenge edging up fast.

"Let me walk on all charges, and I'll tell you what really happened the day they disappeared."

"You ready to give up everybody?" asked Jenkins.

"Yep."

"Call Kliner. I'm not leaving the city till we have this conversation," said Nevada, staring a hole through Liddy's skull.

Helping Nevada to her feet, Jenkins motioned for the guard to return Liddy to his home away from home. "Nevada, let's go for lunch. I'll call Director Kliner first. He might be a while, papering up this kind of offer," he said.

Making the short walk to Delmonico's, Nevada dodged any questions from Jenkins. Could her prayer finally be answered? She had stayed faithfully on the path, as instructed, rocky as it was. With the driving force picking up momentum, she could feel his love. Ordering a sub sandwich, she waited by the window for her number to be called. She was now more of an outsider, her roots firmly planted in the dirt of the prairie. She longed to leave the city, to wash all her misery off one last time.

Grabbing an empty table and brushing the crumbs to the floor, she fought for patience. "Jenkins, will we hear back today?"

"If anyone can get it done, it's Kliner," said Jenkins, taking a bite out of the pastrami.

"Was he mad?"

"Not really," Jenkins lied, sliding the pastrami back under the bun. He could still hear Kliner's screams in his ear.

Washing down her last bite, she said, "Yeah, right."

Waiting it out back at the Sherry-Netherland apartment, could she handle the truth when it came tumbling out? Like the dog who chased cars every day, what would it do if it finally caught one? Fueled over the years by the chase for the truth, would the knowledge

DIVINE MEMORIES

finally heal her open wound? She grabbed the phone. She needed reinforcements.

"Problems?" Jack asked upon answering the phone.

"Jet will be landing in Shallimar in thirty minutes. I need you by my side, Jack."

"What's wrong, honey?"

Clamping an upper lip begging to betray her inner strength, she said, "Liddy. Liddy, the guy we are dealing with. He...my god, Jack. He knows what happened to my parents. Oh, Jack. I want this in the worst way."

"I'm packing."

Locked in interview room 5 for the last hour, waiting for who knows what, Jack was her only bright spot. "How was your flight out?"

"Smooth sailing," said Jack as he caught her arm on lap 8. "We'll get through this, Nevada."

Giving the pacing a rest, she squeezed his bulky shoulders as she leaned down. "Anytime Jenkins is nervous, I tend to worry. He is definitely worried this time for some reason."

Finding a hand, he pulled it in. "What are we waiting on?"

"It's a government operation. Who knows?"

Moments later, busting through the door, the missing answers came. The cast of characters, trailed by Jenkins's long face, took their seats. With a room full of too much executive branch material, failure was an option. Not accustomed to working the night shift, they came armed with attitude and stiff necks ready for the chopping.

"Nevada, this is Rance Chandler of the US Securities and Exchange Commission," said Director Kliner.

She gave him a cordial nod, and the jockeying was off to the races. Holding the reins tight on her mouth, she waited to swoop down. Meant to strike her with fear, the man's presence would be short-lived if she had her way.

"I tried to explain our needs, and Rance is reluctant to step in and give a free ride to one of the principal defendants in one of the agency's largest investigations," explained Kliner.

Uncorking with a slow nasally East Texas tilt, Chandler said, "Ma'am, I can't be letting all the fish out of the barrel. First, you

231

slip the charges. Now you want a second. I need some compelling reason."

"Kliner, what does this man know about me?"

"Only that you are under the State Secrets Protection Act."

She leveled her eye on Jenkins, but the weak link brought no comfort as he diverted his eyes downward. Lining up her sights on the bureaucrat, Nevada said, "Kliner, you know the rules. Better warn your friend. I need a break." She grabbed Jack's hand as she rose.

Sucking down the fifth Diet Coke for the day, she longed to escape back to the Yankee Mansion. She was tired of the journey, never slowing to enjoy the days, powerless to change course until their discovery. Recharged by the nectar of the gods, she powered toward the interview room once again with Jack in tow.

With a sour face hanging on the weak link when she took her seat, the prospects of taking the easy path went down the sewer. Waiting for the government's response, she felt little sympathy for them. Any obstacle in her path would receive her wrath, whether friend or foe. Stacking up the body count of those that made her prove her gift existed would rise once again.

"Ma'am, Director Kliner explained that you would require some kind of mental game with me before you would reveal any—"

She shut down the diatribe. "Yes. Are you prepared to do that?"

"Rance, think twice before answering. This isn't a game," warned Kliner.

Rubbing his five o' clock shadow, he never saw the force that would end his comfortable way of life. Mistaking overconfidence for wisdom, he walked willingly into the lioness's cage. "I'm game for it," said Chandler, waving off Kliner's warning.

"Chandler, place your hand flat out in front of you. No, the one with your wedding ring on," said Nevada. Bracketed between Jenkins and Kliner, the future ex-chairman had nibbled too long on the bait. Springing the trap, the hand was soon snared.

"Now what?" asked Chandler, leaking a bead or two down his forehead.

"After we play this *game* as you called it, I will analyze the findings and determine if it is safe to reveal why the government has an

DIVINE MEMORIES

interest in me. Fair enough?" asked Nevada, releasing her hold on Jack's hand under the table.

"Fine."

"Good. Good. Now close your eyes and think back to a time when you crossed the line between right and wrong. Times when you have cheated the system or betrayed those that trusted you. Bring the memories tumbling back. Don't hold back. Release them, letting them flow freely. That's it. Yes. Yes." Summoning the gift's awesome power, touching the trembling outstretched hand, she sifted through the memories, extracting dark secrets hidden long ago—the ones man would never, alone, discover.

Cringing at the newest victim of her power, Jenkins was still trying to wrap his brain around the wonder of her abilities. Dangling from one of her webs himself, he knew he got off easy. She drew lines in the sand that one crossed at the expense of their own personal peril. Watching Kliner shake his head for an old friend's fall, Jenkins sat back, waiting for the verdict.

Taking her gift to another level, Nevada penetrated through the resistance. Making the sign of the cross on the back of his hand, she pulled deep on the gift. Casting layers of deception aside, secrets long buried floated to the light. She said, "We're done here."

"Well, that was painless," said Chandler, not fully baptized yet.

"Jenkins, pass that legal pad and pen over here," said Nevada, searching for Jack's hand under the table. Clicking the pen several times and pulling her hand free from Jack's, she began scribbling furiously, shielding the words from their prying eyes with her free arm.

The suspense was interrupted by the jarring tear of the legal pad page. Taking her time, she folded the page. Sliding the list over, she now had a millstone forever shackled around his neck. With one finger pinning the simple sheaf of paper, she said, "I can see people's memories. If you allow that knowledge to escape your lips, I will take out a full-page ad with the twenty biggest newspapers in the United States of America detailing these words."

Treating the paper more like an IED, fearful of its destructive forces, he came apart at the seams as his brain acknowledged the words. Worse than an IED, the death it offered would be slow and painful. Seconds from ruin, his brain squirmed, looking for a new hiding place. Bathed in pure light, the darkness had been stripped away from the sins of the past. The blood was draining fast, only stopped by the double-tied wingtips shaking under the table. Ashen-colored, his heart pumped faster than a runaway locomotive. Gathering enough strength to tear his eyes from the list, his life instantly transformed into a sticky morass.

He folded up his life neatly, one crease at a time, to never be revealed. Scooting the chair back with a loud scrape, he said, "Ron, give her what she wants."

*****

Liddy was snatched out of prison under the cover of darkness. Traveling through the night, they brought him to his new home nestled under Mount Porcelain, one of the government's best-kept secrets. Suffering the next three days housed in the secure facility, his mouth sank more ships than the battle for Pearl Harbor, earning him brownie points with each sinking ship.

Making the most of the three-day break, she waited out the time away from the cold winter of her Yankee Mansion. Wading up to the bar, she thought the umbrella shading the colorful elixir looked refreshing. Dropping back on the floating lounge chair and running her nails down his hairy forearm, Nevada asked, "Are you ever sorry you met me?"

Sliding the shades down a notch, he replied, "The only thing I am sorry about is that I didn't meet you sooner."

She ran her finger across the scar emblazoned across his chest—a constant reminder of the price of freedom. Straying into his own misery, she asked, "Even before Sorena?"

Sliding the shades back up, the memory of their deaths still brought a mountain of pain. "Ummm, I don't think so. Sorena gave without asking. She was everything I could dream for. Without her, I don't' think I'd ever left that military hospital. When she and my dad were killed years later, I checked out. Back then, you and I wouldn't have given each other the time of day. But if it weren't for you, I don't

DIVINE MEMORIES

know where I'd be today. We crossed paths at the most perfect of times," said Jack.

"I hate it when you're right," said Nevada.

"Hate's a strong—"

She splashed a wave over his way, drowning his glass of beer. "I know. Been told that several times," she said, smiling at the ease between them. Lying back, she soaked up the warm rays as she left the world's ugliness at the back door till tomorrow.

Dumping the beer water on her thigh, he said, "You ready for tomorrow? I mean really ready?"

She splashed some water on her leg. "I know the words are going to hurt. But I won't shy away from it. I need it."

*****

Earning his ticket to freedom by sinking every ship he could think of over the last three days, Liddy sat alone. Dressed once again in civilian clothes, he had escaped the confines of his former government housing. The smirk came alive as she took her seat.

Wondering what the punishment would be for wiping it from his face, Nevada held her contempt at bay. Maybe there would be an opportunity someday, she hoped. Studying his ugly mug, pockmarked and ruddy, she knew he was loyal only to himself.

With a sour taste at the thought of any concessions, Nevada asked, rolling her new ring around her finger, "Jenkins, what deal has he got?"

"Total immunity for all crimes listed under the contract, including any participation in the disappearance of your parents. Homicide is not included," said Jenkins with little enthusiasm for the generous terms.

Shifting back to the man of the hour, she asked, "What about unspoken ones?"

"Free game for the prosecution."

"Jenkins, do you have the list of crimes he has locked in under the agreement?"

"I don't think she needs that!" popped off Liddy.

235

"Thank you, Jenkins." Looking at the impressive list of carnage perpetrated against the common man over the years, she nodded. "Any crimes uncovered from this point on are able to be prosecuted?" asked Nevada.

"Exactly, ma'am."

Interlocking her arm to Jack's, she gave the green light. "Let's hear what you know."

With fifty-six hard years under his belt, mostly spent looking over his shoulder, the three-day marathon interrogation had taken its toll. Soon to be the most sought-after rat at the mercy of the government's witness protection plan, he couldn't wait to see which Mayberry town they deposited him in. Scratching the stubble on his chin, he looked closer to seventy and aging fast as he saw the unwavering murderous look aimed his way. "Ms. Barrington, what do you care what my deal is? I'm gonna honor it," said Liddy, looking for the trapdoor in her words.

"Buddy, I suggest you start talking," said Jenkins with a slice of ice in his voice.

Crunching a breath mint with a high degree of annoyance, Liddy said, "We're all on the same team here, agent."

"That'd be laughable if one could get around the fact that you really believe it's true. Liddy, you got five seconds to start, or I am packing up and your deal goes up in smoke," warned Nevada.

"Okay. Okay. Where do you want me to start?"

"The morning they disappeared." The mention of that ugly day brought an all too familiar wave of pain, one that walked with her every day. With seconds before the curtain was to be flung back, revealing the guilty, one drunken night when she begged and pleaded for this day flashed to the surface.

Liddy began. "Okay. That Sunday morning, uh, Lawrence had arranged for your parents and Charles to visit the construction site of the new Barrington Garden Center. You know, for a progress check. On the way there, two men blocked in their limo and kidnapped your parents. But what you don't know is…Charles planned it all. Then he—"

"What!" screamed Nevada, coming across the table.

Snatching her by the waist, Jack wrenched her back, saving Liddy's face from the vicious swipe.

"Lady, we ain't even got to the worst yet."

"Continue, Liddy," said Jenkins.

"My brother Amos and me were the guys responsible for stopping the limo, but we had nothing to do with their murder. Well, anyways, we followed the limo to an abandoned factory, and Charles killed the driver there and tortured your parents. Amos and me left when it got too brutal. A few hours later, he called and wanted to meet back at the factory. When we got there, the limo driver and your parents were gone. Charles had my brother shoot him in the leg to make it look like he was a victim too. Only, Amos was nervous, and the bullet hit a bone. As you know, he suffered a limp after that. We left him there and made an anonymous call to the police so he could be saved."

Beyond tears, beyond anger, Nevada whispered, "Where are my parents?"

Shaking his head, blowing the candle of hope out, Liddy muttered, "Only Charles knows where their bodies are."

Heaping on more possible misery, she had to know. "Did Lawrence know about the plan?"

"Charles had something on Lawrence, but he didn't know anything about it. I'm sure he had suspicions afterwards," said Liddy.

"In all these years, he never once mentioned where he hid the bodies?" asked Nevada.

"Nope. He's too smart. Amos and me got in over our heads with Charles."

"Let's go over this one more time. Lean back and close your eyes, Liddy. Think back to when you first started doing serious crime. Let your mind focus on those crimes you got away with."

With a bit of a dreamy smirk, he gushed inside at his years of cleverness, unknowingly swallowing her hook. "But I already—"

She picked his brain clean like a Christmas turkey, but she still needed the last piece of the puzzle. "Shh, just concentrate. There, that's good. Let them all come flooding back. Slow down. Whoa! Whoa! Back up. Back to the armored car. Unbox that for me. Think of the details, names, places. Ahh…yes. Step back. Look at the house. Now go to their hiding place. Good job!"

Coming out of the light trance, Liddy bellowed, "I'm done here! No more." He was feeling the sharp point of the hook tugging him back to his home away from home.

"Liddy, a personal question, if you don't mind answering?" asked Nevada.

Grinding the life out of the butt in the ashtray, he said, "Can't stop ya. What?"

Sliding closer, unleashing a softer tone, she asked, "What's a guy in your predicament going to live on?"

Opening a mouth better suited shut, he would soon be mounted on the government's trophy wall. "Got a bit rat holed back."

"I think that about wraps it up for me, Jenkins," said Nevada.

Watching Liddy lumber out of the room, oblivious to his blunder, she couldn't muster up any mercy for the career criminal. "Jenkins, pull up Google Earth and type this address in."

Sliding the tablet over, he said, "Here you go."

"Jenkins, did he reveal being involved in any armored car heists?"

Rifling through the interrogation notes, he answered, "Well, I don't see any. About every other crime, but I don't see anything dealing with armored cars. Why?"

Huddling over the tablet, Nevada said, "I saw that house in his memories. I also saw flashes of a Tri-State armored car. I also clearly saw him looking at bundles of cash in a hidden compartment in the wall."

"Let me log into the database. You said Tri-State?"

"Yeah.

"Okay. I have two. One back in…no, wait. That was solved already. Okay. Here is one back a few years earlier. Both guards murdered and the thieves made off with over four hundred thousand. No arrests to date and money never recovered. Best news we have, some serial numbers are on file."

"Sounds like that might be our boy's work. Hate to hear it. The world's not going to be the same without him in it." The words didn't get any sweeter. Two down, one to go.

Drawing the files in, Jenkins said, "Yeah, I'm really torn up myself. Let's get you out of here."

"Jenkins, can you file charges on Charles and revoke his bond?" asked Nevada.

"Way ahead of you. Got legal on it already." Jenkins grinned.

*****

As the weeks racked up into months, she waited for the call of his arrest, restless to take that final elusive piece of the puzzle and pop it into place. It was the one that would finally complete the picture of her parents' final days on this earth. One that would answer a thousand prayers so passionately flung skyward over the last couple of decades.

Alone in the Yankee Mansion, the funeral was still fresh in Nevada's mind. Barely reaching her ninety-second birthday, Lillian would forever be a bright chapter in her life. Another guiding light snuffed out of her life too soon. Stepping out into the morning sunshine, her remaining light was making his way up the sidewalk.

"Morning," said Jack as he leaned in.

"Morning back to you." Moving into his embrace, she asked, "How long will you be in court?"

"Should take a couple hours tops. This should be, thankfully, the last case I have any involvement with."

She liked the addition of the beard, even with the salty spots here and there. She dragged a nail across his cheek. Shaking off the shiver, she held tight to her future. "Hurry back."

Leaning on the column as she watched him disappear around the bend in the drive, the walls closed in. Grabbing a cup, she headed to the gardens.

Walking through the shafts of sunlight sneaking down through the pergola, she hesitated to deadhead a geranium bloom. Life was good in her part of the planet as she watched a jet etch a vapor trail against the spotless blue sky.

Dragging the chair out into the full sunlight, she planted her head back, allowing the sun to compete with the early morning chill.

Soaking up the warmth, she loved the rejuvenation as the comforting warmth radiated through her body. It bathed her eyelids as she closed her eyes, drawing in the sweet aroma of the honeysuckle fragrance floating about. She dreamed of all its potential, secretly planning the most important day of her life. Sucking in the peace and quiet, she dismissed the first faint scrape. As she was putting the finishing touches on the dream, the stolen sunbeams brought her back to life.

Shielding one eye, she peeked at the intrusion. The soulless grin shattered her world in a thousand pieces. With motive and opportunity lying there for the taking, pure evil prepared to lay waste against her. Cornered, she tried to harness her imagination as she envisioned the worst.

"Well, well. Isn't this cozy." His voice was dripping with revenge.

Swallowing down fear as her heart rattled out of control, she refused to whimper for mercy. She refused to give what evil sought. The pistol, looking more like a child's toy, came up.

She said, "Charles, just get it over with. You'll get nothing from me."

With payback seeping out from behind the hideous smile, no mercy was on his radar. His disheveled appearance, the results of six months on the run, deserved punishment. "All in good time, you little piece of filth. I intend to make this painful. You should know that."

"I guess torturing my parents wasn't enough of a low bar on the human scale for you. Couldn't take it my dad was a better man. Still didn't get what you really wanted though. Huh?" asked Nevada, pushing smug to a new level.

The small pop stung as she doubled over. The results were immediate as the warm stream rolled down her right arm. She gasped for air as the searing pain roared through her body. Clamping the small hole in her chest, she fought all that should be, pushing fear to the back corner of her mind. Gritting teeth, hell-bent on survival, they sought out a victim.

Launching all her strength forward, swiping his smile into next week, she made a desperate attempt for the pistol. The second pop brought no pain as she held on for dear life. Taking vicious punches at the expense of holding the pistol at bay, her strength faded. The ringing in her ears threatened to bring an end to her fight. Airborne, pitched headlong into the rose bed, she had no answer as her body shut down. Too weak to break the clutches of the rose thorns, she rolled up, waiting for the next bullet to find her. As his voice reached her ears, darkness draped over her as she gave in to the pain, bringing a merciful end to further horrors.

Planting every ounce of strength behind his 230 pounds, Jack's fist found the jaw of all that evil could conjure up for their day. The fight was over as soon as it began, dropping evil in its tracks. Turning, his stomach fell. She lay face down, lifeless, tangled among the rose-bushes' spiny limbs. The sight of her blood-soaked chest was more than the veteran could handle. He started ripping the rose barbs from her. Cradling more than a woman, more than a body, she was his true reason for existence.

"Nevada! Stay with me, honey! You're safe now." Brushing back her bangs, he longed to hear the cavalry coming. Checking her wounds with the skill bought and paid for on the battlefields he so hated, he said, "Come on, sweetheart. Hang in there. It doesn't look that bad." Ignoring the steady flow of blood rolling down her chest, his heart raced as the first moan escaped her lips.

"Jaaack, hold...me." Fighting a fight she never wanted, losing the struggle, Nevada was slipping back into darkness.

"Come on, baby. Stay with me...please! Don't go." Stanching the flow as best he could, the lone wail in the distance brought him hope. Horrified at her battered face, he pushed away thoughts of serving a much-needed sentence to the guilty party. *Lord, don't take her!*

Catching movement out of the corner of his eye as the suspect stirred, Jack fought every instinct to seek justice. Drawing his weapon, he eyed the nickel-plated pistol lying in the dirt next to the man. "Mister, nothing and I mean nothing would give me a greater pleasure. Go for it!"

Grinning the best his split lip could muster up, Charles mumbled, "I'll take my chances in court."

Packaged up in minutes, the air evac launched Nevada to the trauma center for yet a third time. Coming to in the chopper, she fought to stay among the living. Flailing about, she placed demands for her man.

"Ma'am, he's coming right behind us. Lie back and let us help you. We're just a few minutes out. You can see him then," promised the flight nurse.

*****

An old hand at pacing waiting rooms, Jack checked the wall clock again. Two hours into her surgery; he should call family. The harsh scathing from Momma Webster the last time was still vivid. When she comes out of surgery maybe. As two hours turned into four then six, his worry found another level. As worry took command of all he knew, the news was headed his way.

"Are you Jack?" asked the doctor, still in full scrubs.

Praying that her luck had one more lucky spin on the wheel of fate, Jack asked, "Yeah. How is she?"

"She's one lucky girl. The bullet shattered a rib and deflected out under her shoulder. If it would have continued unabated, you would have been saying your goodbyes already," said Dr. Findley.

Taking a hard swallow of relief, he said, "Can I see her?"

"She should be out of recovery soon. Don't expect much. She's got some painful days to get through."

Once again helpless, she had now been shot more than most combat veterans. Looking down at the destructive force man could inflict, she had suffered so much. Fighting to come out of the anesthesia, the contorted face acknowledged the pain. Marrying moans to the futile attempts to fight the bandages and restraints, only time would end the misery. Hours later, wearing the button out on the morphine pump with a vengeance, she wasn't sure survival was all it was cracked up to be. With every part of her body crying for relief, few would escape her scorn.

Waiting for the next dose of euphoria, she said, "Jack, I wish you had let me die."

DIVINE MEMORIES

The broken days came swimming back as he drew down on the dark period. "When I got shot, I woke up saying the same thing."

"Just warning you. Keep sharp objects way from me." She gasped out through gritted teeth. Striking the button on the morphine, grimacing, she fought through the sharp bite of pain from shredded muscles. Closing eyes tired of the rocky path she had traveled, she silently dialed up the complaint department. "Lord, how much more do I have to endure? I am weak. I..." Drifting off, she found relief.

Days later, the knitting muscles still complained, but the howling pain had subsided. She was not ready to compete in a twister tournament, but the focus of her life had returned. She shook off the news of her needing to be a guest for another week. Smiling a rare smile as he entered, she brushed hair back, reaching for the outstretched hand. "Just the man I want to see."

Setting the flowers and balloon by the window, Agent Jenkins asked, "Nevada, how's it going?"

Ignoring the niceties, she went straight for the meat. "Where is he?"

"Right now, still locked up tight in the Noble County Jail until he's transported back to New York."

Had the gift slipped from her grasp? She needed to know as she felt helpless to continue the journey. Rolling to her side, the pain was immediate. Moving back, she stared up at nothing. "Calvin, please keep him there till I get out of here. Can you do that for me?" Her words were more plea than question.

She had never uttered his first name before. It was tough to see the power-driven woman so broken. Raising a guard to his heart as he squeezed her hand, feelings that should never be released beckoned to be freed. These were the ones that, left unchecked, led to ruin. "You know I will. You will have your day with him, no matter what."

Leaving nine days later, Nevada, in a wheelchair, halted by the car door. Lurching forward, no pain would keep her another minute. The ride home reignited her passion to attack. The days blurred by pain and fear needed clarity. Pulling into the KFC parking lot, she longed for the extra crispy.

Latching on to the drumstick, the taste was as advertised. Wiping the grease away, she said, "Are we ready to talk about it?"

"I'm working on your timetable," said Jack, digging into the mashed potatoes.

Polishing off the drumstick, she was blessed in so many ways. Too many to acknowledge, most were taken for granted. For the one across the table, she would happily hand over her billions to hold each night. He was one that she knew she didn't deserve.

Nevada said, "When I opened my eyes that morning and that crazy-eyed psycho was grinning back, I've never felt fear that horrible before. But when I felt that bullet strike me, I forced that fear to anger." Reliving the moment brought her to the brink. The sights and sounds lingered, building the horrible memories. "I felt my life slipping, and I was so mad he had the opportunity to rob me of a life with you. I remember falling and maybe...for a minute, I gave up. I heard your voice. I knew I could just let go."

Watching the train wobble on the tracks as her eyes welled up, Jack said, "We're lucky my court case was postponed that morning. I saw you fighting for your life in the garden, but I didn't see the gun at first. Good thing. You would never get a chance to pick his brain about your mom and dad if I had." He was blessed with more than a sinner his size deserved. "Nevada, I'll always pick you up when you fall."

"Take me home and hold me. I mean it. I am done with this world."

Perking up at the tone of her voice, she was never one to throw out a profound statement lightly. "What's that supposed to mean?" asked Jack, afraid of the answer.

"You'll see later."

He folded his disposable napkin, carefully matching the corners together. The answer couldn't get any scarier. Her frequent mystery trips held the key. *She did promise to marvel me*, he thought, not bothering to try and guess. "If you're done, let's get on home."

Mending for the next month, she was restless to finish it. Sticking like glue, he never strayed far from her. Self-imposing the gardens as off limits, she missed their serenity. Asking for the umpteenth time if there were any signs of the struggle remaining, the

DIVINE MEMORIES

answer remained the same. Wishing the roses a speedy recovery, she wouldn't let Charles dirty up her most beloved setting any longer. "Let's go out to the gardens?"

"You betcha."

Strolling among the plantain lilies, she scouted out ahead to the upcoming rose garden. Halting by the snapped-off limbs of the once spectacular display, she felt the wind sailing from her lungs. Eyeing the high-pressure watermarks on the stone pavers, she cringed at the thought. A sympathetic pain in her chest lurched her forward, forcing her to take a seat on the stone bench. She had been robbed of the peaceful pleasure of the gardens, and he would pay.

"I'm ready to face him. Can we do that this morning?"

"Are you strong enough to face the answers?" Jack asked.

"You know I am." Casting a glance over her shoulder, she continued, "I'm going to miss these gardens the most."

"Huh?"

Crushing a finger against his lip, she silenced the oncoming interrogation. "Let it unfold my way. I made a promise to you, and I intend to keep it."

*****

Waiting out in the car at the sheriff's department's parking lot with her shoulder on fire, she withheld the pain medication. Leaving it no chance to interfere with the gift, she fought through the pain. Using it for fuel, she waited to be unleashed.

Accompanied by the new sheriff, Jack signaled her to come out.

Struggling with the door handle, she could all but feel the final puzzle piece in her possession. She recognized few of the deputies lingering near the door to get a glimpse of her.

Placed in interview room number 8, she wrangled with the chair leg locked into the next chair's leg. Pulling, she winced at the punishing reminder of his handiwork. Alone, not trusting Jack to mind his manners, she summoned strength. *Lord, give me the strength to finish this journey. Lord, protect all I love from harm. I long to know the answer. But more than that, I long to be different, Lord.*

Opening her eyes, Charles sauntered into the room, cuffed in front. He was fighting to display the lopsided taunting grin through the fractured jaw, courtesy of Jack. Holding his boney hands out, he allowed the deputy to run the cuffs through the eyebolt in the table.

"Deputy, can you leave one of his hands free and handcuff the other to that bolt thing?" asked Nevada.

Cocking his head, knowing their history, Deputy Mattison asked, "You'll be comfortable with that, ma'am?"

Refusing to blink first as her last living relative stared back, Nevada could see he was sorry for his failure and was already conniving for a redo someday. She said, "Absolutely. And can you set that case on the table for me?"

"If you need anything else, hit the red button on your side over there, and we'll come running."

Flashing a smile toward the young deputy, she said, "Thank you. And, Deputy, make sure all recording and listening devices are turned off in this room."

Halting at the door, he nodded. "Done already, ma'am."

Seated 2.5 feet away from her was everything that was wrong in her life. Charles was no longer a powerful figure who could break people's lives with a hushed call. Now he was only a gaunt, hollow-eyed, beaten-down old man who was living for revenge. Squaring up in his seat, trying to rack the sore jaw in a better place, his voice was hoarse but clear. "What can I do for my dear niece today?"

Playing his game for now, she said, "Let's have a chat, dear uncle."

Seconds slipped by before the sound of teeth sucking assaulted her ears. "About?"

"This and that," said Nevada, hoping he didn't take too much pleasure in the faded black eye she still sported from the nose surgery.

The dull bloodshot pools stared back, void of love, compassion, or pity. "You know every molecule of my body hates every molecule of yours?"

Slicing the first cut, she asked, "Did that go for Mom and Dad too?"

Pulling a sympathetic look out of his bag of tricks, he said, "Your mother, my dear brother...heavens no."

With the skill of a surgeon, she tested the flesh. "Word has it that you might have had some involvement with their disappearance."

Sucking the enamel faster, he muttered, "Nevada dear, that hurts. That was your beautiful mother and my dear brother."

Ratcheting down her knuckles around the corner of the desk, the lioness circled, ready to sink her teeth to the bone. "Where are they?"

"Who?"

Pulling the case over closer, she said, "I guess we'll have to do this the hard way. You're broke. I am willing to pay you a million dollars for your assistance. I'll need about a minute or two of your time, and it's painless."

Stroking an earlobe, he was wary of her dangling carrot. "Describe this assistance."

"Simple." Nevada drew a small circle on the table between them. "You place your hand on the circle. I place my hand on top. You remain silent during the time my hand is on yours."

With one last suck of the teeth, Charles asked, "That's it?" He was nibbling near the cheese.

Shaking her new perm, she casually popped the locks on the case. The packs of Benjamins stacked neatly within spoke his language. "All yours as long as your hand stays under mine. Pull out early, you get nothing."

Running his fingers through the bundles, he said, "Cheat me and there will be a third try."

Tapping a fingernail on the circle, she said, "Remember the rules and you'll be set for life."

Leaning forward, invading her personal comfort, he stated, "Let's summarize this offer, dear. I place my hand on that circle, remain silent during that time. You take your hand off mine and I earn one million dollars free and clear?"

Holding it together while the baited animal tiptoed closer, she nodded. "Exactly. Your hand comes out first and you don't even go home with a consolation price for playing the game."

He slammed his hand down squarely on the circle. "Agreed!"

With one last roll for all the marbles, she would leave nothing to chance. Her voice low and to the point, she whispered, "Lord, be with me in this room. Give me the power of your might." Warm to the touch now, she began. "I want you to go back twenty years, three months, and six days to the morning. You are with my parents, going to the new gardens center they are building. You are in the limo with them. Let your mind drift. Let the memories of that day filter back. That's it! Just let them flow. You are stopped by the Bankhill brothers. You are responsible for the attack, and you murder the limo driver and...my parents."

She pressed with all her might down upon his hand. "Recall their final resting place. Bring back their grave site in your mind. Let it show! Let it come back!" Faltering, unable to overcome his lack of a conscience, she runs to him. *Lord, give me the strength! Bring the vision to me, Lord. Let me have them back.* Gathering strength, the walls began to crumble, allowing the good to prevail.

Trembling beneath hers, she called forth all. Silent and impassive, she smothered herself in the answered prayer. She unleashed the full fury of the gift, draining it all upon him. "Looks like I have some Calacatta marble to break up, don't I?"

Worried and unsure, he began to feel the discomfort. Contorted, he squirmed in the seat as the heat began to build. She remained motionless as the heat poured from her. "Nevada, my hand is burning! Let me loose. Nowww!"

"Remember the rules, Uncle Charles."

Gritting his teeth sent pain rippling up through his jaw. Yanking his hand out in defeat, the look in his face was murderous as he threw a roundhouse punch her way. Taking the glancing blow, she stood unfazed as the door flew open, jarring against the doorstop.

Holding up her one good arm, she said, "Don't touch the pathetic animal. Let's go live a wonderful life, Jack." She took one last look at the animal. "I thought it would feel better to flatten your life. How could you kill them?"

Straining away from the deputies, he screamed, "I'll get you for this!"

Snapping the case closed, Nevada shrugged. "Good luck with that. You had your chance. Where I'm going, the world's not invited."

DIVINE MEMORIES

Numb, lost at the end of the journey, she stood rigid when the ground-penetrating radar signaled their last known resting place. With an abundance of care, the backhoe operator slowly peeled back the precious Calacatta marble that had entombed her parents for the last twenty years. They were buried all these years in her mother's own gardens. She could only wonder if her mother appreciated the irony of resting in such a place—one she had hoped would bring beauty for others to enjoy. Father would be a different story. Murders with no one's gain. Tortured at their being ripped from her life too soon, they were now only distant memories being brought home with dignity. So much time and joy stolen, denied by one man's greed.

They were buried three days later, and she said her final goodbyes. The coffins were lowered back into the earth, holding her parents together forever. With the bittersweet victory, she was no longer shackled to the cause and was finally free to seek her own freedom. With the closing prayers wrapping up, a gentle breeze stirred her mourning veil. Surrounded by Jack and company, she lifted her veil. "Enough of this sadness," she said, clearing her eyes. Taking the hand that held her life together for the last two years, she said, "Jack, most of your closest friends and family are here for two reasons, unbeknownst to you."

"Two?"

"Yeaaaah. Seeee, we're all jumping on a jet and going to an island I had built for you and me to live on. Also, it's where I am going to marry you."

"What if I'd said no?"

"Yeah right, Jack!" yelled the newest sheriff of Noble County from the back of the pack.

Coming out of the embrace, he said, "You never know, Randy."

"Yeah, we do," said Candy.

*****

Buzzing the island, she was pleased. Looking down at the eight miles of pristine beach and forest, she searched for it. Peeking out from the forest canopy, the roof was just visible from the air. Pointing it out, he could only shake a bewildered head at the construction. The Robinsons would be jealous. Guarded from the world, she would be its queen and he its king.

"How on earth did you accomplish all this?" asked Jack.

"By overpaying for every aspect of this hunk of dirt. What do you think? I even had a Casey's gas station and a Dollar General store brought in to make you feel at home."

"Will it really be all ours? I'm afraid it's all just a dream and I'll wake up any second." Noticing the massive structure going up on the mountain peak, Jack asked, "What's that?"

"God's house. The only place we won't own."

Touching down on the airstrip, the brakes fought hard to halt the plane before the jungle got a chance to. Remaining on the aircraft, allowing the wedding party to exit, she retreated to the rear of the plane. Running her hand down the front of the wedding gown, the weight of the world found her shoulders. The twisting, turning path had been rocky and treacherous, the journey often interrupted and bent by evil players intent on bringing down harm on the innocent. Straying neither left nor right from the path, she only had her heart to follow.

"Father, why me? There were so many more deserving. So many loving you their whole lives with every fiber of their body. So many that had no doubt about you. I could claim none of that, Father… until now. Father, thank you for their bones. Father, thank you for this life. Amen."

Walking up the aisle, the rustle of her gown alone was to be heard. Jack's grin lit up as their eyes met. He was held in place by Randy's hand on his shoulders. Balancing out her side, Matty gushed as her beautiful queen, dressed in a dazzling white Alexander McQueen dress, strolled toward them.

There, under the sun of the tropical paradise, she came to terms with her new world as Pastor Rick held their hands tightly. The world she would never have dreamed of as a little girl, but could never fathom living without now, unfolded before her eyes. As the words and promises were exchanged, she realized the tumultuous journey was worth the prize.

Turning the king and queen to the crowd, Pastor Rick said, "It's my pleasure to introduce Mr. and Mrs. Jack Webster."

For only her ear, Jack whispered, "I'll never let you fall."

Standing on tiptoes, her words sealed the deal for life. "And I'll never let you go."

The End

About the Author

James F. Bender, born and raised in the Midwest, came back home after serving in the US Air Force as a security police narcotics canine handler. Joining the sheriff's department, he retired after nearly forty years of combined law enforcement and related services. Drawing from these years, he combines a healthy imagination and life experiences with his love of the Lord. With *Divine Memories*, he strives to unleash his readers' desire to see another realm of possibilities. Now living in Illinois with his wife, Kim, he enjoys the challenge of taking a blank screen and finding a story to tell.

Printed in the USA
CPSIA information can be obtained
at www.ICGtesting.com
LVHW092115051024
792985LV00001B/96